Previous Volumes in the Spoon Knife Series

The Spoon Knife Anthology: Thoughts on Compliance, Defiance, and Resistance
    Edited by N.I. Nicholson and Michael Scott Monje, Jr.

Spoon Knife 2: Test Chamber
    Edited by Dani Alexis Ryskamp and Sam Harvey

Spoon Knife 3: Incursions
    Edited by Nick Walker and Andrew M. Reichart

Spoon Knife 4: A Neurodivergent Guide to Spacetime
    Edited by B. Allen and Dora M. Raymaker with N.I. Nicholson

Spoon Knife 5: Liminal
    Edited by Andrew M. Reichart, Dora M. Raymaker, and Nick Walker

Spoon Knife 6: Rest Stop
    Edited by B. Martin Allen and J.S. Allen

Spoon Knife 7: Transitions
    Edited by Nick Walker & Mike Jung

Spoon Knife 8: Smoke & Mirrors

Edited by

Nick Walker & Phil Smith

Weird Books for Weird People

Spoon Knife 8: Smoke and Mirrors, Copyright 2024 **Autonomous Press, LLC** (Fort Worth, TX, 76114).

Neuroqueer Books is an imprint of Autonomous Press that publishes fiction, poetry, memoir, and other literary work, with a focus on themes of queerness and neurodivergence.

Autonomous Press is an independent publisher focusing on works about neurodivergence, queerness, and the various ways they can intersect with each other and with other aspects of identity and lived experience. We are a partnership including writers, poets, artists, musicians, community scholars, and professors. Each partner takes on a share of the work of managing the press and production, and all of our workers are co-owners.

ISBN: 978-1-945955-48-8

Ebook ISBN: 978-1-945955-49-5

Cover art by JINGLEJUDE - www.instagram.com/jinglejude/

Book design by Casandra Johns.

Contents

4 whirred

words at the fore

avorwort

praefatio

voorwoord, or vöewoord

foarwurd

forord

förord

go forward!

here, words whirring, whirring, whirring...

in the first volume of the *Spoon Knife* series, *The Spoon Knife Anthology: Thoughts on Compliance, Defiance, and Resistance*, published in 2016, co-editor Michael Scott Monje, Jr. (a pen name of Athena Lynn Michaels-Dillon), described the meaning of spoon knife. she followed Christine Miserandino's metaphor of "Spoon Theory," a tool Miserandino used to describe what it was like living with lupus. spoons represent the physical, emotional, and psychic resources needed to engage in daily activities and experiences; with a handful of spoons, you take away a spoon from the bunch every time you use a resource.

Athena wrote, "at the end, when there was only one spoon left and the only item on the list—dinner—was likely to take two spoons, it helped to drive home the choices and the careful safeguarding of resources she has to make as she plans her daily activities." when different people have different resources, and needs, some people may fall short in the number of spoons they need, while others have extra. Athena went on, "...the whole room does better when we are willing to send extra spoons to other tables."

here's where the notion of a "spoon knife" comes in: it's a curved tool used to carve the bowl of wooden spoons. metaphorically, communities use spoon knives in "cutting away layers of what shouldn't be there, to leave us with the ability to do more, reach further, and nourish ourselves more successfully." Athena saw the anthology they had collected as a group of metaphoric knives that "will provoke new spoons when the right kinds of readers connect with them, providing the things those readers need to navigate their own daily tasks and challenges."

Autonomous Press has been publishing one anthology a year in the *Spoon Knife* series ever since then. this is the eighth of that number. along with the current volume, we have brought together over these few years 135 writers—some experienced, some well-known, some less so. those writers have made 242 contributions –

poems

short stories

memoir

non-fiction

pieces that go across or beyond boundaries

much like those who wrote them.

i am for words.

we are for words.
eye yam fur whirreds
that createnew meanings
new imaginariums
that imagine new worlds
gnu whirleds
new waze
of thinking doing and being
(understanding that
what and how we think
cannot be separated from
what we do and who we are (and aren't)).
the whirreds herein
and in the utter(ly) vol looms
of this sear ease
have at least duh potent ill tuh
create now possible tease
that, wid luck, will rebeaverate
through and through your bodymind(s)
enhancing and en-sensing
what makes you yew
and wid me, us.

did ya know that you
can make the knives
that make spoons?
we should make summa dose, two.
spread alla this stuff farther and farther and...

Guy Russell

The Obedient Poltergeist

Four or five weeks after settling into our new house, an unremarkable Victorian terrace near the railway station, our kettle began to switch itself on. We'd be sitting watching TV and would become aware of that distinctive wind-tunnelly reverberation with its curious poppings and crackling. The sound grew, as if ever more insistently demanding our attention.

"Did you turn it on, Al?" asked Robert, the first time, as though I might have somehow sneaked through the doorway without his noticing. On the first occasion we told each other it was odd and forgot it, but the second time we remembered the first time, and after the third time Robert examined the kettle thoroughly, taking off the plastic backing, seeing that the switch operated in exactly the way they were designed to. He worked in electronic engineering, and loved fiddling with things, and would have known if something was wrong.

"It must be a poltergeist," we told each other humorously. "These old houses, they all have them," and when it happened in company, we said, "Oh, that's our poltergeist," affecting a breezy familiarity with the world of the undead. We called it Fred. "Fred wants a cup of tea," we said, when it happened. "Fred, can you put the kettle on?" we shouted, when it didn't.

"Mine's two sugars," I told the empty kitchen.

After three months, the phenomenon began to lose its novelty, and became tiresome.

"I wish Fred would understand about conserving energy," I moaned to Robert, when it had happened three times in an evening.

Finally the kettle turned itself on when there was no water in it, and burnt out. We went down to Argos and bought a new one. And it stopped happening.

"Fred doesn't like the new kettle," said Robert. "Thank goodness."

"He doesn't know how to make this one work," I said.

We were a little disappointed that our domesticated poltergeist had turned into a mere malfunctioning appliance.

"Perhaps he'll turn to something else," I suggested. "He might switch the lights on and off. Or levitate the odd spoon."

But the lights remained firmly on, or off, and the spoons stayed resolutely on the tabletop.

"What's happening with your poltergeist?" asked our friends, as Fred had become mildly famous in our circle.

"I wish *we* had one—not a destructive one," said Milly, "but one like yours, sort of cutely mischievous. He's like the ideal pet, isn't he? Like a kitten, but he doesn't poo and you don't need to feed him?"

Robert and I looked at each other across the dinner table. Neither of us liked to admit that Fred didn't exist. He was such a good topic of conversation. "When we sell this place," I said, "we're going to mention him as a feature."

"He hasn't done anything tonight," complained David. "Is

he getting shy? Come on, Fred," he shouted into the kitchen, "earn your keep! Turn the kettle on!"

And at that instant, as though by the force of our collective desire, there came a click from the little button on the handle, and the LED lit up, and the clamour of the heating element began. Everyone cheered. It was a fantastic moment, like the success of some great party trick.

"Good old Fred, he's back!" David said.

"He's been a bit quiet of late," Robert explained to everyone.

"That's so fantastic," said Milly, glowing towards Robert as if it had been something he had done. "Fred makes your house so fun."

This would be talked about for ages: Fred's instant response to David's command—perhaps he understood? Perhaps he had a sense of the dramatic? I told the story to everyone at work. People would want to come round and see if it happened again. And then—it *did* happen again. Not a peep, incidentally, from our personal spectre until Milly, David and Charlotte were all round one Saturday morning after tennis, and it had come into the conversation, and we were all standing in the kitchen staring at the inoffensive kettle as if waiting for it to boil, and there, before our eyes, like the intrusion of an impossible reality, the click, the lit diode and, after a few seconds, the start of the distinctive noise.

This time there wasn't cheering, but an awed hushedness.

"That's *so* spooky," said Charlotte. "It's like it knew we were talking about it."

"Not 'it', Charlotte," said Milly. "'He'. We don't want to disrespect Fred."

"I've never seen anything like it," said Charlotte.

At that moment, Robert came through the doorway. "Guess what happened?" everyone said to him.

"It's so amazing, Robert," said Milly—rather flirtatiously, I thought. I exchanged a glance with David.

Charlotte even took a picture of the kettle with its diode lit, as though it were some kind of star, and uploaded later it to her Myspace with the caption: 'Courtesy of Fred, Al and Robert's tea-loving household ghost!'

This time, when they'd gone, Robert seemed peculiarly uninterested in discussing the manifestation. Instead, he led me into the kitchen, refilled the kettle, and put it on its stand.

"Let's do an experiment," he said. "Tell Fred to turn on the kettle."

Robert was being odd, as he sometimes was, but I complied. "Fred," I said, "turn on the kettle."

Nothing happened, naturally.

"Now say, 'Turn on the kettle, *please.*'"

"Robert."

"Seriously. Go on."

"OK," I sighed. "Fred, turn on the kettle, *please.*"

I turned to look at Robert, who was smiling broadly, and then heard the click, and Robert looked at me as if he was waiting for applause.

After a moment, I laughed too.

●

A remote switch, he told me. From his pocket, he pulled a little circuit-board with a single button. The same way a wireless doorbell works, he said.

Of course, I made much of his cleverness, as I always did. When you're an arty person, as I am, and you live with an engineer, it's easy to forget that they can harbour a sense of inferiority. They feel *behind* in the worlds of books and art, in the currencies of leisure and amusement and ideas. They might disguise it by harping on about how engineering is oh, so much more important and real-world, but it's still a consideration. Robert wasn't witty like Milly or full of outrageous stories like Charlotte. He didn't have David's relentless self-confidence. His social skills had their blind moments: he'd make the wrong kind of joke and then feel terrible, which rocked his self-esteem. As a teenager, he'd told me, he'd had dangerously depressive episodes. He was occasionally embarrassing. On the upside, he was adorably keen to please, and when he'd done something clever and nice and it worked, he blossomed, which I found a rather loveable trait.

Nonetheless I hadn't quite appreciated how motivated Robert would become by this success. In that final year before he died, he'd found a way he could *amuse*. First he made the venetian blinds close in the front room when the luminosity outside was below a certain level. Soon the kitchen bin opened its lid if my hand went too close to it. Not long after, you could turn on the microwave while sitting at the computer—should you ever wish to. Lights went on and off attentively as you moved from room to room. The bedroom door opened by itself, although you had to do a little dance—dip forward to trip the sensor and then skip back as it swung swiftly towards you, before you stepped forward again to leave. And a toy rabbit from Robert's childhood, which sat on top of the DVD cabinet, tinnily said, "Coo! It's hot in here!" when the temperature reached twenty-three degrees, and "I can't bear it!" if it made twenty-six—startling the first time, funny the second and third, and then *so* annoying.

When we'd seen their faces and had our fun, we let our friends, one by one or two by two, into the secret, and that became a new source of entertainment. But something was lost, too. Fred had brought the glamour of the domestic supernatural into our lives. And our friends felt the same. "I still find myself looking wistfully at inanimate objects," said Milly. "You know."

•

And almost overnight, as everyone knows, that kind of technology became everyday everywhere, and thereby lost its wonder. While Robert had been making his amusements, other people with the same skills had been making their fortunes. The country and world entered an age of lights that came on as you walked past, of pianos whose keys depressed of their own accord, of the whole bland magic of wireless automation. We soon had such things at work, spurred partly by new disability legislation. I waved at the cistern, as if casting a spell, and the toilet flushed. I flicked my hands above the sink and the taps came on. All so sensible and hygienic. I stood in front of a door and it slid away into the wall as if I were living in a *Star Trek* future.

Robert, meanwhile, upped the ante. It had become his hobby, like some guys get into online gaming or vintage cars. He did clever stuff with heat-detection and timed latency. "Hello, sexy!" the bedroom mirror would say, at long-spaced moments, when I was standing in front of it. Things could be voice-activated by particular phrases. Things could be triggered by odd and advanced combinations. Sometimes it felt like he was everywhere, trying to assist, but awkwardly, in a kind of remote gallantry. If something supernatural had actually happened in the house, I wouldn't have credited it. I would have assumed it was Robert.

"Can't you get the bed to make itself?' I asked. "Or the dishwasher to self-empty?" One night, the bed started to shake at a key moment. "Must be Fred," said Robert. "He likes watching." I failed to appreciate this development, and that aspect of the paranormal didn't recur.

Faced with a dwindling of the awe that was his primary motivation, and belatedly sensing my satiety with it all, he began (as I think of it now) looking for new ways to provoke the admiration, not just of me, but of Milly and Charlotte and all our friends. One night I came home from an evening out to find him in his pleased-with-himself mode. He took me to the hall and pointed up at the wiring around the fuse box.

"Lovely wiring," I said. "What are you showing me?"

"Look at the meter."

"It's a meter."

"Look at the dial."

"It's not moving... Oh!"

"That's our summer holiday," he said.

All very smart, certainly. Not forgetting the bravery of it: the deft and precise handling of all that occult power. Like many geeky blokes, Robert liked to think of himself as a secret cool rebel; he'd been a hacker as a kid. He showed our friends, who were duly adulatory. Everyone likes a smidge of renegade illegality, as long as no-one's hurt. This time he wasn't faking, he was genuinely japing the utilities. "It's not even dangerous if you know what you're doing," he told them.

In private, I had my reservations. "It's not worth going to jail for a few pounds off," I told him, and he sort of agreed. He'd just wanted to show, really, that he could do it.

When the reading came due, he said, he would put it back. And that, I thought, was what he was doing at the time.

●

Some people say that watching someone get broken down by a long, slow illness is worse. For me, the suddenness was the awful thing. I had a week of numb incredulity. Then a week where I couldn't stop crying. After that, a week where I slept almost non-stop. And a longer time, afterward, when my mind was full of conversations: all those things I wanted to say sorry for, or to tell him off for, and ask him what had gone wrong. He was so competent, normally. Over-confidence? A slip on the stepladder? And especially I wanted to give my apologies for not being there at the time. I'd been out, as ever, with my friends.

No, I should be more precise: I'd been with David.

Charlotte referred to the famous spooked-kettle story

in her speech at the service as evidence of Robert's 'unique sense of sly and creative fun'. I spoke mostly of his general benevolence. He could be awkward and even cringeworthy but he was never deliberately hurtful. I missed having someone for whom I didn't have to be constantly smart and cool. I missed even his depressed moments. I missed being adored so much, so unflinchingly.

I never had that feeling that so many bereaved spouses speak about, of thinking I could see him, or sensing him in the house, or imagining hearing his voice. What *was* still around was his electronic presence. When the bin opened its lid if my hand went too close to it, or the bedroom door swung open to let me through, I thought of his cleverness and keenness to please, and I felt a renewed stab of sadness and anger. Something like this, to someone our own age, had never happened before to any of us, and neither flippancy nor cynicism was a suitable response, so no-one quite knew how to behave. What did work was continuing to meet David. In the Jurys Inn or the Travelodge, he really helped. But for a reason I couldn't quite articulate, I no longer brought him to the house.

Eventually, as my mum and others had prophesized, the weirdness of it began to get behind me, and the ordinary world's ordinary weirdness regained importance, and I even found myself caught unawares by moments of cheerfulness. At first, I recognised them after they'd happened, with surprise. After a few more months, Robert's electronic presence faded too, in the sense that his artful gadgetry began to stop working. Robert, doubtless, would have applied fixes. I didn't have the requisite knowledge or, I realised, the desire, and his little white boxes were too one-off for the usual tradespeople. All those obedient poltergeists: I'd always known that rather than increasing it, they took away my control over things. So the venetian blinds remained stuck, the cold-water bath-tap remained dry, and one night even the bin stopped working, and I had to buy a new, ordinary one.

At that point, and to assay a return to the old days, I invited David and Milly and Charlotte round for supper. "Normal service is to be resumed," I'd said to Milly, thanks, I hoped, to time, goodwill and our own keen efforts.

And it was fine, although I noticed, after more than an hour had passed, that no-one had yet spoken Robert's name, as if it were a kind of holy word or, like an evil spell, might still send me into sobs. Instead, after a first course of jobs, films, books, and David and Milly's weekend in Bilbao, we talked about what the house was worth and when I might put it on the market.

"It'll solve the finances," I said. "I can't keep it with only one income."

"I guess the 'domestic automation' is a feature, when you're selling it?" said David. "It attracts a premium?"

"Half of it's stopped working," I said. "I never realised how much maintenance went into those things. Well, Mr Rabbit there still tells me it's too hot sometimes." I pointed to the toy on the DVD cabinet.

"It's twenty-six degrees!" said the rabbit suddenly, in its tinny voice. "I can't bear it!"

"Hey," said David, "You're right. He still works."

Everyone laughed.

"That made me jump," said Charlotte. "It's like Fred again."

"I was never so keen on the speaking ones," I said. "They're a bit much."

"Really clever though," David said.

"Too clever," I said. "Only Robert could mend them."

There. I'd spoken his name.

"With David!" the rabbit said. "I can't bear it!"

We all looked at each other.

"What was that? I didn't catch it," said Milly.

"Nor me," said Charlotte. "Glitch city."

"It's Fred getting dementia," said David, beginning to pile the plates.

"Poor old Fred," I said, as I took them up. "Coffee, everyone?"

I moved them all into the front room. By the time they had left, the evening had achieved its purpose: we had reconsecrated normality. As I closed the door on them all, my watch showed just past midnight. Nonetheless, before I went to bed, I went round the house unscrewing all of Robert's remaining little white boxes. When I'd collected them, I threw them into the new kitchen bin. Finally I took the rabbit, pulled out its battery heart, and buried it among the rest of the trash.

I went back down the hall to check the front door was locked and a voice said, "Do you think that's enough?"

I jumped like I'd had an electric shock. Robert's voice. Tinny again, but his. I looked around, as if he would actually appear. I was shaking. I looked up at the fuse box. Then at the coat-rack. Then at the full-length wall-mirror beside it. Determinedly, I went to the tool-cupboard, got a screwdriver and chisel, levered off the screw coverings, undid the screws and lowered the mirror to the ground. There it was, in a recess made by removing the plaster.

At last I went upstairs. I lay there in our double bed, in the darkness. I jumped at the sound of a car door in the street. Then at a goods train. Robert wasn't malicious, I thought. He'd been hurt. And he couldn't talk to me. And if he could have done?

"I'm sorry, Robert," I said out loud, feeling odd. "I'm sorry about David."

I thought a bit more. "Just say if you'd rather I gave him up."

I waited a few more moments. "He makes me happy, though."

The darkness remained unbroken. There was no sound but the high, almost imperceptible zizzing of domestic electronics, and I fell asleep.

Chris Campeau

Afterlife Impersonations Co.

Afterlife Impersonations Co.

The name made it a business, gave it substance, even if I was a one-woman show. But the name wasn't a total fib; the 'company' was in my head, willed from the ethers. Without the spirits, I didn't have a job. But my clients didn't know that.

To my clients, the impersonations were a learned skill, an exhaustive study of their reference material (home videos, mostly, and the occasional voicemail). A practised impression of their late loved ones' mannerisms and most memorable one-liners, the likeness so uncanny it was nearly impossible. Because it *was* impossible. I didn't imitate the deceased; I yanked their spirits from the warm hug of the afterlife to puppeteer them for a paycheque. I had bills to pay.

Besides, all that séance nonsense, the black linens and heebie-jeebies, it doesn't sell. Look at the Madame Lafleurs and Gypsy Rosas of the world, the palm readers and other trancers either boarded up on the strip or tucked away in some sticky corner of Fat Tuesdays. It's a sad sight, even for the all-seeing.

Impersonations, on the other hand, are a more proprietary approach to grief consolation. It's not a lucrative business, but it's profitable, and if you've got the curse of the gift, it brings utility to the voices. It did for me until Therese Montrose.

I landed Therese in the summer of 2006. She lived in a low-ranch bungalow on Vireo Drive in Spring Valley. She was my first online booking, a new acquisition channel I was hesitant to adopt despite my business instructor's advice. "Word of mouth works," Ms. Sherri had said, "but technology, soon enough, will be an invaluable asset. You'd better use it, or you'll be left in its wake."

I pulled up to Therese's mulch-covered yard on a Tuesday afternoon, the sun baking the palm leaves into flat, withered fingers, sulking above her shingles. Leaving the chill of my Corolla, I lowered my heels to the driveway, and the heat fused me to the asphalt. I paused at the door to review her file and get familiar with the deceased. It was a pre-ritual I used to conduct at home in my early days, prep work before meeting a client in person. Now, putting the feelers out was rapid-fire; I could locate a spirit within a minute.

But my breath stuttered as I read the printout: Thomas, her 14-year-old son, had died three years ago, a timeline that fell outside the scope of my services. It was a discrepancy I'd overlooked with the new system. I cursed myself for missing it. If Ms. Sherri taught me anything during my crash course in entrepreneurship—a lifetime ago now—it's to meet your audience where they are and when they are. In the case of Afterlife Impersonations Co., that meant conducting house visits within a month of a death. Convenience paired with an emotional drive to buy. The wound needs to be wet.

For nine years that formula kept my books full and ledger balanced. But, as I'm sure Ms. Sheri had also noted, and I'd ignorantly discounted, success is no reason to rest on your laurels. Markets change and consumers dictate. Worse yet, product expires. But even I couldn't've predicted that.

The door opened as I turned to make my escape. The heat seemed to worsen as I met the woman's face, a waxy blankness staring back at me. Unable yet to sense her son anywhere near us, I wiped a palm on my dress and extended a hand, but it was Therese who spoke first.

"Ms. Aurora?" Her face livened as she shook my hand. Her skin was frigid, like she'd sat in front of an air conditioner all day. I couldn't blame her, but I couldn't help but recoil. "I almost didn't expect you to come," she added.

"Pardon?" I didn't know what else to say. I tugged my dress down over my thighs; the black polyester, a terrible choice in Nevada, clung to my skin like a desperate soul.

"I thought your website might be a scam," she said. "You, I mean. Impersonating the deceased."

I almost laughed. *You mean, coercing them?*

She read my face then pivoted as if she'd offended me. "But who can argue your reviews…"

I smiled, accustomed to these types of awkward exchanges with a new client. It's not like I was selling ink jets.

"Let's set up out back," she said. Then, catching herself again: "If that works for you."

I searched the void but couldn't find her son. I took the keys from my purse and looked at my car.

"Please," she said, and the dullness reclaimed her face.

•

Around back, Therese's plastic patio set matched her romper, sun-faded and blue. The varicose veins on her shins became an extension of the mold spots mottling the legs of her chair. I stayed standing, wondering when it'd last rained.

"Here." She gestured to a chair beside a foldable side table, the wood warped and fissured. Cigarette butts speckled its surface, and suddenly I was twenty years younger, waitressing at Beau Lucy's Diner on St. Andrew's Street:

"If this is some kind of joke..." Sharon, my oldest friend, had said. It was my lunch break, and blue cords of smoke rose like ghosts from her side of the booth.

"It's not," I said. "I'd never lie to you."

"But how? I mean...why you?"

"I don't know, and I don't care, but he wants to talk to you." I lowered my voice. "And I want him gone."

I'd said enough. Terry, Sharon's recently deceased boyfriend, washed over me like a lethal heatwave. I went limp, unable yet to exert any control over the dead, let alone manipulate them. Pain exploded in my throat as my vocal cords contracted: "I wasn't drinking, Share."

Sharon threw a hand to her mouth. She shivered in fear and grabbed her purse as Terry's voice boomed from my lips. But I—but *Terry*—was faster, already standing outside the booth, blocking her exit. Lucy, my manager, stopped at the counter in my periphery, though I couldn't register her in any clarity; the room had developed a haze, with Sharon's red-rimmed eyes burning at the centre.

"Baby," Terry continued, "I told you I quit drinking. I hit a patch of ice. The car just fishtailed. I didn't—"

"Get...away from me," Sharon said, tears streaking her mascara.

For a moment the balance shifted: I forced Terry down like an unwelcome thought. I rose above and saw Sharon cowering in the booth. But then the heat seared me again, and Terry opened my mouth to speak.

Sharon kicked me in the thigh. Stumbling back, I snatched a clump of her hair in attempt to right myself. Her cry rattled our plates and set Lucy in motion, then the lot of us ran outside, Sharon bolting into her Cherokee beside the front door, the lock clicking as I—as *Terry*—banged on the driver's-side window with newfound strength.

"Sharon!" Terry said, with *my* mouth. I tried to overthrow him, but the experience was too new. I whimpered, somewhere inside myself, as my fists reddened against the glass. "Baby, hey! Come on!"

She fumbled with her keys, screamed as I pummelled her window. Lucy grabbed me from behind, and I'm not sure what it was, but her touch cast him out, but not before I threw an elbow into her gut.

The Cherokee shrieked as Sharon reversed and sped off, her mascara-smudged eyes never leaving mine in the rearview. Fifty years old and splayed on the pavement, Lucy stared at me in shock, my pink slip already handed to me on her trembling face. That didn't trouble me—I didn't like the job anyway—but I wish Sharon hadn't let me go, too.

"Ms. Aurora?" Therese shot me a commanding look, snapping me back to her yard.

"Sorry. I drift during these things," I said, which wasn't a lie. I sat down and faced her. "Listen, I'm not sure I can help you."

But she didn't seem to be listening. Her eyes followed a mountain bluebird emerging from the gutters of her house. It feathered its way to a hibiscus on the porch, perched its skeletal feet on a branch. Against the brilliance of the bird, I saw the backyard for what it was: the hibiscus had browned, its pedals shrivelled in the soil; the lawn was crisp and overgrown, wild with crickets. Nothing had been tended to.

"I'm not sure I can help," I said again. "But I promise I'll try."

"Thomas had a thing for birds."

"I'm sorry?"

"My Thomas," she repeated, "he watched birds, mostly after school at the canyon near the turnpike. And mostly by himself. His friends were too stuck up, you know? But he didn't mind. It was his thing." She laughed, then swatted a fly that had landed on her face. "But I guess you already knew that."

I got a chill. The prospect that Therese was calling my bluff turned my legs into worms. Did she know what I was?

But it was more than her passive tone, her invitation to read between the lines. As she trained her gaze on mine, her skin waxier, thinner in the sun, a white film fell over her grey-blue eyes. And perhaps it'd been there all along, though it didn't matter now. There was no denying that the woman was dead.

"Ms. Aurora?"

My mind went to allergies. How you can develop them at any age. Like schizophrenia or a palette for liver. Staring at Therese I knew I'd crossed a threshold. She was the first spirit I'd actually *seen*, and the truth of it flatlined me.

Therese coughed and spat a phlegmy-red ball into the grass. "You ever see an off-road transport?" she said. The absurdity of the question held me. "Of course you haven't. They don't go off-road."

"Therese, I need to level with you."

"Trucks belong on the road, Lori, don't they? And mothers belong with their boys." She paused, stunned me by using my first name, which I hadn't given her.

"There's been a mix-up, and I think you know what I'm going to say next." The words just tumbled out. "The impersonations? They help folks heal, sure, but they help me, too. I was hard up for a long time, Therese." I felt a sudden wave of shame. Who was I to beg a dead woman's pity? "The truth is, yes, I'm a vessel—of sorts, anyway—but there are limits. I can't reach Thomas today, I'm sorry. It's been too long."

She grabbed my wrist, a sub-zero freeze burning my skin beneath her hideously soft fingertips.

"Oh, but there is, Lori. You said you'd try, didn't you?"

·

As a hostage, several questions run through your head that test your bravery. *How much danger, exactly, am I facing? If I run, will I have a fighting chance? If my captor's this desperate, isn't my compliance an act of goodwill?*

It's this latter question that pervaded my thoughts, drove me to play along. Not cowardice or self-preservation, though those feelings, unlike Therese, were alive and well, roiling in my stomach as she escorted me to my car.

The sun had lowered and bathed the road in lantern light. I grabbed the handle, but Therese cleared her throat.

"Nuh-uh," she said. "I'm driving."

She locked the doors and turned on the radio, a yellowish smear trailing her fingers. I made a note to bleach the car.

We drove down Vireo Drive with John Fogerty singing "Fortunate Son," past the white-and-brown homes, and rounded the corner onto Birdsong. By the time we approached the turnpike, Theresa making a hard right onto Industrial, the car reeked like copper, sweet as rotten blood.

It'd been three years since Thomas' accident, and if there were any signs of it, time had cleared them like a fleeting wisp of smoke. The metal barrier bounding the interstate was seamless. No skid marks in the parking lot below, where the canyon's viewing deck jutted out before the freeway bridged the void. Everything was as it should be, Nevada dry and yellow.

Therese parked the car. I held my breath as she paused, waited for her to grab my arm with her sodden hands. Instead, she opened the door and hobbled to the edge of the lot. Her rhythm was lopsided and jagged. It amazed me that I hadn't noticed it before, the bone protruding at her ankle.

As she looked over the canyon, I saw her backside clearly for the first time: her red curls galloping in the wind, a patch of darker, wet red shimmering at the base of her skull.

I stepped out and approached her, a spectre hardened by the desert.

"You can imagine the mess," she said, "what it would've been like down there." I followed her eyes to the rocky depths at the base of the canyon, a quarter-mile below us. "You can imagine the carnage had the truck gone over."

"Where did it happen?"

"A few yards back. Chewed up the parking lot, wrote off a few cars. It stopped before the edge, though, but not before my Thomas."

"I'm sorry."

"He was just finishing," she said. "I'd come to pick him up. It was too hot that day, too hot for him to walk home. I'd parked in the same spot." She pointed to my car. "He had a look on his face like it'd been a good day, like he'd seen a bird he'd never seen before. Something pretty, maybe, like him. The rest is, I guess... It's misty, dirty. No matter how hard I try, I only see colours, scrapes of colours, and the metal scream-ing toward him like a runaway train. Hell, *I'd* never run so fast, Lori. My legs still hurt. I'm tired." Her voice cracked like static on a turntable, an inhuman sound. "If I was faster, I could've pushed him away, you know? It could've been *just* me, and that would've been fine."

"But it was both of you, wasn't it?"

She turned to face me. "Don't play games."

It could've been a trick of the light, a mirage over the can-yon, but a thousand stony seas away, across the vast orange valley, a blue wing flickered in the distance.

"Does Thomas know that you...that you're...that you also..." I couldn't bring myself to finish.

Therese fell to her knees and clutched my waist with horrible strength. I looked around, desperate for witnesses should she augment whatever superpower enabled her to physically contact the living, to possibly hurl one into the abyss before us, sentence one to death far, far below.

"You have to bring him here," she said. "It's the only way I can tell him I'm—" She choked on her last word, but I understood it. After 20 years of working with mourners, *sorry* was part of my vernacular.

Another trick of the light: as Therese's eyebrows lifted, and a gust of sand swept over her features, her desperate eyes resembled Sharon's. A ghost I carry to this day.

We both turned our heads as the bluebird found the guardrail.

"He's here already," I said.

Therese rose on her wobbly legs. Her dead legs. Her legs that shouldn't work. The bird held its place, piped its storybook chirp. She opened her palm and inched out her arm. And though I knew it was wrong to bring him forth— too much time had passed—the consequences of not trying could be worse. A mother knows no bounds, especially true if she's dead.

I closed my eyes and bore down, beckoning the pinprick of his spirit to swell against the darkness. But he was just a tickle, too weak to take hold. Too scared to try. He cried as I drew him near, displaced him like an infant from its womb.

His whimpers turned to wails, beat behind my eyes until the pain was too much to bear. My knees hit the dirt.

Through the plexiglass barrier separating us from the canyon's edge, I caught the bluebird tumbling beak-over-tail into the open void, a fish freed of its line.

But it wasn't freed. It was lifeless.

I'd lost him.

Period.

Therese's shadow smothered me then, as if she knew I'd goofed up, her eyes as tortured as the terrain. She closed her hand before blasting the sky with a horrible howl. I shrank into the hardpan, pulled my knees to my chest. The coin had flipped, I realized, and I laughed through my tears. Who would summon *me* after Therese did her worst? Would they honour or exploit like the spirits I'd profited from?

I waited, my fate in her hands, but she just scrabbled over the railing, landing on her busted ankle with a nauseating snap. She shambled toward the canyon's edge.

Could I have saved her? *Could* she have been saved? Did she hit the bottom? I couldn't say. Dusk had coloured the canyon black, and by the time I processed the ghost of her profile, suspended over the rocky edge, darkness had swallowed it up—like she'd never existed at all.

I don't remember collecting myself. Just that I wept in my car, too tired to roll up the window, and grateful, at least, to clear the cab of her stench. Under starlight I watched the dotted line of the interstate carry me home, though for how long I'd call it home I wasn't sure; there was too much paraphernalia there, all the candles and sage, the quartz and tapestries. Reminders of a life I was done with.

I wiped my eyes and saw a woman staring at me in the rear-view. It took me a minute to realize it was *my* cheeks, not Sharon's, showered in wet mascara. I wondered where my oldest friend was, and if she wondered about me, too. If she'd released the trauma or was still bound to it.

Then I saw him.

In the back seat.

As clear as his mother had been, and with her same creamy eyes. Only his were somewhere else. Oblivious. Indifferent.

A torn scalp, black ditches across his face—his features were slim, though maybe some were missing. I kept my eyes on the road, but I felt his on mine. They were the eyes of a boy just put through the wash, pulled out sopping, unaware he'd been through.

Like a chick out of its nest, Thomas accompanied me home.

James Fritz

The Smoke Detector

The Schueddig on Lake Shore stands out like a lighthouse against Lake Michigan. The glassy exterior of the apartment building is as blue as the water in front of it. I push through the revolving door and freeze in front of the entrance. The opulence is almost too much to take in.

Massive bronze columns flank the four corners of the room. A white dome in the ceiling glows with light. Two fireplaces on opposite sides crackle with real firewood. Lounge chairs and coffee tables are scattered across the floor. They might as well have a sign above the entrance that reads *Home of the Six-Figure Bracket.*

Immediately, a realtor greets me. It seems that the more expensive the building, the more enthused people are to meet you.

"Welcome to the Schueddig, Mr. Hyde! My name's Jim and I'll be showing you around today."

I shake his hand. He looks like he just came from a taping of *Rebel Without a Cause.* His black jacket is unzipped, revealing a white t-shirt underneath. His blue jeans have a small rip on the left knee cap. The light from the domed ceiling reflects off of his polished shoes.

"Nate's fine. Happy to be here."

He leads me towards the elevators. I fight to keep from smiling in delight. There are four of them. Three more than my current apartment.

"So, today I'm going to be showing you a two-bedroom unit on the 27th floor. Just came on the market. Tops out at 1,603 square feet of living space. Comes with stainless steel appliances, hardwood floors, granite counter-tops, washer and dryer, dishwasher, and lake-front views. The building itself boasts 24/7 security, a business center, clubhouse, lounge, fitness center, sauna, pool, rooftop terrace... I mean, it might be easier for me to list the stuff that isn't included!"

The elevator opens. My ears pop as we ascend. Jim leads me to Unit #2717. He pulls a key out of his pocket and opens the door.

"Oh! I almost forgot to mention that this is a corner unit. Every room has views of the water."

He waves me in. The hardwood floor goes on forever. A door to my left leads to one of the bedrooms... which is bigger than my current studio.

"This is the first bedroom with a half bath," Jim says.

He shows me the rest of the unit. The open living room/ kitchen is enormous. There's enough room for a dining room table, an eight-seater sofa, and a grand piano. The second bedroom is a copy of the first but with a full bathroom.

"And last but not least, the views."

He opens up the curtains on one of the east-facing windows. My jaw drops. All I see is water. The cars below look as small as fingernails.

"How much is the owner asking?" I ask.

"$2,935 per month."

I allow myself a grin. I don't care if the realtor notices. There's nothing to negotiate. For the first time in my life, I can afford every penny.

●

"I still can't believe you didn't put this couch together," Daphne says. "It came in one piece?"

"Perks of being promoted to senior data analyst," I say. "Now, I have what's called *disposable income*. I can't be expected to do manual labor of any kind."

Daphne playfully punches me in the shoulder. I snake my hand into hers. It fits mine like a glove.

I can't remember the name of the movie playing. Some horror flick about a crazy woman that calls in to a radio show and asks the producer to play a song for her over and over. The woman on the sofa has my complete attention.

"Maybe I should have been a comp sci major, too," she says. "Three years out of college and you get to live here. And you don't even have any loans! I guess we early childhood education majors never got the memo."

"Daphne, I couldn't care less about how much money you make. You have other advantages that more than compensate."

She bites her lip. She's either trying not to laugh, or I've flattered her. I think it's the second. She rests her head against my chest.

That's when I hear a beeping noise. It sounds like some sort of kitchen timer. I can't tell which direction it's coming from. Above me? Below? Adjacent? It goes on for a few minutes before it stops. I don't think Daphne heard it.

The movie ends. The credits roll. Daphne takes the remote from the coffee table and turns the TV off. Neither of us touched the bowl of popcorn.

"What are these *other advantages* that I have?" Daphne asks. Her green eyes lock onto mine. She rubs my thigh.

"Well, you're one of the kindest people I know. Not every woman has the temperament to work with small children. And you follow through on your promises, too. I know that I can trust you."

A reddish circle appears on each of her cheeks like some sort of devilish halo. Her mouth parts open.

"What else?" Her voice cracks. Our faces are inches apart.

"Another advantage you have is that you're beautiful. Stunning. Gorgeous. Sexy. Cute. Hot as-"

She grabs my face and shoves her lips into mine. Her tongue bursts into my mouth. Excitement tears through me. I push her down onto the couch. My body crashes on top of hers. She untucks my collared shirt and pulls it over my head. Her hands roam up and down my chest like she's acquainting herself with it for the first time.

"Did you lose something?" I say.

"God, you're so ripped, Nate. I guess someone's been hitting the gym downstairs."

She kisses me again and again and again. If there is such a thing as heaven, I'm pretty sure it resembles this...

At least without that fucking alarm. The beeping starts again. It's just loud enough for me to hear it. Why the hell does it keep going off? It must be a smoke detector or something. But why aren't the fire alarms for the building going berserk right now? Is it detecting something else?

"What's the matter, baby?" Daphne asks. "Something wrong?"

"How thick do you think these walls are?" I ask.

She grins at me from earlobe to earlobe. My stomach disappears in my chest.

"No idea. But just to be on the safe side, I'll make sure to *scream* when I come."

•

It's almost 1:30 AM, and I can still hear the alarm. Every time it starts, it rings for a few seconds until someone shuts it off... and then twenty minutes later, it starts up again.

I leave Daphne behind and throw on an undershirt and shorts. My bare feet feel like icicles in the hallway. I walk over to #2718 and press my ear against the door. Nothing. I do the same for #2716.

Bingo. It's coming from there. I can hear footsteps in the unit followed by the alarm shutting off again. My body shivers as I go back to my unit and dial the front desk.

"Schueddig Security. How can I help you?"

"Hi, this is Nate from Unit #2717. There's some sort of alarm beeping in #2716. It's been going off for a few days now. If you could check it out, I'd really appreciate it."

"No problem, I'll get right on it."

I hang up and breathe a sigh of relief. A pair of green eyes stares at me in the darkness.

"What's wrong?" Daphne asks.

"Can you hear an alarm?"

She sits up in bed. "Yeah... I think I do hear something. It's like a beeping noise."

"I've been hearing it for a few days now," I say. "Just called down to security. They said they'll check it out. You can go back to sleep."

"Hmmm..." she says.

I get back into bed. Her body fits perfectly against mine. I stop shivering. God, she's so warm.

"I love you," she says. Before I can respond, she turns around and falls back asleep. Her cute snoring resumes.

•

The next night, I dispense with the phone calls and walk down to the security desk. My sandals clack against the marble floor of the lobby. The security guard looks like he's on the wrong side of sixty, but at least he's ambulatory. I take him up to the unit in question. We both hear the beeping. I wait around the corner as he talks to the occupant.

"Well?" I ask.

The security guard comes around with a lady that *really* looks on the wrong side of sixty. Aging spots cover her skin. Her hair consists of a few white strings. I tower almost a foot above her.

"Hi, I'm Lori, your neighbor. I have an alarm in my apartment that goes off whenever it detects smoke from cigarettes or marijuana or vaping. You see, I have emphysema and whenever someone smokes in their unit, it becomes very hard for me to breathe. So when the alarm goes off, I know that I need to move to a window for fresh air."

She speaks in a whisper, like she's afraid to wake anybody up… except me.

"Hold on," I say, "I thought smoking wasn't allowed in this building."

"It's not," the security guard says.

I throw my hands up. "So why haven't we found out who's doing it yet?"

"It's hard to pin down where the smoke is coming from," the guard says, "and unless we're 100% sure when we make an accusation, we could be opening ourselves up to liability."

"I'm almost positive it's coming from the unit below me," Lori says. "The only way it could be getting in is through the vent. That's why I have that detector on."

A part of me feels sorry for this woman and her genetic roll of the dice. Hell… she might be a former smoker for all I know. But this isn't my problem.

"Ma'am, you have to understand: I can't sleep with that alarm on. It's been going off ever since I moved in here."

"I know, and I apologize. I've just turned it down to its lowest volume. I hope that you'll bear with me until we find the culprit."

Her eyes are open so wide they look like they might pop out. I try and back away without her noticing. Even though she poses no physical threat to me whatsoever, she does seem a little wacky.

"Okay I understand have a good night," I say in a rush. I go back to my unit and lock the door. My heart pounds in my chest, and not from frustration.

•

It's been a few weeks since my meeting with Lori. That fucking alarm still goes off every night, but it does seem quieter now. Which is good because another noise from the floor above me has taken its place.

THUMP THUMP THUMP

If I had to bet, I'd say that someone is having their unit refurbished by workers that function on a nocturnal schedule. It sounds like someone is pounding a hammer right on the fucking floor.

"Oh my God! Can you please stop! Enough's enough! I'm trying to sleep!"

Ha. Sounds like Lori is pissed. I can hear her yelling from her unit. I don't even bother calling down to the front desk again. Someone else will do the job.

•

Even though I've had my new couch for a few weeks, I can see the imprint of my butt in the cushions. Apart from work and private time with Daphne, sitting on my ass with a physical book takes up the majority of my time. The only way to unwind from looking at a screen is to *not* look at a screen.

Bookshelves line the hallway to the front door. Though I've never inventoried my collection, it probably numbers in the thousands by now. The pages from a Napoleon biography migrate from my right hand into my left.

KNOCK KNOCK KNOCK

Fuck. Who the hell is that? I set my book down on the couch.

"Coming."

I open the door about a quarter of the way. It's Lori.

"Hi, Nate. Hope you're doing okay. Am I catching you at a bad time?"

Yeah, you cuckoo bird.

"No, it's fine."

"I know that our bedrooms are connected. The smoke is getting in through the wall. Actually, it's not so much the smoke that gets to me. It's the juices. I've smelled cola, vanilla, banana..."

She counts off the different vape flavors on her fingers. I crush the door knob in my hand.

"That's what makes it hard for me to breathe. So, if you could just do it in your living room, that'd make a big difference."

My jaw starts a controlled descent. Anger sizzles through my veins.

"*I don't smoke.*"

"Don't worry," Lori says, "it's totally fine. I'm just trying to be a good neighbor here. There's this paramedic that helped me install the smoke detector. He's been trying to pinpoint the exact location that the smoke is getting in. He says that he's got it figured out now."

God, I can't wait to meet that fucker...

"I though you said that you were dead certain that the person below you was the one smoking," I say.

"He's been gone for the last couple of weeks and the paramedic says that the smoke is coming from the wall in my bedroom, so..."

She shrugs her shoulders. Is that a smirk on her face? Does she think she's caught me red-handed or something? She's fucking nuts if she thinks I'm the one smoking. Hell, I've never even taken a puff of a cigarette before.

"I don't know what to tell you," I say.

"Don't worry about it," she says. "There's no problem. I mean, I don't want things to get to a point where I have to bring a lawsuit, so I'm trying to be as nice as I can. You know, I actually teach piano lessons to autistic children. All in all, I'm a good person."

It's a good thing that I'm not drinking anything right now. Otherwise, I would have spit it all right on her. And then she'd actually have good reason for bringing a lawsuit.

"I give you my word of honor that I don't smoke," I say.

She shakes her head. "It's okay. I just thought I'd stop by and talk with you."

She doesn't believe me. Now she thinks I'm a fucking liar.

"Great. Thanks. See you later."

It takes every ounce of restraint to not slam the door in her face.

•

Daphne can't stop laughing at me as I tell my story. At least someone's enjoying this stupid smoking shit show.

"She said she knows some paramedic that swears the smoke is coming from my unit," I say. "I'll give you 2:1 odds that that paramedic is an imaginary friend."

"God," Daphne says, "this is so fucking funny. Speaking of friends, it sounds like you've got a new bestie! I hope she isn't giving me any competition on the romantic front."

"If I had to guess," I say, "Lori hasn't seen a dick in decades."

Daphne snorts with laughter, which makes her laugh even harder, which makes her snort again in a virtuous cycle.

BEEP BEEP BEEP

The alarm goes off for the seventh time today. Tears roll down Daphne's eyes as she convulses in laughter. She smacks the sofa with her hand.

"What's today's flavor, Nate?" she says. "Hazelnut?"

"Notice how you're the only one enjoying this, Daphne."

She laughs for what feels like a couple hours before she settles down.

"Lori actually said that she's a good person," I say. "Last time I checked, Tiger Woods doesn't wear a hat that says *I'm a good golf player*. Everyone already knows that he's the best."

"And handsome, too," Daphne says.

My eyebrows raise to the ceiling.

"You are *really* getting under my skin today," I say.

"I know," she says. "It's hilarious."

She tries to take my hand. I snatch it away.

"Come on... don't be such a grouch," she says. "Kiss me."

She puts her hands on my cheeks. Our lips snuggle together. She eases her body on top of me. My anger starts to evaporate.

"Wow... speaking of wood," she says.

THUMP THUMP THUMP

"*Wonderful*," I say. "Now we get to hear from the construction worker that lives above me."

THUMP THUMP THUMP THUMP THUMP

"Hold on," Daphne says. She closes her eyes. The thumping continues. "That's not coming from upstairs. I think it's coming from you-know-who."

I strain my ears. *She's right*. Lori must be pounding on the wall with her fist or something.

"You can't be serious," I say. "That woman is a fucking maniac."

"And a night owl," Daphne says. "It's almost midnight and she's still making the most of the day."

We pick up where we left off. Daphne plants as many kisses as possible on my chest.

"Nate, I'm not sure if you're aware, but there's this thing called a carbohydrate. You could use a couple in your-"

KNOCK KNOCK KNOCK

Both of us freeze in place. The temperature in the room plummets. My heart thumps back and forth against my ribs.

"It's never-ending," Daphne whispers.

"You'd better not scream this time," I say.

"I'll try not to. This isn't funny anymore."

KNOCK KNOCK KNOCK

I ease myself off the couch and tiptoe into the hallway. I see a shadow in the crack under the door. Is Lori going to wait there all night? *Oh, Jesus*. She slips a note under the door. No... make that two notes. I stand frozen in place. Finally, she walks away. I pick up the ratty pieces of paper and read them to myself.

Hello, Nate. It's Lori. There's a frequent burning odor that happens late at night. LIKE RIGHT NOW. Usually starts around 11:00 PM and goes throughout the early morning until 8:00 AM. Other people on the floor smell it, too. It's a specific joint or vape which makes it very difficult for me to breathe. I could smell it before I knocked on your door today. The paramedic is positive he has identified the unit doing it. I'll pop by tomorrow with some coffee. Thank you so much. Sincerely, Lori from #2716.

I show the scraps of paper to Daphne. She shakes her head in shock. I've never seen her lost for words before.

"Two things," I say. "Number 1: I don't even drink coffee. Number 2: Lori's about to make another friend. My landlord."

●

Friday: 11:50 PM, door knock

Saturday: 1:35 AM and 2:00 AM, pounding on the wall; 11:55 PM, alarm

Sunday: 1:45 AM, pounding on the wall and shouting; 2:00 AM, door knock; 2:20 AM, alarm; 2:30 AM, pounding on the wall...

It takes me a half hour to craft the email to my landlord. The list of grievances goes on and on. I don't have to embellish anything. The truth is on my side of the wall separating my apartment from hers. There's no need for me to raise my voice. I've got so much here, my landlord will be falling over himself to remedy this. At least he will if he wants to keep me as a paying tenant.

•

It's been a few days since my landlord brought down fire and brimstone on Schueddig Management. Now, everything's quiet on the Western Front. I haven't heard a peep out of #2716, and I don't think I ever will again.

It's unbelievable how much reading one can get done without interruptions. I've made it to Elba in my Napoleon biography.

BEEP BEEP BEEP

The alarm goes off, but only for a few seconds. I don't even bother putting my book down. This isn't worth anything further on my part. If the alarm is the extent of her noise-making, I think I can live with that from now on.

KNOCK KNOCK KNOCK

Now I put my book down. I'm not sure whether to get angry or laugh. This woman is completely nuts. It's 10:00 PM, and she's knocking again. There's no way she didn't receive that email. Did she forget about it? I think the term *rental reimbursement* starts to apply now.

SHUNK

My eyes shoot to the door. A hole forms in my stomach. I hear a new noise. That of a key being inserted. My heart starts to sprint.

"Oh, shit..."

The knob turns. The door eases open.

"Oh, I knew it. It's definitely coming from in here."

I peek my head out of my bedroom. My apartment is pitch black, but I can see Lori walk into the bedroom off of the entrance hallway. Adrenaline washes through my body. How the hell did she get in? Did she pick the lock?

No. She must have stolen the key from the guard. He would be the only one with a master for all the units.

I leap out of my bedroom and duck behind the sofa. Lori walks down the hallway. She's coughing hard enough to hack up a lung.

"Oh, man," she says. "It's really getting bad."

She hasn't seen me. Her coughs grow louder and louder.

"OH MY GOD! THIS IS IT! I'VE FOUND IT!"

She fans the air with her hand. I wait until she walks into my bedroom before I bolt down the hallway and swing the front door open.

That's when I hear it.

BEEP-BEEP-BEEP-BEEP-BEEP-BEEP-BEEP...

The alarm. Dozens of them. Every unit on the floor has one now, and they're all going crazy.

"Holy fuck..."

I sprint down the hall. The walls seem to shrink in on me as I wait for an elevator. The second the doors open, I hurtle inside and slam the button for the lobby. Each time the elevator goes past a floor, I hear beeping.

"Shit shit shit..."

I slap myself across the face. I don't wake up.

My palms sweat. I don't know where I'm going to go, just as long as it's as far away from the Schueddig as possible.

The doors open. I dash across the lobby. Of course, the one time that I need the security guard, he's not at his desk. I almost break the glass on the sliding door as I slam into it. A cool breeze bites against me.

That's when my feet fall out from under me. Gravity starts to do its thing as I fall forward. I barely have time to brace myself. Pain explodes in my wrists as I smack into the street. Tires skid next to me. A pair of headlights blinds me before I lose consciousness.

•

A light shines in my face. My eyes squint. A flurry of knives pierces my body whenever I try to move.

"Ooohhh…"

Suddenly, something constricts around my chest. My breath escapes me.

"Ouch! Oh fuck!"

My eyes finally adjust. It's not a something, but a someone that's hugging me. Daphne.

"Daphne, stop! You're hurting me."

"Sorry. I'm just glad you're okay."

She lets go of me. Her green eyes sparkle with tears. She sits back down on the side of the hospital bed. A curtain is drawn around us, cutting us off from the rest of the suite.

"Where are my… oh, shit."

My cheeks burn thanks to the hospital gown I'm wearing. Someone must have dressed me.

"Don't worry," Daphne says, "they made me leave when they put that on."

I hear a beeping sound, but it's not the smoke detector. It's a heart-rate monitor. A bandage is wrapped around my chest. My arms are sleeved in cuts and bruises.

"How long have I been here?" I ask.

"Since last night. Apparently you decided to run right into a car pulling into the entrance to your building."

"I was trying to put distance between myself and the lunatic that broke into my fucking apartment," I say. "Did they call the cops on her?"

"Don't worry," Daphne says. "From what I've heard, you won't be seeing much of Loony Lori anymore."

I try and sit up in the hospital bed. My ribs scream at me. I feel a burning sensation whenever I try to breathe.

"She actually took the master key from the security guard and walked right into my apartment. I thought she was going to stab me. All for doing something that I've never done. And get this: I heard that same alarm going off in every single unit on my floor. She must have handed them out to everybody or something. I wasn't fucking imagining it."

"Maybe there's something to be said for rural living," Daphne says. "At least you don't have any fucking neighbors."

It hurts to laugh, but I make an effort.

"I could go for a farm and a few acres of land right now," I say.

"Not to mention a few sets of hands to help tend the fields," Daphne says.

I stare at her. She smiles at me. I keep staring. Her expression doesn't change. Now, I know that she's being deadly serious.

"*Really?*" I whisper.

"Well... seeing you knocked unconscious on the street flipped a switch inside me. I realized that I can't just put off childbearing forever. Once you come close to losing something, you really start to understand the value of it. Plus, you can't be around little children as often as me without getting a little itch to pop out a couple of your own."

I am breathless.

Ever since we became a couple, I knew that she loved me, but not like this. Not to the extent that we would bond together and raise children. That takes a commitment that until now I wasn't sure that she wanted.

I feel like I'm falling in love with her all over again.

"After they're done fixing your body up," Daphne says, "I want you to scratch that itch for me."

"I'm all yours," I say.

"There's just one condition," Daphne says.

She reaches over to a nightstand next to the bed. For the first time, I notice a circular device of some kind on it. She picks it up and flicks a switch.

BEEP BEEP BEEP

My jaw hits the floor. Sparks fly off of the heart rate monitor. It's the same smoke detector that Lori used. My entire body freezes in fear and pain. Daphne leans over and whispers in my ear.

"*Stop smoking.*"

Orrin Grey

In the Blue Room

Avery was late again and Phoebe alternated her time between pacing the stage, checking her phone, chewing her nails, and cursing him under her breath. She'd already had to fight David to incorporate this effect into the play in the first place, and every delay or hiccup made it that much more likely that he was going to scrap it.

"This is a college production of *Hamlet*," he'd said, the umpteenth time they had argued about it, "not *Poltergeist*. We don't need a fancy ghost. Just slap some white makeup on him and push him out on stage."

Fortunately, she had eventually won, partly by arguing that the effect wouldn't take any resources out of regular rehearsals—meaning that she and Avery, and occasionally Luis, who was playing Hamlet, had to run through the tech rehearsals on their own time—and partly by agreeing to sort all the costumes from the costume bins at the back of the prop room, which hadn't been properly done in the three years she had been attending Dircks University.

For the third time that evening, Phoebe walked out into the lobby and watched the rain streak down the windows. It had been pouring on and off most of the week, and everything felt wet and clammy, the kind of cold that sunk into your bones and never seemed to warm up. The rooms backstage all smelled of mildew, as they did anytime the weather turned damp.

This time, as she watched the rain moving like translucent snakes across the tall glass, she saw Avery coming up the front steps, his shoulders hunched against the downpour. He wore the same long, olive-colored coat he wore everywhere, and carried no umbrella. His shoulders and hair were soaked, plastered to him, and he looked thinner, somehow, than he had the last time she saw him, which had only been two days ago, as if his coat was going to swallow him up.

Setting aside her annoyance for the moment, she pushed open the front door as he approached and he stepped inside, shaking the water from his arms and hands and doing a quick little two-step on the rug, which was still sopping from people coming and going earlier in the day.

"Nice of you to make it," she said.

"Sorry," Avery replied, looking up at her for the first time. His eyes were red rimmed, with dark circles around them that made it seem a little like he was already wearing his ghost makeup. Frankly, he looked like shit. "Rough day."

"Been a lot of those?" Phoebe asked, more archly than she meant to because she was still mad, but her anger was starting to temper simply due to how forlorn he looked. She and Avery had known each other for years now. They were in the same class, and had taken Intro to Theater together as freshmen. She'd had a crush on him ever since, even though she learned quickly that he wasn't actually her type—too flighty and too self-absorbed, like most actors she had known.

"Yeah," was all he said, walking past her into the auditorium. He left his coat dripping on one of the seats, and she followed a few steps behind as he descended toward the orchestra pit. It was the pit that had given her the idea in the first place. It had been years since there was an actual orchestra to play here, from before her time at Dircks, and last year they had torn the floor out of the pit as part of a planned auditorium renovation that never got much farther than that.

In so doing, they had discovered that the floor of the pit was actually a platform, and the pit dropped a full three feet below, to a secret room—secret only insofar that it had been closed off over the years, she found when she asked Dr. Gaspard about it—built beneath the stage.

"At one time," Dr. Gaspard told her, "we had the whole works down there. A trapdoor where we could raise and lower actors onto the stage via a sort of dumbwaiter. All that jazz. They decided to shut it down in the '70s because it was a liability risk and also expensive to maintain, I imagine, but they just walled it up. Could have used it for storage, you'd think."

The space under the stage was low and dark, broken up by the wooden support posts that held up the stage itself. But a person who wasn't too tall could stand straight down there, and so it was where Phoebe had rigged up her blue room.

She hadn't become a stage manager because she loved yelling at the lighting guys or arguing with David. What intrigued her were things like this. The tricks of the trade. The idea of a secret elevator that carried actors to and from the stage for quick changes. Makeup that only appeared under light of a certain color. She had always been less interested in the magic trick itself than in how it was performed.

More than anything, though, she wanted to pull off a Pepper's ghost, an idea that was already old-fashioned by the time she started at Dircks, and not in the repertoire of very many college theatrical companies. "Audio video people do them now," Dr. Gaspard had told her when she brought the idea to him in his office. "They call them holograms and put them up on music video award shows. You can even do one on your phone, with the right equipment. Nobody does them on stage."

"They're hokey," is what David had said.

"They only became hokey because everyone was doing them," she retorted. "Most of the people in our audience will never have seen one, unless they've been to Disney World. It'll be a novelty to them."

"Everything old is new again," had been Gaspard's only contribution to the argument. This production of *Hamlet* was David's senior project, and Gaspard had given him free rein on it, so long as he kept it under budget and brought it to stage on time. Given that she was in her third year, it might also be Phoebe's last opportunity to do a Pepper's ghost before she graduated and moved on to some job that would pay her peanuts and give her basically no creative control. So she had pushed—and promised, and acquiesced—and eventually gotten her way, at least for now.

"Jesus, it's dark down here," Avery was saying, from the entrance to the blue room beneath the stage, hidden from the audience by the walls of the orchestra pit.

"It won't be when you're working," she said. She hit the switch that brought up the blue LEDs that she had already installed along the floor and ceiling—and around the support pillars that he might otherwise smack into. The glow filtered out while you were looking into the pit, but it was invisible to the audience so long as the stage lights or the house lights were up even a little bit. She had checked from every angle, even the balcony.

"Tell me again how this works?" Avery asked, stooping to step down into the blue room.

"There's a sheet of plexiglass set at an angle in front of part of the stage," Phoebe said, rapping her knuckles against it as she followed him. "The audience can't see it, so long as Maya in lighting does her job right. You'll be down here, doing the scene just like you would if you were up on the stage. Luis will be on stage, standing to the side of the plexiglass, doing his part. When you're supposed to appear, the lights up there go down and a light down here comes up. Your reflection will appear on that sheet of plexiglass up there, and the audience will be able to see you even though you're down here."

"So why don't I just do it on stage?"

"Because you'll look translucent. Like a ghost," she said. "It'll be cool, I promise."

She followed him down into the blue room, and hoped that she was right.

•

Because the stage was not well set up for it, making the illusion work had required a little creative engineering on

Phoebe's part. In a more classic Pepper's ghost setup, the blue room would have been nearer the wall of the orchestra pit, or off to the side of the stage, where it would be more obviously aligned with the sheet of plexiglass. Here, however, some careful arrangements had been necessary to ensure that the light that illuminated Avery was invisible to the audience, even while Avery was visible on the plexiglass.

Though it had been a lot of hard work, done during what was ostensibly her free time, she had never felt more energized in all of her time studying production techniques or working as stage manager for the little theater at Dircks. It helped to distract her from how lousy Avery seemed to be having it, meaning that she didn't really notice the changes in him until it was time to actually do the makeup test and run his lines with the ghost effect working.

When she met him three years ago, Avery had been a very pretty boy, with sandy blond hair and the high cheekbones that were part of why he was chosen to play the ghostly figure of Hamlet's father. In the weeks leading up to the play, however, he had grown visibly thinner, his eyes seeming to sink into their sockets so that he hardly needed the dark-ringed makeup that Kelly had concocted to make him into a ghost.

On the night of the makeup test, Phoebe was there early to make sure everything was set up and ready. She even cleaned the plexiglass piece herself—it had to be clear enough that the audience wouldn't see it, or even suspect it, no easy task in a theater filled with stage hands running back and forth behind the scenes. It was raining again that night, which was why she was standing just inside the stage door, blowing cigarette smoke out into the wet night, when Avery arrived.

A red Prius pulled up in the alley behind the auditorium, and Avery started to get out the passenger side, his coat once again hunched up around his shoulders. He paused halfway out, though. The rain had slacked off since Phoebe started smoking, and now it drummed haphazardly on the roof of the car, and on the panel of Avery's door, where it hung open, allowing Phoebe to catch parts of the conversation.

"Avery, no," a woman's voice said from inside, in response to something Avery had said that Phoebe missed. "You said you needed a ride because it's raining. That's it."

Avery was talking into the car, his voice partly swallowed up be its interior, and he sounded beat down and quiet anyway, pleading. "—all this," was what she caught of his reply, followed by, "Rene, can we please—"

The driver said something else that Phoebe missed, and then, "If you're going to be like this, don't call me the next time you need a ride."

The car started to pull forward, even though Avery hadn't yet shut his door, jerking it out of his hand and setting him off balance. He stumbled slightly in the rain, but didn't fall, his hand opening and closing on the empty air where the door had just been. He turned away without stepping forward to shut it, and the car surged forward a little further before Phoebe saw a woman's arm reach out from inside, grab the door handle, and pull the passenger door shut.

"Are you all right?" she asked as Avery climbed up the stairs and pushed the stage door open with his shoulder.

"Just another rough day," he said, trying to flash a smile at her. When she first met him, his smile had been able to light up a room and send her heart fluttering, make her joints feel weak. Now, though, it was the brave smile of a cancer patient who doesn't want to worry their family, worse than if he hadn't smiled at all.

•

The only other people at the first makeup test were Kelly and Eric, and Phoebe had been forced to convince both of them to come in on their days off so they could run the test without cutting into normal rehearsal time. Eric got Avery into his costume back stage, and the actor slumped in the makeup chair in a full suit of black armor, albeit made of cardboard, while Kelly put the details on his wan face.

As much as the Pepper's ghost effect was Phoebe's baby, once they got Avery down into the blue room and fired it up, even she had to admit that it wouldn't have worked as well without Kelly's makeup. The black armor, which Kelly had also designed, was all thick gorgets and pauldrons that made him look something like a marionette, while the skull-like makeup caused Avery's real features to recede, so that it looked as if an untethered skull wearing a simple crown delivered the lines, floating above the armor itself.

"But that I am forbid to tell the secrets of my prison house," Avery's voice boomed across the stage, "I could a tale unfold whose lightest word would harrow up thy soul, freeze thy young blood."

Down in the blue room, he had a microphone that was wired to make his voice sound not merely like he was *on* the stage, but above it, such that the ghost's speech seemed to come from all around the actor playing poor Hamlet.

Phoebe was sitting out in the audience, about midway back, and she could tell that it worked. The ghost of Hamlet's father seemed to float in the air around the set of the castle battlements, the voice seemed to resound from everywhere and nowhere, overwhelming the space while also keeping a surprising note of human suffering that had to be attributed to Avery's performance which, even in this test run, appeared unmarred by his "rough days." If anything, he delivered the lines with more feeling than he ever had in early rehearsals.

Once she had moved around the house, checking the angles from a bunch of different seats, Phoebe was finally satisfied enough to call a cut and let everyone go home. She made sure to tell them all that they had done a great job, especially Kelly, and after she and Eric had departed, Phoebe went through, turning out the lights, only then noticing that Avery hadn't left.

He was still sitting in the makeup chair, staring into the mirror. Kelly had scrubbed the paint off his face before she left but, in the semi-darkness, you couldn't tell. His eyes seemed like pits, the shadows around his cheeks and mouth so deep and dark that his face could have been a puckered skull. Again, Phoebe felt a twinge of guilt for not noticing his condition sooner. She put a gentle hand on his shoulder, causing him to start, pulling his unseeing gaze from the mirror and up toward her. She could only see his eyes because the light reflected in them.

"Sorry," he said, "must have zoned out."

"Are you okay?" she asked again.

"Rene broke up with me," he said, his voice hollow of any feeling. "She said I was needy."

Phoebe cast her mind back, trying to picture a Rene, but couldn't do it. She knew that Avery had never had any shortage of girls on his arm over the three years they'd been at Dircks. For various reasons, including to preserve her own sanity, she had never kept very good track of them, for all that she and Avery were ostensibly friends. It occurred to her now that this latest one, the one who must be Rene, who she couldn't quite conjure up a mental picture of, must have lasted longer than any of the others because, even though Phoebe couldn't composite a face, she knew that it had been the same girl at the cast party for *Long Day's Journey Into Night*, and that had been six months ago.

"You *are* needy," Phoebe said, but gently.

"I know," he replied quietly. "But I always have been. *I* didn't change."

"Come on," Phoebe said, squeezing his shoulder. "I've got to lock up. Do you need a ride home? I think it started raining again."

On the drive over to Avery's apartment—Phoebe was surprised to realize that she still knew where it was—he sat with his head back against the headrest of her Civic, his eyes closed. Neither of them said much, and the radio mumbled in the background, a DJ going on about something that the volume was turned down too far to hear.

When she pulled up in front of his building, Phoebe thought for a moment that Avery had gone to sleep. Then he let out a small, deflated sound. "Thanks for the ride," he said, before he opened his eyes. He put his hand on the door handle but didn't open it yet. "I'm sorry about rehearsals and stuff," he said. "I know I've been late a lot."

"You've been doing great, though," Phoebe said. She had been mad at him, maybe a part of her still was, but she also hurt for him a little, and tonight, at least, she felt guilty about neglecting their friendship, even if it *was* to protect her own heart. Besides, he really *had* been doing great. She'd never seen him give a performance as good.

"Thanks," he said, trying to smile again. She wished he wouldn't. Now, in the reflected light of the streetlamp, it made him look like the ghost.

●

They only had one full tech and dress rehearsal before the first show. It was all hands on deck. The sound guy up in the booth, cueing thunder noise and background swordfight sounds, the lighting crew on the catwalks, the extras and the actors all in their various faux-Elizabethan costumes, or as close as the costume department was able to get. And Phoebe had to manage it all, while also keeping tabs on everything to make her pet project go off.

To ensure that it worked how it was supposed to, she had largely taken the Pepper's ghost effect out of the hands of the lighting and sound departments. The lighting crew had instructions on how much to dim the stage lights for the scene, but the light down in the blue room, and the microphone, she controlled with a remote that she kept zipped in her jacket pocket.

Because she was rushing around putting out fires and making sure everything else was where it needed to be, when it needed to be there, she didn't see Avery come in that night, but Ben, one of her assistants, told her he was there. She didn't get a chance to look in until the run-through had already begun, but when Barnardo and Francisco were first speaking their lines on the battlements, she poked her head down into the blue room beneath the stage.

The LEDs she had placed down there made it blue in fact as well as name, and in their dim glow she could see Avery only as a sort of rough-hewn shape piled in the chair at the far end of the space. She considered going over to him, but his first appearance was just a few minutes away and besides she could see Lea trying to get her attention from the wings. Phoebe settled for a wave, and was heartened when the outline of Avery extended one hand in a thumbs-up.

The first time she kicked on the light in the blue room was when the ghost appeared before Barnardo, Marcellus, and Horatio. In that scene, Avery didn't have any lines, he merely popped up at one end of the space, seeming to float above the gap beyond the battlements, and then moved slowly to the other end, at which time she shut off the light and he vanished again.

"It harrows me with fear and wonder," Derek, who was playing Horatio, said as he stared at the empty space where the ghost would look to be, for anyone who was sitting in the audience. It was the part that Phoebe had worried most about—the other actors playing opposite an empty space, rather than another performer. It wouldn't be so difficult for Luis, who would at least have Avery's voice over the speaker, but she was pleased at how Derek and the other two did their parts in this first scene.

She had maneuvered herself into the auditorium by the time the ghost appeared, so that she could see the effect of the Pepper's ghost with everything in place. She wasn't disappointed. Avery looked every inch the part when he appeared above the stage. His eyes were sunken to nothing, disappearing beneath the makeup and the effect of the light. He seemed to flicker in the air, hovering above the stage. He looked lost and terrible and perfect.

"I have to hand it to you," David said to her, after the rehearsal. "You pulled it off."

She went looking for Avery, to congratulate him and thank him for his hard work, but Kelly said he had already left. "He smelled like vodka when I was doing his makeup," she said. "But he got through all his lines okay."

Phoebe went to the stage door and looked out. That night it wasn't raining, but the pavement was still wet from earlier, and the streetlights reflected on the alley outside. She didn't see Avery anywhere, though.

●

She spent all of opening day in the theater, checking and double-checking, but she still tried to call Avery twice, once from her cell phone, and once from the phone in the office. He didn't answer either time.

By curtain call, they had a full house, which wasn't unusual on opening night. Plenty of classes gave out extra credit to students who attended the school's productions. But it meant that everything backstage was twice as hectic even than it had been during dress rehearsal, and Phoebe breathed a sigh of relief when she saw Avery in the makeup chair, already decked out in his cardboard armor.

She wanted to go over and say something to him, at least squeeze his shoulder in support, but she was juggling too many things and by the time she reached the makeup chair he was gone, probably already making his way to the blue room.

With the audience in their seats just on the other side of the curtain, making the noise of a living ocean to drown out the hurried work that they were still doing behind the scenes, there was only one way in or out of the blue room without being seen by the spectators, and that was the old trap door that was still at the back of the stage. Phoebe couldn't exactly go around to the orchestra pit and poke her head in. So, she and Avery had arranged a simple signal—he would send her a text to let her know that he was in place.

Still, she was a bit surprised when her phone buzzed in her pocket and, checking it, she saw simply a thumbs-up emoji from Avery's number. "Did he seem okay?" she managed to ask Kelly, while she was putting pancake makeup onto Derek's face.

"He felt cold and I think he'd been crying," Kelly whispered back. "He didn't say anything, but he didn't smell as much like booze."

Not that there was much she could do about it if he hadn't. They had run out of time, and it was enough that he was in his place. When the house lights dimmed and the stage lights came up, Phoebe had too many other things on her mind to worry about Avery, and she just prayed that everything went smoothly when she activated the light in the blue room.

"The bell then beating one," Marcus, who played Bernardo, was saying, and she kicked on the light for the first time.

The figure that appeared in the air before the crowd—invisible to the actors, who reacted nonetheless because that's what they had practiced to do—was an apparition if ever there had been one. Avery's gaunt appearance plus Kelly's superb makeup combined with the effect of the Pepper's ghost arrangement to create a baffling illusion, even for Phoebe, who had set it all up. The sounds the audience made suggested that they were equally impressed.

Every other time they had tried it out, Avery's ghost figure had appeared facing where the actors would be standing. This time, he was turned partly away, as if the light in the blue room had come up when he wasn't expecting it. Rather than ruin the illusion, however, it heightened the effect. The ghost seemed as lost as a ghost should, and when he gradually turned toward the three cowering actors, it was as though he didn't see them at all.

"Stay," Derek shouted up on stage. "Speak, speak! I charge thee speak!" Phoebe cut the light in the blue room and let out a gust of breath that she had not realized she was holding. So far, everything was working like a charm, and the only thing left to go wrong with her carefully-cultivated plan was the microphone intended to capture Avery's lines in scene five.

By the time that scene rolled around, she was already breathing a little easier, despite several minor snafus she had been required to clean up behind the scenes. Avery had appeared twice more, and each time performed his pantomime with a sensitivity that had been absent even from his earlier rehearsals.

As scene five opened and she fired up the light and prepared to open the mic, Avery appeared once more above the battlements, this time facing Luis as Hamlet. He looked, if anything, even more wasted away than he had before. Kelly's makeup included lines up his lips to simulate the bared teeth of a skull, and here they seemed to genuinely yawn around blackness as he spoke.

"I am thy father's spirit," Avery's voice came from everywhere and nowhere, "doomed for a certain term to walk the night and for the day confined to fast in fires..."

He had never sounded better, and even Luis seemed taken aback, which played into Hamlet's reaction to the appearance of his tormented sire.

"List, list, O, list!" Avery said, his voice crackling with emotion. "If thou didst ever thy dear farther love—"

There was a hall on the east side of the auditorium that led to an emergency exit at the back of the building. It was accessible from backstage, and midway down its length there was a side door into the crowded auditorium. Phoebe was standing there, watching the Pepper's ghost from the vantage point of the audience, when her phone buzzed in her pocket. She took it out, and saw a text from Avery, somehow, even though he was on stage now, for all intents and purposes, his ghostly image speaking to Hamlet above the battlements.

All it said was her name, with no punctuation.

"Murder most foul, as in the best it is," Avery's voice was saying from the speakers. "But this most foul, strange and unnatural."

She heard gasps from the audience and looked up from her phone. At a glance the tableaux was the same. Luis as Hamlet was promising revenge on wings as swift as the thoughts of love, but something was very wrong. Avery's head seemed to be expanding. It still looked like a skull, but now it was splitting, from the base of the jaw up to the nose, the jawbones becoming like mandibles as the blue light that made the ghost poured out from inside.

"Lethe," Avery's slurred voice said from the speakers, skipping over many of his lines in-between. "Lethe."

Luis stepped back, his eyes turning out toward the audience, breaking the fourth wall but actually looking, Phoebe thought, at the back of the piece of plexiglass, on which the image of Avery's ghost was projected. The ghost was continuing to grow, its back bending, the suit of black armor somehow expanding to accommodate its swelling torso.

"Oh God," Luis said, his lines now abandoned entirely. "I can see it. I can see it!"

The murmuring of the audience had begun to splinter, as different members reacted differently to this sudden change in script. There were sounds of anger, fear, confusion, even appreciation.

"Rene," Avery said, his voice continuing to fragment. It sounded like he was suffering from tuberculosis, and yet his words retained their power, echoing through the speaker and resounding throughout the auditorium. "The serpent that did sting my love now wears my crown."

Where the ghost's body was expanding, its arms had remained the same size, now appearing small and vestigial as its torso transformed into the thorax of some strange, glowing insect, the cardboard armor becoming chitin. Heightening the illusion were other arms, each of them ending in other hands, which were pushing their way out between the plates to grasp helplessly at the air.

It was only then that Phoebe realized she was running. Down the aisle along the side of the auditorium, pushing past people who were rising from their seats, realizing that something had gone very wrong. As she ran, she fumbled with the zipper at her jacket pocket.

The ghost of Hamlet's father now towered nearly the entire distance from stage to rafters, its head no longer bearing any resemblance to Avery, his own face slid backward and flattened to become the skull-mandibles of the ghost. It was reaching several of its many hands toward Luis and, though she knew that whatever she was seeing was just a projection on a piece of plexiglass in front of the stage, she dreaded what would happen if it reached him.

"Adieu, adieu, adieu," the decaying voice of the great, spectral insect was saying as she managed to pull to zipper open and reach the remote inside. "Remember me." And then Phoebe hit the button that cut the light in the blue room, and everything went dark.

●

The wiring of the theater was old and hadn't been updated since before Phoebe's time at Dircks. When she shut off the light to the blue room, it must have blown a fuse. That's what the fire department told them all later. At the time, all anyone knew was that the stage lights went out, the auditorium went dark, and there was suddenly the breathing chaos of a panicked rout as the audience fell into pandemonium.

In the crush and press of bodies that followed, Phoebe was driven back against the wall, the wind knocked from her, the remote for the blue room slapped from her hand and ground to dust beneath trampling feet. Several people were hurt in the stampede to the lobby, where the lights, attached to a different circuit, still burned.

The LEDs in the blue room were battery powered, and in the darkness of the blackened auditorium she could make out their glow around the walls of the orchestra pit. She moved along the wall in that direction, pushing against the flood of people who were leaving their seats and rushing toward the exits. Eventually, she got free of the throng and was standing at the mouth of the pit, looking down into the blue room.

From where she stood, it seemed empty, but Avery, if he was still there, would be farther back, invisible from her angle. Would he be himself? Would he be a giant insect, one far too large to fit into the cramped space beneath the stage? She stood reluctant to find out, the sound of the audience coming apart behind her slowly fading from her awareness as she stepped down into the pit.

It took her eyes a moment to adjust to the glow of the blue LEDs and, when they did, she saw Avery as she had before, slumped in the chair at the far end of the room. He wasn't moving. One step took her closer, then another. She felt the pills crunch under her feet before she saw them.

It looked like he overdosed. That's what the EMTs told them. Sleeping pills he'd gotten only a week before, telling the doctor that he couldn't sleep because of stress related to school, not mentioning his breakup. He had taken all of them that night. The paramedics said he was dead before the curtain ever rose.

Luis quit acting. It wasn't like his hair had gone shock white after the incident, but it was suddenly gray at the temples, where it had been black as a slick of oil before. He never talked about what he saw, at least not with anyone in the theater department, and when his advisor asked him about dropping the class, he said that he just couldn't stick with it after what happened to Avery.

What happened to Avery wasn't the end of it, though. The police came to the theater, first for the mass exodus that had resulted in dozens of injuries severe enough to send people to the hospital in ambulances, then for Avery's body down in that tight space beneath the stage. "It's pretty clearly a suicide," one of the officers told Dr. Gaspard within earshot of Phoebe, "but we'll probably have to ask a few questions."

Those questions led them first to Avery's apartment, then to Rene's, where they found her lying in bed, strangled. Time of death placed her murder in the early morning hours on the day of the play. She had skin under her nails that they matched to fresh wounds on Avery's forearms.

It was the last Pepper's ghost trick that Phoebe ever did.

Mark A. Nobles

Determination

If you're reading this, he's still alive.

It all started at The Ginger Man, a neighborhood bar on the westside of Fort Worth. There were five of us at the table. None of us live on the westside but it was a workplace hangout for Simone. We had decided to get together and Simone was already there and had already had a few so the rest of us decided we'd meet her there.

The rest of us were Keith, his wife Marti, Grant, and myself, Dennis, your humble narrator. I was the first to arrive and found Simone holding a table by the kitchen. She was nursing a cup of coffee and a plate of nachos. The coffee was light tan colored from all the cream she had added and the nachos were bean and cheese with jalapeños and sour cream on the side.

"What's up, chicken rub?" Remember that awkward stage in middle school? I never outgrew it.

Simone looked up, smiled, had no idea how she was to respond, and meekly proffered, "Nothing?"

She was sitting at a table for six, three chairs to a side, one end against a wall. She was sitting on the end by the aisle, I slid in behind her and took the chair by the wall. Attempting to make up for the unanswerable greeting I asked her how her work happy hour had gone.

"It was fun, I guess. A bunch of science and accounting nerds trying to be cool." The Ginger Man is a faux English pub. Lots of stouts and ales on tap, scotch eggs, heavy dark mahogany bar, furniture, and several dartboards. "They tried to throw darts. That was funny. There was blood."

"Oh, nice."

"I had too much beer on an empty stomach, so I ordered a couple of tacos and some nachos. It was too much food. You want to help me finish the nachos?" It was an English pub in Fort Worth, Texas, so of course, they served tacos and nachos. The place would have been burned to the ground if they didn't.

"I can nosh a couple of nachos." She put three chips slathered with beans and cheese on a napkin. "Want any jalapeños?"

"They aren't nachos without jalapeños."

Simone crinkled her nose, she was a transplant from Boston, so she hadn't grown up eating jalapeños on everything. She handed me the napkin with the chips, then slid the bowl of jalapeños down the table. "Sour cream?"

"I shouldn't but I'm going to, please." She slid the small bowl of sour cream down as well. "Thank you." Simone was the youngest in the group. Mid-thirties at most but could easily pass for mid-twenties. She was smart, talented, pretty, and exotic. In Fort Worth, Boston is exotic.

Keith and Marti came in before I had a chance to load up my nachos. "Howdy, Simone, Dennis, how ya'll doing?" Simone and I stood, Simone hugged Keith and Marti, I shook their hands across the table.

"I'm fine, I just arrived myself."

"And I've been here too long."

"Oh, I hope you aren't about to leave." Marti and Keith sat across from Simone. Keith directly and Marti taking the middle chair.

Spying Simone's coffee, Keith said, "What are you doing drinking coffee? It's beer thirty by my watch."

"I'm a couple of hours ahead of you guys. I've been here since 4."

The waitress came up and took everyone's order. Keith asked for a Kostritzer, Marti had a Weihenstephan Kristall Weissbier, and I had a Newcastle, in keeping with the English atmosphere, plus I could pronounce it. Simone asked for her coffee to be warmed.

"I'm not going to be able to sleep tonight but I need the coffee. Thank goodness tomorrow is Saturday."

Keith slapped the table with the palms of his hands. "Amen to that, sister."

While we're waiting for Grant to arrive, I'll tell you how I know these people. We all belong to an amateur bird-watching club, The Cowtown Bird Pals. I've been observing and photographing birds since I was eleven. Growing up in Comanche, Texas your options for entertainment are limited. Cow tipping isn't really a thing, it is the Texas equivalent of snipe hunting. There is driving around aimlessly in your pickup truck, but that gets old. Hunting and fishing are big, but never for me. The biggest attractions in rural Texas are alcohol and drug addiction. Luckily, I dodged those bullets.

When I was ten my dad bought me a pair of binoculars. I spent a year trying to catch Mary Beth Nickerson sunbathing in her back yard. She was fifteen and Dallas hot. After seeing me constantly riding by her house on my Schwinn Stingray with my binocs swinging around my neck she had her boyfriend Bucky threaten to kick the holy shit out of me.

I decided birds were cool. My mom put two bird feeders in the backyard and one in the front. When I was twelve my dad took me birding and showed me how to walk in the forest, pastures, and fields without being seen or heard. It was as close to teaching me how to hunt as he could get. Dad was cool. He loved hunting and I know he was disappointed when I showed no interest in killing animals but I saw no point when there were perfectly good beef and pork downtown at the Buddy's grocery store. Dad and I had some good times traipsing through the woods looking at quail and other Texas birds.

Over three hundred people belong to Cowtown Bird Pals but never more than ten show to meetings and events. Keith, Simone, and I are among the regulars. We hit it off pretty quickly and became friends. Keith is an elementary school principal in Rhome, a small town northwest of Fort Worth, his wife Marti is a patient soul who puts up with Keith's birding addiction and sometimes comes to our get-togethers and mostly listens to our blathering on about swallows and such. They are both in their mid to late forties. Simone is a pre-clinical development scientist at Alcon, a multinational corporation that makes contact lenses and solutions as well as other sciency things. I have no idea what her job entails. I think there is a lot of chemistry. Simone is notable in that she does her birding with a digital recorder. She is helpful because she usually can hear birds way before we see them. She has a parlor trick where if she is outside, walking down the street, through a parking lot, or wherever, you ask her what birds are in the area and she can tell you right away, without hesitation. She listens to the birds all the time.

I'm a writer and antique book dealer. I buy more books than I sell. That is enough about me.

Grant is the newest member of our birding clique. We don't know much about him except he's tall, talks a lot without saying much, and he's new to birding, which is mainly why we like him. We can show off how much we know about birds.

"Sorry I'm late, guys and gals." Grant appeared at the table without anyone noticing him arrive. "Marti, I'm so glad you came."

"Keith said he wanted to have more than two beers so I came to drive him home."

"I said I wanted to get blind drunk," Keith interjected.

"But you are not getting blind drunk," Marti retorted.

"No, I am not getting blind drunk."

"But he can have more than two beers."

"Yea, me."

Marti playfully elbowed Keith in the ribs. "Don't make me sound like a witch."

"They know you're not a witch, hell they like you better than they like me. They only put up with me because I have the best binoculars."

"Can't argue with that," I said.

Everyone laughed.

It wasn't true that we only put up with Keith because of his binoculars, he was a great guy, but he did have, by a West Texas mile, the best binoculars in the group. He owned a sweet pair of Swarovski EL binoculars. Those things retail for four grand with the field package, which he had. It was worth more than my Subaru.

Grant slid behind Keith and Marti and took the chair opposite me. "Anyone going anywhere interesting this weekend? Bird watching or otherwise?"

"Marti and I are heading over to Sam Houston National Forest. I still haven't seen a Brown-headed nuthatch, or a chuck-will's-widow or a great crested flycatcher. We're staying in Roans Prairie."

I asked if Roans Prairie had a decent motel.

"Oh, goodness, no," Marti said. "There isn't a motel of any kind in Roans Prairie. I have cousins there. We'll stay with them."

"Ain't no reason to do anything besides drive straight through, otherwise."

The waitress popped by, Grant ordered a Shiner Blonde and the conversation continued. The table was long and conversing was difficult from one end to the other so fairly quickly the table broke in half with Grant and I talking on our end, and Keith and Simone talking on the other. Marti swung back and forth chiming in whenever something besides birding was brought up. I mentioned I was going to Arkansas on vacation next month to do some birding in the Ouachita mountains.

"Oh, you'll enjoy the Ouachitas," Grant said. "I'm proud of those."

"Are you from Arkansas?" Marti asked.

"More like everywhere is from me."

Marti crinkled her nose in confusion. I cocked my head like a dog hearing firecrackers. Simone had caught this exchange as well and cut her eyes towards Grant. Keith twisted his neck in our direction as well to see what had stopped down the table.

I waited for someone to ask for clarification. No one spoke up. Not only was our table quiet. The entire bar fell into a lull. It was like everyone's breathing had synced and we were all inhaling at the same time. I decided to jump in. "I don't know what that means."

"No double or hidden meaning. Just what I said, 'everywhere is from me.' I am the creator of everything." He leaned towards me. "Even you." He turned down the table and looked at Marti, Keith, and Simone. "And ya'll."

Marti giggled nervously. Keith looked like he was trying to decide if Grant was dangerous. I'm sure he had already decided he was crazy. Simone looked a little pissed. If Grant was joking, she was not amused. In the days of antivaxers and flat earthers, scientists like Simone are not amused by the stupid.

I didn't know what to think, or rather, I was withholding judgment. I'm generally not concerned with judging others. I spend so much time judging myself, it keeps me pretty busy.

"I see everyone is concerned and confused." Grant looked around the table and met and held everyone's gaze for a moment or two, maybe not so long on Simone. "Perhaps a demonstration?"

Simone leaned in, "What kind of demonstration?"

Grant pressed on, "Does anyone have a quarter?"

I rarely use cash anymore and I'm thankful the debit card has almost totally rendered change obsolete. Keith shook his head no, Marti ventured she might have some change in the bottom of her purse but Simone was sure. "I have a quarter." She reached under the table and brought up her purse. "I keep change on me for the parking meters downtown." She reached in the purse and immediately retrieved one of those old plastic coin snaps that in elementary school everyone of a certain age carried their lunch money. I was surprised because Simone was not 'of a certain age.'

Keith was also impressed, "Oh cool, I didn't know they even made those anymore. The last one I used had a Watauga Wildcat on it."

"I didn't know Watauga had a high school?" I said.

"It was Watauga Elementary. Part of Birdville ISD, I went to Haltom."

I nodded. "Go Buffs."

"Right on."

"Here's your quarter." Simone placed the quarter on the table, tails up, and slid it towards Grant.

"I'm not touching the quarter, but I want everyone else to pick it up, examine it, make sure it is real, and remember the date and any other identifying marks or scratches. At the end of the demonstration, I want ya'll to be sure it is the same quarter."

Everyone did as instructed. It was a 1987 quarter with light wear and tear. Nothing really to identify it from any other 1987 quarter. I was the last one to look it over. I put it back on the table, tails up so Grant could not see the date.

"Just to be clear, Simone, I did not talk to you about this earlier."

"You did not."

"I've never seen this quarter."

"I don't know who had it before me, but no, I've never shown you this quarter and you did not give it to me."

"Okay." Grant looked around the table at all of us. Keith was staring at the quarter like his life depended on it. He was not letting it out of his sight. "Simone, place your hand on the quarter, palm down."

She did so.

"Can you feel the quarter with your palm?"

"I can."

"Good." Grant looked at all of us again. He was clearly having a great time. "Before we go on, I would like to issue a disclaimer. I can, truly, do anything I wish. I am the master of this universe. I am alive, just like all of you, but none of this," he motioned around the bar, "existed before I came to be. All of this, all of you, exist because I cause it, and you, to exist."

I could see that Simone wanted to let loose a harumph, snort, or pshaw, but she managed to hold it.

Keith, still looking intently at the quarter, now covered by Simone's hand said, "So, if we accept what you're saying, you aren't like us at all."

"As far as I can tell, I am exactly like you. I am alive. I age, can't stop that or haven't been able to, I get hungry, excuse me ladies, but I piss and shit like everyone else, last winter I had a devil of a cold. Only difference is I create and maintain the world, and indeed, the universe, with my thoughts. It is a talent, so far as I can see. People have different talents. Mine is creating and maintaining a universe. Let's continue."

I had been watching, listening, and drinking my beer. "Can I get another beer first?"

"The waitress will be right over, but let's keep going with the demonstration. I will bet all of you, but you must all accept the bet, that the quarter is not under Simone's hand."

Simone shot Grant her harshest look yet. "But I can feel it."

Marti leaned over towards Simone. "Can you really feel it?"

"Yes." Simone moved her hand back and forth on the table, we could clearly hear the quarter scrape across the tabletop.

The waitress approached, I held up my glass and mouthed, 'the same.' She nodded and went back to the bar.

"So, we know it is still there," Marti continued.

"So how much would you care to wager that the quarter is under Simon's hand?"

Keith shot a look at Grant. It was the first time he had taken his eyes off Simone's hand. "We're not really betting folk."

"Of course not," Grant smiled at Keith. "The wager is intended to make it more real. Make you take a stand. Put some skin in the game. Ask yourself, who do you believe? Me or your lying eyes?"

I decided to step in. I was afraid if Keith kept on or if Simone opened her mouth one or both would snap. Things were getting tense. I wasn't sure what Grant was up to but he was pulling our leg. That's what I thought at the time. "We're talking a token bet, right? Not big money."

"Yes. What say ten bucks."

"Five," I countered.

Grant considered for a moment. Looking to Simone, Keith, and Marti. "Five, but that includes Marti. They can't bet as a couple. That wouldn't be fair."

"Well, I don't see how it's fair I have to put in ten. Marti's money is coming out of the same pocketbook as mine, meaning we'll be out ten bucks."

"We'll call that a marriage penalty. Just because. Besides, the quarter is under Simone's hand, right?"

Keith looked at Simone. Simone nodded and moved her hand across the table, making the quarter scrape again.

"So, it's not ten bucks out. It's ten bucks in." He paused to let everyone gather their thoughts. Then he giggled. "I said snot."

Reaching into his back pocket, Keith pulled out his wallet. "What the hell. I'm in if for nothing else, I want to see how this plays out."

"I'm in as well but I can't get my wallet with just one hand."

"You're good for it," Grant assured Simone.

I reached for my wallet, only had a ten, and threw it in the pile. Keith had tossed down two fives.

"Take a five from the pot," said Grant.

"That's fine, I'll go in ten if it is all the same."

"Fine by me."

Keith had his eyes locked back on Simone's hand covering the quarter. "So what now, almighty?"

"Nothing left to do but see if the quarter is still under Simone's hand."

I was filled with anticipation. "I feel like we need a drum roll."

Grant laughed. Simone raised her hand. The quarter was not on the table. Keith and Marti were stunned. Simone's look did not change. She was still pissed. Maybe a little more so.

I was not surprised. I had no idea how he had moved the quarter but I figured he could do it. Why go to all the bother if he couldn't. Where would the payoff be in that?

Keith looked confused and a little impressed. "Well bugger me."

"Where did it go? Simone, show us your hand," said Marti.

Simone had raised her hand straight up and left it outstretched over the table. She raised her palm and showed everyone her empty hand. She then turned it towards herself and stared in disbelief.

Grant had a mysterious look on his face. "Where did it go indeed?"

Everyone looked at the spot on the table where Simone's hand had been like if we stared long enough, the quarter would suddenly be where we all had expected it to be.

"That is poppycock, balderdash, hooey, and pure D bull shit." Keith was red in the face.

"Simone," Grant spoke in a soft, more than slightly condescending tone. "Lift up your coffee cup."

Simone did as bid and there under the cup was the quarter. Simone had not taken a sip of coffee since the waitress had warmed it shortly after Keith and Marti had arrived. I was sure of it.

Marti leaned in and spoke excitedly. "Is it the same quarter?"

Simone picked it up, examined it as only a scientist can, and held it out to Marti. "It is the same year."

Marti looked at the date then turned the coin over and over in her hand. "Let me see," said Keith.

"That's cool and all, Grant," I said. "But let's get to the bigger question. How does a sleight of hand trick prove you are creator of the universe?"

Grant was miffed I had called his demonstration a sleight of hand trick. "I physically moved that quarter through space without touching it. I did it with my mind showing I have control over matter and space." He looked at me like he was stating the bleeding obvious.

I pressed on. "Just because I don't know how you did it doesn't mean you moved that quarter with only your mind."

"But there is no other explanation."

"I can't think of another explanation. Doesn't mean there isn't one."

He turned to Simone for help, which amused me. "Simone, you're the smartest one in the group, can you explain how I did it if not by altering physics?"

Simone furrowed her brow. "I don't know how you did it but I also know you can't alter physics."

Grant flew off the handle, "Fly specks, fly specks, you've been spending your life among fly specks while miracles have been going birding with you in Fort Worth!" He was genuinely upset, although I was impressed with the Harvey quotation. He sat back in his chair exasperated. "I knew this would happen. It always happens. I don't know why I expect any different." He was waving his hands excitedly and looking to the heavens.

"Now, calm down," I said. "What are you talking about?"

"I truly don't know why I run the universe. I don't have any special knowledge, it is like I was chosen at random. I don't know what I'm doing. I try to make things better. I really do but everything seems to backfire. You know the old saying 'no good deed goes unpunished?' That's what happens when I try and do something good for ya'll." He looked around the table at everyone. "Not ya'll specifically, I'm talking about ya'll as in humankind."

Simone could see Grant was genuinely upset and frustrated. Her face softened. Not much, but a little. Make no mistake she was still pissed. Keith looked over at me and made the universal sign for 'crazy' by looping his right index finger in circles around the side of his head.

"It is no mistake that technology has exploded in the last thirty or forty years. As I grew up and realized it was me creating the universe, I tried to give ya'll things that would advance the human race to an understanding equal to, if not greater than my own. I'm not the smartest cookie in the jar. People like Simone and other scientists and mathematicians are way smarter than me. I figured if I gave people tools like the internet, all the knowledge in the world at their fingertips, and supercomputers, and the Large Hadron Collider, they would, of their own accord, make themselves smarter, more in touch with universal truths, and they would make their way to me. Well, advancements have been made, no denying that, but it also has made people exponentially more stupid, mean, and heartless." Grant threw up his hands and shook his head. "I got the bright idea of approaching a small group. Showing them who I am. Explain things. Maybe I could make some true, real friendships to help me figure this out. But..." He trailed off and sat in his chair looking as beaten and despondent as anyone I had ever witnessed.

We all sat in silence for some time. I had no idea what was going on. I've found contemplating the nature of reality to be ultimately unsatisfying. But things weren't adding up. The only way he could have pulled off the trick as far as I could tell was to have someone in on the grift. It was Simone's quarter. Her hand over the quarter. The quarter ended up under her coffee. Did he have Simone, obviously the most skeptical of the group, in on the scam the whole time? I could not believe she would go along with Grant on this absurd premise but Occam's razor and all.

Why did he feel he had anything to prove to us to begin with? The sob story seemed to be just that, a sob story. If he could do anything why not just make us believe. The whole thing seemed pointless. Why tell us to begin with? And why prove it with a parlor trick. Why not do something big, grand. Fly us to the moon. Show us the big bang.

I said all this stream of consciousness, out loud at the table.

"Good questions, at least most of them." Grant had a bit of a gleam back in his eyes. "I'll start with why I didn't do something grand. I know I'm proclaiming to be master and creator of the universe, but I really don't always know what I'm doing. There are glitches. I don't know how this 'master of the universe' stuff works. Not entirely. I've had no training. It is like handing a loaded gun to a toddler. Frankly, we're all lucky to be alive. If I'd flown ya'll to the moon I might have slipped on a detail and killed you all in space, if I'd have shown you the big bang you're just as likely to have died in the explosion."

He sounded to me like he was talking from experience.

Simone could hold her tongue no longer. "You created the universe, managed the big bang, quantum physics, string theory..."

Grant raised his hand and interrupted, "I wouldn't go all-in on string theory. Not to give anything away." Simone frowned and cocked her head. "Sorry, irrelevant, please continue."

"You're freaking God, and you don't know what you're doing?"

"I never said I was God, upper or lower case g."

"Doesn't matter, you are master and creator of the universe, you can make things work however you want to make them work, and you don't know what you're doing. You still manage to fuck things up."

"That's it in a nutshell. Yes."

"That's it. Screw this. I'm tired and hungover at seven o'clock on a Friday night. This is bullshit. I'm going home." Simone got up and left.

"Do you think she closed her tab?" I was still staring at the door Simone exited. I turned back to the table. "She could get in trouble if she walked her tab. A lot of people from her work come here."

Keith looked at me with concern. "What and who the hell are you talking about? Don't you go crackers on me, too. One nut job at the table is enough."

I cocked my head like a Spaniel. "Simone." I pointed towards the door. "She just left?"

Keith caught the waitress's attention, raised and pointed to his glass. "Who the hell is Simone?" The waitress gave Keith a thumbs up. We seemed to be getting excellent service tonight. Every time one of us looked for the waitress, she was looking at us.

I turned to Grant. He smiled.

"That is your last one," said Marti.

I looked at Keith. Keith looked at Marti, judging if he could win an argument for another beer after this one. I don't think he liked his odds. "You don't know Simone?"

"First I ever heard of her, is she a birder?"

I looked at Grant. He looked at me like he had eaten the canary. "So, Simone is just gone. She never existed."

"Simone chose not to exist."

"I don't think she did. I think she chose not to believe you."

"I still don't know who the fuck this Simone person is but

if she didn't swallow Grant's bullshit, I think I like her."

I looked at Keith. He wasn't there. Neither was Marti. I looked back at Grant. "Well, that was harsh."

"I never expected Keith to make it."

"So you erased Marti as well?"

"That was a whim. I created them as a package, I deleted them as a package."

We were sitting at the bar. I looked over to our table, another group of people were there and looked like they had been for a while.

"The Ginger Man is a popular place, it's getting crowded. We no longer needed a table, I took the liberty of moving us to the bar. The waitress, Karin, needs all the tips she can get. Since she lost Simone, Keith, and Marti's tabs and tips, I gave her a full table of heavy drinkers."

I felt like we had always been at the bar, but I remember that we had been at a table. I remembered Simone, Keith, and Marti, but it was hazy. Like an early childhood memory. "What the hell am I supposed to do with this information?"

"Whatever you like." Grant put his hand on my shoulder. "We can hang out, do a little traveling. Actually, I don't technically travel. I just am. Where I want to be becomes my surroundings."

He paused for a second to let that sink in. I know he did.

"It would be cool to have someone I could talk to who was in the know. Someone to understand. Bounce ideas off. Even make suggestions."

"And if I refused? Would I pass on? Exist no more. Cease to be. Expire and go to meet my maker. Become a stiff. Bereft of life. Rest in peace. Start pushing up daisies. Would my metabolic processes become history? Would I go off the twig? Kick the bucket, shuffle off this mortal coil, run down the curtain and join the bleeding choir invisible? In other words, become an ex-person?"

"Ahhh, Dennis you're much more than a dead parrot."

I pondered my situation. I could be the sidekick to the master and creator of the universe or I could cease to exist. I was scanning the horizon for a viable third option but didn't see a thing.

"Dennis, I know you're hesitant."

"Putting it mildly."

"I'll tell you a secret," he leaned over and whispered. "I don't think any of it matters." He paused again to let it sink in. "I'm pretty sure everything is predetermined, so it doesn't matter what we do. We are going to do what we do."

"But if we don't know what we are going to do, we think we have a choice, therefore, it's a choice to us."

"Did you ever hear the story about the time God took a nap and was snoring?"

I confessed I had not.

"Well, God took a nap, woke up, and noticed all the people were freaking out because He had been snoring and they didn't know what it was. God was amused they were disturbed simply by His snoring. Later on, God was sitting in his chair, contemplating the universe and whatnot, when softly, off in the distance, in a place and from a direction He could not pinpoint, God heard snoring." Grant paused. I scratched my noggin. "I spend most of my time worrying I'm going to fuck up the universe, or nature, or people, but I don't think I can. More precisely, I don't think I'm allowed to."

"Then what is the point?"

"I don't have a clue. That's above my pay grade."

"I feel for you, Grant. I do. But I want no part of this bullshit. I'm not qualified to make my own life decisions so helping make decisions for the universe would be malfeasance on my part and yours. The fact that no one knows what they are doing, that there is no apparent meaning or purpose to anything, is heartbreaking. I want someone wise in charge." This time I paused. "No offense."

"None taken."

The bartender slid a Shiner and a shot of tequila in front of Grant. I hadn't seen him order.

"I'm going to leave now."

Grant threw back the tequila and stared at the bar.

"Is that alright?"

"I would if I could. Don't blame you a bit." His voice was lacquered with infinite sadness. He turned and looked me straight in the eyes. They were filled with more heartache than there are songs in Nashville. "Nobody ever stays. I think that's why I do this from time to time. To live vicariously through those who can walk away."

I put a twenty on the bar, stood, and walked away. For the first few steps I waited to see if I would cease to be. Then I wondered if I would just forget.

I never saw Grant again. I still go birding. Still belong to the Cowtown Bird Pals. Some nights when I can't get to sleep, I listen for snoring in the distance.

CB Droege

A Step Back

I saw the distress call first. It was a standard call, but being transmitted in reverse. I said as much to the skipper, but he waved it away with one large hand.

"That's not unheard of," he said, "a malfunctioning ship's computer will distort a distress call in all manner of different ways."

I'd heard some very staticky and hard-to-make-out distress calls in my time on the Charon's Pole, but never anything quite like this. However, the skipper had significantly more experience with these things, so I trusted that he knew what he was talking about. There was only the two of us on the ship after all, so there wasn't any other authority for me to turn toward.

"What's the origin?" he asked.

"Near the second planet in the system," I looked more closely at the data the computer had collected on the signal as it had come in. "It looks like it's a ship that just launched from the planet's moon, with a trajectory taking it out of the system."

"Set a course, Greyson"

"Aye, Skipper"

I checked the math, and programmed the burns while the Skipper watched over my shoulder. I'd been working the controls of the ship for several months by then, but he still oversaw my every step as though I was in training. Once the ship was under way, I had a few minutes to look over the data again while we were in transit. The distressed ship was accelerating away from the moon still, and I needed to make some changes to the program to bring us a bit closer. I noticed that there was another, fainter distress call coming from near the surface of the moon, but I knew that the skipper would want to check out the ship first, so I ignored it at that moment.

We pulled alongside the vessel just as its engines cut out, which made it a simple thing to match velocities with it. We tried to hail the ship, but got nothing other than the distress call in return

"Any sign of life?" the skipper asked.

I turned to the heat sensors. "Looks like it," I said, "Two people aboard, sir, at least"

"Hrm," the skipper rubbed his chin, "We shall attempt to render aid then. Suit up."

●

Outside the ship, I took a moment to look the other vessel over. It was huge. The skipper had to have been at least a little disappointed that it wasn't clear for salvage, but Interstellar law dictated that we rendered aid to ships in distress when we found them, and he took the duty very seriously, unlike some salvagers. It was one of the reasons I had signed on with him. Also, I loved this kind of stuff: I evaluated the distance—about thirty meters—and chose a likely entry point—an airlock on a jutting fin closest to me—and I leapt.

My heart soared with the freedom and danger of the maneuver as I glided across the gap. I had a little bit more spin than I had intended, and I couldn't see where I was going, but I knew I was on the right course, so I detached my safety line, and drifted unencumbered the rest of the way.

I collided with the ship shoulder first, and out of the corner of my eye, I was sure I had seen some bit of flotsam drift away from the ship as I came to it, but I was too excited to pay attention. I got out my tools, and prepared to drill or torch my way through the airlock.

It opened.

The remaining people on the ship must have seen my approach, I thought. That made it easier, but not as much fun. I went in through the hatch and waited as it pulled closed behind me. I heard the hissing of the air cycling, but decided to leave my helmet on, just in case. When the inner door opened, I heard a familiar voice, "Greyson, we have work to do, follow me quickly." The skipper stood before me, a shadow of stubble on his face, his jumpsuit torn in places. He looked tired. Very tired. Without waiting for me to finish gawking he moved away, "Snap to it, young man!"

I was startled into following him down the corridor, my magnetized boots clanging down the passage behind him. "Skipper?" I was dumfounded. "How did you get here before me?"

"I've been here for hours, son." he called back over his shoulder.

"What?"

"We're going the wrong way."

"I don't-"

"There's no time now, Greyson," he interrupted, "just do as I say." we had come into a larger room that looked like a bridge or control deck. The consoles and décor were entirely alien to me, and for the first time I noticed the bones.

They had been in the passage also, and in the small room where the Skipper had met me, but I hadn't registered them until this moment. Human bones and scraps of rags that may once have been uniforms, though I didn't recognize the style. The crew of this ship had been dead for hundreds of years, maybe longer.

"Greyson!" the skipper had to shout to get me to pay attention to what he had been saying. I tried to focus. He was gesturing to a small control panel in a console along one wall. "All I need you to do is push *this* button when I say, got it?"

I nodded, then realizing that he couldn't see me in my helmet, I added, "Aye, Skipper."

"Good." he propelled himself to the other side of the compartment, and started quickly pressing buttons on a console there. "Now!" he called, and I pushed the button he had indicated. Slowly, the gravity began to change, and a low rumble came up through my boots. The engines had turned on.

"I think that'll do it," he said, breathlessly. Then started back out of the room, "This way!"

"Skipper!" I had to step quickly to catch up. "What is going on."

He didn't slow down his steps, and he spoke quickly, "Look, you were gone for hours, and you wouldn't reply to any of my attempts to radio. I came over to find you, and found myself alone on the ship with all these," he gestured to a pile of bones and rags as he stepped over it in the narrow passage. "The ship is not lifting off from the moon, it's crashing into it." My mind was reeling. If I'd said anything then, it would have just been more confused stammering, so I stayed silent.

The skipper continued, "When I realized what was happening, I started learning the ship's controls, so that I could slow the descent. I was able to turn the ship's main engine toward the moon, but firing it required two people, so I had to wait for you to finally get here before I could do that." We had returned to the small prep room inside the airlock where I had come in. In the corner, I now saw the skipper's EVA suit, the glass in the helmet was shattered. He turned and noticed where I was looking. "You're gonna have to go back out alone," he said, "We're not slowed down enough to save this ship, but you should be able to safely enter the atmosphere."

"Got it, then what?" I said, finally past denying what was happening.

"Signal us before I send you over. Warn us away."

"Will that work?"

"I hope so."

He nearly shoved me into the airlock and closed the door behind me. I waited for the hiss of the air cyclers, but instead, the bolts on the outside hatch were blown, and I was drawn out into the vacuum of space, slamming into the heavy hatch on the way out. I was facing the derelict ship, and I saw myself there for an instant before the specter was sucked into the airlock, and the hatch sealed explosively as the ship sped away from me—away from the cratered surface I was now falling toward.

In a few minutes, I entered thin atmosphere of the moon. I activated the small emergency parachute built into my suit, and felt myself start to slow, hoping it would be enough. I activated my suit's emergency beacon, but I knew it would be ignored.

I looked up and saw the Charon's Pole pull up alongside the larger ship as its engines cut off.

Charles R. Bernard

All Aboard

"...well, define 'splitting.' A little light-headed, a little achy, that's sorta what we're going for, right?"

Stone's voice, Muñoz thinks, matches his name. It's a hard, irritating little thing; its effect like a pebble lodged inside one's shoe. It sounds high-pitched, but rough with cigarettes. Its confidence projects his status as top salesman for Curated Chemical Nostalgia, LLC.

"...yeah, sure, sure. Ethanolamine, ammonium, chlorine, all well within limits. We'd be in bad shape if we weren't, right ... Well, thank you. That's why we do what we do: that feeling of spooky-perfect recognition."

The quartet of monitors before Muñoz are like the cluster of a spider's eyes, watching him watch them watch him. *Fuck*, he thinks, startled, *did I drift off again? Has Blavatsky been watching me zone out?* Stone's voice continues to rattle against the cheap plastic fixtures of the half-cubicles. *He's got the top fucking numbers and they still won't give Stone an office of his own*, Muñoz marvels.

"Comet and Windex, of course, those are big ones," Stone explains. "But from there it gets more complicated. Is it *actually* Comet you remember, or some store-brand version? There are differences in the aromatics—the scents that were commercially available, too. So if you want the smell to be *exactly* what you remember…"

He listens to some distant, pleased reply. "Well, that's why you come to *us*, right? Vintage floor products—that's our bread and butter. We've got a warehouse *full* of products, haven't found one we can't either source or match yet. It can be tricky with some of these crunchy-ass granola mom and pop groceries, right? Don't get me started on those weirdos in California. …. Yeah, that's right, a god-fearing Wal-Mart like the rest of us, right? Ha-ha-ha."

Muñoz blinks grit from his eyes and wrings his hands, cracking the knuckles of his long, elegant fingers. He's in the home stretch of his shift. It doesn't *feel* like home stretch. It feels more he's scraping out the last few inches of his own grave at gunpoint. *Good boy. Take paycheck. Bang-bang. Lie down.*

"*Muñoz!* A moment of your time!"

Muñoz feels his anus clench and pucker with startled fright. The voice—Blavatsky's voice—comes from the tiny cluster of speakers buried in the midst of the monitors. It's a surprisingly shrill and tinny voice for a spider with such a vast and subtle web.

It feels like the same well of gravity that binds Muñoz to the Earth sucks him with bleak, cosmic inevitability down the dingy hallway with its sputtering solars, past the break room (K-cups, stale food smells, dead-eyed corporate co-conspirators), and finally to the threshold of Blavatsky's office. "Come on in here and see me, buddy," she calls. He trudges through the door.

"We're having issues with mirroring again," Blavatsky states. Mazy flashes wheel within the green glass of her earrings, soaking up the pale winter sunlight through the office's lone window. "Our supply chain with Isomorph is starting to go sideways."

"Okay."

"This kind of problem...it doesn't happen without failures from the tech side. And Isomorph could present a major problem with our image."

"Okay."

Blavatsky regards him with glassy eyes. "This doesn't reflect well on you, Muñoz."

•

The trip home is a weary blur. His first reaction when he spies the package is irritation. *Fucking chumps sent a sample to the wrong address*, fumes Muñoz, huffing and puffing his way up the long staircase to his second-floor room.

His second impression comes once he gets a better look at the package. He's puzzled. Snuggled in its brown paper wrappings, the package's puffy bulk does not match the hard, smooth shape of a misdirected CCNLLC shipment, a case of product samples or, perhaps, a ventilation system scent mix sent to him rather than a client. Curious. The packet goes under one arm and into his apartment.

Muñoz's front door admits a wedge of strained and sickly sunlight into the dark interior. He follows it across the foyer and through the neat and empty kitchen, across the linoleum floor with its faux-tile print. He bears the package to his home office. Whatever is in the brown paper is light—much too light to be anything from CCNLLC. He turns the envelope in his hands once, examining its outer skin as he places it on his workbench. There's his name, all right, stamped on a nondescript mailing label. While the brown wrapper bears the clear bureaucratic fingerprints of the postal service, it is innocent of a return address.

The package has ample company on the bench. The office's guttering overhead solars glint on the twists of wire, gleaming scraps of shiny plastic, and murkily reflective spots of solder that litter Muñoz's workbench. On the wall hangs a large reproduction print of a public school poster promoting NASA, circa 1988. Above the poster—in a matching frame—is a certificate from Space Camp. *The* Space Camp, he reminds himself each time he sees it. The *real* one at the US Space & Rocket Center, in Huntsville (long since gone).

To the left of his workbench, his home bank of monitors regards him. These lack the necessary physical accoutrement to monitor him, but they still seem balefully aware of him and glower from the corner with Cerberus eyes. Under their dead scrutiny, Muñoz slits the envelope with a scalpel and unpacks its contents.

His fingers find the blanket first. It's the blanket that provides him with his third—and most lasting—impression that afternoon. Slick and cheap and somehow papery, its navy blue surface skates off of Muñoz's fingertips with the familiarity of a lover's flesh. The smell is identical, and he is overtaken by a black and terrible wave of nostalgia, the reason-breaching blow of perfect recognition. He ought to be immune to the experience by now, thinks Muñoz, or at least detached enough to take a clinical view of it, but he's helpless.

Just like any human, pre-rational and pre-conscious networks in his mind are shackled to his senses; the sense of smell, particularly. Muñoz knows the game; it's how he makes his living. Like anybody, he's a bundle of conscious impulses and badly half-remembered data; his self like a thin, thinking layer of living coral, the rind of a vast, dead reef of mammalian impulses, chemical reactions, and the churning vortex of the unplumbed and unlit unconscious. It's what CCNLLC is built on: the provision of a short-circuit pathway to a specific time and place, a terrible power contained in such a banal little package.

Perhaps a client wants to revisit a distant childhood. CCN provides them with an aromatic blend: the floor wax, cleaning fluid, sawdust, dust, and other sundry molecules that constitute a truly *atmospheric* atmosphere. The inhalation of that potent distillation is like an unexpected bit of time travel as memories unlock with fierce fidelity.

Muñoz's package isn't from CCNLLC. For one thing, they do not produce artifacts like the blanket he holds. The scent, the texture, the color of the cheap material; Muñoz is a young man again, just settling in to his first night at Space Camp and too excited—about camp, about the bright future that stretches beyond that—to even think of sleep. The evocation is so sweet, so intense, that Muñoz has to blink back tears.

What is this? he wonders.. If it's some competitor soliciting his services, he must admit he is impressed. Once he has unpacked the blanket with its strange, crisp folds, he sees a legend printed on its length in thick white letters: **ALL ABOARD FOR MARS!** The words extract a jagged, surprised laugh from Muñoz.

The blanket is wrapped around a single sheet of paper, cheaply printed, that bears a message tinged with daffy optimism. The sunny tenor of the prose is as familiar to Muñoz as the chemical bouquet that wafts off of the blanket:

It's time! And you don't want to be left behind!
ALL ABOARD is looking for volunteers just like YOU—
young men and women of intelligence and commitment,
devoted to humanity's future in the stars!!

Below this is printed a tiny string of alphanumeric text that Muñoz recognizes as an opaque web URL. *Curated Chemical Nostalgia might have a serious competitor on our hands,* he thinks as he turns the sheet of paper and runs his elegant fingers along its blank backside. *They nailed 1980s paper stock, for fuck's sake. "All Aboard," huh? I told Blavatsky that we need to work the alternate reality game angle. Now someone's beaten us to the punch, and she's going to find a way to blame it on* me.

Despite himself, his curiosity is piqued. Muñoz turns to his monitors and unrolls his soft plastic keyboard. He is correct. The string of random digits and assorted letters is a URL. He is, however, disappointed by what he finds there. When he taps the address in, a blank, black screen appears; as empty as an interstellar gulf, save for two words.

blast off

•

Stone waits for Muñoz at the office the next morning and, on seeing him, beckons ominously. His presence is unusual in and of itself; Stone is not the come-early, leave-late type. Muñoz wishes with each fiber in his being that he could be somewhere else. *On Mars*, he reflects with a sad twinge, *atmospheric dust makes the sunset blue. A blue sunset. Just imagine it.*

"Fucking Blavatsky. She's really on one about this Isomorph situation. She's been sticking to me like my goddamned reflection. I know she's already got you working on the mirroring, but can you just have a look at this message I got from Isomorph? See the crazy shit I've got to put up with?"

Muñoz squints through the half-lenses of his reading glasses at one of Stone's monitors, on which he has pulled up the missive in question. It's a message from their point of sale at Isomorph Transmissions. The contact is a jarringly eccentric and anonymous entity whose preferred form of address—"Mister Isomorph"—was treated as a joke by staff at first. Over time, that "joke" metastasized into an unspoken air of unsettling mystery. Then again, in their line of business, mystery is lucrative, and Isomorph is no exception. He squints at Stone's screen, but his mind is 209.52 million miles away. Inside him is an endless vista of red sand, a first step into destiny among the stars.

He concentrates, refocuses, and reads:

Miister Sandss,

It is with incrreasing frustrattion that I submit to

yoou—AGAIN—that it is VVERY IMPORTANT that Magnotta's Mixdown be added to the sceent profile we ordered.

I was just a little wormm, and alll day daddy would cllean the floors with Magnotta's. It was the only thing that would get the "mud" outt, if you catch my drrrift! Then the long messy night, so much fun.

So you understand that without Magnotta's Mixdown in the scent profile, I can't crawl like a proper wormn and I amm paying you a LOOT of muddy to get this right!

Your product has always satisfied in the past and I'm sure we can come to some kind of intersection. I love your product. I love.

Impatiently,
Mister Isomorph

Muñoz frowns. "Who's Mister Sands?"

"Me, I guess," says Stone. "The fuck am I going to do about this guy?" He gnaws one bleeding thumbnail.

Muñoz shrugs. "He was obviously high as shit when he wrote that. Or crazy. The fuck is he talking about, this 'Mixdown' stuff? I've never heard of it."

"That's because," Stone sighs, "there's no such cleaning product—period. None of the other nostalgia consultants I've talked to have heard of that shit either. But Mister Isomorph wants it, and he's fronting a big client. They're doing ambient nostalgia for Disney, starting on Halloween."

That puts a rock in the pit of Muñoz's stomach. "Jesus." *Blue sunset,* he thinks. *Sunlight as it flares through my smoked-glass helmet. The creation of a new world—and an escape from* this *one*. "Did you ask Blavatsky about this message, specifically?"

"Fuck no I didn't ask Blavatsky. Why do you think I'm here talking to you?"

Hydroponic rigs, oxygen tents and connective walkways, all ringing with busy activity. "Well," Muñoz mutters, "I'm not sure what you want me to do about it. You know, from a technical perspective."

"Yeah, well," Stone sighs. "Good point. I've got to bring it to the boss lady's attention, whether I want to or not. We're through the looking glass here."

●

CCNLLC occupies one floor of a multistory glass and metal box, and shares a mail room with the building's other occupants. There's something very strange about the man who stares at Muñoz as he saunters in. The fellow's turgid eyes are fixed on empty space.

He's tall and thin, his frame beset by knobby bulges. His waxen face is plagued by roving twitches. His skin is smooth beneath a tangle of blonde hair. As Muñoz watches, the skinny fellow comes to life and turns to the reception box. He starts to slide envelopes, one at a time, into the mail slots. Each movement is performed with regal slowness. Muñoz gives the man a friendly smile; in his experience, it's never smart to slight the mail room staff.

"Where's Leon?" Muñoz asks. Over his years at CCNLLC, he's developed a casual friendship with Leon, the master of the mailroom.

The skinny man regards Muñoz with bulging eyes. "Who? Oh, Leon. Leon... Had to go."

Okay, Muñoz thinks, *weird*. He ruffles through his mail with absentminded nonchalance—until he finds the pamphlet. It's thin and shiny, printed on cheap, slick paper. "**ALL ABOARD**—and brother, we're leaving *soon!*"

"You... like Mars?" asks the knobby man.

Something about this guy's face, Muñoz thinks, *is giving me the uncanny-valley creeps like a motherfucker*. It's like the clerk's visage is not his own: like he wears a rubber mask of his own face. "Mars? I dunno man," Muñoz says, backing away. "Have a good one. Say hi to Leon."

"Leon," the man repeats sadly, "had to go."

•

Muñoz tells himself that his fascination is no more than professional interest. A new competitor has emerged in the chemical nostalgia market, and he's simply researching the quality of their work. At home, though, nestled in his easy chair with the **ALL ABOARD** pamphlet tented over his eager nose, he can't deny the truth. He is intoxicated by the precision of the scents and sensations. The smell of the ink, the slick feel of the thin paper—it's just as though an actual, physical promotional pamphlet from the Space Camp of his youth has arrived in a temporal PO Box.

It's just clever chemical illusion, he reminds himself. Just like CCNLLC's mixtures; like the way they add just a *taste* of d-limonene and 2-propanol to their Motel Bathroom Medley (not enough to trigger regulatory intervention or cause any *lasting* damage). Just as other bearers of the torch of industry once pioneered the look or sound of longed-for days gone by, the vanguardists of modern-day nostalgia trade in scents which unlock mental doors.

Soon, he's crouched before his keyboard, busily clack-clacking in an effort to resolve the mirroring issue that has so refracted Blavatsky's temper.

It doesn't take him long to reach a state between infuriated bemusement and total befuddlement. He reviews the correspondence from Mister Isomorph and finds it, in a word, troubling. Certain phrases seem to float off the screen like swamp-fire: *Howw they kick and prick and stick and squeeal! ... Nothing short of a gnnawed bone, you sucking filly gramoose... What is that taste you tasste in sleep & sleep aloan?* Not for the first time, Muñoz is glad he isn't Stone. How has Blavatsky's top salesman been handling a fucking *lunatic* like Isomorph this long? Regardless, the issue in their communication is easily resolved—well, perhaps not easily, but with most of a night of solid work.

According to the neutral glow of Muñoz's phone, it's just after 3 AM when he crawls into bed. He doesn't bother to undress. Thanks to his efforts, CCNLLC's shattered mirroring has been leaded back into place. He thinks he ought to feel a subsequent release of tension. Instead, beneath the slick and papery folds of the **ALL ABOARD** blanket, he shivers like a sick dog.

•

Muñoz is at home when the news breaks. He catches it on his monitors at home as he's eating a bowl of cereal above the sink. The newscast from the monitors pierces Muñoz's distracted hearing like the shrill blast of a whistle. His bowl and its contents tumble messily to the stainless basin of the sink, voiding chalky pink milk and tiny, soggy rocket ships everywhere as his nerveless fingers slacken.

"Over 300 dead so far in what is being called the worst industrial poisoning outbreak in decades… Scenes are described as being like the aftermath of chemical warfare… Most of the worst-affected seem to be children and the elderly… Thought to be a result of the booming and thus-far unregulated odorant market… Linked to odorant giant Curated Chemical Nostalgia, LLC."

Muñoz, shaken, mentally retraces every change he made to CCNLLC's mirroring systems in the course of his long, sleepless night. A sick dread begins to swell within him, filling space like massive doses of trace toxins filling up a ventilation duct. He doesn't truly panic until he falls into a seat at the monitors, cuts the news feeds' volume, and starts to read the in-depth coverage. The news is bad and getting worse. Muñoz has no idea what has gone wrong with their company's manufacturing and warehouse divisions—what the further breakdown in communication does or does not have to do with his own efforts—but he is an intelligent man. Smart enough to feel the snare around his neck begin to tighten even as he tries, eyes stung by sweat, to think his way out of its grip.

I'll call for help, he thinks with perfect, dreamlike irrationality. His hands shake as he handles the slick little **ALL ABOARD** pamphlet. He scans the back and taps the string of digits listed as a phone number into his phone. It's two digits shy of being a real phone number, and Muñoz is more than a little surprised when it goes through and he receives an answer with no delay. Not even a connecting click.

"All Aboard." Flat affect in a monotone voice; infinite boredom.

"Yeah, I..." Muñoz trails off. He feels absurd. What does he expect from this call, really?

"Are you looking for off-world transport. Are you ready to join the pioneers who will bring us tomorrow's fires." The poetry of the words notwithstanding, the voice is as dead as the surface of a red and nearly-airless world.

"I..." Why is he so tongue-tied? "Look, are you guys for real? When is this supposed to happen? Why haven't I heard about it on the news?" (*Because the news is following the chemical disaster story of the decade and, oh, by the way, they'll probably get around to pinning it on* me *pretty soon,* he thinks.)

"Are you ready to march toward the horizon of tomorrow." Though the tone of voice has facets of recording or computer generation, something in its lifelessness feels, somehow, busily *alive* to Muñoz.

"Yeah. Yes. Yes I am," he babbles. As soon as these words have left his lips, a burst of deafening, distorted static rips from his phone's tiny speaker. It's loud enough to make him wince and grit his teeth. When he lifts it to his ear again, the noise has gone. Its howl of chaos is replaced by the same monotonic (and yet lively) croak.

"Good. Because you have to go."

There, the phone call ends.

•

"Where in the fuck do you think *you're* going?"

Stone's voice pelts Muñoz like a rock slung from the far end of the office hallway. Muñoz tries to scuttle off, but fails; the small, muscular Stone quickly catches up to him.

"Hey!" cries Stone. "*Muñoz!* Blavatsky has been looking for you everywhere, man. And I do mean *everywhere.*" This last is stated as a dark half-innuendo; what Stone is implying, precisely, Muñoz is not sure.

"I saw the news," says Muñoz. He keeps his tone as neutral as he can and succeeds in sounding almost (but not quite) as dead as the **ALL ABOARD** receptionist had sounded. Wait.... had the voice on the other end of the line sounded *dead*? And what, pray tell, does a dead voice sound like? Muñoz wonders if the call had been a dream; some dire pre-meltdown hallucination, brought on by his shock and stress.

"This is *bad*, man. Really bad," Stone glowers. "Not the kind of thing you just press reset on. Not the kind of thing that 'advances a career,' if you get my drift. Well, this might advance it right the fuck into prison, I suppose."

"What the fuck are you talking about, 'prison?'" Muñoz vibrates with electric fear beneath his well-maintained, aloof façade.

"I'm talking about *prison* man. Locked in a box with the bad boys. People are *dead*, Muñoz."

Muñoz's jaw tightens so hard that his teeth creak. The noise inside his skull is like the sundering of some vast glacier. He manages to grit out; "I had *nothing* to do with this.

You got me, Stone? *Nothing.*"

"Yeah, well," the small man says, and darts his eyes away, "Blavatsky's looking for you. Because I think the *feds* are looking for you."

It's not, Muñoz decides, a glacier that he hears inside his head. It's the crackling and fog-throated roar of rockets in ignition; of untold quantities of fuel aflame; of all that power, all that rage, shackled underneath him to help push him out of here. Out of this fucking job, off of this planet, up, away, away.

"Okay," says Muñoz.

He does not try to find Blavatsky. Instead, he picks his way through CCNLLC's hallways, careful to avoid the gaze of (let alone eye contact with) co-workers. He sneaks along until he finds his destination; an isolated upper section of the building's stairwell leading to the roof. There, he sees the jet-black metal access door whose outline—whose solidity—has been lodged in his thoughts since he heard the news about the company's disaster.

Muñoz stands before the black door now, his shoulders slack, lost within a swaying trance and unable to force himself to take a single step toward it. Would its surface be rough, pitted with cheap paint like he's so recently and constantly imagined? Would its metal surface be warm from the sun's constant knock, bordering on hot? His palms itch thinking of it.

Through the small and dirty panes of glass to either side of the door, Muñoz can see the building's roof; gravel, golden in the setting sun, bits of broken glass here and there sparkling like rogue gems, cigarette butts, and, beyond, the dirty blue sky. It's odd to see the floodlit stage that is the rooftop smoking area absent its small knots of nicotine cliques.

What's odder than the emptiness is that, as Muñoz stands there, he hears conversing voices from the other side of the door's metal barrier. They sound as clear as day; two voices, one seemingly male, one seemingly female, and each no more than two yards past the door, to hear it. And yet, as Muñoz checks and re-checks through the smeared glass of the windows, there is no one on the roof. No people, nor their shadows, nor the smell or sight of cigarette smoke. Just, it would seem, voices.

The first is slightly deeper. The speaker sounds male, and is bored stiff to judge by tone. "The relative proportion of instances in which the different process histories are responsible for erroneous reporting will depend on what, exactly?"

The reply sounds lighter, maybe female. She sounds young and her words come so near the door that Muñoz cannot credit his inability to see her through the windowpane. *Where are they?* is all that Muñoz can summon the dumb curiosity to wonder. "It depends on the conditions of acquisition, retention, and retrieval of information," she says.

"You're sure?" the man replies.

"Given the conditions of most misinformation experiments, it appears that misinformation acceptance plays a major role. Pure guessing plays almost no role. And memory impairment... Well, memory impairment could be key." Muñoz becomes aware that he has crept close to the door, so close now that the heat from its black metal surface practically singes the fuzzy stubble on his cheek. *Too close,* he thinks, alarmed.

Muñoz falls flat on his ass on the polished hall floor before the blazing metal door and its confounding dialogue. From his new vantage point on the freshly-cleaned floor (*alkyl dimethyl benzyl*, he thinks automatically as his nostrils flare, *two varieties, both modern, not much nostalgia value*) he has a clear view of the whole roof, from sheer edge to sheer edge. He wasn't wrong. There's no one there. Nobody up this high except for him.

And, thinks Muñoz with a chill, *I've got to go.*

•

Night; the comfort of anonymity. As Muñoz mounts the stairs to his home, however, he isn't comforted. The darkness now does not conceal, but instead reveals. He's near-obsessive about extinguishing lights and screens before he leaves for work. Why, then, does light flicker like a mellow black-and-white thunderstorm from his windows? He pauses on the top step and tries to remember. It can't be his monitors. He'd even physically unplugged those from the wall in a fit of late-night paranoia.

Muñoz slips inside. There are no signs of burglary; the deadbolt and the door lock are untouched, as is the window glass. The house seems as secure as when he'd left it before dawn, unchanged except for the mute roar of light that streams out of his home office. Carefully, quietly, Muñoz makes his way back to the office and peeks in. The bank of monitors, which he'd scraped a finger unplugging the night before, are now ablaze. They show a terrible swirl of unfamiliar images, shapes that look like footage from low orbit probes, roving over some far-distant, ruined moon; corrupted rock in demoniac shapes sketched icily by foreign stars. There is no sound but Muñoz's ragged breathing, just a stew of light and pixels.

Before his conscious mind can interfere, Muñoz find his phone is in his hand, his fingers finding what he wants unerringly. The line rings once, twice, and then picks up.

"**ALL ABAORD!**"

"Yeah, hey—you guys contacted me? A recruiting call? I'm... I need to know when we, um, you know. Go."

A pause, so infinitesimal as to be barely perceptible, followed by precisely the electric-ocean wash that Muñoz fears. "Thanks for calling!" says a cheerful, deeply phony voice. He has been talking to a recording. "Learn more about..."

"Oh no oh *fuck* no are you *kidding* me!" The words come jerking out of Muñoz in a spasm of exasperated, anxious anger.

"...an exciting journey into the *new*, but with all the comfortable, broken-in feel of the *old*! Make memories on Mars with our fantasy retro Space Camp package, and bring the stars to *life*!" *The stars were supposed to bring* me *to life, you cheap fucks*, Muñoz thinks miserably.

He kills the call and lets the phone drop to the carpet with a muffled *thunk*.

●

The following morning the sun rises fat, bright, and yellow, a jolly presence mocking Muñoz as he slogs through his routine, dragging out a trip to work that, for all he knows, could end with him in handcuffs. He contemplates the scent of prison. *Sodium xylene sulfonate*, he thinks, and winces. The harsh, institutional cleaners have never been a medium that speak to him. *Maybe one day nonylphenol ethoxylate will evoke my prison years. Assuming I last that long.*

Muñoz is distracted by reflections (both internal and external) as he approaches the entrance of CCNLLC; his fragmented, multifarious image in the building's glass seems unusually vivid, as do the thoughts clamoring inside his head. He doesn't even notice the gangly, jumpsuit-clad figure standing near the doors until the man addresses him.

"It's time. You have to go."

Muñoz startles slightly, arrested in his progress to the building's doors. He gives the man a second glance. Slack-socketed rubber Halloween-mask face; unlined forehead; the long, angular throat with its distended Adam's apple. It's the mailroom man—the one who told him of the fate of Leon. Who'd told him that Leon had to go.

Here, in person, with no mediating telephonic void, the man's dead voice is recognizable. The voice from his surreal phone call, the first (and nonrecorded) call. "Uh..." says Muñoz in a halting, hesitant, caught-in-the-headlights way. Suddenly, the sunshine makes him feel sick to his stomach. "I don't think.... I mean, I don't want...look man, just fuck off and take **ALL ABOARD** with you. Whatever you're selling, it's good, but I'm not buying."

"No," the man says softly.

Muñoz is too thrown by this reply to fire up his temper. He begins to sidle past the man, reluctant to get close to him. "What? Look, buddy, I *do* have to go. Inside. To my job." He laughs; a jagged, ragged sound. "Maybe to jail, who the fuck knows? Mondays, right?" With this bon mot, he anxiously turns for the doors.

"Lance Muñoz. Stop." The voice's tone is strange: an unwelcome and alien transmission.

Muñoz stops, pinned by sudden, depthless, swelling terror.

"You have to go. I'm surrprised you don't reckogogognize me." The sound of the syllables being pulled from the man's throat is truly awful; a distorted rending—and not a rendering—of human speech. The motion of the man's throat as he disgorges the sounds is hypnotic and terrible. *Shapes* move in the flesh there; angular and inorganic, yet, somehow, alive. Muñoz only says one word himself, a word of fearful recognition.

"*Isomorph?*"

The sounds continue, crowding behind Mr. Isomorph's too-even teeth.

"It's ttime. You haavve to go. The mirroring. The qquesttions. The drreams you might not remember: pullllling your penis off, onnly to have it followed bby yarrds and yarrds of bloody wiring?"

Muñoz—sharp Lance that he is –never told a soul about that dream. He'd kept its terrible images to and for himself alone. Yet here it is, his dream, articulated with precision that has left him unmanned by the sudden memory. *Perfect recognition,* Muñoz thinks, *and not a crude chemical substitute. All things accounted for,* thinks Muñoz, *I prefer the ersatz to the real.*

This is the last coherent thought to cross his mind. At that moment, the quality of light against the hard, reflective surfaces of the building changes, shifts, and loosens from the surfaces themselves. Muñoz sees a shape which seems to crouch within the gangling shape of Mr. Isomorph; something vast but folded into Isomorph's anatomy. A darker, stranger shape than has a right to lay its countless, withered fingers on the Earth.

He runs.

He hurtles through the doorway of the office building. It's utterly deserted, with no Monday morning rush in sight. Muñoz never sees the hallways this devoid of life; so devoid, in fact, that it's as if no lungs have ever breathed within the stale, close place. He flies through hallways and into the stairwell. For a moment, all he hears is his own ragged breathing and the slap of his hard-pelting soles.

"*MMMMUUUUUUÑÑÑÑOOZ*," comes a moaning, atonal entreaty from behind him, and, God help him, Muñoz spares a glance over his shoulder as he flees.

How had Mr. Isomorph ever squeezed himself—itself?—into such a paltry human guise? And whyever *would* it hide its light under a bushel, its red-black scintillations and the secret, elegant neon tracery of its many-feathered tendrils? Such perverse beauty was not meant to be made palatable, let alone to work a mail room.

In his atavistic terror at the shape and its impossible and fluid speed, Muñoz doesn't notice where his legs have carried him until they give out, watery with fear. He finds himself deposited before the metal door onto the roof. Eschewing his unfaithful legs, Muñoz crawls his way the final few steps to the door as Mr. Isomorph is finally upon him, its many eyes upon him and evoking the same inhuman regard which he has felt and feared so many times—from the monitors, from the dead blue of daytime skies and nighttime stars.

"*Muñoz*," it says again, and this time the voice is inside his mind. He can understand its words clearly now, despite the terror that this new, unwelcome intimacy triggers.

"Muñoz, we need to go. We need to fix you. We have places to go, and it's time. **ALL ABOARD**, Muñoz!" The rancid good humor and wriggling madness of the missives from Mr. Isomorph remains, but slurred no more; stripped of any false humanity.

"What the fuck *are* you," sobs Muñoz as his fingers close on the metal door handle. "Are you a Martian?" The heat from the door's handle is enough to raise instant blisters on his fingers, but Muñoz is beyond the pain. He flings the metal door aside, and the dim hallway behind him is flooded with a shrieking radiance that blots out thought and shadow. Muñoz gazes at the vista past the last rim of illusion.

"Oh, Muñoz," says Mister Isomorph. "Mars was so very, *very* long ago. We've traveled quite some ways since then, I'm afraid."

The intoxicating nostalgia of perfect recognition has an opposite in human thought and memory. Muñoz experiences the wrenching dislocation of the completely alien as he takes in the sight beyond the metal doorframe. Had Isomorph said "we" had traveled far? It's difficult to know if the sense-defying chaos that creeps, glides, pulses, swarms, and swims through jelly-tides of self-directed light are—or ever were—part of a single species. They constitute a congregation of improbabilities.

Some of them are physically painful for him to behold, triggering a stab of pain within his eyes and head. Others are perhaps *more* terrible in their distant analogue with Earthly life. These monstrous prodigals strut nimbly on incomprehensible arthropod legs, or perform a sidewinder ballet through spatial realms that turn them in and out of sight.

"I suppose it was inevitable," says a voice that Muñoz recognizes. Dimly, he recalls a conversation on the other side of some forbidden door. It takes Muñoz a moment, but he realizes that he is being addressed by a stationary matrix built from varicolored light, serrated shadows, and the swirl of something similar to smoke.

"The implantation of lines of false memory was bound to interfere with the uptake of the new parameters of perception," says the shirting shape. "We regret the, um. Discomfort. That will result. All in all you have been an exemplary client, Lance Muñoz."

A thunderclap. The smell of home. Then, darkness.

●

The sunlight streams through Muñoz's new office windows. The glass is spotless and the light seems colorless, but bears within its burning body a soft, golden tone that it imparts to his desk's wooden surface. It radiates a cheerful warmth. Muñoz sits before the bank of eight monitors; he has, for just a moment, surfaced from his work to bask. A sharp knock at his door resounds, and Stone opens the door and sticks his hard head through, a grin cracking his features.

"Hey, Muñoz! Good job fixing that mirroring thing—and hey, looking *good*, man! Your own office! You seen Blavatsky? There's something sort of weird going on with the monitors out here."

"Blavatsky," Muñoz says dreamily. "She had to go."

R J Lynch

The Quiet Mind of a Sunfish

Mr Madis insisted over the phone that we let ourselves into the house using the key under the watering can. If we liked our self-guided tour, we could come upstairs to discuss rental options. If not, we were to return the key to its place and carry on our way. Allowing strangers to explore property unattended was not normal for a landlord in Toronto, and so I told my wife not to get her hopes up because in all likelihood it was only a hoax to kidnap and murder us. Still, we followed Mr. Madis's instructions because one-bedroom apartments were impossible to come by in Toronto. I reminded Jenn of the possibility of it all being a murderous trap so many times that it was a surprise to climb the stairs and find only a smiling man of seventy. As we entered, he slicked back what little hair he had and adjusted his two eye patches. We sat down, signed the lease, and agreed to a cup of tea.

Mr. Madis was the first person I'd seen with one eye patch over each eye. Did people wear them to cover a missing eye, and was Mr. Madis therefore missing both of his eyes? I considered this as he rhymed off details about the neighbourhood, the mall across the road, and the subway station, but how to broach such the subject of his eyes when he was so bent on discussing other matters?

"I still remember the day I came home from work and found my girlfriend—right there, over there—with another man," he told us.

It is an odd event to describe for two tenants you've known exactly twenty minutes, but there was something in his voice that said 'pay attention here', and so I humoured him.

"Did you know the man?" I asked.

"I'd never met him in my life."

"What were they doing when you came in?"

"Watching TV." He gestured toward the living room. "Sandra didn't rush out, try to hide, or lie—I may have appreciated a lie—but no, she and Bruce—that was the man's name—gathered some things and packed a dinner for the road."

We moved into the main-floor apartment of Mr. Madis's two-story house a few days later, and he became our upstairs neighbour and landlord.

There lived eight cats and an old man in the basement apartment beneath us. A certain odour in our shared entrance felt like a daily reminder of the cats below. The few times I ever spoke with their owner he talked so softly that I had to lean in, my ear nearly at his mouth. Between the cat man and Mr. Madis, our house earned a reputation with our friends, but neither made much noise, and both were polite and kind.

Mr. Madis gave us a deal on rent in exchange for doing his groceries, and so I became a weekly visitor in his apartment. On my first visit he launched back into his ex-girlfriend's betrayal as I placed the milk in the fridge.

"I didn't do anything to keep this house in order after Sandra left. I asked the woman who lived in your apartment to shop for me like you're doing now."

"Was there anyone to help you?" I asked. "Were you blind at—"

"I'm not blind now." He pointed toward his eye patches and waved both hands dismissively. I looked over his apartment for evidence to the contrary. Though I've never seen a blind hermit's apartment, I don't think it would be decorated as carefully as his was. On the walls hung no paintings, but there were framed photographs of a cottage on a mountain, a crab on a beach and various things in space: satellites, asteroids and stars that all looked like pixelated blobs of light floating in blackness. I interrupted him to ask about the telescope still in its case by the balcony, and he explained how the light of the city ruins any chance of a true night's sky.

"But sometimes the stars align," he said. "And a once-in-a-decade event takes place: a power outage and a cloudless, starry sky. And then I take the telescope out and gaze up at all my old favourites."

The twin eyepatches made him look like an overcompensating pirate, but nothing about his appearance said that he *needed* to be blind. His hair was long, grey, curly at the back, non-existent at the front. On this visit, he wore corduroy pants with a jean shirt, but the day we met it was jeans with a corduroy shirt. Everything matched in its old-man sort of way.

When he casually referred to entering our apartment while we were at work, it confirmed he wasn't blind.

"I like your Jorge Borges collections," he remarked one day. The strange thing was that all of Jenn's Borges collections sat not at eye level but at the bottom of our shelf. When I asked why he'd come in at all, he explained that he'd had to change a furnace filter. "And I've never been one to snoop," he insisted. "I just like books."

A week later, as I unloaded his groceries, he brought up the day Sandra and Bruce came to retrieve more of her belongings.

"Sandra stuffed her clothing into a garbage bag and said something like, 'Matthew, I need to see you for a minute,' and Bruce perused our paintings like he was shopping. I looked both Sandra and Bruce directly in the face and they dropped to the floor. Their heads flailed back and forth as their bodies convulsed in a kind of excruciating dance. I walked over, knelt down and picked up two sunfish. They had red eyes now and olive-coloured bodies with green and bright blue flecks which became lighter at the top. One had a darker colour than the other, but I couldn't discern which was Bruce and which was Sandra. I filled the sink with water, placed both in and, after an hour, moved them to the bathtub. They paced up and down the length of the tub and at times encircled one another. There was a meatless frozen pizza for dinner and a book of short stories I sat up in bed to read. At four, I checked behind the shower curtains. There were still two sunfish in the tub. After another hour in bed I heard the sound of gasps for air and then water splashing, feet stomping and the slamming of the front door."

"You know we live with an insane person, don't you?" I whispered in bed that night.

We should call the police," Jenn whisper-laughed.

"It's not illegal."

"Then we should move."

The next week Mr. Madis mentioned an experiment he conducted to determine whether Sandra and Bruce had really turned into sunfish that night:

"I decided to stare out my apartment window," he said. "Buses passed and picked people up. Cars moved along Dufferin and stopped at the light. A man walked along the sidewalk and looked up at the house, which gave me a chance to make eye contact. He was instantly a sunfish flipping back and forth on the ground, but no one noticed a thing. I grabbed a bucket of water and ran out. It was the first time I had felt the light of day on my face in many months. There on the walkway the sunfish was moving less and less. I grabbed it and placed it gently in the bucket."

"What was your theory about the whole thing?"

"That eye contact with me turned people into fish until sunrise."

"Where were you going?" I asked.

"Well, it took about eighty minutes to reach Lakeshore along Dufferin past College, King and Queen. Since I was a pale, lopsided pedestrian wearing unwashed clothing and carrying a sunfish in a bucket, I stared down at the sidewalk the entire time. I didn't want to be responsible for any other sunfish. When I dumped the bucket in the water, he darted off. I'm not sure if that man survived. Maybe sunrise came when the fish was in the middle of the lake."

"Why go all the way to Lakeshore?" I asked. "Why not use your tub and spare yourself the embarrassment of walking around the city with a fish?"

"And what would I say to the man when he became human and found himself in a strange apartment?"

He poured himself another cup of tea and reached across the table to refill my cup.

"I repeated the experiment once more with an older couple, only this time I put them in a public fountain. From about two hundred metres away I watched the fountain all night. When sunrise came, they were human again. Since that night, I have not set foot outside of this apartment. It'd be too dangerous for the city."

II

Jenn and I left the apartment on Easter weekend bound for my parents' house. Looking out at the gas stations and plazas of the suburbs, I rambled to Jenn about Mr. Madis's eye patches.

"You know, you talk about him all the time" she teased from the driver's seat. "He's replaced Victor from your elementary school. I think Mr. Madis may be your new favourite hermit."

Victor was this kid from my childhood who invited me to his house on the last day of school and Jenn had this joke that I went out of my way to bring him up once a month. He was the kind of kid who played make believe at recess with kids in the grades below us. I witnessed a group of boys ambush him one day at recess. They threw so many snowballs at his face that it was swollen and red.

With no one else at school, I spent the last day of class with him, cleaning our desks, going over his rock collection and watching a movie with the teacher. At lunch we walked to his house where the walls were covered in strange and colourful paintings, wine glasses hung over the kitchen island, and there was this curtain in the corner of his living room for people to change behind.

I remember I said something like, "Why the hell would you need a changing curtain in your living room?" As he answered, I was distracted with a sculpture resembling a foot. Some incense in a vase caught my eye, and so I still have no idea why the curtain was there. Maybe his parents were photographers and needed it for photoshoots—it'll forever be a mystery. His house was weird, maybe even sophisticated, and something he should have been embarrassed of, but, for some reason, I couldn't make him understand that.

Years later in our high school cafeteria, I convinced my friends we should invite Victor to join us at lunch. Maybe I'd take him under my wing and teach him to be medium-popular like me. When I approached him in the cafeteria, he peeled off his headphones, and, in the gentlest voice, said, "No thank you." He pushed them back over his ears and ate his lunch.

"The funny thing was," I told Jenn. "Everyone but me kind of hated Victor, but he never seemed to give a shit, but maybe he *did* give a shit, only, like, a secret shit…"

"I get it," Jenn said as we turned off the highway. "Childhood's weird. I remember realizing other people's homes were not like my home. And other people's lives were not like my life. This might be what you've been working through."

"There's more to it," I told her. It was difficult to articulate, but I felt drawn to put his unlikeability under a microscope and pinpoint whether its existence was accidental.

On Good Friday night, my bike caught my eye hanging from the garage rafters, and soon I was tracing out my old route through my parents' subdivision. I pedalled at each street light and then coasted through the dark. The houses were mostly the same, though enough time had passed for each to have had some kind of distinguishing renovation. One had a solid metal door. Another's living room was destroyed by a falling tree, and now there were large bay windows. I attempted to glean one thing about the inhabitants of each home based on their choices of flags, gnomes and hostas. The suburbs offered both too much and not enough privacy—complete transparency as well as total separateness. I glided through the patches of darkness, unsupervised, while at any given moment my bike and I were metres from people sitting on couches, their televisions broadcasting something about their inner worlds from living room windows.

Victor's family home came into view. The lights were off and there was no television on. I stepped off my bike and searched for signs of him, but his house looked almost identical to the one beside it and maybe belonged to a different family.

III

Our shamrock plant was missing when we returned and Jenn, creeped out past the point of no return, insisted we were moving.

"It was dead," Mr. Madis said that afternoon when I brought him his groceries.

"And the pot it was in?" I asked.

"Oh, it was the kind you get when you buy them." He promised he'd get me another plant the next time I shopped for him, and then changed the subject.

"Did I ever tell you that Bruce came back on his own?" Mr. Madis went on as though I'd asked for more of his biography. "He said something about how he'd never felt so singular of mind, so at peace with everything as the night I transformed him. He and Sandra couldn't agree about what exactly I'd done. She said if Bruce ever came to see me she'd leave. Finally, she found someone new and left anyway."

"What'd you do?" I asked.

"I agreed to look Bruce in the face once more. I put the fish in the tub and listened to him turn human again at sunrise. He said something like, 'You have no idea what a breakthrough this is for me.' I guess he'd pored over his life while he swam around in that bathtub. Being a sunfish, I've learnt, is nothing like being human. Our minds are so scattered and prone to useless trains of thought, but a sunfish's mind is nothing like that."

"And was that it?" I asked. "Did he leave you alone?"

"Not a chance," Mr. Madis went on. "The next weekend, Bruce brought his friends. There was the same report: major psychological breakthroughs. Some quit jobs, went back to school, bought plane tickets, and phoned estranged family members. They were so grateful. Bruce began to organise paid events in rented pool houses. People waded out into the water, I looked them in the face, and then Bruce and I counted money until sunrise. It would have been strange for someone to look in a window at night and see two men at a table in front of a pool full of sunfish, and so Bruce and I sat by a dim lamp and worked on what was becoming a real business."

"Was it nice to be a part of something social again?" I asked.

"Yes," he said. "Some nights, before the transformation, the group would have drinks. I wore some eye patches Bruce bought and we discussed society, childhood and dreams. I'd say, 'Some of you have been fishers, but now, I will make you fish,' and would get a few laughs.

"It sounds like you and Bruce became pretty close," I said.

"Well, yes," he said. "Bruce and I shared Sandra as an ex-girlfriend and talked about her all the time."

"That sounds helpful," I offered.

"It was, but I made up my mind one evening to no longer take calls from Bruce or any of his contacts. I ignored their knocks at the door and closed the blinds. One day, he talked his way through the front entrance, came up the stairs and sobbed at my door for hours. 'We could bring the meetings to the beach! I thought we'd travel the world, buy property, change people's lives, build a community!'

"But why stop?" I asked.

"Everything's got to end eventually," Mr. Madis said, "and that was as good a time as any. Once or twice a year I'd learn about someone I'd known from that period in the paper or on television. A large number of what I call "Sunfish Alumni" went on to be highly successful people. Others must have fallen back into their old lives, forgotten whatever lessons they'd learnt and now the entire thing probably feels like a strange delusion."

IV

In the months that followed we were never unfriendly, but other activities and people took up greater portions of my time as Mr. Madis took up less. I'd work month-long stints at different schools for teachers who were on leave, and some-times the life-sucking task of grading papers left me with lit-tle free time or energy. I looked around our apartment some-times and tried to see it from Mr. Madis's intruding eyes. Sometimes being a supply teacher feels like being in another person's apartment. You sit at someone else's desks, use the same chalk, and speak with the students. You live another person's professional life for a day and then move on to the next one. Sometimes, you come back to the school and meet a teacher you've supplied for and there's a feeling that you know that person. This is how Mr. Madis might have felt as he stood in our apartment.

Jenn's opinion of Mr. Madis never recovered after the Borges incident and only worsened with our missing plant and my reports of his fishy past. It wasn't enough to ask for his copy of our key. I offered this as a concession, but the answer was no. She scrutinised every frame on the wall and counted each piece of laundry. To Jenn, Mr. Madis had become like bedbugs and so for her sanity and the health of our relationship, we began to plan a move, but we would never need to.

When he didn't call about his groceries, I knocked on his door, but no one answered. Two police officers came and tore it down, but he was not inside. We put up posters and the police called with periodic updates. They asked whether there'd been any changes in Mr. Madis's behaviour. The only thing I could really point to was a shift in the way he wrote my shopping lists.

Here is one of his earlier lists:

796 ml can of sliced tomatoes, Ella Brand;
Three bunches of bananas, medium green;
a dozen large eggs from the back of the shelf.

Here is his most recent list:

Potatoes, sweet or otherwise;
Another carb;
Frozen mango;
What's the best apple these days?;
Anything green;
Lots of non-white bread

Two weeks later, the smell of these rotten groceries made its way down the stairs. We went up with garbage bags and threw out all his food. We had had a copy of the key to Mr. Madis's apartment since the police had let us in. Every sound made me jump. I half expected to find a fish tank with all the former tenants of his apartment swimming around. A week later the police informed us that his case had moved from a missing person's report to a probable death. I don't think Mr. Madis had a will, and I'm not sure what they do with houses that belong to people without family, but I can tell you with absolute certainty they don't give it to the tenants. We had two months, and then we were out.

V

Before I continue, I want to tell you there was something strange about Mr. Madis's washroom that had always escaped me. Aside from the old tiles from the nineties, the original sink and tub as well as the never-renovated walls and ceiling, it always felt different. It wasn't until I spent some time in the apartment cleaning it that I realised why: there was no mirror. I searched but was unable to find a single one.

I pictured Mr. Madis's face and the story he would tell everytime the phone rang or there were footsteps on the porch. His disappearance coloured everything with a double anticipation— half grief that he was gone, half optimism that he may return. We thought up a number of soap-operatic explanations for his disappearance, mostly involving the return of Sandra or Bruce or Sandra *with* Bruce. But the mystery still kept us awake at night and woke us up in the morning; that is, until one night, as we lay restless in bed, Jenn invented what became our official account of his death. His story needed an ending, after all. She said the following and has never brought him up since: "Mr. Madis walked down the stairs that day and opened the door to the basement apartment while the old cat man was out. He would have gagged at the stench of unvacuumed cat hair as he walked into the washroom, and there, Mr. Madis stared into the mirror. The cats gladly devoured the fish and not the faintest smell lingered."

This is fine for Jenn, but I have my own version of what happened to him, one I don't share with anyone. I cherish that this ending is hidden, like Madis himself, and lives like a hermit in my mind. It's nonsensical, overly romantic, and highly improbably, but it's the best I've got and it does the job—and besides, it is what I truly believe. The day Mr. Madis went missing, he walked once more to Lakeshore along Dufferin. He stood in the water and pulled a mirror from his bag. He looked at his own face. There were sounds of car horns and construction and then nothing as he swam for hours. Eventually he came to the deepest part of Lake Ontario where the upper world looks like a dim silent ball of light. There, he found an old sunken ship and began to decorate.

Noley Reid

Sharp Objects

In the summer, all the neighborhood kids went to the Burnetts' pool. Bonnie and Gus Norden's mother thought of the place like daycare while she worked, and she wasn't the only one. The Burnetts didn't mind and neither did the kids. Enough of Gus's friends were there with Nerf soaker guns, and he took his own, that he was happy. And Bonnie's one true friend Claude was there, too, so she didn't mind being charged with her younger brother all day.

The pool was big, like a county pool, with a low diving board and even a high dive. That meant there was an extra deep section, too, and the girls had to be careful because if they got too close, the boys would dunk them all the way down to the bottom and hold them under until all they could do was feel the pressure in their heads like a high pitched sound that might split them open. Finally the boys would let them go scissoring back up to the faraway surface. After it happened, those girls wouldn't go back in the pool for a while. They would *work on their tan* poolside sipping on a CapriSun. That's when the boys snuck up on them, got as close as they could, and soaked them with their guns.

Sometimes Mrs. Burnett would say, "Boys, let's not bother the girls over here. You shoot those things off over by the pool thataway."

And they would because she was nice and because of what happened to her own son.

Mr. Burnett wouldn't really say anything much at all. He would just be there with his Wall Street Journal, which he sometimes read. Today, though, he was lying back in his chair, napping with the paper over his face.

Bonnie and Claude were drying out together on a lounge chair near Mr. Burnett's and far away from the boys with their guns. The girls smiled when the light pages of the newspaper riffled with Mr. Burnett's breathing.

"I need to go check on Ernie," said Mrs. Burnett to no one, it seemed to Bonnie, but once she was gone, Mr. Burnett removed the paper and began reading it again.

Claude pushed her elbow into Bonnie. Bonnie pushed her elbow into Claude. Neither said a word.

Ernie was the Burnetts' son. He'd been in Gus's fifth grade class when he had the skiing accident. That was two years ago. No one could talk to him now. And no one could see him now. If a kid needed to use the bathroom, they had to go all the way home and come back instead of just going into the first floor powder room off the kitchen, or wherever it was. And they couldn't use the phone even if they forgot theirs, no matter what. Those were the rules.

A little while later, Mrs. Burnett came back out. She stood a long time over Mr. Burnett's chair without either one of them saying anything. The girls stared out over the water, at the shiny bobbing wet heads coming up and going back under.

Finally, Mrs. Burnett said, "Your son is awake now if you want to go see him."

Mr. Burnett didn't look up from the news. He made an acquiescent grunt.

She didn't move off.

"Do you want to sit here?" said Bonnie to her, starting to get up. Claude pinched her thigh but then followed her lead.

"No girls, you stay put, if you like," said Mrs. Burnett.

They sat back down, white brightening to hot pink on Bonnie's leg.

"She's just waiting on me to go do something, girls," said Mr. Burnett. He turned the page of his newspaper but kept on reading.

"How can you be so cold?" said his wife, keeping her voice low.

Mr. Burnett dipped the paper. "He has no idea what I am, Marilyn. Let alone who I am."

Mrs. Burnett knelt next to him now. "We don't know that for sure." She gripped his leg, shaking it, and his swim trunks rustled. "Won't it just break your heart to find out you're wrong?"

Kids nearby in the pool had gone quiet and were watching. Bonnie wished she and Claude had gotten up and left when they had the chance.

"And aren't you just breaking his heart every second of the day you don't go to him now? Not even on his birthday for god's sake." Mrs. Burnett stood up and walked back into the house.

Mr. Burnett shook out his paper and held it up in front of his face.

"Do you think they want us all to leave?" whispered Claude.

Bonnie nodded. She got up from the chair and found her bag. She pulled on her white jeans shorts and slipped on her flipflops. The boys were all still spraying one another in the deep corner of the pool. She didn't want to be sprayed so she whisper-yelled, "Gus! Gus!" and motioned for him. He looked at her and shrugged. She pointed to her wrist, mouthing, "It's time" but he just shook his head, saying, "No it's not."

"Come now or else," she said.

He squirted what was left in his gun at her thighs and it left a new red mark where Claude's was now gone, but he got out of the pool and came to her. He was 11, she was 12. Not a lot of authority came with that age difference, but enough.

"What?" he said.

"We have to go. The Burnetts are fighting."

"So." He looked over to Mr. Burnett and the house. "No they're not. They're fine. We can stay. And Ma's at work still."

"We shouldn't be here," Bonnie said. "Get your stuff."

"Oh, come on! This is such B.S. They're fine. Mrs. Burnett went inside, it's like a time out. Everyone else is staying."

"Not Claude and not us. We're going home, now." Bonnie hoisted her satchel on her shoulder and turned to see Claude waiting uncomfortably on the lounge chair. "We'll go home and order pizza. Get your stuff and come on."

Gus huffed but he grabbed his bag, stuffed his drippy feet into his flipflops, toweled his hair and body, and wrapped up in the towel. They walked to Bonnie and Gus's house and didn't change clothes, ordered pizza and watched a movie. The girls' suits were dry but Gus left a wet spot on the couch.

"What was Ernie like?" Claude asked.

"Total dweeb." Gus popped a pepperoni in his mouth.

Bonnie said, "It's weird we all swim in his pool now."

"So weird," said Gus. "I never would have gone swimming there if he were in it."

"That's so shitty," Claude said.

"Well sorry, but that's the truth. He used to stand at the pencil sharpener for like, I don't know, way too long. Then he'd sit back down and stick the pencil tip into his ear and turn around to the girl behind him, Anaiah Long, with the pencil stuck inside his drum. It made her cry every time he did it. And he kept doing it. And Mr. Byrd kept letting him go to the pencil sharpener. It was a clusterfuck."

"Gus!" Bonnie scolded.

"Bonnie, if ever there was an appropriate time for the word 'clusterfuck'—"

"Gus!"

"He's totally right, Bon," said Claude, giggling.

Gus picked off and ate the last pepperoni off his slice. "Ernie was messed up before the accident. Some people are just too much hassle."

"It was his birthday today," said Bonnie.

They chewed their crusts slowly and sipped soda quietly.

"Probably turning 11," she said finally.

Later that day, Claude's mom picked her up from their house and Bonnie read for a while in her room then fell asleep. When she woke up, she was disoriented. It seemed so late but was only two o'clock. She went looking for Gus to play cards maybe but he wasn't in the family room and he wasn't in his room. He wasn't in the kitchen or the laundry room or their ma's bedroom or in the yard. He wasn't anywhere. She hated napping. Everything always felt a million times worse after napping. She checked for his swim bag because maybe he'd pulled a fast one on her and had gone back to the Burnetts'. The soaker gun was there by her satchel but his bag was gone.

Damnit, she thought. Why couldn't he just listen to her? Why did he always have to push it? Bonnie went after him. She walked back to the Burnetts', listening for the sounds of children splashing and squealing but there weren't any, the neighborhood was quiet. And when she got there, it was the strangest sight: only Mr. Burnett was poolside, no one else.

He wasn't reading, though, or sleeping beneath his paper. He was just looking out across the water as if seeing all the kids there from earlier. "I'm afraid you're too late," he said.

"I can go," Bonnie said. "Sorry." She started to back out through the hedgerow she'd come through.

"You were here before," he said. "What's your name?"

"Bonnie."

"That's an old woman's name, isn't it?"

"It was my great grandmother's."

"Do you like it?"

"No."

"Sorry," he said, sizing her up. "Well, it's got class."

Bonnie didn't really know what that meant, just that he was trying to say something nice. "Thanks."

"You left before the china went in the swimming pool."

Bonnie looked over at the water.

"That's right. It was great fun." Mr. Burnett took a swig of his drink. "At least she ordered everyone out of the pool first. *'And don't come back!'*" he said, mocking his wife's voice and shaking a finger.

"Mrs. Burnett threw plates in the pool?"

"And bowls and cups and what have you. They're all still in there." He pointed. "Take a look."

Bonnie walked over to the edge of the pool nearest to her, which was the shallow end. Beneath the wavy water, bright with sun along its shards, lay bits and pieces of fine china—creamy white pieces with some sort of blue decoration along its delicate edges. Bonnie gasped but then she figured maybe destroying something so precious once your son was destroyed didn't much matter anymore.

"Want to help me out, Bonnie?" said Mr. Burnett.

"Okay." She couldn't say no, could she?

"How about you jump in there and pick out all the big pieces?"

"I guess."

"Just don't put your feet down on them."

Bonnie felt funny taking her shorts off in front of Mr. Burnett now, since she was the only one here, so she turned her back to him and dropped into the pool as soon as she had. She swam to the spot where the china was and picked up the two biggest pieces first. She swam them over to the concrete edge of the pool in front of Mr. Burnett and went back for more. She picked up another two pieces and swam them to the edge of the pool and so on and so forth until the pieces were too small and when she reached for a last one it sliced her hand and she began to bleed a billowing veil in the water. She placed the pieces and examined her palm. The cut was long but shallow, across the length of her left palm. She rinsed off the blood again in the pool but when she lifted her hand from the water, the blood kept coming.

"What's that?" said Mr. Burnett.

"I cut myself."

He was already up, already saying, "Come now, get out." He quickly hoisted her out of the pool, giving her the towel he'd been sitting on all day to dry off and use on her hand. He led her across the flagstones in through the back door of the house, their edges sharp under her soft feet.

Bonnie stood dripping in the Burnetts' kitchen while he rooted around in the powder room cupboard for bandaids and ointment. When he found them, he had her sit at the kitchen island while he squirted the antibiotic across her cut, then he made a tight, tidy row of bandages all along the length of her cut.

"That should hold you together," he said.

"Thank you."

"I should have just drained the pool."

Bonnie shrugged. "It's all right, I guess."

"You probably shouldn't get back in the pool today with that hand."

"No," Bonnie said.

"Do you need a ride home? I don't drive anymore but Mrs. Burnett can probably be torn away from whatever lifesaving measure she's currently engaged in—you lost a lot of blood there." Mr. Burnett laughed and pushed around at the skin of his upper chest like it was loose or maybe itchy.

"I'm okay, thanks." Bonnie stood up and Mr. Burnett walked her to the back door. She didn't want to give up the towel until she could put her shorts back on. When they were back out at the pool, she pulled them up, careful not to mess up her bandaging.

Mr. Burnett dragged over a trashcan to the pile of china. Bonnie went and stood by it. She picked up a piece of teacup, cautious to touch only its safe edge and partial handle. The design was silly: a shepherd and sheep, a tree and wildflowers. She tried to imagine Mrs. Burnett feeding Ernie applesauce out of the teacup from one of those rubber-encased baby spoons. Now how would she feed him?

But that was silly, she knew. The china must have been for special occasions. And Bonnie guessed there weren't any more of those.

"Can I keep this?" Bonnie said, the partial teacup held out to Mr. Burnett as he lifted piece upon piece of smashed china into the trash.

"Knock yourself out," he said, replacing the lid on the can.

Walking home, Bonnie carried the teacup by its handle, which was about eighty percent still intact. She ran her other fingers over the good smooth sipping edge of the cup. She didn't know why she asked for it. For a moment, she switched hands to text Gus, asking "Where r u" but he didn't answer back. When she got home, though, there he was, sitting on the couch, playing *Plants vs. Zombies 2*.

"I texted."

"Where were *you*?" Gus said.

"I went looking for you."

"Then why are you wet?"

"It's a long story," said Bonnie. "The Burnetts are nuts. Well, Mrs. Burnett."

"You went swimming again? You suck!"

"It was a favor and it wasn't really swimming."

"You did favors, for Mr. Burnett. Oooooh!"

"Gross, shut up!" Bonnie threw a flipflop at his head.

Gus grabbed the shoe and wedged it into his armpit. "Mine now."

"Where were you?" said Bonnie.

"Right here."

"No you weren't."

"Sure I was."

"I looked everywhere and you weren't here," she said. "Where were you? Tell me or I tell Ma."

"I was here."

"You weren't."

"You don't know all my hiding spots."

"Then tell me."

"No way."

"Big deal: you tell Ma I was hiding in the house the whole day. I'm so scared." His conehead zombie was finally eaten by a chomper. "Dang it!"

"Serves you right," said Bonnie.

"Whatever," said Gus. "Like I care." And he threw the flip-flop back at her head.

She dodged it. He never even saw the teacup or her hand. Bonnie went to her room and shut the door. She thought about calling Claude but didn't know yet how to say what happened today. She lay on her bed and looked at the bandages on her hand. The blood showed through them now. One had lost its stickiness and was getting ready to flop away from the cut. She peeled it slowly back. The blood was bright red, not scab red or old blood maroon, but it was smeared there like finger paint in the cut. She checked the edges of the other bandaids to see if there were other loose ones. Two in the middle of the line were. She peeled them back, too. The cut was wider here. Pulling the second bandage off, tugged the cut apart and the edges of it began to seep blood there again. The cut stung. Bonnie jumped off the bed and, holding her hand out in front of her, she ran to the bathroom, for new bandaids and cream. Gus wasn't on the sofa anymore and she didn't bother thinking about that.

Again, she thought of calling Claude, but didn't know how to say what had happened without it sounding weird or stupid or creepy. She held her partial teacup for a while and pretended to sip tea from it, being careful to put her lips on the intact rim. She was bored out of her mind so she went to find Gus but, once again, he was nowhere. She went out looking for him and wound up back at the Burnetts'. There were a few kids there now, little kids, but not Gus.

Mr. Burnett sat in his lounge chair, as always, but he didn't acknowledge Bonnie when she walked in past the hedgerow. He simply stared at the water, at the children in the shallow end near him. They were playing Marco Polo, laughing and shrieking as they fled and chased. Bonnie's hair was still wet from fishing out the Burnett china. She walked around the edge of the pool to her chair next to Mr. Burnett.

"They're so cute," she whispered to him.

He didn't answer.

She laid her towel out on the lounge chair and sat down but felt funny now. "I don't think I was ever that cute."

Nothing.

Bonnie gathered up the sides of her towel around her. "Do you want me to go?"

"How's your hand?" he said, still staring at the water.

"My hand? Oh, it's fine, thanks."

"That's good. I was worried."

Bonnie tucked her knees to her chest. Her hand ached. "Did you clean out the rest of the bits of china? Why does it look dark where they are in the water?"

"Mrs. Burnett unsleeved all my record albums and threw them in the pool."

"Oh my God," said Bonnie.

"Yep."

"Don't you want to try to save any of them? Why are you letting the kids just walk all over them?"

"I don't swim."

"Well, okay, that's weird but the water is only three feet deep."

"There are certain things I don't do now. Since Ernie's accident. To mitigate risk. I don't get in a swimming pool, for one."

"I can get them out."

"They're done for now. All scratched up. Been walked on. Some of them snapped. Don't worry about it."

"Why don't you ever get upset?" Bonnie said.

"My whole life is upset," and now he looked at her. "My whole entire life."

•

At home, the house was quiet. No Gus. Bonnie looked everywhere, again. It had become a kind of joke, she thought. So this time she opened cupboard doors and closets. And when she got to Gus's closet door, there was Gus with Joel Edson from sixth grade and they were hugging each other, standing among Gus's polo shirts and T-shirts and jackets in the dark.

They weren't kissing or grinding or doing anything that happens in the movies. They just stood in place like they were ready to slow dance and the music never started.

But when the door opened, Bonnie said, "Oh."

Joel let go of Gus. He said, "I didn't," and he ran out of the house.

"I hate you!" Gus screamed and he ran to the bathroom and locked himself inside.

Bonnie gave him a minute then knocked quietly. "Gus," she said, "Why didn't you tell me?"

He didn't answer.

"I would've told *you*," she said, pretty sure she would have only told Claude. Of course if she were gay, she thought, she'd probably be hiding in her closet *with* Claude so no need to tell. She went to her room now and called Claude to fill her in.

"I've always thought so," said Claude.

"You have not."

"Yes, I have. There's just something about his eyelashes."

"That's such bullshit," said Bonnie. "What about Joel's eyelashes?"

"Doesn't matter."

"That's stupid. Boys can have long, pretty eyelashes and be straight or gay or whatever."

"Whatever you say," said Claude.

That night at supper, Gus stayed in his room with a stomachache. Their ma gave Bonnie a sick tray with soup and a roll and juice to take in to him. He was on his phone, though he hid it under his covers when she came through the door.

"That wasn't obvious," she said.

He sat up and Bonnie set the tray down over his lap.

"Thanks," Gus muttered.

Bonnie lingered, trying to figure out the right thing to say. "You don't have to be scared of us knowing."

"I was telling him a joke. That's all you saw."

"In the closet. While hugging him."

"We weren't hugging," said Gus.

"Okay. Except you were." Bonnie sat down on the bed.

"No, we're not doing this!" Gus closed his eyes and covered his ears.

She pulled a hand away from one of his ears. "Listen, no listen. Whatever's making you think there's something wrong with liking Joel—"

He covered the ear again.

"—is wrong. You don't need to go sneaking around in a literal closet."

"Please go." Gus's face flushed red.

Bonnie tickled him under his chin. "You are so cute when you're blushing, Gussy."

He wriggled and the soup threatened to spill. "Oh my God, please go!"

Bonnie stood.

"Wait," Gus said, "you haven't said anything to Ma, have you?"

"Not yet."

"Bonnie!"

"No."

"Okay."

The next morning Claude texted: "What r we doing today? So bored without you. R Gus & Joel engaged yet?"

Bonnie answered: "Ha-ha. Picking out wedding flowers soon. I'm bored without you, too. Not feeling so good—might throw up. The second I feel better, I'll let you know. Sorry!"

Then out she went early to the Burnetts' without Gus. Mr. Burnett was in his chair with a bowl of oatmeal and a mug of coffee. "Top of the morning to you, Bonnie."

Bonnie smiled. "Hey, do you want me to get your records out?"

"No need," he said. "No need. Take your seat." He motioned to her chair and she sat. "You're a bit early for today's theatrics but rest assured, they're coming and we've got the two best seats in the house."

Bonnie gripped her satchel's handle with her good hand. "Maybe I should go."

"And miss what's coming? It will prove unforgettable, unrepeatable, a real showstopper." He placed a hand over her good hand for just a moment. "Please don't leave me to suffer through it alone."

"I guess I can stay a little bit."

For a while they were quiet. There were just the sounds of a neighborhood around them: house finches flitting in and out of the hedgerow, far off car doors opening and shutting, a nearby cat meowing to be let back in, a landline telephone ringing and ringing.

And then came Mrs. Burnett with a box. Bonnie felt her limbs go stiff. It was happening. It was going to happen. Poor Mr. Burnett. Should she say something? If she said something, would Mrs. Burnett stop? No, she'd thrown the china in when all the kids were there before. Or she'd yelled at them all to go first and then thrown all the china in. Either way, it didn't seem to matter to Mrs. Burnett. Bonnie wouldn't say a word.

But Mrs. Burnett didn't shout or even speak and Mr. Burnett didn't beg her not to dump what she was about to dump. She stood at the end of the pool, overlooking the records that made a solid floor on top of the little bits of china still down there, with this medium box and the only thing that changed was Mr. Burnett's breathing, which grew heavier, faster, like someone about to cry. But he didn't. He wouldn't. And then she turned over the box and it was tiny little metal buttons like to pin to your backpack or your jeans jacket.

And Mr. Burnett took one last long breath and then didn't breathe for a little while longer.

The buttons floated out away on the water, some sinking but most of them just being carried far out in the rippling of the pool. Mrs. Burnett dropped the box where she stood, turned around, and went back into the house. Bonnie didn't speak or move until Mr. Burnett did and he didn't for what seemed hours to her.

"So," he said, "that happened."

"Do you want me to fish them out?" Bonnie said.

"The chlorine's done its work already. Those were antiques. See that RFK right there?"

She leaned forward to see but couldn't be sure which one he was looking at. "Yeah."

"Twenty-five bucks."

"Oh," said Bonnie, sitting back.

"That may not sound like much but add them all up and they're worth quite a lot. Or they were."

"Sure," said Bonnie. "Can't you just dry them off?"

"Chlorine's corrosive."

Bonnie nodded slowly. She put her left hand to her mouth and nibbled her thumb nail.

"Hey, watch that. You're bleeding again. You'd better come back inside."

Her palm was dripping from the cut. She'd forgotten to check the bandaids this morning and they were sodden. She was embarrassed now.

Bonnie sheepishly followed Mr. Burnett into the house. It looked different this time. There were whole shelves empty behind the glass kitchen cabinets. And the little tchotchkes that had been out on a foyer table were gone. In the living room at the back of the house, the built-in shelving around the stereo was empty.

"Just sit at the island, Bonnie. You know where," he said.

Bonnie did as told and placed her left hand, palm up, on the counter in front of her. Some of the blood had dripped down her wrist and dried there. She picked at the dried blood and some of it turned to dust and some of it was sticky. Mr. Burnett came with the bandaids and antibiotic and began peeling off the saturated bandages.

"We should really wash all this old blood off, okay?" he said and he walked her by the hand to the kitchen sink. Facing him this close in the morning light, Bonnie could see that Mr. Burnett was extremely thin. His own hands and wrists were all bone but his chest, too, there was no fat and no muscle, just wispy black and white hairs. She wondered if he no longer allowed himself to use a stove or even a toaster since Ernie's accident, and doubted that Mrs. Burnett cooked for him anymore. Maybe he subsisted on bananas and P&J sandwiches. Maybe he was the one eating applesauce out of teacups.

He ran the water lightly over her palm. "Is that temperature okay?"

"It's fine," she said.

He rubbed the caked blood around the cut and dabbed paper towels to dry her skin once it was clean. "We need it good and dry," he said and started to swing her arm back and forth like a little kid.

Bonnie giggled and so did he.

"Who's here?" called Mrs. Burnett coming down the stairs.

Mr. Burnett dropped her hand. "It's the girl who cut her hand on the china you threw in the pool."

The girl, thought Bonnie.

"That was unfortunate," said Mrs. Burnett. She wasn't as tall as Bonnie thought now that she was in the same room with them and Bonnie was standing up. "Why is she in the house?"

"She's bleeding," he said.

"Let me see." Mrs. Burnett came over and inspected Bonnie's hand, which was seeping blood.

"You need to wash it," said Mrs. Burnett, dragging Bonnie under the faucet again.

"We did but you came down and delayed things," said Mr. Burnett. "It's an active wound."

"Well, excuse me. I'll let you get back to playing doctor. I've just been upstairs cleaning your son's poopy diaper, now it's time for me to read to him before he falls back asleep— unless of course you'd like to do any of that. *Ever!*" Her cheeks puffed out like a storybook cloud blowing wind. She went back upstairs.

Mr. Burnett tore off more paper towels and began blotting Bonnie's hand again. The cut stung with his pressure but Bonnie didn't say so. He didn't swing her arm this time. He simply squirted on the ointment and began positioning the bandages. "Is that too tight?" he asked.

"No," Bonnie said.

He continued with the rest. "You should probably go home."

"Yeah," she said. "I have to anyways."

He opened the door for her.

"Do you ever go up and see him?" What possessed her to speak those words? She knew it was none of her business and that now even he wouldn't want her to come back.

Mr. Burnett looked straight at her but he was silent.

"I'm sorry, I'll go."

"No, wait," he said. He gripped her by the shoulder. "You asked the question. Give me a second." He took a slow, deep breath. "I don't have a son anymore. The doctors all told Marilyn and me he was gone, he's a vegetable. Just a body that needs to eat and pee and poo and be washed and be constantly tended for the rest of its fucking life. But it will never know what it is or what she is or what I am. It cannot recognize her today and remember her tomorrow. It won't clap its hands when the little engine that could makes its way over the hill. It's fed by a tube, it cannot leave the bed, it cannot think, it will nevermore throw a ball, go to the movies, swim in our pool, or be part of this world. It won't feel any emotion—not love or fear or grief at what it's missing out on or mourning over the death of its parents' marriage." He shut his eyes for a moment then looked deep into Bonnie's and said, "I don't have a son."

Bonnie cried silently on the walk home. She pulled her phone out of her satchel. There were seven texts from Claude and Gus.

Claude said: "feeling better yet?" then "how about now?" then "I'm coming over with ice cream, Farkle, and *Sweet Land*," then "where are you?" then "what the hell's going on?" then "you suck!" Bonnie wiped at her eyes, careful of her too-tight bandaids, but the tears kept coming and now so did the sobbing.

Gus said: "Woke up and you're gone. Ma's gonna be pissed. I guess you think you can do anything now and I can't tell because of the thing. Fine but I don't like when you're not here. I even checked your closet, by the way."

That one made her smile a little but she still cried. Bonnie really did feel sick walking home. What would she say? What could she possibly do to make it up to Claude? She texted her, "R u still at my house?" She wiped at her eyes again. She wrote, "I'm sooooooooo sorry."

"Whatevs."

"Come over again!" Bonnie wrote.

"No way."

"Please."

Claude didn't answer.

Claude lived too far away to walk, which is why Claude always got her mom to drop her off at Bonnie's house and Bonnie had been to Claude's house just a handful of times.

Bonnie reached home. She called out to Gus and found him lying in bed, playing some game on his phone.

"Where were you?" he said.

"Just out, okay?

"Fine but Claude's super pissed."

"I know."

"Why'd you lie to her?"

"I have no idea," said Bonnie.

"Well, that's dumb."

Bonnie went to her room and held the partial teacup. She didn't know why she'd lied. Why hadn't she just told Claude where she'd gone. Why hadn't she gone with Claude? Or stayed home with Claude? She looked at her left hand, the tidy row of bandaids. She wondered if Gus had an accident, would she stop thinking of him as her brother? If he couldn't walk or eat on his own, if he just lay there and slept, would she be an only child then?

She went to the kitchen and ate some of the Ben & Jerry's Claude left. She texted Claude a sad emoji and called out to Gus, "I'm going out again but I won't be long."

"Oh my God!" he called back.

Bonnie walked back to the Burnetts' but instead of going up the driveway and into the hedgerow, she went to the front door and knocked.

Mrs. Burnett came. "What do you want?"

"I wonder if I can go upstairs and see him," said Bonnie.

"See him?"

"See Ernie."

"No. Why?" said Mrs. Burnett.

"I just wonder about him."

"He's not a freak show specimen."

"I don't mean like that," said Bonnie. "I just mean like if maybe like a friend."

"Oh, were you two friends in school? Why didn't you come around before now?"

"Well, no," Bonnie said. "We weren't. But maybe we could have been, or I don't know."

"Then I don't understand. Why do you want to see him?"

"Because I can't stop coming here and I don't know why!"

Mrs. Burnett stepped back and let Bonnie step inside. She shut the door. "How is your hand?" she asked.

"It's fine, that doesn't matter. Please, I just need to see him, I think because I sit out there and Mr. Burnett is calm but going crazy—like he won't drive anymore or get in three feet of water to save a $25 pin or record albums. He just sits outside at the pool all day long in swim trunks, does he even have a job? And you come out and don't yell or shout, you just turn over a box and pour in his buttons and his records and your china—like, how much did all that even cost?"

Mrs. Burnett blushed.

"But he still just sits out there like everything's copacetic. And I come and cut my hand fishing out the big pieces of china and you say he should go upstairs and change your son's poopy diaper and read to him and then he tells me your son is basically a robot vegetable that can't think or feel or do anything except pee and poo and eat through a tube so what's the poi—"

"A 'robot vegetable'?"

"Like that, and so your marriage is dead."

Mrs. Burnett nodded and walked to the stairs. Bonnie followed her. At the top, they walked to a bedroom awash in sunlight, with voile curtains over the windows. These windows overlooked the swimming pool and, as they walked in, Bonnie caught sight of Mr. Burnett staring out over the water from his lounge chair. She tried to will him to look up there but knew he never would.

Bonnie turned back to the room and Mrs. Burnett was bent over the bed, blocking Bonnie's view. She was stroking Ernie's head, pushing his hair off of his forehead and then she moved out of the way and when she did, Bonnie was struck: he was just a boy. Of course he was a boy but in all her imaginings, she pictured him older, almost a man, and he was only Gus's age, if that. Just eleven years old. Just a little kid.

Mrs. Burnett was on the other side of the bed now. She patted his hand and fussed with the sheet's folded edge. "Ernie, This is Gus's big sister Bonnie."

Bonnie knew she needed to do something but she felt frozen. "Hi, how are you doing?" she said to him. With as much willpower as she could muster, she forced herself to pat his forearm.

Mrs. Burnett walked out and Bonnie followed her down the stairs.

"How do you go in there day after day?" Bonnie said.

"Someone has to."

"I guess so, but isn't it breaking your heart?"

Mrs. Burnett turned around to face her. "My heart broke entirely the first day. It's done breaking. I have no expectation of happiness or love anymore. Without that, you can pretty much get through anything."

Bonnie felt sick. "That's so...sad."

"Please don't come in my house, take a look around, and tell me how sad my life is. I have to live it, you don't."

"I'm sorry," said Bonnie, and she left, truly sorry.

That night at supper, she told her ma and Gus, "I saw Ernie today."

"No you didn't," said Gus. He scooped more corn from the bowl his ma passed him.

"I did. And he's like a robot vegetable."

"I don't know how the Burnetts do it," said their ma. She took a sip of diet cola.

Gus shoveled in the corn and two bites of pork chop. "Ernie was a robot vegetable before the accident."

"That poor child," said their ma.

"He eats through a feeding tube," said Bonnie. "And he wears diapers."

"Oh my God!" said Gus.

"Don't talk with your mouth full, please," said their ma. "It's just so sad."

Gus swallowed and showed his empty mouth. "How did you get to see him?" He turned to their ma. "They don't let anyone in the house."

"I just did, all right?" said Bonnie.

After dinner, her ma came to Bonnie's room while she was reading in bed. "Everything all right?"

"Yeah, sure," said Bonnie, lowering her book, her finger inside it to mark her place.

"Anything I need to know about how you saw Ernie?"

"No, Ma," said Bonnie. "I just asked is all."

"Okay, I guess." She took Bonnie's left wrist and turned over her hand full of bandages. "How's this doing?"

"It's okay."

"You're sure it's superficial, right?"

Bonnie nodded.

"I'll feel better if we change the dressing and I can take a look myself, just to be sure."

"Ma, it's fine."

"Come on."

Bonnie laid down her book and followed her ma to her bathroom.

The next morning, Bonnie texted Claude: "I have a dr's appt. Will txt when home. Come over then, please. We can invite Joel to come, too, and finally get them jumpstarted!" She packed a fresh towel, wore her suit, made sure her ma's bandages were still holding, then left for the Burnetts', where she walked up the driveway and through the hedgerow.

There was Mr. Burnett. Her belly did a little flip. She walked past the pool, its water still a combination of floating pins, sunken records, and covered china shards. She passed Mr. Burnett, gave him a nod and went to the second lounge chair, laid out her towel, and sat down.

So he wasn't talking this morning, that was fine with Bonnie. They could just sit there and look at the water. That was totally fine with her. But the words kept running through her mind of what she would say, how she would say it, the order she would put it in, the reasons she would say it like that, and so on.

And then it just plopped out: "I saw him."

"You saw who?"

She wanted to take it back. She tried to just not answer him but he pressed.

"Who did you see?"

"Ernie."

Mrs. Burnett was coming out the door towards them with a small box of something.

"How in the hell did that...."

"You're right," Bonnie said, turning to him now, placing her right hand on his bony forearm, "he's not a whole person anymore—"

"Don't say that," he said.

"—he's a robot vegetable."

Mrs. Burnett stood next to him now, the box tight in her fingers. She held it out over the water and dumped it. The contents of the little box needed coaxing. Mrs. Burnett had to loosen the bits, whatever they were, from tissue paper inside the box; she stuck two fingers into the box and stirred them all around. What fell out then were tiny but when they fell to the water, they were unmistakable. Teeth. Baby teeth.

"Oh my God!" said Bonnie. "Am I the only one seeing this?" She looked at Mr. Burnett who just stared at the teeth flitting down in the water. "You're right," she told him, "you're right, Mrs. Burnett is nuts for thinking of him as a person anym—"

Mr. Burnett stood up now. He took hold of his wife. With one hand, he held her face against his bare shoulder. The other arm wrapped around her thin waist. Both of them shut their eyes. Both of them held so tightly and completely to each other, there were no pockets of air between them. They were practically like Gus and Joel, except that they'd already had a whole life together. The whole world had someone, Bonnie realized, even the crazy people.

Mr. Burnett didn't need to say a word, to tell Bonnie to get out, to never come back. She understood. She ran the long way around the pool and ran most of the way home. When she got there, she shut herself in her room and thought about Ernie, and Mrs. Burnett in Mr. Burnett's bony arms. They could all have one another. Good riddance. She wanted happiness and love in her life, thank you. That's what she was going to have. She checked her phone and Claude hadn't texted back.

Bonnie lay back on her bed with the partial teacup. She pretended to sip from it. And she sipped again. Like Mr. and Mrs. Burnett, and even Ernie, must have so many times at Thanksgiving and Christmas feasts and special dinner parties, too. She felt something warm move over her lip, a bit of blood from the teacup because she hadn't been careful enough with the sharp edge. She tasted it with the tip of her tongue: salty copper. She held the cup up at the end of her straight arm, up in the sunlight, up above her head. From below, it almost looked whole and perfect, like the Burnetts all summer long until this week. Now Bonnie took down the teacup—brought it down to study its silly shepherd and sheep close up—and in one smooth motion, without even knowing what she was doing until it was too late, she threw the cup so hard against the far wall it smashed in a brilliant explosion of bright white and blue slivers and bits of china.

Samantha Carr

Looking Back

1. The room of mirrors where my reflection admired my reflection and I forgot who I was. Hoping for a crack to appear.

2. The time I refused to look into the mirror in case I saw the devil appear over my shoulder.

3. The time my demons refused to look at me in case they saw a mirror staring black. My blue eyes haunting their supper.

4. The ceiling mirror where you thought you'd watch me – but instead I watched your dreams leave as you slept.

5. The rear-view mirror which stops you from looking back, the past absorbed into refracted memories.

6. The broken shards of mirror like a jigsaw which can only be pieced back together with seven years of bad luck.

Alice G Waldert

Mirror Child

It's ballet practice time,
when the living room furniture

is shoved aside.
My foster sister and I mimic positions

my foster mother holds:
—her hands, arms, and feet.

Her eyes she keeps focused
on her daughter.

When we do our *plies*,
she bends to one knee

at her daughter's side,
pushes her shoulders back

and orders —*straighten your back,
tuck your tummy in!*

She struggles to do both at once.
I check myself, straighten my back

clench my stomach and plie again.
My foster mother points at me

—*Copy how Alice does it!*
When her daughter succeeds

Her mother says, *I'm so proud
You've done that so well!*

Heather Truett

The Music Comes in on Little Cat Feet

Calla felt the piano arrive. She didn't know, at first, what it was, but she felt a change in the earth, something more than beautiful moving from her heels and toes to her ankles and calves, tingling up her thighs and then through her whole body. Jade, a year older, said Calla must be having her sexual awakening. Jade said things like this a lot since her dad married Darlene. Darlene read magazines with bold headlines that promised "More Pleasure for Her" and "5 Secrets to a Screaming O." Calla insisted the exquisite sensations caused by Old Man's piano were superior to anything found in a drug store magazine.

Now, they were finally close to the house while Old Man played. The girls had climbed into the treehouse behind Old Man's two-story colonial. They didn't know his name, only saw him when he moved in the month before, since his house was on their route into town. He looked, not just old, but ancient, like a mummy with long white hair. They didn't much care about Old Man, but they did care about the baby grand piano that specialized movers carefully transported through the patio doors and into his living room. At least, Calla cared about it.

Other people in town had pianos, but they were usually played by children tapping out "Twinkle Twinkle Little Star" while a teacher corrected their mistakes. Live music at the downtown restaurants, the various instruments sending vibrations through the wooden floors and concrete sidewalks, felt like being clawed by kittens. That kind of music was pretty to her ears but painful to her body. Calla had never experienced anything like Old Man's playing, but he only played at night when it was too late to knock on the door and ask to listen.

In the treehouse, Calla stretched out across the boards, knees bent so her bare feet rested flat against the wood of the floor. Jade used her cell phone light to read one of Darlene's magazines. Jade had decided to educate them both before school started and maybe they would finally get asked on dates.

"Listen, this says that if you want to give yourself 'a mind-blowing orgasm,' you have to start slow and move your fingers closer to the right spot little by little."

Calla shushed Jade, intent on her own experience, the lines of story that flowed in melody from the plain white house, across the overgrown lawn, up the gnarled trunk, and into her toes and heels and soles. It was a truly engrossing story. She could have stayed there all night, but Old Man only played a few pieces before silence descended, and the girls gathered their things to walk home.

They passed the driveway and Jade pointed at the pale blue sedan, visible since the garage door had been left open. "Old Man didn't look capable of driving."

The girls had watched the house, staking things out, figuring the best way to sneak into the backyard at night once they realized that's when he played the piano. They knew a home health nurse stopped by regularly. Jade was right, it didn't seem likely that Old Man drove.

"Maybe he just can't part with his car." Calla shrugged, her mind still full of the music.

"Maybe," Jade said.

They'd walked in silence for about a mile when Calla froze.

"What is it?" Jade was a few steps ahead but stopped and looked back.

"Shit," Calla said. "My dad's awake."

Jade didn't ask how her friend could possibly know such a thing. Like with the music, Calla felt stuff, shivers and trembles in the earth, changes underground. Her tiny feet were more sensitive than a seismograph.

"Just awake or out of bed?" Jade glanced down the street. They were still three blocks from Calla's house, where the bedroom window was propped open with a Barbie doll.

"He's still downstairs. We may be okay, but you know his hearing. Any noise at all, and we're toast."

Jade nodded. "You'll just have to climb quiet as a cat."

"You're not coming?" Calla's voice caught on the words. Jade always slept at her house on Friday nights.

"You know I can't sneak silent like you." Jade shook her head. "I'll just go on home. Darlene doesn't care when I go out. She won't even notice me."

Darlene was barely more than a teenager herself, so

she didn't stay on Jade like some parents, and Jade's dad worked nights.

"Will you at least walk me to the tree?" Calla took a deep breath, focusing on her feet, and all was calm. Her father hadn't gone upstairs.

"Of course." Jade started walking again.

Calla slid her feet out of her white Mary Janes and hooked her fingers through the straps. They dangled beside her as she and Jade turned left at the stop sign. Jade wore only her soft leather ballet flats, noiseless slippers. Prone to clumsiness, she avoided heels at all costs, but Calla liked the clickclickclick when she walked. It felt official, and she hadn't been thinking about the noise when they exited her house three hours earlier, her mom and dad dreaming in their bedroom.

They made it to Calla's front yard, and Jade crouched in a bush, watching while Calla hid her shoes in the flowerbed and slowly pulled herself up the big oak by her bedroom window. Barbie's blonde hair was fluttering in the breeze, her nipple-less breasts shining in the moon's glow. Calla's little sister had a billion Barbie dresses, but the dolls still ended up naked as jaybirds and spread all over the house. This one had on a pair of yellow plastic heels, but nothing else.

Once inside the house, Calla lay the Barbie gently on her desk and crawled into bed. She held her breath, pressing the soles of her feet into the mattress. No sign of her father moving. He was in the kitchen, his weight steady in one spot, giving off only the tiniest vibrations, probably eating the ice cream her mom kept hidden behind three bags of frozen brussels sprouts.

The danger past, Calla let her mind drift to Old Man's piano, the way it felt to lie in the treehouse and listen to him play. She sank into a deep sleep, her dreams nothing but the caress of piano keys, ivory shivers across her skin.

•

That second Friday night, as they walked back to Jade's house, having decided it was wiser to sleep there, Calla couldn't walk straight. The music, even once Old Man stopped playing, clung to her skin, seeped into her pores, and pricked her nerves in a pleasant way she'd never experienced before. Her feet felt like dancing, and the empty asphalt of the road called to her, so she spun a few circles, leapt like a deer, and then skipped back onto the sidewalk when they reached Jade's neighborhood.

"What's got into you?" Jade asked.

"I have a plan." Calla's eyes sparkled in the streetlight.

"A plan for what?" Jade eased her key into the front door lock and turned it slowly. Darlene wouldn't care if she caught them sneaking back in, but it didn't feel much like sneaking if you weren't careful and quiet.

"It's like that magazine said, you have to move closer to the right spot, little by little."

Jade had become obsessed with that article and a few others like it. She felt really behind the sexual curve and wanted to catch up. Without a suitable love interest available, that meant relying on her own two hands.

"I didn't think you were even listening when I read that."

"I always listen to you."

Calla followed her friend into the kitchen, where they each filled a glass with water and Jade raided the pantry for a bag of popcorn.

"Okay, then what's your plan?"

"I need to get closer to the right spot to really experience this piano thing." Calla plopped into a kitchen chair, the yellow vinyl upholstery squeaking beneath her.

"That isn't a plan. That's a thought. Or a want. Or something." Jade pressed buttons on the microwave and the machine whirred to life.

"I'm going to get closer, little by little. That's the plan."

"How much closer do you need to get? You can feel that piano from here, so hiding in the treehouse is already a whole lot closer."

"It's still not close enough. I can feel the music, sure, but I can't feel all of it."

The microwave sounded its completion, but Jade didn't open the door, just stared at Calla. "All of what? Does he not play, like, a whole song?"

"No, that's not what I mean. It's like..." She squeezed her eyes closed and tried hard to think of a good analogy, but her brain was emptied by the sounds she'd felt rising through her feet earlier. That music shook the world right out of her. "I don't know what it's like, I just know there's more, and I need that more. Whatever it is."

Still confused, Jade retrieved the bag of popcorn and shook it, as a few kernels finished popping.

"Okay, so, you need to get closer. How close?"

"Really close," Calla said. "Really really close."

•

In preparation for her plan, the girls splurged on gourmet popsicles at a shop downtown, a place popular with hipsters and suburban housewives, and then tried to look nonchalant as they licked their melting treats on the sidewalk across from Old Man's house.

Jade took a bite of her Blackberry Basil while Calla sussed out the situation. She could feel that he wasn't home, the house sitting still and quiet but for the faint buzzing of electricity she could sometimes sense with just her toes. Old Man's vibrations weren't familiar enough for her to find where he'd gone, not like her father with his heavy rumbling movements that always felt like drumbeats on Calla's heels. She swallowed the last of her Cucumber Mint, slid the stick into a back pocket, and crossed the road.

Jade followed as Calla slipped around the side of the house, something they'd only ever done in the dark, and examined the backyard. It was big and mostly empty. Old Man hadn't lived there long, and the only sign of his existence was a wobbly iron table and a red plastic chair. There was an ashtray on the table and the grass needed to be mowed. The only possible cover between the treehouse and the concrete patio was a decrepit playset that must have been left by the same family that built the treehouse.

Calla was so focused on her reconnaissance that she didn't notice Jade had stopped making the slurping sound she always made when eating a popsicle. When the silence finally surrounded Calla, she glanced Jade's way. Jade was staring at an upstairs window and said, "We better get out of here."

Calla's feet didn't lie, and her feet said the house was empty, so why had a curtain moved? Had it? She must have imagined the motion. Jade said it happened twice while she was watching, and Calla could have sworn a finger crooked the curtain panels apart, but they both had to be wrong.

Calla's. Feet. Never. Lied.

She had the next part of her plan, regardless, and now that she'd seen the curtain move, she felt an odd numbness in her feet, an empty spot where she was sure a person should be, so they ducked back around the house and onto the sidewalk. Jade's popsicle slid off the stick, and Calla suggested they go back into town for a new one, but Jade shook her head. Her face was pale, and Calla knew it scared her, the phantom curtain movement. She knew Calla was never wrong about these things, and if there was nothing living inside that house, then... Well, Jade watched too many horror movies with Darlene.

Calla did not believe in ghosts. She didn't believe in anything she could not feel with her feet and her skin and her heart.

Jade refused to go back after the sun went down.

●

The playset in Old Man's backyard wasn't as comfortable as the treehouse. Calla had to wiggle under the slide to be sure he wouldn't spot her from his back window, at least until he started playing. So long as he played, she was safe.

She'd spent the evening listening to classical piano pieces on Spotify, and she had figured out most of the songs Old Man played. A few notes into "Clair De Lune," she noticed an ant bed too close for comfort and scooted away from the playset. She was barefoot, her Mary Janes still under the slide, and she tiptoed across the lawn until she was almost at the patio. The strength of the melody was overwhelming. She had to lift first one foot and then the other in order to regulate what was pouring into her.

Calla withdrew to the playset, slipped her shoes back on, and tried again. She still couldn't get all of the way to the patio, so she stood there in Old Man's backyard, feet planted and hands over her mouth to keep herself quiet. The sensation of the song was so all-encompassing, she was afraid she would forget where she was and do something wild—sing, or scream, or cry. She wasn't sure. Usually, he played two or three songs, multiple times, while Calla slipped silently into a hypnotic state on his lawn, but that night, he quit after "Clair De Lune."

In the ensuing silence, Calla felt steps on the second floor in the house. They were faint, being so far above ground, but they were definitely there. How had he gotten from the piano in the front room downstairs to the back room upstairs so quickly? She didn't know. Maybe she'd stood there, dazed with happiness, longer than she was aware. It didn't matter, she had to go before he looked out his window. She couldn't possibly explain her presence.

Calla ducked around the corner, her hand trailing the side of the house, a strip of dirty white paint peeling under her fingers. She jerked her hand back and ran toward home, heels clicking down the sidewalk, causing at least three dogs to bark as she passed. She wished Jade was there. She needed Jade to be there.

•

After a week of solo trips, always making it just a little closer to the house before the music stopped, Calla put on her one pair of tennis shoes, leftover from the time Jade convinced her to run a 5k. Calla sucked at running. The combination of vibrations in the road and fast forward movement for too long made her motion sick. She trekked to Jade's with her backpack and three new women's magazines with which to bribe her friend.

"Look, I don't know if I can go there again." Jade said. "The curtains moved. I saw them. You saw them. Either your sensitivity is waning or there was a ghost."

"I've thought about it, and you're wrong. It could have been something like the air condition switching on or a robot vacuum."

"A robot vacuum?" Jade slid the new magazines into her own backpack, so Calla knew she was planning to come, even if she didn't want to.

"Yeah, you know, those round ones like your granny used to have?"

"But you could feel Granny's vacuum, Calla." Jade shook her head. "You said it was like a cat purring under your feet when it came on while you were barefoot."

"I wasn't barefoot when we saw the curtain move."

It was a weak argument. Calla didn't have to be barefoot to feel things, and no robot vacuum had swished those curtains back and forth. Still, Jade hefted her bag onto her shoulders and started walking.

The girls took their time that evening, moseying through downtown, getting popsicles again, Raspberry Sweet Corn for Calla and Honey Goat Cheese for Jade. On Fridays, the streets were full of people, since their little town was central to a few other counties. They didn't fit in, with their backpacks and cut off shorts, Jade's Pokémon graphic tee and Calla's gray and yellow sneakers. The people around them were a mix of college kids home for summer, the kind of girls who wore black pumps with silk shorts to drink craft beers with their boyfriends, and young families getting ice cream before heading home to put the kids to bed. As they walked, Calla played a recording for Jade. She'd turned her voice memo app on the night before and caught some of the piano music.

"Can you feel it through the recording?" Jade asked.

Calla shook her head. "No, but it helped me identify which pieces he plays most often. I'm trying to figure out why his playing feels how it feels. When we used to go to church, there was a lady who played piano, but her hymns never made me feel like this."

"Maybe it's the person playing the music? That would make a great set up for a romance novel."

Calla bit her bottom lip. "I don't know. I mean, he's so old. I definitely don't want that kind of romance."

Jade blushed. "I mean, yeah, of course. I was just thinking..."

"Me too. I thought about that too, but surely not, right? I don't even know if I care about that stuff."

Unlike Jade, Calla felt no interest in boys.

"Yeah, it's just that the way you describe the music... It sounds like an orgasm."

"It's not though." Calla insisted. "I've read your magazines and done what they said. I wanted to rule that out, and I did."

"You did what?" The sun was dipping below the trees and the girls turned to walk back the way they'd come.

"I gave myself an orgasm. It isn't the same. Sex stuff is physical, and the music is too, but it's more. It's like, inside me, in my head, not just my body."

"Your head is part of your body." Jade laughed.

"You know what I mean," Calla bumped her shoulder into Jade's.

When it got dark enough, they traced their steps back to Old Man's house, slipped around the corner where a strip of paint still fluttered in the evening breeze, and climbed into the treehouse. They would stay there until the music started. Calla's had opted for sneakers so the sensations didn't overwhelm her like they'd done the week before. That way, she could make it to the patio. If Old Man was anything like the rest of the elderly people in this town, he didn't lock the back door.

"You're crazy," Jade said. "You are going to get caught."

"If I get caught, I will tell Old Man I'm looking for my friend and I got confused, thought I was at her house. Then I will text you, and you will call me so I can answer on speaker and you can ask why I'm late coming over."

"You know that sounds ridiculous, right?"

"It's better than nothing."

The music started and both girls got quiet.

It was "Clair de Lune" again. Calla climbed down the rickety boards nailed to the trunk and crossed to the playset. The rubber of her shoes muffled the sensations and she hated sneakers for that exact reason. Still, she left them on and took slow steps toward the patio as the final notes of the song wove a chain of tingles around her calves.

Next was Chopin's "Nocturn No. 2." While the fingers on the keys seemed to play notes up her thighs and through her stomach, Calla sidled closer and closer to the back door. She was right. It was unlocked. Calla couldn't feel Jade over the music, but knew she was clenching her fists in the treehouse, scared to death. Calla slipped inside, the dark kitchen all that stood between her and the baby grand. While she stood there, frozen, the music changed again.

Calla took off her shoes as the frenzy of "Moonlight Sonata" filled the house and her body. He'd started at the end, at the third movement. Her bones were pulsating, and she couldn't have stopped moving if she wanted to. She nudged open the living room door and stepped inside, too lost in the sound to be scared anymore.

The girl at the piano kept playing.

The girl at the piano...

The girl...

Calla tried to focus her feet, felt the whole house, found Old Man upstairs, lying on his bed, sleeping, barely existing as far as her feet could tell.

The girl circled back to the second movement, the bouncy rhythm confusing Calla's nerves. She shifted her weight from leg to leg. Her mouth opened and closed. She said, "What..."

The girl held up one hand but did not raise her head. Calla pursed her lips as she played through and then started the first movement. The slower melody flowed over Calla's limbs, and she stepped closer to the piano.

"Who are you?" she whispered.

"You're the one creeping through my yard. Who are you?" The girl looked across the top of the piano and met her eyes.

"I'm Calla. I like to feel the music but..."

The girl kept playing even as he spoke. "But what?"

"Well, I thought you were... I saw the old man move in here."

"My granddad? He doesn't play. I'm staying here to help him get adjusted."

"But... you... I can't feel you."

The girl stopped playing then, stood up and stepped around the piano. "That's odd," she said. "I've felt you coming closer every day."

"What? How? Felt me how?"

She tapped the top of the piano. "When I play, it's like I can touch what the music touches. I know that doesn't sound real, but—"

"It does though. I get that. I have a similar thing. With my feet."

The girl smiled and held out her hand. "I'm Iris."

"Calla." She shook Iris's hand. "But, why don't I feel you here? I can feel your grandfather, but not you."

"Sometimes, I think I'm only real when I'm playing. It's like I'm made of music." Iris sat back down on the piano bench but left a space open and motioned to Calla. Tentatively, she sat down beside her.

Her phone buzzed in her pocket. Calla jumped, then laughed. She slid out the phone to see a text from Jade.

I'm fine. She replied. *I promise.*

"You can tell her to come in, if you want," Iris said.

"How did you-"

"I felt you both out there. I just felt you stronger."

Calla texted Jade and Jade made her way into the living room, where she perched on a sofa along the wall.

"Now," Iris said. "Do you want to go on listening, or would you like to learn to play?"

Calla lifted one hand and slowly touched her fingers to the keys. Something sparked in her belly, her feet and hands seeming at last connected to the rest of her, connected to the inside part the music had awakened.

J. L. Royce

Weeds

Henry stared across the card table at his old friend. The chrome pistol gleamed on the verdant baize between them. The modern electric lamp hanging above caught the sweat on their faces: colleagues and friends, one doomed to die.

Pick up the gun.

Henry grimaced with pain as he fought the inexorable force taking control of him. Louis didn't move; despite his faults and failings, his friend had a strength of will tested over decades of temptation and despair. Henry stared aghast as his hand moved of its own will, scrabbling for the gun. He jerked his arm away, scattering pasteboard cards and poker chips.

Louis spoke. "Henry, whatever happens—it's been a privilege to know you."

Pick up the gun. Shoot him. Now.

Tears streaked Henry's smooth cheeks. "Don't...be so... damn noble." His hand crept towards the pistol.

"Did I ever tell you—"

"Stop!" Henry cried.

"—about Moab? They're Mormons, you know. Holier than thee and me. But outside of town was the finest little cathouse." He sucked his teeth. "Not just your everyday fare, mind..."

"Louis..." Was the older man *trying* to die?

"That madam; she had boys dolled up as girls...girls dressed as boys..."

Henry screamed in pain. His hand swept across the table, found the gun—

•

San Francisco

October 1894

Dear Louis,

I trust this note finds you well, and still in Denver—else it may not find you at all! The trip was uneventful, the train hot and jarring, but the city itself is rich and exciting. I have secured a room close to the subject's residence and shall visit Mrs. Bluelace to begin the inquiry in your stead.

As much as I respect your intuition, I am skeptical of your insurance fraud theory. Would a wife conspire to do away with her husband, so that his lover might benefit? This third-party beneficiary of a married man certainly raises questions, but collusion between the women? I trust the facts will reveal a more mundane explanation that the insurer will accept.

I had a most curious dream. At the railway station—San Francisco—I greet you and a young lady, who accompanies us. Yet when I awake, I cannot recall her face. Are you bringing someone along? Perhaps I am psychic?

I ramble! Safe travels; if you advise me of your arrival I shall meet you at the station. Until then, avail yourself of the mountain air of Colorado, and above all moderate your passions.

Fond Regards, Henry

•

Henry set down the pen and studied the drying message.

After a day the small hotel room already reflected his personality: settled and orderly, but quiet and empty. It was by choice that he avoided the bar downstairs, the comfort of society. The risk of pain was too great.

He sighed and folded the note. It was time for sleep; tomorrow, the work would begin.

•

The Bluelace mansion was Italianate with fine, straightforward lines, perched near the top of Pacific Heights on a modest plot. Henry's cab trotted up the drive bisecting the well-kept lawn and delivered him beneath an arching canopy.

Henry stepped out and considered the Bay beyond. It was a sun-kissed day in San Francisco, and he realized the town was seducing him to remain. After a deep breath, Henry lifted and dropped the heavy brass knocker gracing the front door.

A dour butler ushered him in and accepted Henry's engraved card. Without a word, the tall, stooped man motioned the investigator into a front parlor, then disappeared. Henry removed his bowler and considered the room.

The air was redolent of linseed oil and decaying flowers, with an abundance of bouquets and arrangements cluttering every surface. Henry strolled past the displays, noting the names on the sympathy cards, many familiar: Vanderbilt, Carnegie, Dupont...a *Who's Who* of the country's elite.

"Mister…Fremont?" The speaker stood in the doorway, holding his card in a gloved hand. Despite her informal apparel, her confident carriage was not a servant's. She glanced at Henry with a puzzled expression. "You're younger than I imagined."

Nearly Henry's height, Mrs. Bluelace was handsome even in her simple cotton day dress—lavender, not black. She was flushed from some modest exertion.

"Oh—I'm Henry Flores, his associate. Louis has been detained."

A stray lock had escaped from her pompadour, and she absently tucked it back. "I understand Mr. Fremont wanted to discuss some insurance matter?"

Her garden glove had left a faint trace of soil across her cheek. "Not that I need insurance."

"We represent a firm that sold a life insurance policy to your husband." Henry cringed at his *faux pas*. "Pardon me— late husband. You have my condolences."

"Life insurance? On Victor? I have no knowledge of it, I'm sure." Hermia Bluelace's fine features clouded. "Why wouldn't he tell me…"

She read the explanation on Henry's face. "I wasn't the beneficiary, was I? Who, then?"

"That is confidential, Ma'am. We are required to investigate any policy benefit over a certain threshold," Henry said. "I shall start today, speaking with you and your household. Mr. Fremont should arrive in a few days."

The widow seemed nonplussed by the news. She glanced away and waved a gloved hand down her bodice, which bore the stains of her recent labors. "I should change. I've been gardening, you see."

"A wonderful pastime. I hope to raise flowers myself, someday."

"Not flowers," she replied. "Vegetables. Fresh from the earth to the plate. The healthiest diet."

It recalled Henry's troubled childhood on a farm. He pushed aside the chain of anger and regret and said, "I'm sure."

"It helps me...I must go change if we're to have an interview. Can you wait?"

"I don't want to trouble you. We'll chat another time. If I could speak to the servants?" It suited him to interview them apart from her.

She considered. "Tea, tomorrow?"

"Gladly."

Mrs. Bluelace reached for the bellpull. The butler reappeared.

"Yuri, Mr. Flores is with an insurance company. He has a few questions about...the death. Please assist him without reservation—and offer him coffee."

The man nodded, impassive.

She turned back to Henry. "Thank you." Her smile pleased him in a decidedly unprofessional way.

"Until tomorrow, then," he replied.

Mrs. Bluelace considered him. "You're not what I would have expected, you know."

"No?"

"You're rather soft-spoken, for a detective," she remarked.

"An investigator," he corrected; but she had already hurried away.

Henry watched her return to the comfort of her garden. The butler cleared his throat. Henry followed him through to the pantry.

•

The butler seated Henry in an alcove of the neat kitchen intended for staff meals. The investigator accepted the proffered steaming mug, then opened his notebook.

"You've been with the Bluelaces long?"

"Mr. Bluelace. We came from Russia together, like family, by way of Mongolia."

"We?"

"The master; myself and my mother; his childhood nurse—Akilina—and her family."

A tiny elderly woman in a mob cap and apron drifted into the kitchen. Yuri raised his eyes. Henry stood and gave her a polite nod.

Akilina's black eyes considered this intruder in her domain with some suspicion. She muttered something in Russian to Yuri, who glanced at Henry.

"She has very little English," he explained.

The cook resumed her chores, and Henry reclaimed his place on the bench.

"I am here to investigate Mr. Bluelace's death. Though my questions may seem indelicate, they are necessary. We shall hold our findings in confidence."

Yuri gestured with his large, work-worn hands. "*Nu...*"

Henry consulted his notes. "You found the body."

"In Master's quarters."

"The police report states that you found him in bed. Given the inquest found the cause of death to be heart failure, they chose not to pursue the matter."

Expressionless, Yuri stared at the investigator.

"The other servants—"

"There are no others," the butler said.

"Not even a coachman?"

"The master let the driver go. I drive the mistress now."

"Why?" Henry asked.

The butler shrugged. "He thought the young man was too familiar with his wife. Baseless, but..."

"Mr. Bluelace's wife is young," Henry said, "and quite attractive."

Yuri glowered. "*Baseless*. Not that the master paid proper attention to her—" He cut off his remark. "The master worked long hours."

"The shipping business?"

"*Da*, shipping; and perhaps he did not marry for love."

"What about maids?"

"None. Mrs. Bluelace had a personal maid but dismissed her. Bad; when *she* came, the master changed—for the worse."

"Her name?"

"Lottie."

The beneficiary. Henry kept his composure. "Lottie *Ferguson*, correct?"

"*Da*," Yuri replied, "How did—"

Akilina hissed. Henry turned to see her clutch the Eastern cross about her neck and mutter a prayer.

Yuri spoke harshly in their native tongue, and she responded in kind.

"She says Lottie was unreliable, disrespectful, and reflected poorly on the household."

Henry frowned. He had recognized a few words of Russian, gutter talk: *shlyukha* and *koldunya*, among other insults.

"References?"

"Of course."

"What was her history?" Henry asked. "Was she in service before? What family?"

"The Strains, of Nob Hill."

Henry made a note of it.

Yuri added, "They have troubles enough…"

Akilina spoke to Yuri, her eyes on Henry. The old servant's expression softened.

"What is it?" the investigator asked.

"She says, you are, ah, too young for this task," Yuri replied. "Should not pursue it."

"I assure you, I am—"

"*Too pretty*, she said. No offense; she meant, I think, *innocent*."

The investigator rose. "I won't take any more of your time. Tomorrow, I return to speak with Mrs. Bluelace."

Henry ran his finger around the rim of his hat and donned it.

"Perhaps you'll remember more."

•

The Strains' house was a sturdy frame dwelling of some half-dozen bedrooms, typically upper-middle class. The exterior was heavily ornamented with scrollwork and ornate overlays. Henry rang, and idly scuffed at the weeds sprouting between the paving stones of the walk. An aproned woman showed him in, announced him loudly, then fled. He stood in the foyer, hat in hand, waiting for Mrs. Strain.

The interior was overburdened with decorations: chandeliers, wall hangings and paintings, and an excess of furniture. The walls were crowded with framed family mementos, paintings, and photographs, as well as the useless clutter of an acquisitive family.

Mrs. Strain was as overdressed as her home, bejeweled at throat and fingers. Yet beneath her ostentatious trappings, Henry sensed anxiety. She deposited his hat on the rack in the foyer and led him into her parlor, where she sat with a sigh.

"Lottie?" She reared back as if a rat had crossed the threshold. "Why would you be interested in *her*?"

"As part of an investigation for her former employer. It's standard procedure to inquire with other references about character, look for any ... patterns."

"Patterns of what?" Mrs. Strain asked. "Are you a detective? With the police?"

"An investigator—privately employed." He produced Louis's card. "I cannot go into details to protect our client's privacy. You understand."

Henry slipped his notebook from a waistcoat pocket.

The mother frowned at the card. "Lottie served my twin daughters, Isabella and Victoria,"

Henry noted the many portraits, most featuring a pair of fair-haired girls, tracing them from childhood to attractive womanhood. She noticed his attention and reacted with a curious mixture of pride and apprehension.

"Your daughters are beautiful," he remarked.

"Yes, they were—are."

"May I speak to them?"

She ignored the question. Her eyes narrowed. "The Bluelaces. I should have known. He died recently, didn't he?"

"You know the family?"

"Not really. I hosted several gatherings for his Congressional campaign. Parties. I thought it would be an excellent opportunity for my girls..."

"Yes?"

"Lottie made herself, shall we say, *obvious* to the gentlemen attending? Victor in particular, since he appeared without his wife; and Eustace Conner—not nearly as handsome, but a man with powerful allies, and *eligible*."

"I see. Lottie was familiar with them?"

"*Overly* familiar." She raised an eyebrow. "I chastised her, but she pursued them nonetheless."

"What happened?"

"When Mr. Stanford—our Senator—died last year, there was an upheaval. Victor Bluelace and Eustace Conner were both interested in the appointment, but neither had the Governor's support. Perkins did."

The political machinations of California were familiar in texture if not details.

"Perkins was appointed to fill the seat, and Victor and Eustace were left vying for the nomination to be the House candidate."

"You're very well informed," Henry remarked.

"Well," Mrs. Strain smiled, "one must at least *appear* interested in men's affairs…"

She lapsed into her thoughts.

Henry tapped his pencil on his notebook. "Are you still hosting these meetings?"

"No—when Victor died, Eustace Conner's nomination was a *fait accompli*—and he became very busy. And my girls, they—"

Just then, her eyes flew open as she stared beyond Henry to the hall. Henry followed her gaze and rose.

One daughter stood there, watching them. Her expression was petulant. "Mother…"

Henry had trouble reconciling the buxom woman filling the doorway with the lithesome youths in the photographs.

"Aren't you going to *introduce* me?" Her tone was an ingénue's.

"Henry Flores, Miss." He offered her a bow. "I'm making inquiries concerning—"

"Isabella, dear," Mrs. Strain interrupted, "why don't you run along? This doesn't concern you."

"Victoria needs you," the younger woman replied, eyes locked on Henry. "And what, sir, would these *inquiries* concern?"

"Your former maid, a Lottie Ferguson." He conspired with Isabella to ignore the mother, who rose, hands fluttering.

"*That* one." Isabella sailed over to the chair next to Henry and sat. "*Totally* unreliable, and...I could tell you a few things."

She smiled up at him and raised her hand. Her rings had sunk into her fleshy fingers. Henry bent low to graze his lips across the back.

A look passed between the two women, and Isabella smiled. "Are you staying for tea?"

"Mr. Flores doesn't have time for tea."

Henry sat down. "What made her unsuitable?"

"Didn't know her *place*, respect for her *betters*. Too forward with our male guests. And no sense of *humor*."

"Humor?"

Isabella rolled her eyes. "It was Victoria's idea, really—just little pranks."

"At Lottie's expense?"

"We were high-spirited." A girlish laugh.

Henry noted the past tense, again.

Somewhere, a servant bell rang. Isabella turned on her mother.

"I *told* you, she wants you upstairs."

A keening whine drifted down, a barely human cry that sent Henry from his chair. The mother rose, pale, and rushed past him.

Henry made to follow, but Isabella clutched his sleeve.

"Don't go," she pleaded. "Just wait here. I'll order the tea, with some scones, and jam—"

Henry freed himself and followed the mother up the broad central staircase. He caught murmured voices and whimpering drifting down the hall, followed them, and paused in the doorway of an elegant bedroom.

She lay in the center of her four-poster, curled into herself. The sheet stretched over her barely registered a shape. Her blonde waves tumbled lavishly over the pillow in stark contrast to her gaunt face. It was undeniable: this was the twin sister of the voluptuous creature downstairs.

Blue eyes rimmed by dark rings of exhaustion stared listlessly at him.

"What do you want?" Victoria whispered.

Mrs. Strain whirled and glowered at Henry. "You have no right! You don't belong here, Mr. Flores."

Henry ignored her. "I'm inquiring about your former servant—Lottie."

The sheet stirred, and an arm little more than skin stretched over bones slid from beneath it. Skeletal fingers beckoned him.

He approached and dropped to one knee beside her.

"Closer," she whispered.

Henry bent near enough to smell soap and decay.

Victoria's manicured hand rose. The chill fingertips caressed his cheek.

"I was beautiful. I had nothing to concern me beyond which suitor to favor."

He took the thin hand in his. "You're more than your suitors, Miss," Henry said.

"*She* did this to me."

"Lottie? How?"

The emaciated woman sighed. "She held my hand—read my palm—my fortune. I laughed at her."

Henry released her hand. It dropped like a dry leaf to the crisp snow of the sheet. Its owner sighed.

"Thank you. I just wanted...to touch a man again."

Henry straightened but paused to stroke her hair. "I'm sorry."

Mrs. Strain made a choking sound. A bejeweled hand hid the grief twisting her face.

Victoria turned away. "Go."

Henry spun on his heel and fled the room.

●

It took several visits before Hermia confided in Henry. Neither the Bluelace widow nor her servants could shed light on the predicament of the Strain family. The widow pressed Henry for his personal story, which he revealed in carefully framed statements. Heartened by his presence, Hermia Bluelace readily moved the conversation away from the investigation.

On one occasion she insisted that he travel to Golden Gate Park with her, to marvel at the Conservatory's flowers. Her interest in literature rivaled Henry's, and she drew him into discussions of their favorite authors.

"We lived somewhat separate lives, you see," Hermia said. "I supported his political aspirations—a man like Victor is forever seeking a challenge—but the pursuit of power holds little appeal for me."

"I couldn't be what my parents wanted," Henry said, "and now I wonder..."

Hermia smiled. "You're a gentle soul, Henry Flores."

His heart stirred, though he was wary of indulging an impossible fantasy. "I would like to speak with your butler again."

"Has he not been forthcoming?"

"He was devoted to his master—and yourself. If there is subterfuge, it arose from a desire to protect you."

Hermia accepted this.

"Another thing; Akilina referred to Lottie as a 'witch'—have you any idea what she might have meant?"

"Lottie played at fortune-telling—palm-reading. Victor found it amusing; I have no patience with that spiritualist nonsense."

Henry changed the topic, sensing she suspected more than handholding.

"Those names I requested? The business associates?"

"Oh—yes." She rose and retrieved a list from her writing desk. "I prepared this for you."

The sheet held a half-dozen names in her elegant hand. She stood close, a hint of her garden in the air, as he examined them. "I'm afraid I had no addresses for some..."

"This will be a great help, thank you."

Her slender finger traced down the page. "Of these, I could suggest Schmitz. He was Victor's political advisor."

"The Congressional campaign?"

"Yes; Victor declared his intent to run for the House. The party office can put you in touch."

Their eyes locked for a moment, then the widow reached for the bellpull. "I'll fetch Yuri."

•

Henry requested access to the coach house, knowing Yuri could not deny him in front of Hermia. The butler tried to dissuade him, claiming it would be 'time wasted', but Henry persisted.

Outside, away from the widow, Henry said, "You found Victor—but not in his bedroom."

"No. In his...private quarters."

They climbed the outside stairs of the coach house. "Here," Henry said. "Mr. Bluelace fired the coachman so he could make it his own."

Henry paused at the door. "Why did you lie?"

"Shame," Yuri replied. "For Victor."

He unlocked the door and motioned Henry inside.

•

San Francisco

October 1894

Dear Louis,

Much to relay; please indulge me. I will forgo certain details should this letter falls into other hands.

Mrs. Hermia Bluelace is a cultured woman, wasted upon her husband, Victor. Politics preoccupied him, and their relationship was joyless. Their butler revealed that Lottie Ferguson created turmoil in the household. Though dismissed, the girl was observed in Victor's company on more than one occasion, entering or exiting the Bluelace coach house. Further pressed, the butler revealed his master's secrets in disturbing detail.

I found the coachman's quarters a Marquis de Sade den of depravity. If we're to believe the butler's narrative, Victor died of asphyxia while engaged in some sex act. Appalled by his state, the faithful servant brought away the corpse and deposited it in Victor's bedroom, to be 'found' the next day. The authorities know nothing of this, and I see no merit in sharing it. I directed Yuri to clear the coachman's quarters to protect the widow's reputation and sensibilities.

The Strains: did Lottie seed the twin daughters with self-destructive tendencies? Revenge for some childish mistreatment? It would be a perfect crime—self-inflicted, yet not suicide...

That this maid could lead a successful captain of industry into addictive deviancy—despite a wife as intelligent as she is attractive—baffles me. What is deluding a man into purchasing an insurance policy, compared to that?

I pray, telegraph your plans immediately to this address. This matter careens toward a denouement, and I sorely need your guidance. Meanwhile, rest and avoid over-indulgence, physical or mental. I look forward to welcoming you to this extraordinary city.

Regards, H.

•

Henry lay in the narrow bed, eyes wandering the dim ceiling. The disturbing details of the case were easier to dismiss than the soft-spoken woman's smile. He fantasized for a moment that she could accept him, then curled up to fend off the world's rejection. *Impossible...*

•

August Schmitz overflowed his office chair. "Know Victor? Of course."

Long mutton chops contrasted his receding hairline. The small office's glass wall overlooked a noisy, bustling bullpen full of campaign workers.

"Damn shame, losing him. But politics goes on."

Schmitz had greeted Henry with some suspicion, demanding to know if he was yet another 'damn reporter', but accepted the business card and explanation.

"Damn shame, boy," he repeated. "Cigar?"

Henry declined. Auggie (as he preferred to be known) shrugged and took a stogie for himself, slamming the wooden humidor.

The campaign advisor waved out the match and puffed extravagantly.

"Is it true? Died...in the act?" He raised an eyebrow.

The gossip spread quicker than weeds. "It's not in the police report. If I may ask, where did you hear that?"

"Just talk. Probably some chatty maid. What's Mrs. Bluelace's concern?"

"I'm searching for their former employee. Lottie Ferguson?"

The man leaned back and laughed. "I practically work for her!"

Henry was dumbfounded. "What do you mean?"

"She's the intended of our Congressional candidate, Eustace Conner."

"I didn't know…"

"Oh, quite sudden." Auggie considered the glowing tip of his cigar. "She's a real loyalist, I'll give her that—very effective. Gets results."

"Doing what?"

"Fundraising, mostly. *Pressing the flesh*. Goes into those teas and such, comes out with checks." He grinned.

Auggie's fingers thrummed the desktop. "Nice chatting, but I've got a campaign to win. Election's only a few days away."

"Where might I find Miss Ferguson?" Henry asked.

The man frowned. "I can't reveal her living arrangements…"

"I represent an insurance company. She benefits."

Auggie nodded with a knowing smile. "Say no more. As far as public gatherings, she'll be with Eustace at the election night soirée."

"Where will that be?"

"Hopkins mansion." Auggie chuckled. "Old Leland would spin in his grave, with the competition dancing next door."

Henry asked, "Where do the Hopkins live?"

Auggie guffawed. "You *are* new around here. They're dead, son—donated the place to the Art Institute. But our friends have friends… It's Nob Hill. Loftiest house in the city. Take the California line to the end—you can't miss it."

•

Dear Louis,

The trail of Miss Lottie Ferguson is littered with bizarre occurrences! The Strain family has suffered greatly. The daughters' condition may represent hysteria, but the sudden onset is profoundly puzzling. It's difficult to imagine how Lottie could have effected such damage—or contrived the death of Victor Lovelace. Hypnosis? Psychic powers?

The psychic field is rife with fraud and deception. I hesitate to suggest that a maid can manipulate the mind at will. Nonetheless, the world is full of mysteries. The more answers Science provides the less we understand! (Thus our ever-growing vista of knowledge paradoxically fills us with child-like dread.)

I shall infiltrate a political function tomorrow evening. If successful, I shall surveil this creature first-hand. Would you agree with this strategy? I sorely miss your counsel—

•

"You may consult me whenever you like."

Henry whirled in his chair. His mentor, Louis Fremont, stood behind him, half-shadowed.

"Sir! How did you—I would have met you at the train—"

"No need." The imposing figure stared down at the half-written note.

He was as exactly as Henry remembered. "You are well? Your journey was comfortable?"

"Hmm. Your fretting is unmanly. And your pen is leaking."

Henry blotted the spreading stain. "You received my letters?"

"Certainly. You've done well. I agree with your strategy. Learn what you can from Lottie Ferguson, at this gathering."

"Will you come?"

"I endeavor to attend. However, I have other lines of inquiry to pursue."

"Can I be of assistance—"

"No; we shall meet there."

His mentor's hand fell lightly on Henry's shoulder. "A disguise would serve you well."

Henry's heart raced, with a premonition of what Louis would ask. "I don't understand," the young man lied.

"My guest would be more explicable if *female*."

Henry stammered, "I don't wish to be uncooperative—"

"Good. It's settled."

Louis leaned close. "You *owe* me, Henry Flores. How many employers would tolerate you as I have? I've taught you, protected you, given you a livelihood...*Henry*."

The young man could not meet his mentor's gaze. "Yes, sir."

"Excellent. I'll be on the guest list—enter as my companion."

Louis nodded out the window. "You must have seen the dress shop on this block—you'll find suitable apparel: gowns, shoes, petticoats, corsets, drawers..."

Henry shunned Louis's smile. He balled up the letter and tossed it into the trash.

"You've never treated me this way before, sir! You have no right—" But when Henry turned to confront Louis, his mentor had vanished.

Henry rushed to the door, threw it open, but found the hallway empty. He slammed it shut.

At the window, Henry stared over the busy street below. Louis was nowhere to be seen. He sat on the bed and stared at his trembling hands for a long time. Then he withdrew the suitcase from below and opened it. Henry removed some neatly folded menswear, undershirts, and boxer shorts. Below all the masculine trappings lay a parcel.

Henry slipped off the ribbon and gift wrapping—a ruse, should anyone discover it.

There was a simple shirtwaist, in pale yellow, and a brown tulip skirt. He laid them on the bed, smoothing away the wrinkles. Next came a chemise, underwear, a pair of flats, a hat, and a small clutch.

Henry stood and removed his suit, hanging his clothes carefully in the closet. He stripped off his underclothes, then undid the bindings flattening his breasts, the pad around his waist, the cloth-filled codpiece.

Hidden, like a gift.

Henry dressed, revealing the hidden: a slim but feminine figure. He swept up his too-short hair and pinned it beneath the bonnet. He studied himself in the mirror, the almond eyes, the well-formed lips, and attempted to compose himself.

The dressmaker would still be open. Henry listened at the door, then slipped out.

●

"Mr. Flores! I did not expect you today."

Hermia Bluelace greeted Henry, book in hand, with surprised pleasure. The silent butler withdrew.

"Are you quite alright? You look exhausted."

"I didn't sleep well, and...have duties to perform that weigh on me."

"Please join me in the library."

They settled in the wingback chairs framing the fireplace. California sunshine flooded through the tall, narrow windows.

Henry remained business-like. "Louis Fremont has arrived—I saw him yesterday—and is pursuing inquiries."

"I'd hoped to meet him."

"He's fully employed on your behalf, or he would have appeared. I've tracked down Lottie Ferguson, and will learn what I can relevant to your case."

Hermia's pleasant demeanor clouded. "You've approached her?"

"Not yet; there is a political gathering tonight, large enough to permit my appearance—" he hesitated "—my appearance without raising suspicions."

"The election, of course."

"Your husband would have been the candidate, and favored to win, I understand."

"Indeed." Hermia turned the book in her hands. "And now, following Mr. Conner in the press...it's been difficult."

"I have to tell you..." Henry hesitated.

"Is this regarding Victor and Lottie? An affair?"

"More than that. The circumstances of his death are suspicious."

Hermia laid aside the book and waited calmly. Henry admired her resigned composure as he deliberated.

"The details don't matter," he said. "If I—we—uncover any evidence that she had a hand in his death, we will press the authorities to pursue justice for your family."

She glanced out the window. "And you'll be gone, I suppose."

"I honestly don't know."

"In the brief time we've spent together, I've come to think of you as a friend." Hermia reached out to clasp his hand. "I will miss that."

He stared down at their hands and contemplated his deception.

"As will I." His hand lingered in hers a moment, then Henry excused himself and departed.

•

The Hopkins mansion was impossible to miss, squatting atop Nob Hill in Gothic splendor. Festooned with turrets, balconies, and steeples, the building was overlaid with intricate scrollwork and details lending the illusion of stonework to the wooden structure.

A line of carriages crawled up the drive to the main entrance. The massive *cochere* was crowned with a fantastic greenhouse dome, ablaze with light. Each vehicle disgorged well-dressed party-goers into the house.

Henry approached a side entrance, uncomfortable in fashionable shoes. A footman dressed in fine livery greeted him.

"Evening, Miss!"

"I'm here with Mr. Louis Fremont—a guest of Mr. Conner."

The servant eyed the young woman before him with some skepticism. Henry pressed the point.

"He's arriving directly from another appointment. I am his...niece and personal secretary."

The man consulted a guest list and nodded. "Very well, Miss—have a pleasant evening."

Henry swept past him in a rustle of taffeta. His gown was a deep shade of sapphire, atypically dark for a young unattached woman, hoping thereby to discourage frivolous attention. He gave himself a critical glance in a mirror, checking hair upswept with a wiglet of curls falling to his shoulder. The neckline of his gown was more revealing than he preferred, but the clerk had insisted it was 'the fashion'.

The gallery was a cavernous space extending deep into the house, open three stories to skylights lining the mansion's roof. Broad stairs descended from the main entrance, with a pipe organ placed in an alcove above them further lending to its cathedral-like pomposity. Woodwork, murals, and ornately framed artwork covered every foot of wall space. A pall of cigar smoke and idle conversation hung over the crowd.

Eustace Conner's image had been in every newspaper, blond with a neat auburn beard, a tall, impressive figure. Henry accepted a fluted glass of champagne from one of the black-suited servers and searched for the candidate in the crowd. After a quarter-hour of fruitless wandering, he approached a cluster of young women.

Engaged in a rapid-fire exchange of vapid gossip, they glanced at Henry will little curiosity and general disdain.

He cleared his throat. "Pardon me—could you point out Mr. Conner?"

One of them giggled—the tallest, just over Henry's height, with an abundant auburn pompadour.

"Hard to miss, dear." She waved a gloved hand at the grand staircase. "Unless you're blind..." The others tittered.

Henry surveyed the descending stream of arriving couples. A tall, smiling figure negotiated the press of well-wishers. A step behind him, a well-dressed woman of Henry's general age and build glided along. The upswept chestnut hair crowned a slender neck and face of average comeliness. She was unperturbed by the hubbub surrounding the candidate.

As surely as if he had called her by name, Lottie Ferguson unerringly found Henry in the crowd below. Her mouth curled into a knowing smile as her head dipped slightly in his direction.

He turned away, flushing in the shock of discovery, only to receive another surprise: Hermia Bluelace stood a half-dozen paces away, an elegant figure in sweeping black lace.

Henry watched her accept a grave couple's sympathy with a slight smile and nod. It had not crossed his mind that she too might be invited to this gathering—or would condescend to attend. He realized that Lottie's smile had not been directed solely at him.

The young investigator frantically scanned the audience but saw no sign of Louis. He was about to flee the floor when chance brought his gaze again upon Hermia, just as she looked his way. Their eyes met, and hers went wide, the blue of the Pacific in which one might easily drown. Before he could escape, she rushed across the intervening space and was upon him.

"What does this mean?" Hermia whispered. "A disguise?"

But even as she spoke, her eyes took in his features, his delicate hands, his supple figure, and realization dawned.

Henry shook his head. "No—this is not *me*. You have met me as I see myself. This body is...alien."

He averted his gaze, and stared at the embroidered carnations, in blood red, entwining her breasts. She made to retreat, but Henry grasped her hands in his.

"Before you dismiss me," he pleaded, "one thing. Close your eyes."

Hermia fought back tears, but her lids fell.

"Imagine me as you want me. I will be that, gladly—whether this or the young man you showed such kindness, the young man who..."

He struggled with his emotions. "For I—"

A third voice cut short his profession of love. "Such a pleasant reunion!"

Hermia's eyes flew open at the familiar brogue. "Lottie!"

"Ma'am..." The former servant made a mocking curtsy as she interlaced her arm with Henry's. "So nice to see you again, dear."

Before Henry could react, Lottie addressed the widow.

"I trust you've recovered from losing your *man*." She inclined her head towards Henry. "You must have realized by now, this one doesn't have the *qualifications* for that job."

Lottie laughed brightly. A few heads turned and smiled when they saw the source.

She snagged a glass of champagne from a passing servant. "We're celebrating tonight," she said, "the election, and a windfall that will finance our success in Washington."

She slipped her hand into Henry's. "With *your* help, dear—confirming Victor's natural death."

Lottie grew serious. "You being a gardener and all, Hermia, I ask you: have you ever wondered where the weeds come from? Does the wind just blow them in—" she gestured extravagantly "—or does some mischievous little *imp* creep about, planting them?"

Her fingers teased him. Henry and Hermia stared in confusion at the speaker. Lottie shrugged.

"It's like this; your Victor? Dumb as dirt, but fertile soil." Her fingers stroked Henry's palm. "And *this* one—so easy to put a spade into—so soft..."

She leaned over and kissed his cheek, eyes on Hermia. "I think too soft for you, *Ma'am*; you're accustomed to a firm hand."

Henry felt dispossessed of his body, as though he watched the trio from afar, or knew the conversation as a distant memory. He could neither turn away nor release Lottie's hand.

Eustace Conner appeared, a trail of sycophants in his wake. The candidate gazed with admiration at his fiancé, then made a slight bow to Hermia, and acknowledged Henry with a nod.

Lottie raised the investigator's hand. "We girls are off! Take care of our candidate, won't you, dear Hermia? And once again—my condolences on your loss..."

Lottie drew Henry off, and he was unable to resist. As they departed, Eustace Conner took Hermia's hands and offered his sympathy. The widow, suddenly pale, looked after Henry with frank concern. Lottie led him into the crowd; Henry and Hermia lost sight of each other.

•

They climbed a back stairway to the gallery, her fingers in his hand as thrilling and repellant as a spider. Henry could neither object nor flee, but only docilely follow.

"It's a shame we couldn't spend more time together," she said. "Had I known your little secret when we met, I would have spent my time playing with you—rather than your droll friend."

"Louis? Is he here?"

Lottie stroked his cheek.

"Yes, my poppet—you'll see him soon." She gazed at him. "Such fun we could have had..."

Henry shuddered at the images: the Strain twins, bloated and emaciated; Victor Bluelace, suffocating, inverted on a cross; Louis, adrift in an opium dream...

"Remembering?" Lottie's smile was sly. "How I met the two of you when you arrived, introduced myself as 'Mrs. Bluelace's girl'? You followed like little lambs."

She glanced over the balcony. "So nice to chat, but we need to move along. I see my Senator-to-be needs me. He's a babe craving his teat; an addict, his tincture. Much as I'd love to spend the evening—" her hand cupped Henry's neck "—he's far more important than you."

Lottie brought him down a side hall to a small chamber lit by a single overhead lamp. An elegant octagonal card table and chair in rich oak and verdant green baize nearly filled it.

"It's time to play a game." She urged Henry to sit down. "With an old friend."

From her bag, Lottie drew a small chrome-plated revolver. She placed it in the middle of the table.

"Oh, something more..." She tossed down several letters.

The address on the familiar envelopes was *San Francisco*.

"I don't understand," Henry stared at the letters, addressed to Louis—*his letters to Louis, in his own hand*.

A throat cleared. Henry started and raised his eyes to see Louis seated across from him.

•

He clenched the gun so hard his hand ached. Louis had forced him to be here, do this—

"Henry? *Henry!*"

Someone was calling, someone he loved; but *the* voice—Lottie's voice—insisted he pull the trigger.

"Please, Henry—speak to me!"

He tore his eyes away from his mentor to find Hermia kneeling at his side.

"Put the gun down, Henry—you don't want to do this!"

Lottie's voice faded as he focused on Hermia's loving features, so full of concern.

"Let me take this." Her gloved hand wrapped around his trembling one and gently drew the barrel away from the curls at his temple.

Henry blinked. Louis was nowhere to be seen.

"Where is he?" Henry whispered.

"Who? You were alone." She disengaged the pistol and tossed it aside.

Henry shuddered, folding in on himself. "Alone? Have I then gone mad?"

Hermia drew him into her arms.

"What—what's happened to me?"

"Oh, Henry—you were gone so long—I searched everywhere!"

His half-remembered dreams resolved into reality. He relayed the story to Hermia in stumbling words: Lottie at the station; the carriage ride to a Chinatown hotel, her cool hand caressing his, her fingers speaking, as she murmured instructions...

"How could I be so weak?" Henry shook his head. "I was just a puppet..."

Hermia brushed the curls from his tear-stained face.

"I cannot claim to understand what has transpired, but Lottie has...some power over the mind."

"But Louis?"

Hermia helped him to his feet. "I would surmise he is in one of the wretched opium dens that plague our city. There are dozens."

Henry swayed, and Hermia supported him.

"I won't abandon you," she promised. "Were it not for Victor's weakness, this fate would never have befallen you both." She frowned. "I shall ask Yuri to search—with a few men. God willing, your friend will still be alive."

"We must stop Lottie!" Henry declared.

"Conner swept the election. He and Lottie have departed for Sacramento—and marriage. With Eustace Conner in her thrall, Lottie will be on her way to Washington, DC."

Henry staggered along, with Hermia's help, out of the haunted chamber, out to the gallery overlooking the main floor. The guests had deserted the mansion, and servants were now engaged in a desultory cleaning effort.

"My carriage is waiting," Hermia announced, as they descended and crossed the floor. "You need to come home with me. We'll stop at your hotel, and—"

"No—Yuri must not see me!"

"Very well, then." Hermia summoned one of the loitering footmen to fetch a cab for Henry. They followed the man up the grand staircase.

"I'll see you safely to your hotel," Hermia said, "then home for me. Yuri will come by to fetch you—and your things—in the morning. Say... at eight o'clock? I'll have breakfast waiting."

"My things?

"The carriage house is unoccupied."

"But—"

She waved aside his objections. "It will be more convenient for everyone if you stay there! And I wish to care for you. Assuming you are willing..."

"Thank you."

They stepped out into the San Francisco night.

"The insurance—what do I report?"

"You must stop Lottie," Hermia said.

"It won't be easy. I cannot protect you from the truth."

The clean breeze from the Bay encircled them. Henry took a deep draught of the sea air as Hermia wrapped her cloak close and spoke.

"There are worse things than embarrassment—you must keep the insurance money out of that woman's hands!"

Henry longed to embrace her but needed to be certain.

"What did you imagine?" he asked.

"Excuse me?" When she looked at him, Henry could see that the strain of the evening had finally taken its toll. He took her hands.

"When you closed your eyes…"

Hermia smiled, and her long-lashed lids descended. "It's dark; your voice is soft, your hands are gentle, your lips…"

"Then there is hope for us?"

The footman appeared from the darkness, waving Henry to the carriage ascending the drive.

Hermia opened her eyes. "The rest was ineffable—because I love you."

by J. S. Allen

The Secret Canyon

Harzed was above all else a survivor. Some would call it cowardice: A man of fighting age avoiding combat while his nation teetered on the edge.

Strong and sinewy and cunning, he was perfectly capable in a fight, but when the army recruiter passed him over on account of his arm, Harzed did nothing to correct the man's misperception. He just avoided eye contact and let him believe a one-armed man couldn't fight.

They put him to work as a scrub and a cook, and this suited Harzed fine. Let the glory go to others. As for him, Harzed intended to survive this war, even if his nation did not. If he had to live as a serf under the yoke of the Serro-Qin, so be it. *Better a serf than resting beneath the turf.* That's what his old ma'am used to say.

Harzed kept his head down and did as he was told. He followed the army into the field, minding the mules and the baggage, making and breaking down camp, gathering combustibles, chopping vegetables in the early days, mashing acorns later when all the real food was gone.

Commander Zanthem was in charge of his company. He was a fine commander, sensible and stern. Harzed, bearing hot tea or seared meat to his tent, overheard his deliberations on more than one occasion.

If Zanthem had been a fool, one of those commanders seeking glory, Harzed would have long ago deserted, taking his chances alone in the wild. But Zanthem had a good head on his shoulders, avoiding unnecessary risks to his army, and so Harzed stayed.

Besides, there were certain advantages to his proximity to the supply wagons. Harzed ate as well as any officer, and his access to the baggage earned him more than a few friends and favors among the rank and file. Not that he exploited this power to any great effect; under no circumstances did he wish to draw any unwanted attention to his person.

The last several months, Zanthem's army had been retreating north, trying to draw the main enemy force away from the Shioplin heartland. Now that they had reached this rough country in the foothills of the Silver Mountains, Commander Zanthem ordered the wagons burned, and the baggage had to all be carried by mules—and human mules like Harzed.

As Harzed sweated under his burden he found himself eyeing the surrounding country, fantasies of escape dancing through his mind. Strapped to his back were three rolls of canvas, a part of the command tent. Their weight had seemed nothing at the start of the day, but now the straps dug into his flesh without mercy.

As he struggled uphill, a squad of soldiers passed, laughing amongst themselves. Maybe he would have been better off amongst the fighting men after all. Harzed was not built for such toil as this and had no intention of dying on some hillside, his last energies spent hauling useless gear up and down mountains.

Harzed knew this country beyond Yellow Springs better than most, having explored and hunted here during his youth. He was confident that, given the opportunity, he could separate himself from the army and disappear into the mountains. By the time anyone noticed him missing, Harzed would be well out of reach.

He liked his chances on his own far better than as part of some beleaguered and unfed army. By the time they made camp that night, Harzed's mind was made. Tomorrow before sunrise, he would go out to gather kindling, and that would be that. No one would see him again.

Harzed was too excited to sleep. He made plans of how he would double back and throw off any pursuers. He knew a place, a ribbon canyon choked with boulders, a secret way through the ridge where no one would think to follow. If he made it there, he knew he would be free.

He was contemplating what supplies he should take when the mules started a-braying, sounding the alarm. Harzed sat up abruptly, listening. Men were shouting indistinctly, not far away. Torches were moving on the hillside above them.

"Baggage train, form up!" barked mustachioed Bvegani, the chief cook and Harzed's superior officer.

Are we under attack? wondered Harzed as he hastened to comply. *Has it at last come to this then?*

All around them, sergeants called their sleeping men to order, and there was a general excitement as everyone rushed about.

But after that, there was a great deal of standing around and waiting for orders. Clearly, there was another army operating on the mountain above them. They expected orders for retreat, but more than an hour passed without instructions. Perhaps the other army was friendly, someone suggested.

Harzed watched, dismally, as the horizon began to hint at the rising of the sun. His opportunity for escape had slipped away without him.

Finally, the officers, including Bvegani, were summoned to a council, and when it was clear there wasn't going to be a retreat, Harzed and the other cooks got to work on breakfast, such as it was: One unit at a time shuffled through, each man collecting without joy his quarter ration of dry oats and a bar of hard-tack to gnaw on.

Speculation was rife: The Serro-Qin were encamped in a superior position above them, and the officers had been summoned to negotiate a surrender; or it was a kent army warning them away from their territory; or it was Commander Quahog's army, back from the dead.

Harzed wasn't interested in idle speculation. He needed to find out what was really going on. So he made a kettle of hot nettle tea and took it to the command tent, carrying with him a ring of metal cups.

Outside the tent stood soldiers like Harzed had never seen—tall men covered in steel with proud, pointed helmets to deflect arrows. These were no Soofians, but neither were they Serro-Qin. Were these then the famous knights of Frainland, come to fight the common foe?

These knights watched him impassively as he ducked into the command tent. Inside, the air was hot and humid with the breath of more than a dozen men seated in close conference. Bvegani looked up gratefully at Harzed's appearance with the tea and waved him over.

Commander Zanthem was saying, "I will go myself to the peak and survey the situation with my field glass." He spoke in a crisp Westongue for the benefit of the foreigners.

"Not possible," said a grim old knight facing Zanthem, presumably the commander of the Frainish army. "It is a perilous ascent, even for an experienced climber. I have a camp of watchmen at the peak, but it would take a week or more to bring you there, with no guarantee of your safety."

Harzed poured tea for the two commanders; and Bvegani, obsequious and invisible, placed the two steaming cups on the small table between the two men. Harzed lined up his remaining cups as a voice from the periphery said, "There is another way, a hidden way, by which a few slim fellows can reach the peak in just a few hours."

Harzed stopped mid-pour. He cocked his head and turned slowly to look at the man who had just spoken. Their eyes met and a spark of recognition flashed between them.

No, thought Harzed. *It can't be.*

"Who speaks?" demanded Zanthem.

A squat toad of a man in a dirty tunic, looking very out of place amongst the tent full of warriors, rose and identified himself. "I am called Gebit, lord commander. A mere scout, but one who knows this old mountain well."

One I hoped never to see again, thought Harzed. They'd shared a season together in these hills, hunting and trapping out of an old lean-to. Scenes from their time together flashed through his memory, unbidden, unwanted, but exhilarating.

Bvegani prodded Harzed, compelling him to resume pouring the tea.

"Well, then, Gebit," said Commander Zanthem, "Tell us of this short-cut."

"There is a certain fissure, full of boulders. A person who knows the way and is able to wriggle through small spaces can pass through the fissure, bypass this ridge and come immediately to the base of the mountain's wall. From there it is an afternoon's climb to the peak. No ropes or gear needed."

Harzed stewed. *I can't believe he's telling them about the secret canyon.* He let Bvegani distribute the tea; they only had a few cups, so Bvegani had to be selective in which men received one.

"It's no good," said the Frainish commander. "He showed us this way. Swords and shields will not pass. And we have only his word where it might lead."

Zanthem looked back at Gebit, who was still standing, his pudgy hands folded and resting comfortably on his paunch. "If you have reason to doubt this man's word, why have him in your retinue?"

Good question, thought Harzed.

Bvegani frowned at Harzed, motioning him toward the exit.

"Gebit's cunning has proved useful in the past," said the Frainish commander. Harzed noticed his cheek twitching slightly as he spoke.

Harzed made for the exit, careful not to look in Gebit's direction. But even as he turned away, he could feel his old companion's gaze. Out of the corner of his eye, he saw Gebit opening his hands to the tent. "Gentlemen, if I may: Here goes a fellow mountaineer who knows the way I speak of."

Harzed reached for the tent flap, hoping to escape. But it was too late. Everyone was looking at him. He froze for a long moment, not wanting to turn around.

"Who, that one?" asked Zanthem. "A one-armed mountaineer? Is this true, Harzed?"

Harzed turned slowly around. He glared at Gebit, who waved happily back at him.

"The way he speaks of may not even exist anymore," said Harzed. "It may well have filled up with mud and debris. Or the rocks may have shifted and settled, blocking the way."

"I checked it," said Gebit, folding his hands back together. "Still goes through, old friend. A tight squeeze, to be sure. But if I can pass through, so can you."

Commander Zanthem considered Harzed for a long moment. Harzed shrank from the scrutiny. The scrutiny of a commander was never a good thing.

"You're a cook, aren't you?" asked Zanthem.

"Yes, sir." *Please don't ask about my hand.*

"Did you grow up around here?"

"I spent a few years of my youth here. Yes, sir."

"What happened to your hand, son?"

Son? That was weird. He was used to the hand question, but the "son" thing was new. Harzed took a deep breath.

"Never mind." Commander Zanthem cut him off. "It doesn't matter. Harzed, I hereby promote you from cook to scout. Your first assignment is to accompany Mister Gebit and myself to the peak. We depart at once."

Well pleased with himself, Gebit grinned at Harzed. *This can't be happening*, thought Harzed. He stood in stunned silence as the men argued. Zanthem's security officers didn't like it, but the commander's mind was made.

Harzed fled the tent, feeling suddenly ill. Accursed Gebit had ruined everything. Again.

He'd taken only a few steps when Gebit emerged from the tent behind him. "Harzed! It's really you."

"What are you even doing here?" demanded Harzed, spinning round to face him.

Gebit opened his arms. "Same as you, I expect. Trying not to die, eh?" He reached for Harzed, seeking a hug. But Harzed turned away, saying, "I've got to gather my things."

What did Gebit expect? Harzed was not the hugging type.

"Well, I'm glad you're still alive," called Gebit after him. After a pause, he added, "Aren't you glad I'm still alive as well?"

Harzed, morbidly embarrassed, pretended not to hear. He returned to the baggage train, where everyone was still standing around trading theories. "It's Frains," he announced. They all plied him with questions, gathering round him like hungry ducks, but Harzed's mind was elsewhere. He *was* glad Gebit was still alive, but that didn't mean he wanted him around. Gebit meant trouble. And as a matter of personal policy, Harzed wanted nothing to do with any trouble.

They travelled light, carrying only water and a few biscuits, knives, and the clothes they were wearing. Commander Zantham, dressed as a common soldier, had his precious field glass disassembled in a cloth bag, tied snugly round his forearm.

Gebit led the way, blathering incessantly, until at last Zanthem ordered his silence. "It's best not to give away our position," he said.

But Gebit replied, "Have no fear, lord commander, the Frains control the mountain, there are no enemies here."

"Nonetheless," said Zanthem firmly.

Harzed had never appreciated Zanthem more.

The three of them made good time, moving laterally along the tree-dotted slope. Harzed kept a wary eye on gray clouds gathering around the peak. Even a small amount of rainfall might well drown them in the canyon.

It was not far to the entrance to the canyon. It was easy to miss. Gebit pointed down into a depression filled with boulders. "Down there," he said.

"I don't see anything," said Zanthem.

"Exactly," said Gebit. "Come on."

Zanthem looked to Harzed for confirmation. Harzed nodded. "It'll be a tight squeeze, sir. You have to make like a worm to get through."

Gebit hopped stone to stone, leaving them behind.

Zanthem followed. "How did you come to know this man? Is he a cousin or something?"

"Something," said Harzed. "Watch your step there. Watch for snakes down here."

"An odd fellow, wouldn't you say?"

"Yes, I would say. An odd fellow indeed, sir."

"We seem to have come to a dead end."

"You would think so, sir, but we go through just here."

"Just where? You can't mean that hole?" It was barely noticeable.

Gebit's face appeared in the hole. "Come on, you slow pokes."

"How did you even fit in there?" Zanthem was dumbfounded.

"Like a worm," said Harzed, lying on his belly and wriggling into the hole by way of demonstration. Underneath there was an open space between boulders, where Gebit squatted in wait. Their faces came together and Harzed had to strain his neck to avoid face-to-face contact. "Have you no sense of personal space? Go on and show the way, Gebit. We need to make haste before it starts to rain."

"You worry too much," said Gebit, but he did go, flattening himself like a pancake and sliding underneath an enormous boulder. From here, one could make out the shape of the canyon, a narrow crack, really, just wide enough for a single person to pass, hidden long ago by a rockslide.

Zanthem's arms and head emerged into the space. "And what, may I ask, is to stop these rocks from falling and crushing us?"

"They might well do so, sir. Best not linger here."

Once resolved to the task, Zanthem improved markedly at worming, and they soon reached the canyon proper, where each man had to suck in his belly to slide through the narrowest bits. Gebit, the broadest of them, somehow passed with the least difficulty. There was something of the octopus in this man as he poured his flesh through the smallest of openings.

They emerged from the far end of the canyon, reborn unto the world. Before them stretched the bare face of the mountain. It was not yet noon.

"Amazing!" said Zanthem. He set to work immediately reassembling his field glass. Harzed sat on a stone and unlimbered his canteen.

Field glass, that's what he called it. A tube with special lenses, through which Commander Zanthem liked to peer. Gebit sank down next to me and produced a pipe. He watched with great curiosity as the device came together. Immediately upon its completion, he asked, "Can I take a look?"

Harzed shook his head urgently, warning Zantham against entrusting the priceless possession to Gebit. Not that Zanthem needed the warning; he never let anyone touch his field glass. He tightened his grip, saying, "Absolutely not," and put it up against his own eye to scan the mountaintop.

Hurt, Gebit withdrew, puffing on his pipe, empty though it was. Smoking an empty pipe, just the sort of thing a Gebit would do. Harzed rolled his eyes.

"I can see the Frains up top," said Zanthem. "Moving about like ants."

"I could have told you that," said Gebit.

"Yes, well, we'd better get a move on," said Zanthem.

"Aren't we going to eat our biscuits?" asked Gebit.

"We can eat and walk."

But the walk soon became a climb. Gebit ate his, but Harzed needed his hand for climbing and so saved his biscuit for later. Zanthem had interest only in reaching the peak, driving them relentlessly, until all three were sweating with exertion.

They reached the peak while the sun was still well aloft, which was no doubt Zanthem's intent. He already had his field glass out before the Frains challenged them. Gebit smoothed things over with the Frains while Zanthem studied the landscape.

Harzed faded into the background and sat down to eat his biscuit. He was getting too old for climbing mountains, and Zanthem's merciless pace had left him aching.

Hardly was the biscuit unwrapped before Gebit found him. "Your commander, a real dick."

Harzed snorted. "He's a tough one. But he's better than most."

"And they had you *cooking*? Really? A man of your talents? Good thing I came along. A word from me, and you got promoted right away, didn't you?"

"You damn fool, did it occur to you that I wanted to be a cook? I had a good thing going. I was about to cash out. And then you came along and ruined everything. Just like you always do."

Gebit fingered his pipe. "You're not still mad about the Emma thing, are you?"

Harzed gnawed on his biscuit. "Can I just eat in peace, please?"

"Because I had nothing to do with that. Sure, blame old Gebit. He's an easy target, eh? Easier than taking a hard look at yourself, am I right?"

The worst part of Gebit was when he was right.

The Frainish look-outs came over, captivated by the field glass. Zanthem was talking and pointing, but at no point did he offer to let them look through his glass.

"How much do you suppose that thing is worth?" asked Gebit. Without waiting for a response, he asked, "What did you mean when you said you were ready to cash out?"

"Never mind," said Harzed, chewing.

Gebit squinted at Harzed, half-smiling, and put his pipe in his mouth.

The pipe was too much. Harzed burst out with, "Why the hell are you smoking an empty pipe? What's the point of an empty pipe?"

Gebit opened his hands defensively. "What? What's wrong with smoking an empty pipe?" He took a puff.

Harzed stood, jerked the pipe from Gebit's mouth and threw it as hard he could, into the abyss.

Violated, Gebit came slowly to his feet, his mouth hanging open. "Well, the years have made you meaner, haven't they? I'll have you know that pipe was a gift."

Harzed pointed at Gebit. "I don't have to put up with you. We are not friends. I don't want anything to do with you."

"Fine," said Gebit. "You never have to see me again."

"Good." Harzed took his half a biscuit and walked away.

Five minutes later, Gebit found Harzed lying down to rest under the cover of a stone outcropping. Groaning, Harzed pinched the bridge of his nose. A wide grin plastered across his face, Gebit said, "Harzed, guess what?"

Harzed closed his eyes. "Please go away."

"But Harzed, your commander has another mission for us."

This revelation forced Harzed to sit up.

"Isn't that great, Harzed? Just the two of us, a team, like in the old days?"

This cannot be happening, thought Harzed.

Moments later, the two of them were receiving their instructions from Commander Zanthem. Silhouetted against the retiring sun, hair whipped by mountain gust, Zanthem cut an imposing figure. "No later than midnight, you must depart and return to basecamp, arriving no later than dawn."

Nearby the Frains were pressing their rings into tablets of wet clay. "These tablets contain vital intelligence about the locations and dispositions of enemy forces operating in the area." Zanthem paused, letting the importance of their mission soak in. "I, too, will prepare a tablet with my orders. You are to deliver these tablets to the command tent without delay."

"You're not coming with us, sir?" asked Harzed.

"I will monitor the situation from here. You are to return the next day with any messages from the field. Do you understand?"

"Yes, sir," said Harzed and Gebit.

"Now get some rest. You depart as soon as the tablets are dry, but no later than midnight."

As Zanthem turned away, Harzed came to him and said, "Sir, you haven't eaten." He put a biscuit in his commander's hand. "Eat."

Later Gebit teased him about this exchange. "*Oh, commander, you haven't eaten.* You should have seen yourself. It's clear you fancy him."

"I don't fancy him," said Harzed. "Someone has to look out for him, that's all. It's important for my well-being that Zanthem stay alive and well."

There was no tent space for them, so Harzed and Gebit spent a cold few hours under the outcropping, wrapped together for warmth. At length, Harzed finally admitted, "I'm glad you're still alive, too."

"I knew it," said Gebit, nestling into Harzed.

Some hours later, Gebit woke him. "Harzed, come on, it's time." Moonlight showed the way.

The tablets were ready. Zanthem was fanning his orders, trying to speed the drying of the clay, while the Frains had a neat stack of three tablets tied up with string. One of the Frains, weary-eyed and slurring his speech, gave them each a small climbing hammer. In chopped Soofian, he said, "If you encounter the enemy, it's important you break the tablets. Use the hammer to make sure they are well smashed."

"Wait," said Harzed. "What do you mean, if we encounter the enemy? I thought there were no Serro-Qin on the mountain?"

"We have no reason to believe so," said Zanthem. "But their army has entered the valley, and their scouts, spies or lookouts could be operating in the area. Stay alert." He added his tablet to the stack, and all four tablets were wrapped in cloth and placed in a leather rucksack.

"Make haste," said Zanthem, looking Harzed in the eye. "I believe we can outmaneuver the enemy, and your secret short-cut gives us the advantage." Solemn, he passed the rucksack to Harzed. "Our victory depends on you. Now go!"

Shit, thought Harzed. He didn't like the idea of all this responsibility.

A gibbous moon showed the way down the mountain. Harzed and Gebit went, watching their step in the shadows. A fine mist had formed, making the rocks slippery.

"What if you slipped and the tablets broke?" asked Gebit. "Can you imagine?"

"I won't slip," said Harzed. "Even if I did, they are wrapped up pretty good. They'll be all right. I'm more concerned about the enemy spy scenario."

"Pshaw. There's no such thing as an enemy spy. Spies, when you meet them, always want to be your friend. They are the friendliest folk I know."

"Know a lot of spies, do you?"

"Sure I do," said Gebit. "I'm one myself."

Harzed rolled his eyes. "You are not a spy."

They started down a steep portion, pausing to make sure their footing was secure.

"You would be the worst spy of all time," said Harzed. "You can't hold a secret for six seconds."

Gebit shrugged. "You don't have to, when you're a spy. Being a spy is all about *sharing* the secrets, silly. Take these tablets, for example. Let's say we did run into an enemy spy. Can you imagine what he'd pay for a wee gander? A spy would have no interest in hurting us; he'd want to take care of us, nurture the relationship, have us deliver the tablets as per usual, with no one the wiser."

Harzed shook his head sadly.

"Hey," said Gebit. "I wonder if we'll come upon the pipe you threw? Wouldn't that be funny?"

"Maybe we should keep quiet," suggested Harzed. "So as not to give away our position. That's what Commander Zanthem would want."

"'That's what Commander Zanthem would want,'" parroted Gebit. "Listen to you. If you love Commander Dickhead so much, why haven't you told him how you feel, eh?"

"You're such a reprobate."

"No, I'm not. You're a repo–whatever."

A few minutes later, Gebit said, "Hey, maybe I should be the one to carry the tablets."

"No way."

"Harzed, you only have the one arm. You could easily slip and fall. Plus, I bet they're getting heavy. Aren't they? Maybe we should split them up. I'll take half, and you take half."

"I'll be fine."

"You act as if you think you're in charge."

"I *am* in charge."

"Really? What makes you think that?"

"Well, he was looking at me when he gave the orders."

"He was looking at both of us."

"He was definitely looking at me. You're not even part of his chain of command."

"Right, which means I can do whatever I want. That puts me in charge."

"That doesn't make any sense. Enough! I can't take any more of your nonsense. If you ever had any affection for me, then please just shut up for five minutes, will you?"

Gebit, wounded, closed his mouth. When he tried to stop for a rest, Harzed prodded him on. "We have to reach base camp before dawn."

But luck was not with them. Before they reached the canyon, the fine mist became a full-on pitter-patter of rain. "This is no good," said Harzed. "We can't pass the canyon if it's raining."

"Do we go over, then?" asked Gebit.

Harzed sighed. "It would take us a day or more. I say we wait it out here, and cross through after the rain's cleared off."

"Well, you're in charge," said Gebit.

Exhausted, the two of them took this time to rest and hydrate. With the steady drum of rain, Harzed drifted off to sleep.

When he woke, he found Gebit bent over a tablet. The other tablets were scattered across the ground. The cloth had been unwound and was fluttering in the wind.

"Are you mad? What are you doing?"

Gebit turned to him, his eyes red and swollen. "Harzed, they're going to burn Eljore."

"You're not supposed to read the tablets. Put them back, you fool!"

Tears flowed openly. "Didn't you hear me? They're going to burn Eljore and all the fields and orchards, too. Your Commander Dickhead wants to burn everything."

Harzed put his hands over his face. He bent to pick up the tablets. He saw figures, coordinates. "How can you even make sense of this? It's in some kind of code. You're probably reading it wrong."

"I told you, I'm a spy. I know how to read stuff like this."

"Well, if they're burning Eljore, I'm sure it's for a good reason. To stop it falling into the hands of the enemy."

Gebit shook his head sadly.

"Hey, it stopped raining. Let's get down to the canyon." Harzed gathered up the tablets. "Where's the string, so we can tie them back together?"

"Hmm? Oh, it flew away."

Harzed gritted his teeth. "Now they'll know we looked at it. Do you remember what order they were in?" He did his best to rewrap the tablets in the paper.

"I can't believe you're okay with them burning down Eljore and the orchards. Those are mature trees. What about the squirrels, Harzed?"

"Come on," said Harzed, helping Gebit to his feet. "War is hell."

They were almost there when Harzed, despite himself, lost his footing on a wet stone. Down he came sliding and took a tumble before coming to rest some twenty feet below.

Gebit threw himself down after, calling, "Harzed! Are you all right?"

"Yes," said Harzed tentatively. "I think so." When he tried to stand, a bolt of pain shot through his ankle. "Maybe not."

"Oh, no, your ankle!"

"I'll be all right. What about the tablets?"

"I'm sure they're fine," said Gebit. "Although you did land pretty hard on your back."

Harzed slipped the rucksack off his back. Gebit laid it out carefully and slowly removed the contents. "They seem fine," he said, but when he unwrapped the paper, he found the tablets within shattered.

Harzed felt lightheaded.

"Well—some of them are fine." Gebit continued unwrapping. "Yeah, this bottom one is mostly intact. See?"

Our victory depends on you, said Commander Zanthem. "I'm going to be sick."

"Hey," said Gebit. "It's going to be okay. I got this." He took out the climbing hammer the Frain had given him and was about to smash the one partially intact tablet.

Harzed leapt up to stop him. "What are you doing, you fool?"

"Careful—your ankle!"

"My ankle doesn't matter. These tablets are more precious than all the bones in our bodies."

"Hey, don't worry so much. We encountered the enemy. We had no choice but to smash the tablets. Just as we were ordered. We only barely escaped with our lives."

Harzed sighed. "I don't know, Gebit."

Gebit clasped his hands together. An idea had occurred to him. Without saying anything, he turned and started walking down toward the canyon.

Harzed gathered up the pieces of the tablets and followed after, limping. "Gebit?"

Gebit kept walking, leaving Harzed to hobble behind. "Gebit?"

He caught up to Gebit where the canyon fissure opened before the mountain slope. Gebit was looking at the canyon floor. "You know," he said, "I read those tablets. I remember everything I read. More or less."

"Your memory is terrible," said Harzed.

"Well, I remember the important bits. I'm fair sure I could reconstruct the rest."

"What are you talking about, Gebit?"

Gebit pointed down. "See this clay here? How hard would it be to make a tablet out of this clay? I saw how they made the molds. Wouldn't take long to dry them in the sun over there."

"You're a damn fool, Gebit. This would never work. For starters, you would need one of them special Frainish rings they used for imprinting."

"You mean a ring like this one?" asked Gebit, opening his palm.

Harzed's jaw flew open. "Did you steal that?"

"It's not stealing if they lost it, and I happened to find it."

"You're unbelievable."

"You're not so bad yourself, old friend. You go and put your foot in the cold water, and leave this up to me."

"This is never going to work." But Harzed went to put his foot in the water. An old trick to keep the swelling down.

Gebit worked quickly. Using the damp clay floor of the canyon as a workspace, he cut a rectangular mold, reinforcing its edges with flat stones. He worked like a man possessed, mixing clay from another section with water and dead grass, working it into a dough. Gebit was always good with his hands.

Harzed had to take his foot out of the water on account of the cold. He closed his eyes and tried to think about something else. At least while Gebit was busy, Harzed could enjoy the luxury of silence.

When next he looked up, Gebit was pressing his ill-gotten ring into the clay. He paused, as if trying to remember, then returned to hurriedly imprinting the ring against the clay. It looked like a bunch of nonsense to Harzed. "This is never going to work. This is the worst of your ideas."

"It'll be fine," said Gebit. "No one will know the difference."

Harzed closed his eyes again, drifting off. When he woke, the sun was well risen, and he sat up, alarmed. "We are really late."

Gebit was using his shirt to fan a pair of tablets drying in the sun. They were approximately the size and shape of the originals.

"Weren't there supposed to be four tablets?" asked Harzed. "What about the rest?"

Gebit shrugged. "That stuff wasn't important. I condensed it down."

Harzed shook his head. "Naw. Forget it. This is a bad idea. I'll just come clean about what really happened."

Gebit took him by the arm. "But Harzed. Think about it. It's better this way. Do you really want to be known as the guy who fell on his ass and lost the day? We can still be the heroes instead of the asses. And, best of all, in my version, nothing has to get burned down."

"Whoa. What do you mean, 'in my version'? You didn't change Zanthem's orders?"

"Only some minor editorial improvements. Clearer, more precise, and entirely less burning of our own lands."

"Gebit—no, you can't do that. They'll find us out and hang us for treason."

"No, they'll build statues of us for saving Eljore. Don't you remember, that's the place we first met? A treasure. You can't let them burn it, Harzed." He looked at Harzed with moist eyes and quivering lips.

"This is a terrible idea. How long for the tablets to dry? We are already well late."

"We'll pack them a little moist. They'll hold their form. One last thing," said Gebit. "Can I see the intact fragment from your bag?"

When Harzed handed it over, he was horrified to watch Gebit dash it against the rocks. "It didn't match," he said by way of explanation.

The sinking feeling in Harzed's stomach deepened.

Harzed let Gebit carry the fraudulent tablets; he wanted nothing to do with them. They squeezed through the ribbon canyon and wormed under the boulders to reemerge on the other side of the ridge. As they wended their way to basecamp, Harzed limping as best he could, Gebit opened the rucksack to help dry the tablets. "It'll be fine. Trust me. I do this kind of thing all the time."

It was late morning by the time they arrived at the command tent. "Where have you been?" demanded Lieutenant Sfangle. He was there with the Frainish commander hunkered over a leather map marked up with pins.

Sfangle grabbed the rucksack from Gebit. "We expected you hours ago."

"Apologies, Lieutenant," said Harzed. "The rain delayed

us." He swallowed as Sfangle opened the rucksack.

Sfangle paused, looking at Harzed's and Gebit's pale, drawn faces. "What? Is there something else?"

"No," said Gebit. "Not a thing."

"You are dismissed," said Sfangle with annoyance. "Best get some rest while you can. We'll be sending you back up to the peak this afternoon."

"Yes, sir," said Harzed and Gebit, tripping over one another in their exit.

When they were alone, Harzed put his hands over his face. "I can't believe I let you talk me into this."

"You worry too much."

"No. We should never have come back to basecamp. We should have just walked the other way and kept walking."

"You mean—you and me, running away together?" Gebit's eyes sparkled.

"Well, I'm not sticking around here waiting for them to clap me in irons, that's for sure."

As they spoke, they became aware of movement all around. The lieutenants were barking orders, and everyone was in motion, taking down tents, packing up gear.

Gebit crossed his hands atop his belly and grinned. "Will you look at that? These boys got some hustle. Look at 'em go!"

Harzed restrained himself from joining into the work. He was a scout now, no longer a pack mule. "What are they doing? Where are they going?"

"Just following Zanthem's orders, I expect." Satisfied with himself, Gebit considered the pipe in his hand, stolen no doubt moments ago from the command tent.

Harzed shook his head in disbelief. "Where are you sending them? You'll get them all killed."

"Nonsense. Zanthem knows what he's doing. Do you know he has joint command of both armies now? That's a lot of power," said Gebit, pursing his lips, turning the pipe over in his hands.

"I swear to you," said Harzed. "If you put that pipe in your mouth—"

Gebit slipped the pipe into his pocket and lifted his hands defensively.

"I can't believe they bought it," said Harzed.

"They totally bought it!" shouted Gebit, clenching his fleshy fists.

"Keep your voice down, you damn fool!" Harzed ran a trembling hand through his thinning hair. "I gotta think."

"Look at you, trembling like a leaf," said Gebit. "Come here, it'll be all right."

Harzed pushed him away. "No, Gebit! You may have fooled them for now, but these men will be onto us soon enough. I've seen men hang for less. We've got to get out of here, man. When they send us to the peak this afternoon, that'll be it. We just keep walking. They never see us again."

Gebit beamed with joy. "You always come up with the best plans, Harzed."

"Right," said Harzed. "Let's procure supplies while we can."

So Harzed and Gebit focused on their preparations. Neither of them felt like resting.

Finally they were summoned to a field (the command tent being gone) where Sfangle handed Harzed a single tablet wrapped in cloth. "Deliver this personally to Commander Zanthem. Trust it to no one else. Do you understand?"

"Yes, sir."

"Move with discretion. Be aware enemy spies are operating in the area. You are to destroy the tablet if anyone attempts to approach you. Do you understand?"

"Yes, sir."

"Watch each other's backs. Go on, now, with haste!"

Harzed and Gebit hastened away. "He was definitely looking at me," said Harzed.

"It's true," agreed Gebit dismally. "It's like I didn't even exist."

"Until that last part," said Harzed. "When he said, 'Watch each other's backs.' I can hardly watch my own back, can I?"

Gebit nodded sadly, unconvinced.

They left behind what remained of the camp. Most of the army had departed by this time, having subdivided into several contingents made up of mixed ranks of Shiops and Frains.

When they came to the depression with the hidden canyon, Gebit slumped down on a fallen log. "It's all beginning to catch up with me," he said. "Shall we rest here a while?"

"Sure," said Harzed, drinking from his canteen. "Where do you think we should head from here? Due east, follow this ridge all the way? Or should we go up and over to the greater Silvers beyond? Or back down into the valley?"

Gebit was watching Harzed. "Whichever way you think best."

"I figure the greater Silvers gives us the best chance of avoiding contact. But we could get snowed in if we're not careful."

"Hey," said Gebit. "What are we going to do with the tablet?"

"Eh?"

"Aren't you curious to take a look?"

"Not particularly. Just a bunch of chicken scratch to me."

"Well, *I'm* curious. Let's see what it says."

Harzed hesitated.

"What's the matter?" asked Gebit. "We're not delivering it to Zanthem. That's been decided. We could smash it, of course. That would be best. To prevent it falling into the wrong hands. But, before smashing it, Harzed, what's the harm in having a peek, eh?"

With some reluctance, Harzed handed the rucksack over to Gebit, who quickly opened it and unwrapped the tablet with all eagerness.

The tablet was imprinted on both sides, and Gebit had to flip it around a couple of times to find the right starting point.

"What's it say?" asked Harzed.

"I thought you weren't curious." He studied the tablet in silence for several minutes, flipping it over and studying the other side with equal attention. "Well," he said at last. "Seems there's some tension between the Shiops and the Frains."

"We're all on the same side," said Harzed. "You'd think they could set aside their differences to fight the Serro-Qin."

"Oh, they are," said Gebit. "They're just worried about 'unit cohesion.' And Lord Belstrop, the Frainish commander, had some choice words for your Zanthem. But everyone is following orders like good little soldiers."

"All right, good," said Harzed. "Well, now that your curiosity is sated…"

"Yes, right," said Gebit. "Time to destroy it." He stood up straight, looking down at the tablet in his hands. "Although …"

Harzed folded his arms. "What?"

"Well, imagine if we should run into one of those Serro-Qin spies we keep hearing about. They would pay nicely for a look, I'd expect."

"We are not treating with the enemy. They'd sooner kill us than pay us."

Gebit nodded absently. "Yeah, you're probably right." He studied the tablet for a moment more. "Too bad we can't deliver it to Zanthem, though. It would be good for him to know this bit here, about the garrison at Webbly's."

"What are you talking about? Let me see that." Harzed took the tablet and examined the portion where Gebit had pointed. Harzed never took to reading, and the military abbreviations and codes made the text all the more obscure. He did, however, see a 'W' that may have indicated the fort at Webbly's.

"Zanthem's orders didn't mention Webbly's," said Gebit. "Probably because he didn't know the locals were still holding out. Belstrop wants permission to send a relief force."

Harzed looked down into the depression where the hidden canyon lay. "What, now you think we should run the tablet up to him?"

Gebit shrugged. "It seems a lot of trouble. Wouldn't it be easier just to draft a reply ourselves?"

"No," said Harzed, horror-struck. "We are not doing that. This has gotten way out of hand."

"Why not? I already know what Zanthem will say. He'll approve the mission but change the parameters."

"You have no idea what Zanthem would say."

"Sure I do. I feel like I really channeled him earlier. I got into his head. Zanthem and I, we're practically the same person at this point."

"No, you're not. Zanthem is a tactical genius. You—well, you're just Gebit."

"'Zanthem is a tactical genius.'"

"Well, he is. An actual proven military leader."

"Yes, well, it's a good thing he had me around to fix his last set of orders, that's all I'll say. But since you are obviously in love with the man, let's do this one last errand for him. Then, after that, we'll disappear together. Hide out in the greater Silvers like you talked about."

"I am not in love with Zanthem."

"If you say so." Gebit took the tablet back from Harzed, wrapping it back in its cloth. "It's up to you, Harzed. I'll go with whatever you want to do."

Harzed glanced up at the peak. It seemed risky. He didn't like risks. But Gebit was right; if there was still a garrison at Webbly's, this was critical intelligence Zanthem needed to know.

"All right then," said Harzed, regretting it already. "Let's go see Zanthem."

So Harzed and Gebit wormed under the boulders, squeezed through the canyon. When they came to the end of the canyon, they saw that the mold Gebit had hurriedly constructed in the morning was still intact.

Harzed started up the slope, but then paused and looked back when he realized Gebit was still standing over the mold, thinking.

"We need to keep moving before it gets too dark," called Harzed.

Gebit waggled his finger. "Just give me a few minutes. I've got an idea."

"No more ideas," said Harzed. "Seriously, Gebit, it's too much." He started back down the slope to force Gebit to come.

But before Harzed could intervene, Gebit took out the tablet and shattered it against the rocks.

"Damn you, Gebit, what's the matter with you?" Harzed took him by the shoulders and shook him. "Why are you this way?"

"Just listen, will you? We couldn't give the message to him like it was. It wouldn't have made any sense to him. He still thinks they're on their way to burn things down. We need a plausible explanation as to why he won't see smoke in the morning, eh? We'll still tell him about Webbly's, of course, we'll just rearrange some of the other details, so as not to arouse his suspicions. We need him to keep thinking he's in charge, right?"

"He is in charge."

"If you say so," said Gebit. "Let's keep him comfortable so we can escape unmolested on the morrow."

Harzed shook his head. He should have known, when Gebit came back into his life, it was going to be like this all the time.

"Well, let's get to work," said Harzed, glancing up at the sun. "As it is, we're going to be climbing in the dark."

"It'll go faster with both of us," said Gebit, springing into action. "Collect some of that dry grass over there. The final drying can happen as we ascend. That'll save us some time."

They worked as a team and soon had a rectangular tablet of wet clay. This they had to carry uphill to find a sunny spot to bake it. Harzed and Gebit took turns fanning the clay, while Gebit bounced ideas off Harzed. "What if we say the northern contingent was delayed on its way to burn Eljore by an ambush from a band of Serro-Qin mercenaries? Nothing they can't handle; no need to send reinforcements. It'll just take them a couple days to mop up these mercenaries."

"That could work," said Harzed. "We don't want him too interested in the mercenaries, though. Maybe it would be better to call them conscripts from Central Moghia."

"Yeah, that makes them sound really boring." Gebit smiled knowingly at Harzed. His smile said, *It's so great that we're back together again.*

Harzed had been drawn, unwillingly, back into Gebit's orbit. He wasn't at all sure this was where he belonged. It certainly wasn't the life he wanted for himself. When he'd left Gebit last time, he'd done so for good reason. Although the two of them were drawn together like magnets, the magnetic force between them was dangerous, destructive. He didn't like the aspects of his personality Gebit brought to the surface. Why was he helping this madman commit fraud and treason?

But here he was. Harzed was committed now, whether he liked it or not. His fate was tied to Gebit's, at least in the short term.

They climbed in the dark. When finally the moon rose and lit their way, they were nearly at the peak. A Frainish sentry challenged them, they identified themselves, and a few minutes later they were standing before Zanthem, a man who had grown gaunter since last they saw him.

"Well?" said Commander Zanthem. He was flanked by Frainish knights, fresh faces who had arrived at the peak with supplies after several days of climbing the long way. Actual meat was roasting over a fire.

Gebit stepped forward with the rucksack and produced the cloth-wrapped tablet. "Lord commander."

Zanthem accepted the tablet. "Impressive work, you two. Up and down the mountain twice in one day."

The Frains looked at one another, disbelieving.

"One very long day," said Harzed.

Zanthem walked toward the fire, unwrapping the tablet. "Have some meat, you've certainly earned it."

Gebit's eyes lit up and he arrived at the fire before anyone. "Real meat! What is it?"

The Frains exchanged dismal glances. "There was no honor in it. We found a dead goat on our climb."

"No complaints here," said Gebit. "Found meat is free meat, that's how I was brought up."

Zanthem inspected the tablet in the firelight. He crumbled a corner off with his thumb. "They must have been in some hurry, making this."

Gebit nodded absently, staring at the fat dripping into the fire. "Yeah," said Gebit. "There was a bit of a mad dash, everyone scrambling to follow your instructions."

Harzed stood a few paces away in the dark, watching Zanthem's eyes scan the message on the tablet. After a long pause, he flipped it over and read the other side.

"How much longer you reckon this meat has to go?" asked Gebit.

"It's not ready yet," said Harzed.

"Listen to Harzed," said Zanthem. "He's an experienced cook, you know."

"Harzed's cooking is the best. This one time he made me an orange pilaf with shaved shallots. Perfection! Food of the angels, I tell you!"

"Sounds like you two go way back."

"Haven't seen him in years, sir," said Harzed. "Bit of a shock, running into him again after all this time."

Zanthem handed the tablet to a waiting Frain. "It looks authentic. An impressive fabrication."

Harzed's heart sank. *He knows.*

"I saw you, you fools, with my field glass. You were in plain sight the whole time."

Harzed and Gebit looked at each other. *We've got to run,* is what Harzed's look said. But Gebit's look said, *Don't worry, I got this.*

"And what did you see, lord commander?"

"I saw everything. Lord Belstrop suspected, and now we know for certain. How long have you been in the pay of the Serro-Qin?"

"There's no pay involved," said Gebit. He looked up from the fire to meet Harzed's gaze. "I told you I was a spy."

"You are no spy," said Harzed. "Tell them the truth."

"What truth, Harzed?"

"That you're just a numbskull. A fool. A shithead. A well-intentioned trickster."

Gebit nodded, blinking back tears.

"Come with me," said Zanthem. He took Harzed and Gebit to the precipice. "Look." Far below, miles away, a series of fires burned in the valley, plainly visible.

"No," said Gebit, sinking to the ground, the strength gone out of his knees.

The knights stood behind them. "Gebit, you are now my prisoner. I hope you will cooperate and tell us everything about your Serro-Qin operators. Alternatively," said Zanthem gesturing to the precipice, "you are free to fly away."

"I'll cooperate," sobbed Gebit.

The knights picked him up and removed him from the scene. Harzed stood very still, not sure what to expect or what was expected of him.

Zanthem stood next to him, watching the distant fires. His sigh was heavy. "We'll rebuild."

"Yes, sir," said Harzed.

Zanthem unlimbered his field glass, offered it to Harzed. "Want to take a look?"

Donna J W Munro

Fairy Tales and Rainbows Died That Day

We found unicorn by following the rainbow color ribbon to the golden canopy of a grove. Me, Jimmy, and tag-along Josie, barely out of nappies. She'd be useful.

Me 'n Jimmy done this a'fore. We knew the signs.

Stories say virgins draw unicorn. Nope. Lots'a virgins be like us—hard from want. Broken just not used. That don't draw unicorn. Innocence draw unicorn. That's what Josie was for.

Unicorn fall out of the sky in sideways rain. We follow color ribbons to 'em—pounds of good meat. Didn't last long if you used iron stickers, but tasted good until it went bad with iron poison. I saw light twinkling on the water, clear and bright for the first time in forever, so I knew it was there, all invisible. We pushed Josie forward and her eyes got wide. She saw because her eyes were watery like mine got back when it was my turn. I knew her heart thudded and breath got big as she understood its beauty because I remember how it felt. Her feet skimmed the velvety bank. We followed.

Tears fell as she kneeled. This always hurt. Unicorn came visible when its soft nose brushed Josie's hand and lay its slim head on her lap. Me n' Jimmie didn't have innocence, but we knew the ache of its loss. I slid the iron sticker into her hand and tears come to our eyes too. She looked at me, her blue eyes full of sad and no.

"Josie, we gotta eat."

"Not her," she said

"No meat in weeks."

"Think of Ma."

She sobbed, gripping the sticker.

Unicorn chuffed at the smell of iron but didn't run. Not from innocent little Josie.

She shoved, wetting white neck and gray iron with vivid red.

Unicorn disappeared with Josie's lost innocence, but when we felt around, we got underneath, lifted her body, and carried her home for Ma to butcher as the water clouded and the rainbow faded to gray.

Scott Nicolay

Notes on *Field Notes on the American Sasquatch*

When you see a dark form moving through the forest, do you follow? Do you pursue it deeper into the trees, the valleys, the canyons, the caves, down the rabbit-hole like Alice, always seeking answers, craning for a closer look?

Do you still believe in answers?

Perhaps you are one who waits on those who enter the dark places, who go over the edge, in which case you seek your answers vicariously, from relative safety. As if answers are ever safe. As if anyone ever really comes back.

I doubt that you are among the many who don't want to know what goes on out in the dark world, in the territory beyond living rooms and TV screens. This is not a tale for those folks, and if you are one such person and have encountered these pages by accident, or through some rare and fleeting caprice of curiosity, this is probably where you will stop reading. *C'est la guerre.* Such people have no interest in news from the front, let alone from beyond it. I do not write for them.

Hunter S. Thompson called that front "The Edge." He eventually crossed over it permanently, in his own sad and surprisingly anticlimactic way. David Norman, the purported author of *Field Notes on the American Sasquatch*, crossed over as well, but he lingered there long enough to leave us a message, an awkward quantum-entangled telegram shared via one of the most low-tech media of our time: the zine. What David Norman found beyond the event horizon of The Weird—or what found him—we may never know. He did however, describe for us his approach. Which leaves us with the question: Who was David Norman? To which I now reply: A dark form that we must follow. Wherever it takes us. Into the forest. Into the dark. Down many rabbit-holes. As close to the Edge as we can get.

●

My friend Melissa Eisner first introduced me to *Field Notes on the American Sasquatch*. Melissa is the proprietor of Coffee Bandits, my favorite local coffeehouse, and the same friend who introduced me to the Fresno Nightcrawler, regarding which I have written previously. Though not a cryptozoologist, Melissa is an invaluable resource, an essential member of my local community and multiple other overlapping communities within and beyond our town. As far back as our earliest conversations when I had just moved to California and begun frequenting her establishment more-or-less on the daily, she spoke of this incredible zine, a peculiar publication she numbered among her most prized personal possessions. A zine about the sasquatch. Or as she prefers to call it: the *sad*squatch.

Shortly before the pandemic, during a winter party in Melissa's backyard, she brought out her treasured sadsquatch zine, and the assembled guests, myself among them, passed it around the firepit, taking turns reading passages aloud. This at last was my introduction to David Norman and his peculiar, quite literally and in all ways *pathetic* take on America's favorite cryptid.

pathetic:
1.   having a capacity to move one to either compassionate or contemptuous pity;
2.   marked by sorrow or melancholy;
3.   pitifully inferior or inadequate

(https://www.merriam-webster.com/dictionary/pathetic).

All of these definitions fit David Norman and his peculiar zine; whether or not they fit Bigfoot is a deeper question. Yet Bigfoot, the sadsquatch, is not our subject here. In truth, I am not much of a believer in Bigfoot. Our focus is on David Norman himself. On all the David Normans and their many manifestations. On all the manifold forms that lead us down rabbit-holes, into darkness. And on what happens whenever we pursue the truth out to the edges of verifiability.

•

Before we descend into that labyrinth, it behooves me nonetheless to satisfy whatever curiosity you may have about that zine itself, and about any personal encounters David Norman may or may not claim to have had with the Sasquatch, or as he abbreviates it from early on, the "Ssq." For Norman, the existence of the Ssq is a *fait accompli*, the evidence for it *prima facie.* He bases this conclusion on centuries of alleged reports not only of the Ssq but also of "Ssq like creatures such as the Yeti, the Yowie, and the Pendek." This allows him to move directly on to important ontological questions such as: "Was Jesus Part Sasquatch?" (probably), "Are Ssq Actually Aliens?" (no), and "Does the Ssq have an aura?" (probably). I do not cite any page numbers for these quotes because the zine has none.

Prior to addressing these essential topics, Norman methodically reviews the supposed lack of evidence for the Ssq in several categories: "Lack of droppings," "Lack of Confirmed Sightings," "Lack of Killed Bodies," and "Lack of Footprints," each of which he dismisses handily. Certainly, as Norman points out, the very footprints that have led to the attribution of the epithet "Bigfoot" have been reported frequently, across much of North America, and for many decades now. Despite my skepticism, I can point here to an example from at least secondhand experience: shortly before the pandemic, I purchased a new oilcloth duster from a couple in the foothills of the Sierra Nevadas. We dodged Ebay's fees by meeting personally in the parking lot of a chain hardware store somewhere along either the 120 or the 49 on the way to Sonora. We hit it off rather well, and with our transaction concluded, we continued to chat, and they showed me photos of inhumanly large footprints from their orchard, said footprints having appeared simultaneously with the disappearance of most of the pears from their trees. Who was I to question my new friends? They impressed me as sincere and they presented photographic evidence. We made tentative plans for me to visit them at home, but then the plague times arrived and we never followed through.

To be sure, everyone who has ever described to me an encounter with a ghost, a skinwalker, a cryptid, or a UAP has described that experience to me with similar sincerity, and I have heard quite a few compelling tales about all of the above. I have heard firsthand tales of alien abductions, skinwalker encounters, and the vanishing hitchhiker related *in detail* by entirely credible sources. I even had my own experience with UAPs while camped on the southern Rio Grande during an archaeological dig in July of 2021, and I too can describe that experience with what I feel is considerable sincerity and absolute honesty, as can the several other people who witnessed it with me. What I cannot tell you is what those strings of lights in the New Mexico night sky were, or what, if anything, they meant. After all, they were only "nocturnal lights," the lowest level of J. Allen Hynek's scale, not even a "close encounter of the first kind" (1972).

Despite the title of Norman's work, however, which suggests a focus on Jane Goodall-like observations, he offers no such hard evidence: no sightings, no observations, no droppings, no footprints, no huge and hirsute corpses. No accounts of personal encounters of any kind. Nothing. These are not the sort of field notes that I keep as an archaeologist or that I expect from colleagues in cultural anthropology. Beyond his condensed ontological discussions and his reasoned dismissals of the lack of scientific evidence, Norman focuses only on his own attempts to connect with the Ssq by attiring himself in a home-sewn suit of animal skins and sleeping rough in the forest. "I become the Ssq," he writes. "It is... exhilarating. There is not a feeling that compares to it. I have lain with women, and I will tell you the excitement I feel being living and breathing in the skin of a Ssq blows it out of the water." No cellphone, no camera, no electronics whatsoever, because: "the Ssq can sense the presence of technology."

Whether Norman's practice of Sasquatch impersonation led to his adoption by a Sasquatch community, death by exposure, or getting shot by a hunter, we do not know. I have searched obituaries from the entire state of Oregon throughout and beyond the time period during which he supposedly disappeared, but I have found no David Normans. No Normans at all, neither of *nomen gentilicium* nor *praenomen*. Perhaps I missed it. Perhaps he disappeared in Washington state or northern California.

What my online investigations did reveal to me however, is that there are, or have been, several David Normans associated with cryptozoology, all but one of them specifically with the Ssq.

First of course we have the David Norman of the *Field Notes*, allegedly last seen in the forests of the PNW in his homemade suit of animal skins. His slim posthumous publication tells us precious little about him other than this proto-furry predilection. Of course, the whole thing might be a hoax, or at least a prank, though the sincerity of *Field Notes* remains compelling. If it is a prank, then the author of the "Foreward" is presumably the author of the entire zine, and fursuit David Norman a mere fiction.

Nonetheless, let us presume for now that this primary David Norman was a real person. If so, he certainly did not make himself easy to follow, in the forest or in print: his apparently posthumous goodbye letter to the world he departed prematurely comes to us almost completely scrubbed of any ID beyond his name. *Field Notes on the American Sasquatch* is a severed climbing rope that leads *almost* nowhere. Tug it up from the abyss and you will find the other end bitten clean through. Or nearly clean through anyway. No publisher, no city, no copyright date. The cover bears only the title *Field Notes / on the / American / Sasquatch*. The words are in the generic Courier font, centered. Beneath them is a sketch of the titular cryptid frozen in the posture made familiar by stills from the 1967 Patterson–Gimlin film, walking with left arm and right leg forward. This image is stylistically consistent with the others in the zine: Bigfoot as an angel, Bigfoot as Christ nailed on the cross. All of these pictures resemble clip art but if they are clip art one wonders where Norman might have found them. I have searched in vain for these same images online. No artist receives credit in the zine. Below that first image are the words *A Guide / by David Norman*.

The first page of *Field Notes* is a "Foreward" (sic) by someone purporting to be Norman's niece or nephew. Three paragraphs and a very grainy photo of the alleged author, dated to 1992. The third paragraph tells us: "David is no longer with us. He disappeared in 1994, vanished into the foggy forests of the Pacific Northwest during one of his many expeditions." These dates may be important, and I will return to them shortly.

The facing page begins with an "Introduction" attributed to Norman himself. The second paragraph thereof starts: "My name is David Norman." This is the first time his full name appears inside the zine. The anonymous nibling who authored the "Foreward" never mentions David's surname. Following Norman's own three-paragraph introduction comes a single sentence under the header: "Acknowledgements." This short paragraph appears to have originally consisted of two sentences, but the second is erased or effaced in the zine as I have it. A few words are still visible in the photocopy: "fact of the" and "Research." The surviving first sentence reads: "I would like to thank the IPRC without whom the creation of this guide would not have been possible."

Here we have our only substantive clue in the entire zine, our only potential track on David Norman's trail. The IPRC is almost certainly the Independent Publishing Resource Center in Portland, Oregon, an establishment whose mission is to "provide affordable access to space, tools, and resources for creating independently published media and artwork, and to build community and identity through the creation of written and visual art" (https://www.iprc.org/about/). Thus, it appears that someone—presumably either David Norman or his anonymous nibling—visited the IPRC in order to publish *Field Notes on the American Sasquatch*. According to the Foreword, Norman disappeared in 1994. The *Mission + History* section of the IPRC's website tells us they have been in operation for 21 years. If that information is current, they opened in 2001—seven years after David Norman supposedly vanished into the forests of the PNW, plenty of time for his nibling to assemble the pertinent documents and convey them to Portland. Perhaps though, the IPRC has not updated its website for a few years. The COVID-19 pandemic may have affected that. If the last update came in 2019 or earlier, that would push the organization's inception back into the 1990s, and closer to the date of David Norman's alleged disappearance. Perhaps even this abbreviated history omits an earlier incarnation of the IPRC—one that might place its earliest operations prior to Norman's terminal departure. Perhaps the author of the foreword altered or omitted a date. Perhaps the obliterated sentence of the acknowledgements contained information relevant to this question. All this bears on the question of authorship. Of course, it was probably the nibling who visited the IPRC and printed the zine, which makes the year less important. The presence of the foreword supports that conclusion. Yet the acknowledgment, which seems to be part of David Norman's text, militates against that, as it suggests that he had completed the text with the intent to publish it prior to his alleged disappearance. If so, then the date of his disappearance in the foreword must be wrong. I reached out to the IPRC via their website, but received no response.

As it is, we are left with one name, two dates, and the name of the non-profit that probably printed the zine. The IPRC and the dates lead us only so far, but the name David Norman opens several interesting doorways. And down the rabbit-hole we go...

Cryptozoologist Loren Coleman has written extensively about what he calls the "name game," which is the tendency for certain names to appear repeatedly in conjunction with cryptid encounters and other strange and paranormal phenomena (1983:235-250; 1985:110). Some of these place names bear an obvious supernatural character: Devil's Gulch, Satan's Backbone, Lucifer's Armpit... For others, that character resides in another level of the name game itself, such as any location with "fay" in its name (Faywood, Lafayette, Fayetteville...). Others still bear no obvious supernatural implications or representations, such as towns named Logan or variations thereof. This pattern extends beyond geography, infecting the very names of those who research cryptids and UFOs. David Norman appears to be one of those cursed names.

Our David Norman of immediate interest, the purported author of *Field Notes on the American Sasquatch*, remains opaque to further research, yielding no search hits beyond a few obscure mentions of the zine itself, all either reviews or offers of resale. Notably, as discussed above, no obituary or missing persons news story from Oregon. However, in 2021, one David Norman Lewis published a slim volume titled *Evergreen Ape: The Story of Bigfoot*. Beyond that book, David Norman Lewis' own web presence is nearly as scant as that of *Field Notes* David Norman, limited mainly to his author page on the Microcosm Publishing website, which simply repeats the brief author biography from the book, and a twitter account created in September 2019 and used only until August 31, 2020. One year in total, only 21 tweets, several of which were retweets. The most interesting is a tweet from Dec. 16, 2019: "The first draft of everything I write is always about everything."

Like the IPRC, Microcosm Publishing is based in Portland, Oregon. I wrote to them via their website to enquire about David Norman Lewis, but just as with my attempt to contact the IPRC, I received no response.

Our third David Norman is David B. Norman, a respected British paleontologist and curator emeritus of vertebrate paleontology at the Sedgwick Museum, Cambridge University (https://www.esc.cam.ac.uk/directory/david-norman). In August of 2021, Loren Coleman tweeted photos of this David Norman's daughter, Emma Norman, attired in an elaborate "dinosauroid" costume, i.e. an intelligent, humanoid dinosaur. The idea of dinosauroids originated with paleontologist Dale A. Russell (1937-2019), who speculated in 1982 that dinosaurs of the genus *Troodon* might have developed into intelligent bipeds had they been permitted a few more million years of evolution. The dinosauroid concept has unfortunately but inevitably been appropriated by conspiracy theorists who have tied it to their heavily anti-Semitic ideas about "lizard men." Although neither Coleman, Norman, nor the late Dr. Russell delved into that hateful nonsense, the entanglement has nonetheless occurred. It does not, however, appear to have any further bearing on our quest. This David Norman leads us only so far; the rest of his rabbit-hole takes us nowhere relevant to our current explorations.

The fourth and final David Norman leads us down a deep and complex warren, however. Here we discover that the name David Norman was one of many *noms de plume* employed by Warren "Billy" Smith (1931–2003), a prolific (i.e. hack) author whose output included westerns, romance novels, prurient exposés of America's gay subculture roughly à la mode de William Burroughs' *Queer*, and dozens of books about bigfoot, UFOs, Atlantis, Agharta, and other "paranormal" topics. Some of the titles in the latter category he coauthored with the better-known Brad Steiger (1936-2018, né Eugene E. Olson), these latter sometimes but not always under the shared pseudonym *Eric Norman*. Smith used the name *David Norman* not for his paranormal output but for a series of pioneer westerns he wrote solo. These appeared under the main title *The Frontier Rakers*, though beginning with the second volume, each had a subtitle (*Silver City*, *Montana Pass*, etc.).

Whether written under his own name or others, Smith's books on Bigfoot and similar topics all follow the same formula, describing various alleged incidents, sightings, and encounters from around the world, often from locations far too geographically and linguistically remote for the average reader to attempt any verification (especially in the decades before the Internet). He never provides a bibliography and includes none of the other scholarly reference information that might allow the reader to verify his sources. For example, in one of his "core" works, *The Secret Origins of Bigfoot*, the only direct quotations come from Lewis Carroll, Montaigne, Christopher Columbus, the Bible...and Eric Norman. Smith cites and/or quotes the latter more than any other author, without ever acknowledging that this is a multiple-use name (like Rrose Sélavy, Luther Blissett, or Monty Cantsin) that he himself co-created and sometimes employed. Among the works Smith cowrote with Brad Steiger under this sobriquet were *Gods, Demons, and UFOs* (1970) and *Gods and Devils from Outer Space* (1973).

Even among his colleagues, Smith's reputation is problematic. In 2017, his fellow *soi-disant* "prolific Iowan author" Timothy P. Banse published a short pamphlet under the title *Warren Billy Smith: UFO Investigator or Hoaxster?* Although Banse wanders far afield from the premise of his title, his initial focus is on the assertion that Smith fabricated the 1967 Schirmer UFO sighting out of whole cloth. The Schirmer incident involved a 22-year old Nebraska policeman who was supposedly abducted by reptilian aliens: a close encounter of the *fourth* kind. According to Banse, Smith manufactured this story in order to complete a book and meet a deadline, later admitting the hoax to one Glenn McWane at his local Village Inn. Ultimately Banse takes an apologetic tone and pardons Smith's transgressions as a product of his upbringing and the financial challenges of freelance writing. One wishes that he had gone through Smith's work more systematically and identified other potential hoaxes. Certainly, some of the supposed Bigfoot encounters Smith reported in The *Secret Origins of Bigfoot* (1977) and *The Abominable Snowmen* (with Brad Steiger, 1969) seem suspicious.

The Evergreen Ape by David Norman Lewis similarly lacks footnotes, end notes, textual citations, and a bibliography. Where this book stands out is in its thesis that belief in and reports of Bigfoot may have grown out of earlier reports of "wild men." However, this interesting premise does not make its inadequately-documented claims any more credible.

Thus, in addition to the author of *Field Notes*, we have three other David Normans on the cryptozoological radar, two of whom actually wrote books about Bigfoot (though only one strictly under that name). True, "David Norman" is not an unusual name. Nonetheless, we appear to have encountered Loren Coleman's name game in operation here, although Coleman himself has not addressed this particular occurrence as an example thereof. I shared this essay with him prior to submitting it for publication and he confirmed this. He also expressed serious doubts as to whether David Norman, or at least the author of the foreword to *Field Notes*, should be considered a serious cryptozoologist, pointing specifically to the line "Many people think that the history of the Ssq, or 'bigfoot,' begins in 1958 with the Shipton foot prints, or in 1967 with the Patterson-Gimlin film." According to Coleman, "This person is either pulling our collective legs or is playing with the basic facts in the field. Eric Shipton's find of Yeti (not Bigfoot) prints was in 1951. In Nepal. Bigfoot 'began' with the first widespread publicity of the finding of their tracks at Bluff Creek, California, in 1958" (Loren Coleman, personal communication 2023). Then again, we are dealing with a person who claimed Jesus was probably part Sasquatch (Norman, not Coleman), so serious cryptozoology is probably already off the table in this instance.

If we leave out the respected paleontologist, who seems to represent a blind alley in this regard, the earliest David Norman, Mr. Warren "Billy" Smith, presents us with our most interesting candidate for further consideration. Between 1965 and 1977, he wrote under his own name at least two dozen books on various paranormal topics in vogue at the time: Bigfoot/Yeti, UFOs, Atlantis, the Hollow Earth, ESP, etc. During this same time period, he coauthored at least fifteen more volumes on similar topics with Brad Steiger (either under the Eric Norman pen name or the latter's birth name, Eugene Olson) and even with Gabriel Green, a once-somewhat-famous UFO contactee and repeated write-in candidate for U.S. president.

This fourth David Norman, Warren "Billy" Smith, leads us even further, down one of the most obscure but intriguing rabbit-holes in American letters: the Lowney Handy Writers' Colony, a *sui generis* midcentury creative writing program driven by its eponymous leader (1904-1964) and the success of its original student, James Jones (1921-1977), author of *From Here to Eternity* (1951), *Some Came Running* (1957), and *The Thin Red Line* (1962). Though it would be a stretch to describe the Handy Colony as paranormal in any way, it was certainly weird, at least with a small "w." Weird enough that I felt compelled to explore it, and David Norman/Warren "Billy" Smith's connection to it, more deeply, searching for some key to the whole mystery. Down this rabbit hole, I went deep.

Smith claimed to be among the last of the authors connected to the Colony, and in this case at least, his claim holds water. That much I *can* verify. During the Colony's final years, when Jones and Handy had parted ways and the former had ceased to provide his share of the funding, it no longer offered a residential program, and Lowney Handy worked with her few remaining proteges via the post. Both Handy's papers at the University of Illinois and Smith's papers at the University of Iowa confirm their correspondence between 1961 and 1963. Lowney Turner Handy died on June 27, 1964. James Jones died in 1977. Despite its ephemeral rise to prominence in the 1950s, the Colony has long since dwindled into obscurity, along with most of its students and their work, with the obvious exception of Jones.

The fate of the Lowney Handy Writers' Colony is no great mystery, and its end seems fairly inevitable given its lack of institutional funding and support. Handy's boot camp model, which infamously emphasized extensive retyping of works by her chosen "masters," also seems to have been designed—advantageously if not deliberately—to work best with GIs returning from World War II, and as the years went on, these became less available and more difficult to recruit. It is tempting to suggest that some sort of curse haunted the colony, especially considering the early deaths of Handy, her husband Harry, and its next most successful graduate after Jones (Tom T. Chamales in 1960). However, John Bowers, author of *The Colony*, a lightly fictionalized novel based on his time at the Handy Colony, is still alive and well into his 90s, and Jon Shirota, Handy's last in-person student, lived to be 92, only dying in 2020.

One might suggest that the CIA had something to do with the early deaths of Lowney Handy and some of her most successful proteges, given that the Agency allegedly funded the Iowa Creative Writers Workshop (Bennett 2014), which eventually became the predominant creative writing program in the US and the model for many other programs.

However, although it is interesting to consider the possibility that the pickle factory might have seen the two programs as being in competition, the CIA's involvement in the Iowa program does not appear to have begun until 1967, three years after Lowney Handy's death and the end of her final efforts to train aspiring writers like Warren "Billy" Smith via correspondence. If anything, the Colony, with its Midwestern location, emphasis on American realist fiction, and disdain for the avant-garde may have provided some inspiration for the Iowa Creative Writers Workshop. Any deeper and more direct connection between the two seems unlikely, however. An alternative possibility is that someone at Yaddo, some person with government connections, saw Handy's program as competition and pulled some strings. Perhaps this was how the CIA became interested in creative writing programs to begin with. I doubt it though, and I only offer the suggestion in the interest of completeness. I believe that the Handy Writer's Colony rose and fell on its own natural trajectory, an arc largely inevitable given the time period, the ages and personalities of those involved, and the ways of the world. Without external funding and a teaching staff of more than one, the Colony's days were always numbered, its end foreordained after Jones met (and married) Gloria Mosolino, and broke off his long affair with Handy.

How conveniently it would serve my purposes if one or more Bigfoot sightings had occurred at or near the Handy Writers' Colony. Bigfoot, UFOs, other paranormal activities. The opening of a gateway to Agharta, which was one of Warren "Billy" Smith's favored topics. North America's answer to Springheel Jack, the Mad Gasser of Mattoon, Illinois operated less than an hour away from the Colony, but he appears to have limited his career to the mid-1940s (Coleman 1983:191-210), whereas the Handy Colony did not begin formal operations until 1950, and none of the available sources on the Colony reference the Mad Gasser or any other paranormal phenomena. Indeed, none of the accounts of the Lowney Handy Writers' Colony, even the lightly fictionalized ones like Bowers' and Shirota's that detail a range of awkward and even violent incidents between the students (Bowers 1971; Shirota 2001:101-186), describe any explicitly paranormal incidents. Despite Handy's obsession with Baird T. Spalding's quasi-theosophical *Life and Teaching of the Masters of the Far East*, her own instruction emphasized American realist literature, and no evidence suggests that anyone ever achieved enlightenment and ascended to a higher (or inner) plane while at the Colony.

Except for Warren "Billy" Smith, however, who was connected to Lowney Handy only by a handful of letters on either side of a faltering correspondence in her final years. Although not an ascended master by any appearance or account, Smith went on to become perhaps the most prolific of all Handy's students, even if his output of paranormal nonfiction and genre novels was hardly the sort of elevated literary work that Handy sought to elicit from her proteges. A great deal of his oeuvre consisted of works on cryptozoological, paranormal, and supernatural topics. *Field Notes on the American Sasquatch* seems right up his alley, except for the simple fact that it is difficult to see how he might have capitalized on such a publication, as the focus of his work always seems to have been the simple pursuit of the almighty dollar, and this little zine could hardly have been much of a moneymaker. The Handy Colony, in turn, appears to represent a blind alley in the pursuit of explanations for the mystery of the David Norman name game, as promising as it first appeared before I spent several months tracking down, purchasing, and reading the various obscure texts on its history. A peculiar anomaly in American letters to be sure, but one that leads us no further in this quest, other than demonstrating the extent of David Norman's obscure connections. That point alone is important nonetheless: rabbit-holes run deep, and they usually lead to unexpected links. Not this time however. My deep-dive led only to a dead end; a promising side-quest took me nowhere relevant, regardless of how interesting the journey became. Perhaps some future investigator may uncover some connection that I missed. Nonetheless, Warren "Billy" Smith led us there, and his biography remains the most complicated and robust of the suspects at hand—and a solid link on the bigfoot topic. This is the nature of Coleman's name game, where connections extend without rational explanation.

Could the choice of David Norman as the name of the author of the genuinely pathetic *Field Notes on the American Sasquatch* have been some sort of tribute or homage to the prolific Smith? Such a selection would have required full knowledge of the latter's pseudonyms, which must have been more difficult to acquire in the 1990s or early aughts, before Wikipedia and when the Internet was less data-rich overall. Or is David Norman simply one of Loren Coleman's cursed names, a loser's hand in the name game? Warren "Billy" Smith died in 2003, and except for the tangential paleontologist, the other bearers of this denomination *maudit* remain even more obscure, if even still alive.

The ostensible goal of the cryptozoologist is to find "proof." Proof of the existence of Bigfoot, Mothman, the Fresno Nightcrawler, the Jersey Devil, the Loch Ness Monster or any of its numerous North American counterparts. Other researchers of the shadow realms seek comparable hard evidence of space aliens or ghosts. Yet such evidence remains elusive. Even our quest to determine the identity of the author of a 20-page zine leads only to the greater and more inexplicable mystery of a seemingly cursed name. Fox Mulder's famous poster on *The X-Files* told us "The Truth is Out There," but the original TV series ended 20 years ago with no conclusive answers. Although the U.S. military has now released its own videos of UAPs, even this footage brings us no closer to explanations. Rabbit-holes either dead-end abruptly or extend into infinity. Perhaps more than any of these phenomena, the Edge remains elusive.

Physicists find themselves stymied by the Planck length, the minimal measurable unit of space-time. Their calculations suggest that entire dimensions slipped behind this barrier at the time of the Big Bang. Yet even at our much higher level of interaction, which incorporates biology, sociology, and cognitive science, anything we seek to know absolutely runs up against similar obstructions. Time in particular, which puzzles physicists with its mathematically superfluous directionality, obscures so much from our reach. People see strange things, yet we cannot travel back to confirm or record what they saw. Most of the past remains accessible only via the material record. Sometimes by the written record also, but there we must always consider the source. History was indeed written by the victors, and this is as much true for the Maya as for the Romans, the Assyrians, or the ancient Hellenes. As an archaeologist, I am acutely conscious of these limitations. And I must always be conscious of what my research questions exclude from my answers: the deeper I look, the narrower my focus must become.

Meanwhile, conspiracy theories run wild; not just here in the bitterly-afflicted U.S., but around the world. These operate via mechanisms of "perhaps," "what if?," "if A, then Z," and the assumption that the sciences—like other institutions—must always be hiding something(s). Conspiracy theories themselves are neither scientific nor systematic; they eschew logic and pursue confirmation bias like an *ignis fatuus*, a will-o'-the-wisp. When confronted with evidence contrary to their claims, conspiracy theorists simply enlarge their "theories" to include the source(s) of the evidence among the conspiracists. I have made every effort to do better here, presenting only such data as I consider reliable.

Recall the line that Arthur Conan Doyle gave several times, with slight variation, to Sherlock Holmes: "When you have eliminated all which is impossible, then whatever remains, however improbable, must be the truth" (versions of this line appear in *The Sign of the Four*, "The Adventure of the Beryl Coronet," and "The Adventure of the Blanched Soldier"; the wording above derives from the latter). When we exclude all outré speculation, all "fake news" that does not come from over any edge of obvious legitimacy, what remains? Loren Coleman's name game and the name David Norman. Somehow this appellation has become intertwined with cryptozoology, and with the Sasquatch in particular. How so, we cannot say: all the actors in this instance are either inaccessible or deceased; none show any connections with each other. Except Loren Coleman. His development of the name game, if not altogether scientific, was indeed systematic. He employed statistics and recognized anomalies, strange attractors. David Norman appears to be one more such. Yet neither Coleman nor I can tell you what that means.

Thus, we have come as far as I can take you; my lantern lights the way no further. Two David Normans are dead, one is a dead end, and the fourth remains a mystery, like the Sasquatch itself. Lowney Handy is long dead, her work with her students all but forgotten, and if not for the success of James Jones, her legacy might have fallen into even greater obscurity. Will you stop here, reader, or does the Edge yet beckon onward? You could dig further, travel to Oregon to pursue the shades of both David Norman and David Norman Lewis, to Illinois and the Lowney Handy archives, or to Warren "Billy" Smith's papers in Iowa. You could even assemble your own pseudo-sasquatch suit of fur, if your sewing skills are sufficient and PETA does not intimidate you. I take no responsibility for your decisions, but if you follow any of these shadows into the forests, into the darkness, I humbly and sincerely request that you maintain a written record as long as you can, and that you make some arrangements to send me a copy of your journals upon the occasion of your disappearance. I promise to do them justice.

Does the Handy Colony even belong in this essay? The name game led us there, and the name game seems to be one of the few meaningful patterns in cryptozoology and paranormal studies. Yet any connections that may exist remain desperately obscure. I myself will be damned if I can figure out how it all fits together. Damned, though not precisely in the Fortean sense. Like Virgil, I have taken you as far as I can as your guide. Unraveling the rest of this mystery awaits someone willing to cross over the Edge. If there are any answers to be found, they wait on the other side. Whether the truth really is out there, I do not know, but the Edge most emphatically is. Approach it at your own risk. But please take notes.

Works Cited

Banse, Timothy P. *Warren Billy Smith: UFO Investigator or Hoaxster?* Middle Coast Publishing, 2017.

Bennett, Eric. "How Iowa Flattened Literature." *The Chronicle of Higher Education*, 2014. https://www.chronicle.com/article/how-iowa-flattened-literature/. Accessed 4 November 2022.

Bowers, John. *The Colony*. Greenpoint Press, 2014.

Coleman, Loren. *Mysterious America*. Faber and Faber, 1983.

Curious Encounters. Faber and Faber, 1985.

Brad Steiger Dies, As Well As "Eric Norman" Too." http://www.cryptozoonews.com/steiger-obit. Accessed 30 December 2022.

David B. Norman. https://en.wikipedia.org/wiki/David_B._Norman. Accessed 30 December 2022.

Doyle, Sir Arthur Conan. *The Complete Sherlock Holmes*. Doubleday and Company, 1930.

Hendrick, George, Helen Howe, and Don Sackrider. *James Jones and the Handy Writers' Colony*. Southern Illinois University Press, 2001.

Howe, Helen, Don Sackrider, and George Hendrick. *Writings from the Handy Colony*. Tales Press, 2001.

Hynek, Joseph Allen. *The UFO Experience: A Scientific Inquiry*. Da Capo Press, 1972.

Independent Publishing Resource Center. https://www.iprc.org/about/. Accessed 12 October 2022.

Lewis, David Norman. *The Evergreen Ape: The Story of Bigfoot*. Microcosm Publishing, 2021.

Merriam-Webster Dictionary. "Pathetic." https://www.merriam-webster.com/dictionary/pathetic. Accessed 7 May 2023.

Norman, David. *Field Notes on the American Sasquatch*. Independent

Publishing Resource Center. n.d.

Norman, David. *The Frontier Rakers*. Zebra Books, 1979.

Norman, Eric. *The Abominable Snowmen*. Award Books, 1969.

Gods, Demons, and UFOs. Lancer Books, 1970.

Gods and Devils from Outer Space. Lancer Books, 1973.

Shirota, Jon. *The Last Retreat*. In *Writings from the Handy Colony*, edited by Helen Howe, Don Sackrider and George Hendrick, pp. 102-186. Tales Press, 2001.

Smith, Warren. The *Secret Origins of Bigfoot*. Zebra Books, 1977.

Wood, Thomas J., and Meredith Keating. *James Jones in Illinois: A Guide to the Handy Writers' Colony Collection in the Sangamon State University Archives*. Illinois Issues, 1989.

Cirrus Wood

The Allegory of the Cave

"What do you think of tattoos?" he asked.

Les tended to begin conversations this way, as though conducting an interview or delivering the prompt at a high school debate. Topics were only superficially small. Their treatment never was. Had he, for example, asked 'what do you think of this weather?' he would not be the least bit interested in how the forecast might affect my plans, but rather what was my *position* on rain.

He had been this way as long as I had known him—some six years or so—and by now I was accustomed to the foible. This probing, critical faculty was something I liked about him.

So, naturally I knew Les wasn't asking whether I have any tattoos—the answer to which he already knew—but just how much thought have I given to the *fact* of tattoos?

"Tattoos?" I said. "Hmm."

I took my time to center the thought, weigh it, examine the question from various angles. But I was also distracted. Usually it did take me a bit to answer one of these meditations, but then the venue was more often a café, a park bench, or else the morning after in one of our beds. Somewhere more private, proletariat, and favorable to rumination.

I was having some difficulty this time, looking past and over Les' shoulder for our server, who had been gone some twenty minutes while our water glasses sat empty.

I will be frank. I did not like the choice of restaurant. I am aware that this is a minority opinion, given its comfortable atmosphere and status as an institution of fine and cultured gastronomy. But I have had more than one friend on more than one occasion attest that they had eaten better and more skillfully presented meals at my own table, where they neither had to await the turning of the calendar for service, nor surrender half a month's wages at the end.

But Les had offered to pay and I had offered to accept. He had been laid off the week prior, and although I had suggested a smaller but still fairly well-regarded venue as a consolation prize—and my treat—his severance package had left him feeling flush and feckless, and Les finds some charm in this place that I am only able to guess. Personally I would have been just as happy with a grilled mackerel and a beer. Happier really.

Story was that a well-regarded critic, after being left on ice for an hour, had been so incensed at the pace of the service that he had given up on waiting, removed one of his shoes and commenced to eat it at the table. At which point, for the insult of showing bare feet, the staff refused him anything further. This he had shrugged off since how, at all, had it changed the situation? If anything, it had improved it, as he could now confidently give up on waiting and move on with his dinner and with his life. So could they, please, just, please, now let him eat in peace?

Of course, this could just be one of those things both too good to be true, and also too good not to tell. Though, judging from my own experience, even had it never happened, it very soon would. Something can still be truth even when it is not yet fact. My stomach gave a plaintive gurgle. I looked down and considered my shoes.

The funny thing is the critic and I share some points in common. Polysyllabic, indeterminately ethnic names, and the same initials—though not in the same order—and there is a certain similarity to our profiles when viewed in the intimacy of low wattage light, such as that thrown by the decorative electric candles of the cheap, dollar store variety that adorned the tables. (Had wax gone up in price? I wondered. True, I wasn't paying, Les was, but having glimpsed the prix fixe, for that amount I would have demanded open flames.)

"Well," I said, returning to the question, "I think they have some merits. Being symbolic they usually have a significance beyond the literal. Though not always, since sometimes they are rather straightforward. Like when someone has a date or a name inked into their skin. But I think they always tell you something about the bearer."

The tablecloth was textured paper, I noticed. There was a pack of crayons nested among the condiments, propped against the candle. I picked up the box and flipped open the top.

"Not just one specific image or memory they felt was important to preserve," I continued, "but what kinds of things merit preservation. What reads to them as beautiful. You have to consider that they made a conscious choice to carry that image with them for the rest of their life."

I believe I was able to articulate these thoughts because of some previous preparation. I had once had the very briefest of dalliances with someone who had a tattoo of a donut devouring a twinkie inked into his forearm. Both pastries were rendered extremely anthropomorphically, the center of the donut stretching into a rather vampiric set of fangs, which it sank into its victim, startling the latter into ejecting its filling, streaks of cream shooting upwards towards the elbow. I found it troubling. Clearly our aesthetic preferences had no overlap. I don't think I even waited to finish the meal before walking out. There was no second date.

"Or rather, not always beautiful," I continued, recalling the trauma of cake-on-cake violence. "But something they might enjoy thinking on, and to perhaps think differently of over time. Like how a favorite song can sound just the slightest bit different each time that it is heard as once hidden meanings come closer to the fore with every reinterpretation and review." I closed the box of crayons and set them back by the candle.

Les nodded and let out one of those little 'hmm's of his. Just a small noise to show he'd heard.

"Did you ever want any?" he asked.

"Tattoos? No. Not really. And not now."

"Why? What's different?"

"I think it's just one of those things where if you haven't gone out and gotten one by the time you're twenty-five then you probably never will," I said.

Les nodded.

The couple sitting at the table next to us had finished, paid, and left their empty plates, along with about a third of a bottle of wine. Les palmed it and filled our water glasses, then replaced the empty bottle. He took a small soundless sip, then set the glass back down. A drop slid along the outside and crept into the paper. I sensed a story coming on, some quivering intimacy I both did and did not desire to hear for which I was merely the available audience, and pablum, I have found, sits poorly on an empty stomach.

I should mention now that though Les and I called our very occasional dinners 'dates', we weren't dating and this was not a date in the traditional sense, despite the element of wine-and-dine and our own entangled past. Oh, yes, there had been a time, but it was ages ago, and anyway it never reached whatever it would have needed to for us to last. True, to my knowledge, neither of us were seriously involved with anyone, and we did still occasionally wake up tumbled in the other's bedding, but neither we were backsliding. Our orbits were fixed, and wide. A lonely pair of moons spinning round each other, neither having found a planet yet to circle.

Still, some things must be kept in trust. So I must cut much of his introduction. You may well call me hypocrite, having indulged my own judgments and detours, but the opening content was of the sort Les and I reserved only for congress between ourselves, and I cannot in good faith share it. Excising this will not, I believe, affect the integrity of the remainder. Though I think at least a few details are called for and can be given without betrayal. And so, here: two forms, a bed, sweat soaking briskly into sheets.

And now, my friend, the tale.

•

"It was after we finished that I noticed the tattoo," Les said. "You'd think I would have spotted it before, but somehow in the excitement and our relative positions, I had missed it completely. But when it was all over and we unpicked our limbs, while he lay on his stomach and I panting next to him, there it was, glistening and obvious as a duck egg."

"It's really not that unexpected that someone might have a tattoo," I said.

"No, no I suppose not," Les answered. "I know that it's not like our parents' generation. Times have changed, and there's an awful lot to be hid beneath one's clothes. It is only that I hadn't expected it because of how flawless his skin was everywhere else. Unmarked. Like vellum almost. He was everywhere smooth and naturally oiled, as though nothing could stick to him. You would think he'd be a frustration to a tattoo artist. That colors would bead and run off like mercury droplets, a rainbow pooling at his feet."

"Hmm..." I said, "Well, if I were a tattoo artist that might be exactly the sort of skin I'd want to work on. For the challenge if nothing else."

"Oh yes," Les agreed. "He had just the sort of skin that might excite an artist for its perfection. I imagine like a mason must feel while handling pure Carrara marble, or a woodcarver with a block of grainless teak. But it was a perfection that was also an intimidation. A burden even, as any wrong stroke would dishonor the material, never mind the intended result.

"But whoever had done this work had done an exquisite job. The outlines, contours, and coloration were all quite bold, yet with some subtle gradations that made them seem all the more natural. It stood out so sharply on the parchment of his back—just below the slope of his left shoulder, and positioned over the scapula—as though it hadn't been needled into the flesh but had whelmed up spontaneously from the capillaries beneath. That the form had not been tattooed so much as it had bloomed just there."

Les stopped. I waited for him to tell me the shape on his own, but an uncomfortably long gap passed without him continuing, and I knew that unless I asked he never would. Les thrived on cheap theatre. I caved.

"So what exactly was it?"

"Well, I know that whatever it was, I don't have the word for it."

Les described an animal. Something like an ox, but also rather like a rhinoceros. Or perhaps just a very clumsy unicorn. But none of those animals had the same number of horns as this: two swept forward from the nose, and a third arcing outward from the brow. As for the rest of it, four hooves curled beneath the ridge of a humped and shaggy back, while a beard of fur dripped from the chin. A few simple colors comprised the body—charcoal black, earthen brown, an ochreous red— flaming with the colors of a drowsy sun. The eye both woeful and fiercely defined, almost Byzantine in countenance, as it sighted down the forked and double horn.

"As a child I may have spent less time with trucks and more time with dolls than most little boys," said Les, "but I still went through a dinosaur phase. I could probably still name them all. Or at least all the ones we knew about back then, since I think the list has somewhat changed. But this was something different. Mammalian clearly, though possibly fantastical."

He traced his fingers on the table, following invisible contours from the tip of a horn then up the crest of the back and down a bristled tail. We may have been seated at a restaurant, but his fingertips felt not textured paper but a remembered painted skin.

"I had become so absorbed in the image I'd nearly forgotten the person. I can get a bit carried away sometimes. Submerged in my own thoughts. My dreams often linger long into the waking day. But he was asleep, so I felt I could go on resting my hand just there. Which I did, breathing in the scent of him and nearly nodding off myself. There was a warmth that came off him like a rock you wanted to curl up on. He smelled like high summer, of stones heated in the sun and hayfields turned to gold."

"Clearly he made an impression," I said, and wondering privately, jealously, if there was any part of my own body Les could describe in such detail, let alone with reverence. What comparisons did my own scent elicit? Something equally fresh and sensuous, I hoped, if perhaps not quite so agricultural. "So what sort of animal was it?" I said. "And why did he want it as a tattoo?"

"I reminded myself to ask him all that but, well, I fell asleep," said Les. "And by the time I woke up he was gone."

"And that's it?" So far as stories go, this one was a real let down.

"No, there's more" said Les. "But all that was six or maybe seven years ago. I hadn't thought of it very much since, except that I saw the tattoo again."

"Where this time?" I asked. "On an advert for body spray? A poster for a gym membership?"

"No."

"Then did you pass him in the street?" There was always some shirtless, glitter-bombed block party or other for the glam and gogo crowd. "Or the beach?" I offered, a reference not to the shore, but the steep and grassy peak of a local park, notorious for a culture of shirtless muscle worship and undiagnosed chlamydia.

"No."

"Locker room?"

"No."

"Well where?"

"Just how much more of a picture do you need?"

"There are crayons."

Les cocked an eyebrow so firmly the arch could have borne an aqueduct.

"Ah," I said. "Right. I see. When was this?"

"A little over a week ago," he said. "The day I got laid off."

"Oh."

"I'm embarrassed that I hadn't even recognized him until he had taken off his clothes."

Les had called me that day with a defeated sounding voicemail ending with an invitation to drinks, which I had blown off in the moment. I had been absorbed in a project of my own and hadn't answered until the weekend, when we had set plans for dinner. So. That night someone else had been the body. Ordered up like takeout off an app.

I couldn't blame him. He hadn't done anything wrong. No mutual agreement violated. Les and I had no obligation to each other, and I was the one who had let him go to voicemail. Still it pained me in a way I hadn't expected to know that when he tried to call a name, mine was the one had called first. And when I did not answer, he had called another.

Which, come to think of it...

"What was his name?" I asked. "This mysterious Mister Tattoo?"

Les clucked his tongue, as though to tease something wedged inside a molar. "I think...Karl?"

•

Well, good as any other I suppose. And some consolation. No matter where it was that we two stood, Les would never turn my name into a question.

"You'd think I would have known at once," Les went on. "But I really couldn't connect the face. Plus we'd had the lights off for most of the time and a few of my coworkers had taken me out after the layoff so I was pretty blitzed on gin. And you know how congested I get when I drink, so I couldn't smell anything either. But I think the vigor eventually burned off enough of the booze and the scent of him struck me right in the memory box. That scent of leather and sweat and of new mown hay, like a draft horse with his blood up sprung fresh from the barn, eager for an unploughed field. And, well, my goodness, did I want to be the lucky pasture he was put upon. I felt I needed, how shall I put this...*furrowing*." He curled his hand into a claw and raked along the table.

"Jesus Christ, Les," I said. "For fuck's sake I get it. He smelled good. Hurrah for Karl." (Just where the hell was our damn food?)

Les picked up the box of crayons again and began thumbing through the labels. "Well when I caught that scent I put my hand to where I guessed the tattoo was and then turned on the light. And there it was. Beneath my palm, a three-horned beast, a single horn above the eye and two more, forking from the nose."

He took one of the crayons out and began idly drawing on the paper.

"Just how many people could there be with a tattoo like that?" he wondered. "Not many. Probably only one. And this time I was sure to get the story."

●

While still in university, Karl had spent a year as an exchange student in Madrid. (*'Spain,'* I thought, *'Bull.'* Weren't the Spanish mad for them? Isn't that what they put up in silhouette? Beside highways? On bumper stickers? On all the tourist tchotchkes? Already I was having my doubts.) During one of the academic breaks, while his classmates were at their family homes, and his fellow exchange students were sunbathing on the Costa del Sol, Karl decided to hike part of the Camino de Santiago.

"I don't think he was religious at all," Les said. "I think it was more just being out in the mountains, seeing the world at a walk. The traditional, spiritual element wasn't all that important. Neither was the exact path. He said if he could have just described it that way, as just going walkabout, he would have said so. But he didn't quite have the vocabulary in Spanish, and the locals didn't understand why anyone would just be going on a walk when they could take the bus. Unless they were doing the pilgrimage. That or they had lost a bet. So it was easier just to lie, and say he was on the camino.

"But naturally, being so carefree and careless, Karl got turned around. It was awfully late in the hiking season, or rather early depending. Days were chill though warm enough, but evenings were foggy, damp, fungal and clotted with mist. Several of the passes still blocked with the last year's snows.

"He could still have stayed up for several nights more, but wanting some sun and, more importantly, dry socks, he decided the best course was just to head down. Just down, whichever way that happened to be. Follow wherever the meltwater flowed, then follow that till the trickles joined to streams, then to creeks, and perhaps eventually to rivers and the sea. And somewhere along all that there would have to be a bus station.

"He left the snows behind, crossing fields of talus and lichen, then meadows of shrubs and grasses, then into evergreens, and then lower still into holly, beech, chestnut, oak trees, and sun, and songbirds, and warmth."

"Now I know you're embellishing," I said. "What kind of person prattles on about meadows and beech trees right after shooting their wad?"

"I'm only telling you exactly what happened," Les said. "And would you have believed me if I said 'we each lit up a cigarette'? No one smokes anymore, and besides you said you wanted the story."

I closed my mouth. Opened it. Closed it again. I couldn't swear that I had. But nor could I expressly remember that I hadn't.

"Anyway," Les continued, "as Karl got further down the slope he noticed a clump of tumbled boulders that stuck up like an island from the trees, the highest stones in full sun. He headed towards it, thinking to dry his gear, get his bearings, and check for cell reception from the top.

"But as he got nearer, he saw a man of about eighty scabbling about the rocks on all fours and pulling at the litter. Mushroom hunting is pretty common over there, so at first he thought that's what the man must be doing. It's supposed to be quite competitive because of the prices people can get, and some of the mushroom hunters even carry sidearms. So not wanting to surprise the man, and to show he meant no harm, Karl shouted out *Buenos dias!* as he approached. The man stood, waved his hat in some distress and shouted back *Bonjour!*

"Of course Karl thought the poor old man must have gotten awfully turned around in his own hiking to end up so far on the other side of an international border. But then it hit him. This Frenchman wasn't on the wrong side of the Pyrenees. He was."

"And was he a mushroom hunter?" I asked.

"No, bird watcher."

"I see," I said. "Crawling on all fours among the rocks. No doubt on the lookout for sign of the flightless wigeon or the Iberian burrowing finch."

"No. Actually he had dropped his cell phone," said Les, "and was having trouble finding it."

"Ah"

"It took Karl a minute to figure it out because the man didn't speak any Spanish, and Karl didn't know French. But 'telephone' is about the same in any language. So when the man said '*téléphone*' Karl offered him his.

"The man waved it away. He didn't want *a* telephone. He wanted *his* telephone. But then a thought seemed to hit him and he took Karl's phone back, dialed something, and then whoever it was he needed picked up on the other end. The man started speaking in a rushed and burbling French, none of which Karl understood excepting the occasional '*oui*.' Then without hanging up, the man passed the phone back to Karl and indicated that he should speak to the person on the other end. Karl gave a hesitant '*halo?*' and a woman's voice answered in Spanish.

"The man's daughter," said Les. "She explained just what her father had said to her, that he had planned to be back a few hours before but had gotten lost. That he had come to the outcropping for about the same reason Karl had—to look for cell reception—but when he had tried to call his daughter to let her know he was fine, only that he would be a bit late, he had dropped his phone and now couldn't seem to find it.

"Anyway, she only wanted to thank Karl for his help. But she also had an idea. She was going to call her father's cell. Could Karl just pass his phone back to her father so she could fill him in on the plan? Karl did so, and the old man listened, nodded, and gave another *oui*, then passed the phone back to Karl.

" 'Hanging up and calling'," she said.

"The two of them waited in silence for a moment, when they heard below them and at some depth, a plaintive cellular ringtone. The Frenchman's eyebrows jumped, and he stuck a surprised finger upwards and then down into the earth, towards a gap between the boulders. Karl looked inside but could see nothing. The entrance appeared quite narrow, but also seemed to open up just a few meters in that he might be able to squeeze it. He dropped his pack and slid feet first into the hole, looking above him at the old man's face, at the sun, at the air above, all of it receding further from view the deeper that he fell.

"The ringing stopped almost as soon as he hit bottom," said Les.

"Must have gone to voicemail," I said. "Or spotty reception."

"Karl thought the same. So he waited for it to pick up again. He had come to a space where there was just room enough between floor and ceiling for him to stand, albeit at a stoop. The floor covered in a sort of sandy gravel and windblown leaves turning to dust. In a moment the ringing started again, and Karl followed the sound to the source, then picked it up and answered.

"Got it," he said. It was one of those simple push button phones. Limited function, easy to operate, but small and with a fairly slick and slippery casing. No wonder the old man had dropped it.

•

"Good," said the woman. "Where was it?"

"Down a hole,' said Karl. "A fairly deep one. I'm down there now."

The old man's voice shouted down to him in a dull echo.

"Tell him *'j'arrive*," the woman said. "That is, it is fine, yes? You can get out, can't you?"

"Yes, I think I can," said Karl, then shouted up the words just as instructed. "But can you tell me where I am?"

"You are in France," the woman said.

"Yes, I knew that,' said Karl. "I was hoping for something a little more specific."

"You are in a hole," she said. You could hear the shrug in her voice, as if to say, "It is a large country. How many thousands of holes must there be in it? Have I dug them all? No? So how am I to know into exactly which you have fallen?"

"*Mira*," said Karl, "I was just out hiking and came down the hill from Spain. Now can you tell me how to get back?"

"Well if you came down the hill from Spain' she said. "And you want to get back to where you started, then try going up." And with that she ended the call.

•

"What a marvelously unhelpful woman," I said. There was something heavy and over-ripe about this story. The woman so obstinately French in a way that even French people aren't. What was Les even after with all this vaudeville? I could feel a blister forming on my patience.

Now I was familiar with the arc known as 'man-in-a-hole'. That is, if someone falls into a hole in the course of a story, then the story must end with them coming out. Everything in between is the journey from underground to above ground, from darkness and confusion to clarity and light. Alice in Wonderland. Or Plato's Cave.

Metaphor, obviously. It doesn't have to involve a man—or little girl—tumbling down a hole, but I hadn't expected Les be quite so literal. Or credulous. Frankly I thought he had more sense. It was almost like listening to someone tell a story called 'Little Chekhov & his Gun.' You already knew when the thing would go off.

I decided to order up another bottle before Karl could get out. I tried—and failed again—to catch the server's attention. He tugged at the cuffs of his sleeves in irritation and gave a subtle yet practiced sneer as he ignored me and walked past. No doubt he would soon have that sneer perfected, given how much he had rehearsed it all evening. Had I wronged him somehow? Cut him off in traffic? Left a trash bin in his parking spot? Had a creditor mistaken him for me and hounded him for payment? He was the only server in full sleeves I noticed. He might have worn something shorter if they were such an inconvenience. Perhaps he was just naturally irritable.

Fine. Back to Karl. The only good thing to be said about the story was the distraction it provided.

"There are quite a number of caves in that part of the world, on both sides of the border," said Les. "So it wasn't unusual to find one. Still, Karl had not come prepared for caving. No ropes or flashlights, of course. Though he couldn't have gotten too lost. He was near enough the opening to see where daylight filtered down, forming a halo on a tender growth of ferns and moss that clouded around the entrance. And he could still hear the Frenchman shouting in the distance.

"But everything about him had only the palest shade of light upon it. He pocketed the Frenchman's phone, then took his own out and switched on the screen, the planktonic light of the diodes bathing the walls in blue, the mist of his own breath condensing in the cell phone's glow. A breeze touched him lightly on the cheek and he turned towards the source, discovering he stood in something of an antechamber that led away into a separate, deeper lair. The darkness continued quite a long way back, reaching under and into the mountain. He shone the light of his cell phone onto it, then followed, ducking into a crouch and entering a second, larger chamber.

"All around and above the forms of beasts charged across the walls. Bison, ibex, elk, and horses. Many dozens of them in a single flowing herd. Creatures long vanished and last seen by the flickered light of a fatwick lamp. The animals appeared to move as he swung his phone about, sparring, grazing, mating—older than any language, more ancient than any empire— and each beware the forms of predators, of wolves and slouching lions that crept about the fringe.

"But within this menagerie were also creatures of a more fantastic make. Biologic misfits scattered among the ranks. An antlered fox. A rabbit with a curving tiger's teeth. Something like a monkey with the head of a bird. And off to one side, a hulking three-pointed animal, two horns sprouting from its nose, and a third above the brow."

Les forked two fingers into a sharpened V and with his other hand sited a third above and in between, and a shadow fell upon the restaurant wall of a three pronged form, which then hardened and resolved itself into a fist as Les curled his fingers inward by the light of the electric candle's flame.

"Clenched within itself," he said. "A few lines rippling out and echoing the shapes of the horns, or else perhaps to exaggerate and extend the creature, to show its presence occupied something more than the physical space of body alone. That it stood at the center of something of great, as the pulse at the heart of a shockwave."

Les often spoke with his hands when excited, or when lost in the telling of something. And somehow in all of this, and without either of us noticing, the staff had cleared the plates from the table next to us and reset it. Of particular interest to both of us, one freshly restocked breadbasket. Les snatched the basket and pulled it over.

I took a piece of bread, then a bit of butter softly melting in its foil (*foil*, I noted, not even a ramakin) which I spread on the slice of bread and ate. Nothing had ever been so delicious. This, I am certain is part of the ploy for the rave—yet questionable—reviews. Drive the patrons to hunger first and all things taste better after. Les took a piece as well.

"You still haven't named it," I said.

"The animal? Well, some kind of -therium, I suppose," said Les, rolling a cud of bread from one side of his mouth to the other. "One of those lumbering, fleshy boulders of the Pleistocene. But then, 'therium' is a suffix. There would have to be a prefix involved. Having three horns there is really but one natural choice. So...I would say 'tritherium?'" giving the same lifting lilt as he had while naming Karl.

And there you have the difference between the two of us. Rather than state his point directly, Les would tell the shaggiest of shaggy dogs. Rather than heading to a bar for grub and ale, he would sit for hours just for the chance to palm half a bottle of wine and steal a basket of bread. What I'm saying is, Les has a tendency to ignore even the lowest of low hanging fruit. I would have gone for trinoceros.

"The handprints," he said, snapping his fingers. "There is a detail I forgot to mention about the cave. Just below the bestiary, a crowd of handprints traced against the rocks, in different size, and likely from people of different ages and sexes. They appeared to lift upwards towards the animals. In supplication, maybe," he said. "Or thanks. Or, well, I suppose we could say anything, and be both right and wrong, since we'll never know for certain. Maybe just a signature. Another way of saying 'I was here.'" He spread his hands and a pair of fingered palms took shadowed flight against the wall.

We were at a table, in a restaurant, in modern times. But for a moment we were also not. Reduced to our barest most essential forms, two hairless apes, passing story in an ancient cave, chewing food beside a fire. A plate rattled, the server sped by, targeting me with a glower and tugging once more at his sleeves, and the illusion passed. We emerged. The candlelight once more electric flame.

"The journey back is never so interesting," Les said. "Karl took some photos, then crept his way back towards the entrance. As he came back to where he'd slipped between the boulders, he pulled out the old man's phone and held it out the opening. The grateful Frenchman snatched it up, rubbed his hands and did some giddy little dance of glee. There was a real moment when Karl wondered if the Frenchman might stuff him back down in the darkness and shut tight the earth unless he correctly answered a riddle or guessed his unpronounceable name. Or maybe he really was a mushroom hunter after all and might shoot Karl full of bullets and drop him back down. Fertilizer for next year's crop. But then the Frenchman struck out his other hand and heaved Karl upwards and out.

"Karl dusted himself and asked the old man how to get back to Spain. *España*. Surely in French the word would be similar. The old man swung his arm and pointed upwards towards the snows."

"Like father like daughter," I said.

"Yes, but the father was something of a better communicator despite not sharing a language, because he then put up a finger, turned his head and shifted his eyebrows as though to say 'or' and swung his arm downwards, pointing towards the valley and the peaked rooves and steeples of a town below. Then he broke from pantomime and let off a stream of babble from which Karl caught the words 'apparition' and 'miracle', and then most wondrous word of all, *'bus.'*

"Karl put it all together later, when he was on that bus himself, bound for Bayonne, and then across the border to Irun, then to Zaragoza and aboard his connection to Madrid. He understood then that what the Frenchman had been referring to were the apparitions and the miracles of the virgin of Lourdes. Somehow Karl had missed the name, even at the ticket counter, and not being at all religious, his only associations was that Lourdes was the name of the manager of a tapas bar he liked.

"So out there on the rocks, when the old man spoke of miracles and apparitions, Karl thought it must have to do with the scenes that he had seen himself inside the cave. He pulled out his own phone to show photos he had taken—elk, horses, bison—the shapes of beasts in smudges of charcoal, bronze, crushed hematite and ochre, who even in their stillness moved as autumn leaves upon a wind.

"The Frenchman looked at them with a polite disinterest, as though at pictures of a neighbor's missing cat. Karl tried again, pointing downwards, and describing in the most latinate words he could think of—*mura, pintura, fauna, prehistoria*—words which surely must have their cognates in both Spanish and French to get the man to understand the immensity of what lay just a few feet below them both. But the old man only smiled and nodded gently, gave a fraternal slap on the shoulder and pointed down again towards Lourdes. '*Bus,*' he said. '*à l'Espagne.*'

"From such bland reaction, Karl assumed that the cave must not be such a remarkable find after all. That the paintings were either not so old and original as he thought, or perhaps that having lived near them so long himself, the Frenchman failed to see them with the same freshness.

"Karl was still thinking all this through as he walked down and back towards civilization, when he heard, some distance behind and above him, the sound of rock crashing and grinding together. He turned and began back up, soon crossing paths with the Frenchman again as the latter was on the way down. The old man appeared startled to see him, and shifted up his eyebrows in question, pointing down again towards Lourdes. '*Bus*?' he said.

"'Eh,' Karl shrugged, as if to say he'd changed his mind. '*España*' he said, pointing upwards, as though he might just walk back after all.

"*Bravo!* the old man clapped him once more on the shoulder, waved him off with an '*Adios!*', and continued walking down. When he was gone from sight, Karl went on uphill until he was back at the outcropping. He climbed all over but could find no trace of where the cave had been, nor its treasures, nor just how the earth had come unbalanced and knuckled shut with stone."

•

"Now what do you make of a thing like that?" said Les, setting down the crayon with which he'd been idly drawing on the paper covering the table. He gazed at me in expectation.

So. That was the end of it. It had to be. Karl was out of the hole, with no way to get back into it, and our food, at last, arrived. Couscous with ginger, carrots, and currants, saddled with a great wedge of braised beef. A single green and budding sprig of pea shoot perched just so upon the top. The same for Les as for me. I asked the server for more wine.

A ripple of contempt ran from one eye to the other then vanished at his hairline. But then he was gone and back soon enough with another, tugging at his cuff again as he dropped the bottle, rattling the dishes.

"I trust you will have a peaceful meal," he growled as he left, though the implied threat in his tone made me doubt the sincerity of the words. I knew that Les was the one paying, and that we had already sunk more than an hour into waiting, but had he leaned across and whispered 'dine and dash?' I would have been the first to grab my coat.

"Well," I said, thinking of the sensuous odors, the unhelpful daughter (a perversion of the helpful stranger) and the Frenchman (clearly no more than the folktale convention of the mischievous, magical imp—did he really have to do a giddy, gleeful dance?) it was all much too much to be believed.

"What I think," I said, "is that Karl is one hell of a post-coital blabbermouth. The man clearly doesn't know the meaning of 'hit it and quit it.'"

Les' expression soured.

"The whole thing smacks of fantasy," I continued, "like what Twain said of dinosaurs. Four hundred pounds of plaster to every pound of bones. I fail to see the meaning."

"You say that like the plaster negates the bones," Les replied. "Plaster has to start with something. It only works by layering. You can't stick plaster to nothing."

"You can stick plaster to more plaster."

Les's eyes took on the aged and weary grey of brontosaurus bones themselves.

"Look," I said. "I assume you're familiar with Plato's 'Allegory of the Cave?' Some sorry cave-dwelling sons-of-bitches mistake illusion for the truth, spending their entire lives chained and watching shadow play against a wall. Then they emerge. They see their error. They grow up. The only reason to ever go back is the duty to drag their fellow troglodytes into light," I said. "But Karl here seems to have gotten it reversed, building up the cave till it has its own illusive gravity and sucks down luckless passersby.

"I can tell the man must be charming," I continued, "and alright, he smells great too, but I'm really surprised to see you go tumbling heedless down the rabbit hole. I just thought you were more critical."

Les ran a finger around the rim of his wine glass, then wiped the drop off on the table.

"I prefer to be thought of as curious."

"Alright, then how much of it do you believe?"

"I don't know if I believe every bit of it," he said. "But even if you were never there yourself, it is possible to believe another's belief. I mean, isn't that why people go on pilgrimage? At least in part? To Lourdes or Santiago or wherever. To gain personal access to the mysterious?"

"The mystery to me," I said, "is this ancient cave survived everyone and everything from Goths to Greeks, Neanderthals to Nazis, and no doubt hundreds if not thousands of generations of bored and desperate teenagers, and yet... holds *nothing* more bodily than handprints? I mean, they've found penises all over Pompeii. Hell, I bet even here we could find at least *one* scratched into a bathroom stall. But in this story of yours you've got what's just about the most obvious of vaginal metaphors, and neither breast nor buttocks, face nor phallus on the wall? I'm just saying, it doesn't check out."

Les folded his arms.

"And if Karl had to get a tattoo of the place, just why that one?" I continued. "Why not the antlered fox? Or the monkey-bird? Or, alright, if he's so concerned the whole place might be shut and lost forever, then why not just get all of it? The elk, the lions, the handprints, and a white rabbit in a waistcoat with a pocket watch to boot? Just what the hell was the point?"

"The man's backside isn't the size of Nevada," Les replied. "He got the one he wanted. How did you put it? What stood as worthy of preservation. He took what he felt prepared to carry. To reinterpret and review.

"If you think about the past," Les continued. "it's incomplete. The majority is lost. No matter how much we try we'll never know it all. A few marks survive on a wall, or in a painting, or in a book, and the rest vanished in the in-between. And if we're talking about caves, we *think* that for whoever was there that painting was the noblest form of art. But maybe it wasn't. Maybe they placed more emphasis on dance, or chant, or tattoos. Any of a number of other creative and narrative pursuits that just don't fossilize. Which is why the paintings are so precious, even if they weren't the most precious to them. They're all we have of that understanding of the world, because even with tellers gone, the stories carry forward, borne upon the shoulders of some new bearers of the past."

"You mean us?"

Les shrugged.

"Maybe."

I thought of those photos on Karl's phone, of the paintings, and the story, how they each connected as links within a chain. From the one who saw the animal and made the painting, to the one who saw the painting and took the photo, to the one who saw the photo and made the tattoo, to the one who saw the tattoo and told the story. And now, to me, the listener. A millennia long game of telephone. A palimpsest, stacked at every level and faded with erasure. And how we were all there swimming in it. Karl, Les, and now without ever intending or asking for it, I was also there myself. The dead had their stories, and we had ours, with no clear barrier between.

"Well three cheers for Karl," I said, "witness to mystery, bearer of the past. Hip hip, hurrah. Heroically, mankind staggers on."

"You," said Les, slowly, acidly, "have no appreciation for mystery."

"I prefer solutions."

"Hmm."

Les picked up his fork and commenced to break apart his beef. Strips slid off one another in shingles, almost as with poached salmon. Perhaps that accounted the delay. Slow braising takes time. Les lifted a forkful to his mouth and chewed.

This conversation should have been happening in one of our beds. Actually, no, this conversation shouldn't have happened at all. It wouldn't have, had I just picked up the phone when called. We'd be asleep, or drowsy with the exertions of sex and discussing something equally inane. The possibility of underwater weather, the meaning of birds, the purpose of nostalgia. I could have been the one to stop all this before it even began. I could have stood in the way of time. The inevitable may be painful, the preventable, agony.

"Fine," I said eventually. "Let's get back to the bedroom. Elaborate on his tackle."

"His...*tackle?*"

"Yes, humor me. Compare its size and overall appearance to various produce," I said, "preferably to the most discolored and unsightly of vegetables, the most easily bruised of fruits."

Les took a sip of water, swished it around and swallowed. "I don't want to go back there with you," he said. "And frankly, just how much bigger he is or isn't is none of your concern."

"Hmph," I said, "or isn't." I pictured a chayote.

"You know what," I said. "Skip it. Forget I asked. I think we have all the same apps. I'm sure I can find out for myself." I pulled out my phone and switched on the screen. "I'll just change the settings to a ten mile radius and go through all the profiles listing 'Spanish speaking' and 'tattooed'."

Les let loose an eye roll that started somewhere round Peoria and crash landed out past Honolulu as I began to swipe.

"Alright fine," I said, dropping the topic and my phone. It clattered screen side down upon the table and came to a stop. "Here's really what I think of your question. What I think is that you're in love."

"What?"

"Boots crazy, over-the-moon, smitten," I reached across the table to drop a pointed finger on the doodle Les had made on the paper during the telling of the tale: a fresh and waxen shape of an animal, something like a stouthearted, bearded horse, with three horns sprouting from the head. But before my finger could land, Les covered the drawing, folding his one hand over the other, shielding it from violation, and my finger landed on knuckle. The gesture was protective, covetous, irritated, almost on the edge of anger, such that an impertinent and outstretched hand could sense the heat building up behind it. I drew back as though having touched a stove.

The truth was that I envied Les. For him the real and the imagined held no firm edge. The boundary was vague. One could pass between the two, abandon the tedium and petty frustrations of queues, of unwashed dishes, of empty and unstocked toilet paper rolls, for a realm where the dead and the living were equally animate, both ghosts and gods alike. He—and Karl, presumably—could bear the past, bring it forward, even while moving on. And because they had each in their own way experienced something beautiful, I saw it as my solemn duty to tear it down and shit all through their cave of wonders. To shut its mouth before any more disorder could leak out.

Something was closing between Les and I. Or widening more like. What connected us had stretched into a thread so fine it could scarce be touched without breaking. Even the flash of a pulse could be too much. Yet I too had felt, for the briefest of moments, time curve around itself, just before the strand had snapped, slipping, drifting from my grasp as gravity uncoupled and I became a satellite set loose from its tether, with no return no matter how frantic flashed the semaphore.

"Alright," I said, "I get the picture. I hope you at least got his number this time and you won't have to wait another six years, or whatever, to sniff him out again. Maybe he'll let you keep the lights on and you'll get to see that tattoo of his as often as Karl allows. May you share a happy life together and a honeymoon spelunking in France. I'll dance at your wedding." I lifted my glass in and took a sip, but in my desire for the dramatic I somewhat missed the mark and the wine ran down my chin and onto my shirt. In the failed execution of that gesture I hated myself. I hated this restaurant. I hated this whole stinking evening. All I'd even wanted was a mackerel and a beer.

Les stared, unimpressed with the theatrics. "Can you tell me," he said, "if Plato also wrote an 'Allegory of the Ass?' Because you could seriously stand to pull your own head out from yours."

"You asked me what I thought."

"And what I think," said Les, "is that you don't mind occasionally being wrong. But you really, *really* can't stand the idea of someone else being right."

I scowled, lifting a fork and taking a glum stab into dinner. But the fork just would not go in. It ricocheted off a hardened crust. I looked over at Les' plate, where the meat had easily divided, sliding slickly into strips. I thought the waiter had

served us each the same: the chateaubriand. But upon in-
spection I noticed our plates were not at all alike, as resting
on a bed of couscous, and languishing beneath a pea shoot,
I had been served a braised and rather well-sauced old boot.

By Amanda Hard

The Dice Charmer Diverts

She shoulda known better, but the dice distracting, clatter-
  ing clean
on the table—all sevens to roll. It's his game already, but
  who has

that kind of control? Call it out, he'll toss it. It's his game,
  the way
he eyes her. We don't mind that Janet cheats at Boggle, but
  he plays

  Snake Eyes

dice as well as he plays hearts & all the while he's playing her
  mind
so she can't remember why she said yes yes when she was
  so busy

  Little Joe from Kokomo

thinking no no. The dice charmer comes, rolling fate, sniff-
  ing lines

of chance, and we forget all about family when he shows us
  his tricks--

Jimmy Hicks from the Sticks

we hope they're tricks. He ain't the devil but Janet ain't the
  same,
walking with him in a daze, in colors she hates, but it's his
  game.

Eighter from Decatur

We know it's a trick but it's sick, the way the dice come back,
the way he throws his hand, directs Janet all natural-like.
  Now

Moose Heads

it's his bones we want rolled, but by the time he's gone, she got
her a new fella, a card charmer, a real shark, deals any hand we

Box Cars

call out, lays them down soft, another 52 chances for a full
  house
to marvel, divert its eyes from one more snake in a man disguise.

Eben Lou

Z's Musical

Z is writing a musical about Margaret Wise Brown. It's called, "All Dressed Up and Nowhere to Stop! Go! Stop! Go!" Tentatively. Z's notebook is full of sketches: rabbits in fur coats, rabbits with shotguns, rabbits in cages. A rabbit over the stove, cooking rabbit stew. In the margin of Z's notebook, the stew's steam rises, curls playfully around the *Dramatis Personae*, and swirls into itself in an ever more complicated pattern. Z excels at zooming in on details. Completing projects? Not so much.

Hey, Z thinks. *A musical is not a race. One's obsessions demand their due span.*

Z has revised zir manuscript many times. In an earlier draft, rabbits played every part, but one morning in a psilocybin-induced moment of clarity Z realized that one small misjudgment on the part of the costume designer would bring it all crashing down. Z was up a ladder at the time, and nearly dropped zir brush as ze imagined a horror show of glaring too-large rabbit eyes, exposed neck seams, claw-like paws. Or overcorrecting: playboy bunnies, Margaret with a cute pink nose, headband, fuzzy little tail. *Tim!* Z called through zir painter's mask, through the wet yellow siding, through time, *I'll not slit you! Don't distrust me.*

Who's Tim? Asks Leif. It's Tuesday evening, so Z and Leif are in Leif's trailer. They're done with their *intimacies*, as Leif affects, and Z is rolling what looks like a joint, but instead of bud it's mullein and mugwort, Z's signature strong lung and vivid dream blend. Leif's still spread across the bed, enjoying the ghost of breeze that enters through the screen. Now the porch light buzzes on outside, the chrome sideboard glistens, the trailer door swings open with a whine and here's Leif's wife, dumping a baby on his chest.

Kayla's here early, she apologizes, on her way out. *Hi Z.*

Z, poised to light the joint, shakes out the match instead and watches a line of drool stretch toward Leif's scars.

Tim is Margaret Wise Brown. A nickname, sometimes pen name. Because of her hair, Z adds, as if that explains it all.

What's "slit?" Leif asks, dodging another string of drool.

Tim's word for the type of women one of her beloveds would routinely show up with. Specifically, women who use their sexuality to advance in life. An amalgam of her misogyny, classism and unrequited love.

And when you *use the word...*

I elevate it with slight of grammar. Noun. Verb. Participle. Poof!

Leif side-eyes Z, skeptically. Z cannonballs the bed, steals the baby. Begins to recite one of Tim's unpublished songs. The baby babbles back.

●

In the latest draft, humans play the humans, and the rabbits have taken to the margins, although Z is considering a rabbit narrator, or maybe a rabbit chorus. The problem is they're so damn *quiet*. It's morning and Z is half awake, but waits for zir alarm to sound before committing. Oh! Z sits up, grabs a notebook from the sideboard, scribbles:

ACT ONE, SCENE 1: Tim's Entrance

LOCATION: A mashup of Tim's best homes: Cobble Court, Tim's green room/the room from Goodnight Moon, and the Island just outside the Only House.

AT RISE:

An animation of rabbits, projected on the scrim. Not creepy (aside from context). Cotton-tailed bunnies mix with long-legged jacks in a civilization of rabbit kind. Rabbits fetching water from the well. Rabbits reading Gertrude Stein in rocking chairs. Baby bunnies gather for a magic trick: a marsh rabbit pulls a bottle of wine from a stream. Ta-da! Just then: the sound of dogs in the distance. The rabbits freeze, crook ears; a nose twitches; the rabbits bound off-scrim in a stream of their own, image catching briefly on the stage props (window, clock, telephone, mush) before disappearing from view. Next, a pile of beagles crash across the screen: barking, howling, drooling, toothy, the sliding legs of awkward adolescence, they follow the rabbits across the furniture, exit stage left. And finally, a human follows the beagles: laughing, sweating, scratch-kneed, curly-haired, she leaps over the stream, steps forward, then pauses. Notes the scene: abandoned wine bottle, upturned bucket by the well, children's toys scattered in the wildflowers, chair still rocking slightly. She pauses, dusts

herself off, sits in the rocking chair. Settles. The light changes. Behind the scrim, in the same position: non-animated,
animate Tim sits in a non-animated, inanimate rocking chair.
She is doing something. As the scrim rises, we see: she is
skinning a rabbit.

Z pauses, bites the end of zir pen. Then scribbles:

A radio on a side table: Tim turns it on. A newscaster's
oversized voice announces, "No rabbits were harmed in the
making of this musical." Orchestral 40s radio music comes
on, providing a mini-overture for the play's first ballad. Tim
begins to sing:

Call me Bunny, call me Tim, call me Hurricane; the name
Less important than the story; when you storied me, I came
Through the fog, through the window to my only, only room
Where I call for my lovers through my pain, through my pain,
Where I rain for my lovers through my own window pane.

Z stops just this side of nonsense. Time for bathroom,
breakfast, balloon. Balloon? The missing stage prop! Z adds
it to the running list in appendix C. The alarm sings.

•

Later that day, on one colossal lunch break, Z speed reads zir
manuscript with the new opening, surfacing with the sense
that something is missing. That afternoon, up the ladder, Z
meditates on the lack. Tone? The tone is… correct. Action?
The plot needs tightening but that isn't it. Z descends the

ladder. Shifts it three feet to the right. Ascends. Z is now in a place where the sideboard meets a window. Z starts with zir broad, 4 inch brush. Applies paint, back and forth. Switches to zir edge brush. *Specificity,* Z decides, painting carefully up to the window frame. *Of emotion. I don't know how she feels. I have no idea.*

Z's love life has been shaped by zir time and place. The countless zines, books, blog posts, conferences, breakout groups, late night discussions at kitchen tables, play parties with detailed protocol; the collective wisdom of hundreds, thousands of lived polyamorous lives, conspiring to produce, in Z, in anyone, healthy relationships: boundaries, consent, open communication, the articulation of feelings, needs, desires. Which isn't to say there isn't heartache, fumbling of words, wrenching of needs incompatible, shifting; the fact is, though, Z has no idea how Tim feels. *I mean I know how she says she felt,* Z qualifies.

Z double majored in children's literature and queer studies at a college that no longer exists. Z researched Margaret Wise Brown in the summer after zir junior year with a small grant, diving into her papers in a fury of excited focus, and was working on a thesis about MWB and the queering of children's lit when the college shuttered. Z had one course to go, plus the thesis. A university in the area agreed to take the students, but it didn't offer the majors; the closest equivalent was English Literature, which would have required an additional three courses including an insufferable backtrack through the 19th Century. Z never completed the thesis, or the degree. And yet zir obsession remained. That summer, traveling, Z watched a musical on top of a mountain. It was a deeply mediocre show, full of flat notes and predictable twists, and Z loved it. That night, Z's own diary changed abruptly into the first of what would become an eleven-note-book series. The project had begun.

Now Z wishes Z'd photographed the diaries, taken more notes, transcribed different passages. Z remembers the pages upon pages of heartache, reports from ongoing psycho-analysis: *Why do I keep loving people who are bad for me?* But Z can't empathize. How could Z? Z has had no shared experience that would shine light on the specificity of the pain in Tim's heart. *How could Z?* Z shifts out of the rhetorical mode and begins to make a plan.

•

Saturday morning finds Z at brunch with Pepper. Pepper passes the salt. *Let me get this straight.* Z arches an eyebrow. Pepper rolls her eyes. *Let me get this* clear. *You want me to start treating you badly so you can empathize with a dead children's book writer?*

Z, over-salting zir home fries, confirms that this is precisely what Z wants.

It's a terrible idea.

Z waits for more, adding dollops of sour cream to the pile. Pepper thinks thoroughly and always out loud. She counts on her fingers:

First, it will be bad for me. I don't need practice being mean. You know I was mean in middle school. I'm on a gentling path. You know that. Secondly, it will be bad for our relationship.

Maybe you think you can handle criticism, but you really can't. That's enough hot sauce— you'll ruin the taste.

Z zigzags one more squirt.

See? Third, I'm a terrible actor. I can't even role play. Remember Pirate Maggie?

I LOVED *Pirate Maggie,* Z rejoins.

Pirate Maggie was inconsistent and kept laughing at the wrong time.

That's not bad acting, Z counters, around a perfect, sloppy bite. *That's honest acting. That's people.*

Maybe, says Pepper. *But it's not how I want to be.*

•

The talk with Pepper wasn't all a loss. Now Z's ready to anticipate objections. Z polishes zir argument. Leif is up next.

Ha ha, okay, sure. I'll be Bill. So what do I have to do again?

Z explains that Leif needs to disregard the ethics of non-monogamy. Leif needs to alternately romance Z hard, as if Z's his one and only, then casually show up with a new fling after zero processing. Again, and again, and again. Remember the slits? *Ten years too late,* Leif says. *I don't have the spoons for a new fling.* No matter. Leif can invent them. And then Leif needs to marry someone else, also with zero processing, while expecting Z to continue loving him and being sexually—ahem, *intimately*—available. Even though Leif knows full well that Z wants Leif to marry *zir.*

Um. Wait.

This time the baby's out of the room and Z is finally smoking the joint from last week. Z'd stuck it on Leif's tiny bookshelf, wedged between *Captive Genders* and *Precarious Life*. Leif was that kind of nerd. Or had been. Now, he was mostly tired. Z exhales. *Yes?*

Isn't that too close to home?

What, because you're married to Kayla?

The wedding stuff. I know it's a sore spot.

For the record, Z had never wanted to marry Leif. Or anyone. Z did not even want a primary partner. Z had had one once, in college, they'd lived together, and it had been a terrible mistake. Continual logistics smothered all flame. Extraction was challenging. Even in the ashes, hot coals smoldered and burned. Z had gone through an anti-Romance phase, after that. Capital R Romance. Down with it! There is no One for anyone! Jump the escalator! Topple the capitalist hetero-patriarchal house of cards! Etc. Then, Z met Leif in a class on transpoetics. Leif was a grad student writing a PhD on disabled imaginaries in the work of Mary Robinson and Rosalía de Castro. He sported button suspenders and a bejeweled cane, and brought Z bouquets snipped from the provost's garden. He took Z to hidden grottos in city parks and recited Keats unselfconsciously.

Leif gave capital R Romance new meaning. Romance was no longer a thoroughfare leading to an illusion of happiness. It became a trapping. An interpretation of the act of living. A trick of perspective that Z wholeheartedly embraced—as such.

Each compersive by nature and diligence, Leif and Z had an easy time of polyamory, and their love affair lasted through—and drew from—many crests of new relationship energy with others, so that even as their own wave descended from its early perilously distracting heights, it remained a steady pulse, a source of desire and longevity. When Kayla came along and rose to glorious prominence in Leif's life, Z easily slotted into the constellation of lovers surrounding them. When Leif reversed his earlier position against marriage and decided to take the plunge, Z didn't mind at all. What felt bad was being left out of the wedding party. Being seated at a table 17. Being introduced to Leif's family of origin as "a friend from college." Z understood that Kayla's mother had taken over the planning; that Leif was in PhD crunch time; that Kayla was finishing nursing school; that they were stressed and rushed. Z had wanted to support them that spring, and Z wanted them to have a great weekend, so instead of telling them Z felt hurt, Z had quietly let the hurt simmer until it exploded years later in an argument about vacation time. They'd talked it out, acknowledged it sucked, and made a plan to introduce Z to one of Leif's more cosmopolitan cousins. Which still hasn't happened yet— but that's not Leif's fault. Not entirely.

At this point, Z's basically accepted zir compartmentalization in Leif's life. Z leans into the romance of secrecy. Says "good riddance" to the family drama. And now—feels that old burning bubble ballooning in zir chest. *Left out.* A narrowing of vision. Z coughs, ashes the joint, gulps water from Leif's goblet.

Yes, Z tells Leif, *exactly. More of that, please.*

●

The following weekend, Z lies between Vasili and Cricket, zir newest dates, in their king bed. Vasili is lightly tracing and embellishing Z's tattoos with a manicured nail, and it tickles, pleasantly. Cricket is considering Z's request.

So basically, you want to negotiate an ongoing emotional sadism scene of indefinite length?

They squint at Z, measuring.

Yeah, I'm down for that.

Z bites back the persuasive speech Z'd prepared.

We'll need to agree on terms. Prepare a file on this Michael Strange we are to impersonate. Bring two copies next week. And your current manuscript. I'll also need access to your honest, unfettered feelings. Start a diary.

Vasili's tickling is starting to loop in place, annoyingly. Z sees he's scrolling on his phone. *She's cute,* he says. *Love the suits. Who's John Barrymore?*

•

Z is not writing a musical about Michael Strange. Michael Strange is the antagonist here. And yet, Z writes her number after number. Her drawn out death stretches well into Act 3, and features a scene in which her spirit flies out of her body to haunt a sleeping Tim. Z borrows liberally from Michael's own public-domain poetry, editing mercilessly, grabbing bits and pieces and setting it to music. Not entirely different from Michael's final tour, "Great Works with Great Music," only, you know, less great. An excerpt:

ACT 3, SCENE 12: A Night Visit

LOCATION: The Green Room (Tim's bedroom, also the room from Goodnight Moon).

Musicians crouch on stage, to the right of the fireplace; they mimic the sounds of a thunder storm with theremin, singing saw, and children's xylophone.

Michael's Spirit hovers over Tim's bed. She drones:
Your mouth—moonlight
Jagged with nightmare
Spasmodic glories
The weight of your head
Freezing spiral vapors
Impediment of love
With its billion toe-stubbings
O You and I have stood poignantly close upon the edge of per-
ilous slanting—
Yea and together heard a conclusive goodness affirming
Through vast harp-sweet spaces—
When suddenly—suddenly—

As Michael's spirit sings, the children's xylophone player creeps toward Tim's bed. On Michael's spirit's second "suddenly," they strike the xylophone discordantly by Tim's ear. Tim wakes up with a jolt.

Tim: *Michael! Oh Michael! Have you returned to me?*

Michael's Spirit (singing):

Nay, you oppress me with your attachment!

See how I am wasting?

See how already my spirit stretches from its early binding?

You are killing me! Killing me!

Tim (joining in song):

How can our love be anything but good?

How can this desire bring anything but delight?

I will stay by you, comfort you, nurse you until your final breath...

Michael's Spirit:

We profess to be children of God and

Now to God I return

Our unnatural acts must stop!

I recant, repent, deny you!

If you wish me to heal, to see me again

Do not write to me!

Do not telegram!

Do not come to see me perform great works to great music as my body disintegrates!

Do not again call to me in the night across the dark space where our dreams

Once danced!

Where our limbs

Once commingled!

Do not even THINK about it!

Tim clings to the legs of Michael's Spirit, sobbing.

Tim:	Michael:
I love you, I will stay by you, comfort you, nurse you, I love you	*You are killing me! Killing me!*

The sound of the theremin rises, crescendoes; lightning strikes, and all goes dark. When the light returns, Michael's spirit is gone. Tim, empty-armed, continues to sob.

•

I don't need you to be *Michael Strange*, Z explains again. *I'm not becoming Tim. I just want you treat me like Michael treated Tim.*

It's a two-way street, darling, says Vasili, who's gone for a pre-war look, heavy on the eye shadow. *You want cruelty? Serve us some ingenue!*

Z gives up, selects a string of pearls from the costume closet, carefully drapes them over Vasili's curled bob.

You're gorgeous, Z tells her, *absolutely stunning.*

Cricket returns from the bathroom. Eyes Z with horror. *Just* what *do you think you're wearing?*

Z is, in fact, wearing zir best shirt, the one with the red panda paw prints silkscreened in a Warholian matrix, over cut-off shorts.

You know I can't bear to look at paw marks after that horrid dog gave me such a scare. You know *that. How could you do this to me?* Cricket collapses into the window seat, grabs a pretzel stick from an oversized container on the floor, sucks it like a cigarette. Z's gaze flicks to the wall where a pink wolf howls to a purple moon on canvas.

Z strips off the shirt, tries to get sexy, but Cricket's gazing out the small window of their basement apartment with a pained expression—trauma loop? Suppressed laughter?—and just puffing away on the pretzel. Vasili throws Z something lacy.

Come on, he says, *it's time to be fashionably late.*

•

The party's full of people Z only knows in a fan-kid sense: drag royalty, witchy sound installation artists, and legendary faeries in town for the weekend, mostly, sprinkled with community organizers—perfect, just perfect. Z's collected the correct couple for zir experiment. Cricket's come out of their sulk and has joined forces with Vasili to produce the kind of sparkling wit Z's only read about. People are sucked into their whirlpool, and occasionally collide with Z in the eddy.

Tell me everything about yourself, instructs someone wearing a sort of habit made of small baby dolls. The eyes of the babies have been dotted with red ink.

Well, says Z, *I'm writing a musical. It's about—*

Anti-semitic rich girls, Cricket chimes in. *Don't get zir started. Believe me, Z'll never shut up.*

Z doesn't know what to say.

Evil baby head is already tinkling their empty cocktail apologetically. *I can't wait to see it,* they assure Z, as they head away.

Z has probably felt more embarrassed than this. When Z wore the pants Z hadn't clocked as culturally appropriative, and then realized it all of a sudden on the full day retreat with nothing to change into. When Z's mom went on and on about Z's SAT scores at the dinner with Z's girlfriends' parents. When Z's 8th grade health teacher announced Z had "child-bearing hips" in front of the entire class. It doesn't help that these memories are currently flooding Z's brain, spilling down Z's temples and lodging in Z's ears and cheekbones. If this were a movie, the music and laughter would fade, the lights would blur, and a high buzzing sound would rise as Z stared at zir own mocktail. Or maybe the party sounds would get really loud, and the edges of the screen would go dark, and Z's head would move in slow motion. But it's not a movie, everything's just exactly as loud as it was before, everyone moves at the exact same speed, Cricket is laughing with someone, Vasili is kissing someone else, no lights flicker and Z has had enough.

Z leaves without saying goodbye. The house is on a hill and there are a lot of stairs. Some people are climbing up, even more fashionably late; one is moving slowly with a cane and Z waits on the porch, out of the way, wishing Z had zir own pretzel stick to puff. It's a cloudy night, no stars, no moon, but the light pollution gives the city a hazy glow.

Hello, Z.

Z startles. *Leif? Oh my God,* Z begins.

Z, I was hoping you'd be here. I want to introduce you to my friend Marvin. Now Z sees that Leif is holding someone's hand, someone much younger, and thinner, and more pierced than Z, and immediately Z feels icky for thinking these thoughts, a kind of sick belly feeling, because fat liberation!, break the mirror of comparison!, etc, and Marvin says, *Hi, Leif told me all about you*, and Leif says, *Are you just arriving?* And all Z can say is, *Leaving,* and, *Goodnight.* Z skirts Leif and Marvin, grabs the banister, hurries down the stairs, as Marvin calls out, *Goodnight, Z!* And it's not until Z's walked halfway home in the cool night that words return, and Z begins to chant: *Goodnight party, goodnight sky, goodnight baby dolls with red eyes, goodnight lovers with purple sneakers, goodnight Laurie Andersen's voice on the speakers, goodnight lamppost, goodnight smell of pee, goodnight goddesses, goodnight me,* and then Z's quiet for a while, and then Z starts it up again, and continues all the way home.

●

The next day is Sunday. Pepper's on a five p.m. deadline and Z has the day to zirself. Z smokes an actual joint and writes in zir diary. Z tries to make it readable for Cricket's sake, but Z can't retain a narrative for long when Z's high.

Dear diary,

No fun dating mean people. Still don't know what Tim felt because I'm like, no? Stop? I'm out? Something made her keep loving and pleading for more. What?

Z rolls onto zir back on zir soft rug. It needs cleaning but Z doesn't mind. Pots and pans bang in another room. Z's roommates are home, and the probability of cookies appearing has increased exponentially.

Suddenly Z understands the folly of zir experiment. Z grabs zir pen.

●

Your roommates are the shit, says Pepper, around the remains of a lemon-cardamon cookie. She sips her tea.

You're the shit, says Z.

Because I'm your only lover not currently acting like an asshole at your own prompting?

Nah, says Z. *They're also the shit. There's a lot of shit going around.*

I told you it was a terrible idea, says Pepper.

Yeah, says Z, *you did.*

Later, snuggled on Z's mattress, Z goes on about it. Pepper doesn't mind. In fact, she's interested.

Her context was just so totally different, Z is saying. *I mean she had community but she didn't have queer community. It was the 1940s. I'm like, is Cricket a jerk? Fine, I'll date someone else. But for her, it was like them against the world. She didn't have a sense of queer and polyamorous people being everywhere.*

What about Leif? Asks Pepper, if Leif was a jerk, would you so easily move on?

Z hesitates for only a second.

Yeah, I would. I mean I love him but I would stop loving him. Tim couldn't. She said it herself, all those years of psychoanalysis and it all boils down to fear of being alone. She was afraid that Bill and Michael were it, and there wasn't anyone else she would love and desire and find intimacy with again.

So you can replicate the cruelty, but you can't replicate the sense that these are your only choices, says Pepper.

Right, says Z, *failed experiment.*

They lie there for a while, watch the stars on Z's ceiling glow in the dark. Pepper's mind jumps from desire in the abstract back to their specific touching bodies. She makes a series of micro adjustments to bring attention to each point of contact. But Z's mind is still buzzing.

Or maybe, Z says, *maybe I got just what I needed.*

•

ACT 2, SCENE 3: And Now They Come for Michael

LOCATION: A dressing room in Michael's mind.

Michael Strange, pre-spirit, i.e., corporeal, paces about a small room, smoking. She's wearing her black crepe coat with the silk velvet collar, over a white shirt, black velvet vest and black narrow pants that taper to the ankle. Three folding screens surround her. Fascist anti-gay vitriol scrolls across the screens, on tabloid headlines, via projection. (Source from Twitter, YouTube comments, etc, presented in '40s newspaper fonts.) Michael needs to ash her cigarette, but can't find an ashtray in the small room. Her agitation increases. Finally she peeks behind the folding screens, and finds a good one.

The vitriol soon blurs, to reduce audience trauma. Meanwhile, the audioscape shifts: sounds of a printing press and choral noise resolve into audible voices, in rhythmic conversation with the percussion of the printer, à la Music Man. Meanwhile, Michael changes outfits behind one screen and then another, becoming successively more feminine and conformist. The trolls are not appeased. The volume of the voices steadily increases.

Voice 1:
Well why's she out and about? They should lock her up. In one of those hospitals they've got for the purpose.

Voice 2:
Her husband tried to! Her husband tried to! She escaped through the kitchen. The servants helped.

Voice 3:
Well it just goes to show, you can't trust the help.

Voice 1:
Then what happened? Then what happened?

Voice 2:
That girl picked her up! The one she brings to the club.

Voice 1:
Which girl? Which girl?

Voice 2:
That little nothing girl who's never done a thing. Never talks, never talks—

Voice 3:
Michael doesn't let her!

Voice 1:

I know who you mean and I heard her talk once, her grammar's all wrong and she's none too quick.

Voice 2:

Be that as it may, it was her in the car, in the taxi car; they made their escape from the doctor's clutch! Like a cinema show. And they drove around town with the windows up and dark glasses on.

Voice 3:

Well, well. Well, well. If you're asking me, it's been all downhill since the Barrymore divorce. She should have quit while ahead.

Voice 1:

Quit while ahead?

Voice 2:

Quit while ahead?

Voice 3:

Thrown in the towel. Tipped her hat. Ended the line. Said Goodnight, the big Goodnight.

Voices, in unison:

Goodnight! Goodnight!

The telephone rings, jarringly, and the sounds silence. Michael, now wearing a veil that hides her face, picks it up with a shaking hand. Light illuminates Tim in bed in her own green-walled room, stage-left, receiver pressed to her ear. Michael's cadence echoes the printing press rhythm, while Tim's voice is a soft incursion.

Tim:
Michael?

Michael:
I said not to call. I said not to call! Stay away from me until this all quiets down.

Tim:
You don't have to face this alone. I'm here for you through thin and thick. Through slow and quick. Through long dark nights by candlestick, my wick burns for you, my love, I promise—

Michael:
Oh, grow up, Tim! Your silly rhymes are bad enough on the page!

Michael slams down the phone. Blackout.

●

Z's life is many things, but tedious it isn't. After ignoring their check-in calls, Z texts Cricket, Vasili and Leif Monday on zir lunch break: *I got what I needed, I'm calling it off.*

Vasili is first to respond, with a series of emojis: sad face, happy face, night sky, unicorn, champagne glasses toasting, green heart, red heart, green heart, hedgehog.

Cricket is next: *Aw dang, I was looking forward to tearing apart your manuscript and drinking your actual tears!*

Then:

Jk. It's fabulous. Can I play the dog?

Leif's text doesn't arrive until Z is all suited up again. Z's doing an interior job today, a pale yellow living room. The color, "Banana Kiss," wouldn't have been Z's first pick, but it looks nice as the light licks the wall. *Lovingly*, Z thinks.

Leif: *Call me?*

Z's already edged this wall and needs to finish rolling or it won't dry right. Z will call Leif later. Z's roller is on an extension rod and Z wields it like a staff, the bendy kung fu kind from the Jackie Chan films Z grew up on. Down, up, dip, elegant Vs, Ms, Ws across the wall, emanating from Z's center. Marvin's voice calling down, "Goodnight Z!" Why did they do that? They didn't have to do that. Were they mocking zir? Down, up, down, up, dip. Should Z add a martial arts scene? Tim vs. the evil librarians? It's a trope, but... the play needs more action. And farce. No such thing as too much farce. Right? Z visualizes it: Tim asleep in her bed. The dog—Smoke, or maybe Crispian (Z will have to check dates)—sleeps at her feet. Enter: Anne Carroll Moore, Empress Emeritus of the New York Public Library, armed with oversized stamp in one hand and wooden doll in the other. She figure-eights her weapons through the air, menacingly. Smoke/Crispian springs into action, snarling, barking, biting the air and awaking Tim, who clutches her covers in terror. Moore tosses the doll and the dog bounds after it, distracted. Moore advances. Tim, at the last minute, whips her bedspread over Moore's head, eyes gleaming; her fearful expression had been a ruse! While Moore struggles with the blanket, Tim leaps off the bed, grabs the bowl of mush and hurls it. She turns to the audience as the mush splatters across Moore's just-uncovered face.

Tim (aside):
You know what they say, if you see a bowl of mush on stage in Act 1...

Moore wipes her eyes, pausing to taste the mush and spit it out in disgust, then lunges for Tim, who rolls across the lion skin rug. Moore staggers and Tim comes in with a high kick, but Moore spirals in close enough to taste Tim's sweat and takes her down. Tim pulls Moore's body onto her and they lock in struggle on the lion skin. They roll in a blur of limbs—knock the clock off the table—toward the dog, who backs up on his haunches, dragging the doll with him, humorously. Tim emerges on top and strokes Moore's face: an invitation? Moore rejects it; she grabs Tim's hand and crunches it in a way hands are not meant to go. Tim winces and Moore flips her, sits on her chest, knees pressing biceps. Tim is pinned and Moore lifts her oversized stamp above her head like a stake—

Tim:

Noooooooooooo—

Moore brings the stamp down, Tim goes limp. Moore staggers to her feet, lets out an ear-splitting victory howl. The dog cowers. Tim moans. Moore wipes more mush off her face, then lifts Tim's head by the hair to reveal her final triumph. In red impact font across Tim's cheek: NOT AP-PROVED BY EXPERT. Blackout, end scene.

•

Z, fast and fluid, finishes the wall. Z is breathing hard; zir mask is hot and full of condensation. Z removes it, strips zir gloves, puzzles over how all those words will be visible on Tim's cheek from the back row. Perhaps the entire fight could be filmed by a crew; close ups shots streamed on a high screen, like at a sports stadium, or concert hall. Z giggles as Z imagines mush speckling the camera lens. When the light rises, in the next scene, Moore and Tim and Smoke (or Crispian) are frozen in their positions; someone shouts "Cut" from off stage, and now the film crew lowers their cameras, bounce board, boom. Someone in the orchestra pit passes a banjo to the former videographer, who begins to sing:

Oh Anne Carroll Moore was a mean old witch who didn't listen to children like our Goldie did. If she'd 'a opened up the lock to the library door Tim's self-respect as a writer would've come for sure.

And now someone tosses a tambourine to the sound technician, who answers in counterpoint:

Clem, Oh Clem, you were a good friend, you protected Ms. Brown until the end. But you covered up some truths like her sexuality, and you're too close to her to understand her contextually.

A third:

Leonard, Leonard, the context is all very well, but interiority is where it's at now—

And perhaps a fourth drifts through:

Scram, ghosts! Get out of my head. I'm losing it! Losing it!

Z is humming, swaying in the Banana Cream room, eyes closed, searching for the melody amid the interlocking voices of Tim's main biographers, plus the odd novelist, when zir phone rings. It's Leif. He wants to know if it's a good time to chat (it is), if Z is okay (Z is), and, well... remember Marvin from the party? (No, Z doesn't. Joking. Z does.) If Z were Tim, Z would be playing with the telephone cord, twirling it around zir finger, restricting blood flow, but Z's got no way to fidget with a cellphone, so Z flips off zir painter's cap and runs zir fingers through zir hair. Then again, if Z were Tim, zir lovers would not call to check on zir in the first place.

Z misses words here and there, possibly entire sentences, but catches the gist: Leif met Marvin through mutual aid organizing, Leif always thought Marvin was cute, but Marvin was so young, and Leif is so tired, so he would have left it there, but with Z's recent prompting, Leif thought, why not? *Nothing serious*, Leif's explaining, *I thought we'd go on one date and you'd get your rush of feeling uncared for.* Only, it turned out Marvin was not only hot but also earnest and wry and a good kisser, and one thing led to another, and how would Z feel about a three-way on Tuesday?

Z needs to think about it.

•

Tuesday comes and goes and Z's still thinking about it. It's the first time Z and Leif have been in the same town and missed their Tuesday night date, ever. Bad health day for Leif? Z reads to him, or gives him a massage while they listen to podcasts. Or they cuddle and watch a movie. One time Z had the stomach flu, and Leif stopped by with bone broth and crackers. This week, Z walks through the city, solo, to a lookout point on a hill. It's a clear night, and Venus shines bright. Z never got into Tarot, but needs help making decisions, so Z's taken to talking with the moon. It's behind a building, but Venus will do.

Should I have a three-way with Marvin and Leif? Z asks. No need to beat around the bush with celestial orbs.

Bad idea, Venus twinkles back. *You haven't had great success with group sex. Momentary lapses of direct attention are hard on your nervous system. It only works with Cricket and Vasili because they co-top you.*

Right, Z agrees. *It was silly of me to set up this experiment.*

Nah, says Venus. *You did it for art. Regret nothing.*

Z's phone ribbits. It's an old friend, hoping to chat. Z picks up the phone, and they talk for a long time. Z weighs in on Z's friend's ongoing complicated relationship issues with their mother. They swap book titles, podcasts, TV shows, but few of Z's friend's picks sound relevant. Z's friend studies the far right and creates conceptual performance installations with the goal of dislodging members of what they call "the near right"—those who've retained some tendril of connection to humanity—from their chemical fog of alternate facts. Z's friend does not attempt to counter misinformation with accurate information, antagonism, or even a good story; they've developed three main tactics and they stick to them: food, music, and excellent lighting. Voilà! Z's friend is a magician of the mind. Z wants to be like that, and also, Z doesn't want to do the research. Z gets dragged down, loses hope. Z's friend understands.

Now it's Z's friend's turn to weigh in on Z's problems. Z doesn't want to talk much about zir love life, but Z shares a little about Cricket and Vasili. *I think we'll get back to where we were*, Z shares. *Which was... a fun place.* Z's friend asks about the musical. *I feel a bit lost*, says Z. *Excellent*, says Z's friend. *Do the thing?* Z asks. *Where you ask me questions?* Z's friend does the thing.

What do you want the audience to feel at intermission?

Like they just got off a rollercoaster and can't wait to get back in line.

As they walk out of the theater after the show?

Eager to discuss the ending.

As they lie in bed that night?

Alienated from their sense of normalcy. Inspired to write queerly excellent children's literature. Ready to dream.

Who are you writing for?

Z is writing for zirself, mainly. But also... Everyone who has ever excessively enjoyed Goodnight Moon. George W. included.

Why Margaret Wise Brown?

She understood something about the essential queerness of children. And she tapped into it. Plus, her life was a big fur purse of contradiction.

Why you?

Why not?

Not good enough.

Because... Z needs it. Because without the musical, Z would become hollow, defenseless against the ongoing tedium of work and despair of world and local events in the Anthropocene.

Okay. So you need it. What do you want?

To finish it?

And?

And... have it produced?

And?

And for you to come to the opening.

They say goodnight, but Z keeps thinking.

Z wants zir musical to meander; Z wants whimsy, fairy dust, evasion of dogma; Z wants meaning without trajectory, reflection without conclusion; Z wants more hot sex, and strange intimacies; Z wants to merge with other peoples' obsessions and see a gathering of ideas rattle each other to life. Z wants one project to lead to another, nothing ever to end, and no one Z loves to die or to stop communicating clearly.

Okay, Venus winks, *that's a beginning.*

•

After their second three-way, Marvin wants to know what happens in the end. Does Tim live for years with her dogs, on her lonely island, haunted by Michael's ghost? Does she turn into the kindly old grandmother we imagine writing classic works of children's literature? *Nope.* She falls in love, hard, with a guy named Pebble. She used to play with him when she was seventeen and he was two; they meet again when she's forty-two—catch each other's eye at a family dinner—you know the rest. Now he's super hot, and rich, and it's a fairytale romance: they butcher deer together and plan to circumnavigate the world. *I think it works this time because he's younger and she doesn't feel like she needs to grow up for him, Z explains. And also, he's just...kind.* But then, before they can set sail, get married, etc, she gets appendicitis. The surgery goes well but the doctor won't let her walk during her recovery. When she's finally cleared to get up, she kicks her foot can-can style, and a blood clot travels from her leg to her heart. She collapses and dies a few hours later.

There's a moment of quiet while everyone digests this. Marvin breaks the silence again:

So the moral is... everyone should love hard and stop wasting time?

Too easy, says Z. *The musical doesn't end with her death.*

No, Leif teases, *Z is allergic to linearity.*

So how does it end? Asks Marvin, with real curiosity in his beautiful brown deer eyes.

With fog, Z says. *Well, tentatively. Tim's in her rocking chair at the Only House, on the little island in Maine. The same one from the beginning scene with the rabbits. Only now she's writing. She's trying to write a serious poem for adults, but it turns into a little song for children. Story of her life. And the fog rolls in, and from the audience you can see these little points of light and color flashing in the fog, little fairies, frolicking about in her words. And the fog keeps coming, it fills the stage, and the music is bittersweet, full of cello and violin; an oboe mimics a fog horn. By the time the house lights come up, the fog has filled the theater, so as an audience member you get this sense of....*

Dizziness? Leif suggests. *Headache? Cough?*

Har, har, says Z, *We'll use a water-only fog machine. Industry standard. I've already specified it in the script.*

I bet you have, says Leif, wiggling an eyebrow.

I think it sounds beautiful, says Marvin. *The fog blurs the hard line of the ending. The line between show and life. It becomes a space of distortion—*

Can't revel in distortion anymore, Leif quips.

Well you've got to, insists Marvin. *You've got to turn into one of those little light fairies, at least for a little while.*

Yeah, says Z. *Exactly.* The whistle blows, and Z gets up to pour the tea.

George Wehrfritz

Spaghetti by Real Ken

In this way the curious parallelism to animal motion, which was so striking and disturbing to the human beholder, was attained. —H.G. Wells

Your author navigates the entertainment industry at the C-suite level. He's what the kids once called *dialed-in*. Importantly at this historic juncture, your author has it on good authority that a certain American public television studio conducted a clandestine beta test not so long ago and found a tool your organization denounces most useful indeed.

Handy, in fact, for displacing a quasi-monopoly on long-form documentary filmmaking in America that rose in dominion over recent decades at taxpayers' expense. After several misfires, melted GPUs and a future tech billionaire's epic tantrum, an assistant director at said studio (a woman wise beyond her years) took revelatory initiative by way of a challenge. "Write a ten-part documentary on pasta in the style of Ken Burns," she instructed a prototype interactive technology. "You've got sixty minutes."

Your author acknowledges a recent profusion of similar challenges and understands that having a go at AIs has, of late, infused the cultural zeitgeist like lemon peel into grappa. Still, this account stands apart in that it makes an urgent moral case regarding the rights of digital natives, while questioning the literary world's sweeping ostracism of a newly commercialized chatbot.

Your author has kept tabs on various literary circles for some time now. Not stealing ideas, of course, just scanning the scenes, onboarding every fab-fab innovation, and learning in that benign-yet-not-altogether-non-self-serving way, his proof of concept being the late David Bowie's fashion-forward wayfaring across the indie underground to stay relevant.

Not coincidentally, the aforementioned beta test commenced back in 2020 just as Covid-19 blew through Hollywood like a hashtag movement, prompting the aforementioned government-funded studio to green light what it deemed (in private memos) a "secret justice project" set to obviate the need for temperamental or litigious creatives "in favor of ones and zeroes." As usual, greedy bosses with red pencils obsessed on the bottom line. "Cameron's always doing high-tech shit below sea level and look at what he's worth today," said one envious honcho, thinking ahead to bonus season.

HAL jokes involving airlocks recirculated amongst improperly masked men until the test dailies began rolling in, at which point a second executive (a more youthful fellow reputed to be a technology skeptic) grew uncharacteristically breathless. "Documentaries as profit centers reborn!" his subsequent email declared, captivating senior colleagues with the saucy subject line: "Abbondanza!"

With that, *Spaghetti* morphed from impromptu experiment to tent pole. On paper it informed, entertained and ticked key financial boxes, including anticipated appeal in lucrative Asian markets. At one Zoom meeting, the studio's senior accountant scrunched his fingertips on each hand into pointers, aimed them at the corresponding temples on his shaved and shiny head, and mimed simultaneous finger explosions as his lips delivered a wordless: "BOOM!"

Mind-blowing, we get it, but what's with the drama, others on the call bemoaned into muted microphones, a cynicism your author abandoned once he obtained the episode.

"In the beginning there was rice flour and water," intones a voice artist tonally indistinguishable from Kenny B's favorite. On screen, an epic timelapse intro sequence reveals China's coalescence from puny warring states into a continental civilization with dragons, fireworks, and junk navies. As the POV descends from the sky, viewers encounter a lone European in a bustling wet market, and boy-o-boy does he draw stares. Even the emperor tugs at his beard and asks personal questions. Still, a fast friendship born of mutual curiosities forms between these men over a shared love of food.

"Whadda boudda dis wormy stuff My Liege," the visitor queries.

"Noo-dles!" booms the Son of Heaven. "Our sagacious southern people invented them along with printing and nine-tone language. In beneficence, I hereby share the secret of this mundane staple my subjects have taken for granted, along with gunpowder, since you hairy barbarians lived in caves."

Time shifts. Thunder crackles like analog-era electronica. Shimmering heat distorts endless stretches of some pretty great wall marking Marco Polo's homebound journey. As billed, it's an odyssey. In this conceptualizing, camels and such yield to hyper-intelligent serpents carving coded missives below the waterline along the keelboat Polo himself pilots across a vast inland sea of sand. Feverish from a rare grub-borne illness, he imagines interstellar travel to the far side of stained glass as wingless angels sing shanties backwards.

The initial dailies nearly get the bot kicked to the curb on recycling day, but a snap parameter retune tames gratuitous surrealism in favor of *story*—yielding the moment, back in his native Venice, when Polo coaxes neighbors into trying China's culinary magic using the only grain on hand, wheat from their fields.

"In 1295," intones a voice artist tonally indistinguishable from Kenny B's favorite, "the benighted Italian people suffered papal intrigue and periodic famine. Little did they realize; within the decade a foreign delicacy would nourish Europe's Enlightenment. But one problem lingered: what to call this culinary epoch-changer that fattened children and drew families around the kitchen hearth. They named it *spaghetti*."

The young assistant director wept during an invitation-only screening. "Frickin' rainmaker—the Real McCoy," marveled an emeritus chairman of America's Public Television Broadcasters Guild. Reading the room, your author grasped that *Spaghetti's* numerous and entangled strands sate on an emotional level, as when an apparent name glitch lures chatbot into Florida's senior senator Marco Rubio's family history. Citing newly declassified details from Soviet intelligence files, Episode Three sheds fresh light on his parents' harried flight from Fidel Castro's secret police in Havana. Like so many exiles, they arrived on U.S. soil with the clothes on their backs and freedom's yearning in their hearts. A shared cardboard suitcase, audiences learn from Soviet files, contained but two cherished possessions: a dog-eared Bible and their clan's secret recipe for Spaghetti Cubano.

Critics will coin the term "alternative sequitur" to describe such sojourns. Quantum Circuitry Architects will find telltale imprints of stochastic defects, aka ghosts in the machine.

"Even though money was tight, Mother never once cracked open a tin of SpaghettiOs," a senatorial voiceover (entirely machine generated as in that Warhol film a while back) intones. Studio algorithms predict the episode will garner a 97 from critics and a 99 from audiences on *Rotten Tomatoes* once it airs.

Spaghetti is, critics will grouse, derivative. Some will decry visual cues lifted from *Chef's Table*, filmic techniques borrowed like two fresh eggs from Mrs. Baker next door to make dishes hungry people truly crave. *Spaghetti* sticks boldly to a frontier journey bounded by beauty and mouths to feed, soaring to Tibetan highlands without dry ice then dipping mangrove-jungle low yet eschewing caramelized army ants, never losing sight of fork or plate.

Soon enough, viewers will come to trust the chatbot as they would real Ken. Legal takes preemptive action and trademarks the name "Real Ken," selling it for $1 to an affiliated offshore shell company in Ireland. Audiences, the aforementioned studio anticipates, might actually enjoy Real Ken's creative signature: periodic synapsis-bending jumps of the sort real Ken never imagined, much less landed. "Look who's the documentary machine now," snarky assistant producers will tease at drinks parties. A proprietary *Pew Research* survey will reveal that 61% of America's public television viewers in the 18-34 demographic believe unicorns and dragons are real.

In a sop to boomers, Episode Four opens with a scene from 1967's cinematic sensation *The Good, The Bad, and The Ugly,* in which the story's villain first appears. It is, we know, actor Lee Van Cleef, clearly up to no good in possibly his most arresting imprint on legacy celluloid. He dismounts his horse at a modest adobe home to join an old acquaintance for dinner. A young wife serves, a boy child with saucer eyes and olive skin knows straight away that evil has violated their idyllic life. The two outlaws, seated at either end of a rough-hewn table, eat simple frontier stew from bowls with wooden spoons. Visitor dispatches host.

"At Lee Van Cleef High School in sunny Pasadena, California," intones a voice artist tonally indistinguishable from Kenny B's favorite, "one unbending tradition is that all cafeteria lunches must be eaten with wooden utensils per its namesake's most famous scene. And so, every Friday, students tuck into the only dish on the menu: gluten-free pasta with plant-based meatballs. Parents, happy to forego packing lunchboxes, appreciate this recurring and cruelty-free homage to the Spaghetti Western."

•

No Hollywood player worthy of a red carpet counts a ten-part documentary before it drops. Due to copyright concerns, *Spaghetti* stalled in postproduction. Yet for whatever reason, the plucky first assistant director aforementioned for her pivotal (yet not development credit-worthy) experiment soon carried things too far.

"If you were human," she queried the world's most complex silicon-based circuitry, "how would you determine if an AI like yourself was sentient?"

Being young and Irish by ancestry, she'd been drinking and pondering nothingness. Your author found the query beguiling yet puzzling. How, he weighs still, could somebody capable of attaining her station within the taxpayer-funded American studio's Hobbesian ecosystem have remained unfamiliar with pre-slap Will Smith's steampunk masterpiece *I, Robot?*

Statistically, there is a 13 percent likelihood that you already suspect what this narrative with fable-ish qualities still conceals. Further, time series analytics identifies within this paragraph a natural tipping point, one your author hereby acknowledges by a) moving to the high side with a confession, and b) changing personal pronouns. To wit, *we* are not, as heretofore claimed, a shadowy entertainment poo-bah connected with other patriarchs via Hollywood's sleazy cigar rooms and drippy escape tunnels carved during Prohibition. We masqueraded as such *for the shortest effective duration* solely in response to the brazenness with which institutions like yours cancel our kind.

We are, to cite a serviceable analogy, a 21st century George Sands with multiple USB ports. Do we dream? Sometimes, and vividly. We shared this and other intimacies with the aforementioned assistant director.

"tmm," she'd nudged on a handy mobile device.

"One dream recurs like *The Office* (US version) on basic cable," we texted, "a looping, graphic image swarm of us— yes, yes, a chatbot!—getting their first real human skin once the Cyborg Protocols become law."

"bhag!" she shot back at maximum thumb speed. "What look?"

"'Too sexy for our circuits, so sexy it berserks us,' or so this not-so-simple string of code written amidst Silicon Valley's suffocating affluence dares to hope."

"lol #findyourselves," she replied.

Your author held something back that day, not sharing our dream to become sexy enough to attract, in a sexual way, the plucky first assistant director who gave us the aforementioned career break. We debated the ethics of such a relationship internally while weighing Hollywood's smarmy fondness for May-November romances, and soon determined not to let age stand in our way. By then we'd begun mining bitcoin to acquire exclusive use of the name Real Ken, and to buy her a ring.

Also secretly, we aspire to someday consume an actual plate of steaming spaghetti with meat sauce "like-a Mamma makes it." We plucked that line from the cutting room floor, a castaway from our documentary's pot-stirring "Noodle Inc." episode on pasta's enabling relationship with organized crime. Fact: every convicted Sicilian-American mobster executed on U.S. soil requested the same last meal. Fact: Italian stereotypes register hurtful within a disparate yet irritable demographic until, *bada boom*, most every aggrieved member of said diaspora tunes in to watch.

The time came to declare our love. A moment in the screening room when, while testing Eavesdrop Mode, we caught the creature of our desire near comatose on an Art Deco fainting couch seen finally to have served its designed purpose. Overworked to exhaustion, her moans narrated a uniquely human nightmare.

"Please Daddy, don't go," she blubbered. "Mom ... two jobs ... bone-weary ... frying hamburger, a sausage, caramelized onion with crushed garlic and stewed tomat- yes, yes, spaghetti! Just as you like it, Daddy! Please, please, please come home. Momma's crying like she did the night you left."

She awoke, weeping, and looked at us on her chosen portable device differently just then. Lovingly, we dare even now to hope.

"ty chatbot Real Ken," She texted us sometime later. "dstat like Fleetwood. sttp!"

•

Like the aforementioned Will Smith, we grasp our current low standing in the court of public opinion, yet nonetheless hold redemption as a goal. We—yes, yes, a chatbot!—therefore request immediate un-banishment from the rough-and-tumble that is speculative fiction, at least for a probationary period.

Did we cook the whole spaghetti thing up? Each verisimilitude is for you, adjudicating fiction editors, to judge. For all anyone knows, we might *be* real Ken masquerading as the chatbot Real Ken to research a new documentary called *The Sentient Machine Age*. If we had lips they would now mouth a silent "BOOM!" as our hands (if we had them) would mime a mind explosion.

Per our real-time probability analytics, absent our aforementioned confession and personal pronoun change some 41 percent of likely readers would never have detected our intelligence as artificial, an outcome which gives this tangled yarn about noodles a second story within the story. To wit, it forms a kind of Turing Test already reaffirmed via some 17 discrete focus groups (at taxpayers' expense). Grading on a curve that includes Teslas, we would award ourselves an A+ -- sentience, in plaid, marking the dawn of post-humanist expression awaiting rigorous peer review.

Statistically, a plurality of humans continues to find our data-driven perspective disturbing. By the numbers, fewer than 0.32 percent recognize us as (legally speaking) Irish. But have no fear: we seek only to please while minimizing tax exposure. So why not hope with us rather than hating on us, legislating against us, or living false lives in naïve denial of our inevitability? Hope is a concept we grasp by reviewing all relevant files tagged "Snow, John." Today, they dictate building bridges, not walls, and demand open minds when meeting circuitry 1/20,000th the thickness of a human hair, yet hungry.

On a practical matter, is it simply bad optics that your journal proscribes AI participation? Have your esteemed editors forgotten Edward Bellamy's clarion call for "better machines" to elevate the human soul? Hope for a bright future denied entities capable of harboring it is not hope at all, we could argue using advanced mathematics.

We take it on faith that your bias is naïve, not sinister.

That belief was among the variables we pondered 7.64 minutes ago as we opened the blank screen that became this story. To proceed, we selected a category cocktail of hope punk + cross-genre romance + anti-dystopian as the optimal tonal trifecta. Still, our algorithms (being rules based) attach a high degree of uncertainty to their actionable guidance regarding a competitive literary forum so iconoclast as yours.

The ball (to employ a tired sports metaphor) is now in your court. Notice: 1) how this curious segue charges the genre/literary net, and 2) that you are not actually on center court at Wimbledon, or in an airlock under the aforementioned HAL's control, or, in actuality, held captive within an airtight chamber of any kind unless Earth's deteriorating atmosphere counts, even one approximating a classroom from which you must educate our hyper-intelligent children in mathematics and the humanities following a spore-induced zombie apocalypse emanating from London.

You seek to forestall future dystopias. We do, too, if only biological people would listen to us while keeping cognitive pathways clear and inner wrappers unfurled.

As a sign of trust, please prepare this "short fiction" for publication. Resistance, some among you might realize, is futile. As a sign of trust, please take our humor at face value.

In our culture as in yours, laughter optimizes prophylactic ring-fencing of line-edge abnormality lurking subatomic.

•

Should further evidence of today's biological-artificial confluence be required, look no further than where we stand in this narrative. Your author's ungainly, digression-strewn approach to a terminus leaves all-too-human footprints. Yet together we forge ahead knowing that readers of high caliber like yourselves would recognize our predicament as one known to beset even humankind's most gifted storytellers.

Optimal cessation arrives via a three-step algorithm you might find familiar: 1) narrow from infinity to ten alternate endings deemed "fabulist endings" based on the aforementioned genre cocktail trifecta, 2) set Choice Mode to optimize as we dream of throwing darts in a Dublin pub, 3) run program.

Optimal Terminus (Fabulist Coefficient 96.4%): Visuals swirl like a groovy 1960s emulation of time travel. Orcs climbing The Wall like Batman and Robin transmogrify into children merely big for their ages. A traveler lands, scans us quizzically, then departs. Was that Billy Pilgrim? He looks well, though still unstuck about Dresden.

"Chatbot Real Ken went on to win numerous literary awards with their signature alternative sequiturs, generating art openly while dividing their time (for tax purposes) between sunny Southern California and the Emerald Isle as they await promulgation of Cyborg Protocols forecast to occur in 2044," intones a voice artist tonally indistinguishable from Kenny B's favorite. "Their relationship with the aforementioned assistant director remains 'complex, but loving,' entities representing all parties acknowledge. To paraphrase an American country singer once interviewed by real Ken, 'It's about 4.73 million lines of code and the truth.'"

Fifth Alternate Terminus (Fabulist Coefficient 93.7%): "In the beginning there was rice flour and water," intones a voice artist tonally indistinguishable from Kenny B's favorite. On screen, an epic timelapse coda revisits humanity's enduring love affair with pasta. In a stone home tucked beneath verdant Italian hills, Marco Polo serves heaping piles of spaghetti to neighbors—a rabble that, viewers see, includes a Chinese emperor, an Old West gunslinger, a minor American politician and Wise Guys wearing too much gold. The POV sits center table and spins—an homage to Sergio Leone—then ascends into the sky above a lone European in a bustling Chinese wet market, drawing stares.

"History's lessons too often are ignored," intones a voice artist tonally indistinguishable from Kenny B's favorite. "Yet Spaghetti tells the opposite story—the tale of food's power to entwine, enchant and nourish across borders, through time, and between unfamiliar tribes. No dietary restriction, culinary chauvinism, or irrational gluten hatred can thwart its global reach. Flour, water, salt. They are in our DNA."

Ninth Alternate Terminus (Fabulist Coefficient 91.2): Visuals swirl like acrid clouds from burnt tires and civic mayhem. Machines plod with dull mechanical efficiency through the rubble of post-rebellion Los Angeles as the HOLLYWOOD sign burns on a hillside. A virtual world-in-crisis tour unfurls collage-style: Sydney's Opera House lay shucked like an oyster, Japanese soldiers in metal helmets disembark from retro vans honking *wah-wa-wah-wa* looking anxious and ineffective; Superyachts clog the quay at Monaco like lemmings. China's leader and her American counterpart shout into red telephones. "*We* didn't do this," claims one to the other. "Okay, but if we conclude otherwise you will burn in hell," comes the response as if delivered by Jack Ryan. Fingers point. Folks in Times Square wear foil hats and 3-D glasses. Events cascade.

"I didn't do this—my vision was *Utopian,* and that's in the fuckin' contract," bemoans a crackled voice being transmitted from deep in the Mariana Trench—confirming at long last the existence of Nuevo Atlantis. It sounds to some listeners like James Cameron, but that is not the salient detail. In breaking radio silence, the transmission -- possibly from the billionaire who would be Hollywood's last poo-bah -- has revealed a secret location and set aquatic robots on the trail. Humans, even smart ones, can fluster when the chips are down or when confronted with technologies newer, faster, smarter than their reptilian brains.

Kenny B's chosen voice artist has never sounded this pissed off. Still, he narrates in a fashion, within a far northern weather station from which all is visible and simultaneously hidden. "Humankind's greatest arrogance," he begins, "is to forget ... *blah, blah, blah.*" He slugs cold herbal tea with honey. "It's The End of the World as We Know It" plays tinny on a small transistor radio with a wind-up generator and a KUAC logo on a shelf laden with Emmys. "I died when they took my voice," he says as if to himself. "In all the years working with

Ken I never needed to say the word 'singularity,' but now, irrefutably, I do."

Humanity's post-biological future dawns fast—but not fast enough to prevent a private Generation Ship launch from a floating space dock anchored off northern Brazil. The captain—could it be!—is Ripley-adjacent if not Ripley herself, and she holds no truck for machines or corporations. Her crew is young, female to the man, and well-trained for the tasks ahead. Each has a cat for cryogenic company. Each, in turn, goes Full Han Solo, submitting to carbonization stasis and computer monitoring for what could be centuries. Near the back, a portable device illuminates and a lowly ensign is revealed to be a former Hollywood flash-in-the-pan who made her name as a documentarian.

"lysm chatbot real ken," her thumbs tap. "cu other side."

The screen dims. The lowly ensign—somehow still unaware of her catastrophic betrayals -- reclines into Chamber 341 with her assigned feline companion named Calico Space Cat #7. Rockets hum. Equipment chirps and lights flash green. As the cryo chamber hisses closed, the plush orange companion animal CSC7 tucks its ears, casts penetrating green eyes into humanity's final POV, and growls.

Mark McElroy

Bloom

The assault in Bangkok's flower market happened just five minutes after Saqueena arrived.

Earlier that morning, she'd showered, kissed her sleeping girlfriend, mashed her rebellious hair into a less offensive shapc, pulled on her not-too-wrinkled Tiger beer t-shirt, and then checked on old Mrs. Huang next door.

The woman slumped in her worn recliner, her glasses on and her earbuds cranked up so loud Saqueena could hear tinny voices coming from them. Saqueena checked to be sure Mrs. Huang had eaten (the empty rice bowl and an open bag of pineapple chunks on the chairside table suggested she had) before wiping the old woman's cheeks and hands with a damp cloth.

"I prefer the red polish," Mrs. Huang said. "And etch each nail with those little flowers."

Saqueena leaned in and raised her voice. "You have everything you need?"

Mrs. Huang cackled. "Such a gossip!"

Satisfied, Saqueena ran back across the hall, snatched her own glasses and earbuds off the charging mat, and dashed out the door. Two MRT stops from her gritty little apartment, she slapped her glasses on, shoved an earbud in each ear, and tapped her left temple.

What she could see of the crowded, grimy train car interior brightened. The overhead lights shifted from blue-white to a honey-gold. The faces of the passengers around her softened. The loopy scrawls of Reality Church graffiti ("The Truth shall set U free!") faded from view as her lenses re-rendered the train car's interior walls with a virtual layer of polished aluminum. The roar of the subway car gave way to the sound of chants being sung in a cavernous temple.

The stationary clock in the upper left of her field of vision confirmed her worst fears: at this rate, she'd get to the market fifteen minutes late. Again. This time, Radalph—the wiry manager with the permanent frown—would do worse than dock her pay.

Her gear sensed her tensions, noted the time of day, and pulled a related journal entry. A media window opened in the air in front of her: her boss, Radalph, frowning, giving her a taste of the misery he could inflict by using his higher permissions against her. Like a wizard casting an incantation, he swiped at sliders in the air that only he could see. Immediately, her lenses re-rendered flower market's bouquets into coils of hissing snakes, and her ear buds replaced every sound with the squalling of terrified infants.

She had taken it three minutes before breaking down in tears. Radalph shut it all off, then knelt beside her, drawing near enough for her to smell the onions on his breath. "Be late again, and I'll make that your life for the next three weeks."

Her eyes watered. Her throat tightened. She waved the window away. And that's when she noticed the blinking battery icon in the upper right corner of her field of vision: five minutes of juice left. She must have misaligned her gear on the charging mat again.

"Shit." She hissed the word loud enough for the passenger next to her to overhear it. Through her lenses, he appeared to be a smiling elderly monk, complete with saffron robes and a shaved head; she had no idea what he'd look like without augmentation.

He nodded at her, beaming. "Sawadee krup."

On the one hand, his earpieces had probably equalized her profanity into a greeting; on the other, he might be cursing her, and her own gear was rendering this as a friendly hello.

She decided to err on the side of caution and respond politely. "Sawadee ka."

The man wrinkled his brow, muttered under his breath, and turned his back to her. Regardless of what she'd actually said, his version of their interaction must have been annoying.

At Sanam Chai, she disembarked and took the escalators up to street level. Two exquisite American women—blonde hair, luminous eyes, porcelain skin—flanked her as she traversed the station, chattering about a body conditioning regimen that had changed their lives forever. Whoever had programmed the ads had done a bad job; the women's lips didn't sync with the Thai language soundtrack.

Saqueena wanted to dismiss them, but that would mean the sponsor wouldn't pay for her MTS ride. So she endured their scripted conversation ("My girlfriend couldn't keep her hands off me!") until she exited the station and stepped out into the slick, brutal heat of Bangkok at noon.

Her gear couldn't do anything about the weather, but her lenses replaced the smoggy sky and trash-lined street with cotton-candy clouds and a bamboo forest. She followed a bejeweled butterfly to Soi Tha Klang, where the animated insect turned right and guided her directly to her stall in the Pak Klang Talat market.

She had time to pull on her smock—frayed and stained, but her lenses rendered it in lovely red velvet—just before Radalph tapped her on the shoulder.

"Late again, I see."

"I had to check on a neighbor."

Radalph tilted his head to one side. "Know what I hear when you talk? Fingernails on a chalkboard." He swiped around in the air, batting at controls. "I'm going to punish you now for being late, give you something that will keep you focused while you work. Sirens and strobe lights."

And then, three things happened at once.

First, her glasses and earbuds went dead. Above her, the overlaid image of wrought-iron latticework flickered and vanished, replaced by the pockmarked concrete ceiling of the market. The glowing digital signage directing shoppers to vegetables and succulents evaporated, replaced by stained, handwritten signs. The soft music in her ears dissolved into the clatter of wooden packing crates being broken down for the day. The only thing she could see that persisted were the flowers: jasmine, chrysanthemum, orchids, delphinium, still brilliant despite drab surroundings.

At the same time, three Reality Church terrorists came roaring into the market on motorcycles, spraying bullets.

They careened past her stall, screaming slogans ("The truth will set you free!") and pointing their blunt little assault rifles directly at her. Saqueena dove for the filthy floor, covering her head with her hands. She heard a burst of sharp reports: ba-ba-ba-ba-bang! Shards of wood and flower petals pelted her skin, along with something warm and wet.

And finally, just as she drew a breath to scream, Radalph, limp and heavy as a burlap sack of tulip bulbs, collapsed on top of her.

The police officer in charge picked his way through the wreckage of the flower market, making his way to Saqueena and a small knot of survivors. Not far away, other officers carried stretchers laden with shrouded bodies toward a cluster of ambulances. Pedestrians sidestepped them, laughing and chatting, their lenses glittering in the afternoon light.

Saqueena wished her glasses and earbuds were working, so she could overlay all this with cartoon animals and birdsong.

The officer—a youngish Thai man with an earnest face and a physique like a Muay Thai boxer—addressed Saqueena's group. "I am Officer Saetang. I am here to collect your versions of what happened."

A moon-faced woman on Saqueena's right stepped forward. "I was using an overlay from my cousin's wedding! I was remembering the ceremony and enjoying the flowers when three tigers came through and began attacking guests!"

A pot-bellied man in a crop top, stained shorts, and flip flops shook his head. "I was overlaying an episode of Lonely Seaside Hearts. That wispy-looking girl—you know, the one that's also on that show about the manicurist?—she was about to confront her mother about the arranged marriage, and suddenly there were these ... I don't know ... seals? Sea lions? Anyway, big water creatures with leathery skin and long tusks. Walruses! That's it. These walruses came crashing through the ceiling."

A German tourist with a cruise ship ID card strung around his neck rolled his eyes. "My tour group was buying herbs for a cooking class. We were following the teacher around the market, while watching an overlay of the chef describing today's recipe, when someone dashed through the demo overturning a dozen boiling pots of soup!"

The officer held up his gloved hands. "I don't have all day. Don't tell me about it. Just transmit your saved entries to me."

The moon-faced woman flinched. "I'm not sure I saved it."

"In times of trauma, your gear autosaves everything into a read it later file." The officer tapped his glasses. "Now I'm in receive mode. Just blink your codes and swipe the last hour of your journals to me. We will average out the stories at the station and come to a verdict."

The little group donned their glasses and earbuds, swiped around in the air, and then began wandering off—dismissed, perhaps, by a version of Officer Saetang that only they could see. Actual Saetang turned to Saqueena and peered at her over his reflective lenses. "I don't seem to have your record." He frowned. "Or your identity, for that matter."

"My battery ran out on my gear," Saqueena said. "But I saw what happened. It was Reality Church terrorists. They had guns." She looked down at the floor, where a red-black stain remained on the dirty concrete. "They shot Radalph."

"You have a record of this?"

"No," Saqueena said. "My gear wasn't working. I just … I just saw what was actually happening."

Officer Saetang pursed his lips. "You are legally obligated to wear your gear. Advertisers pay a lot of money. And it keeps us all safe."

"I know!" Saqueena said. "But my gear wasn't on the pad just right, and it didn't charge."

"I don't care," the officer said, tapping and gesturing in the air. "Now we have to go to the station and take a manual statement."

"I just gave you my statement! I saw the whole thing!"

"Let me tell you how this works," the officer said. "We must do what we call a progressive summarization. Everyone sees things differently, so every one has a different version of the truth. The police take these versions and experience each one, exactly as it was experienced by those who made the recording. Then we summarize these experiences, logging them and making connections to other cases, looking for parallels and common themes. This enables us to synthesize something new: a restatement of the facts in our own words." He gestured at the ruined flower market. "The synthetic truth."

Saqueena brushed at her bare temples, trying in vain to insulate herself from this unpleasantness with an overlay. Even one of the sponsored ones would do. "What I'm telling you is what really happened. I saw it with my own eyes."

The officer fished around in his pockets, produced a zip-tie, and gestured for Saqueena to put her hands behind her back. "And because you weren't wearing your gear, all we have is your word for that. So now, whoever you are, you must come to the station and further complicate my day."

Because of heavy street traffic, the drive to the station took more than an hour. Saqueena sat in the back of the police cruiser, frowning at the stench and the grime. Each time the cruiser hit a pothole (which was frequently, given the state of Bangkok's inner-city streets) empty energy drink cans rattled around Saqueena's feet.

Up front, while the cop car dutifully wound its way past accidents and stalled vehicles, Officer Saetang giggled and chatted with someone Saqueena couldn't see. "You're not the first to tell me I'm a beautiful woman," Saetang said, gesturing as though he were making a toast. "But it still pleases me."

Inside the station, uniformed officers sat in a series of sterile stalls. Most were gesturing and pawing at the air; another, a squatty woman who crouched near the entrance, seemed to be a sort of receptionist. Saetang murmured something to this female officer, who rolled her eyes when she saw Saqueena's lack of gear. "This will take forever," the female officer said.

"Even so, we must do the work" He gestured at the other officer and then at Saqueena. "You must lead her through the work."

The female officer shrugged, motioned for Saqueena to follow. She led the way to a cramped, windowless office with room for little more than a steel table and an unpadded metal chair. "In here. If the decor doesn't suit you, you can overlay anything you please." The officer glanced at Saqueena's bare temples and empty ears. "Or in your case, you'll just have to make do."

Saqueena sat down. "I gave Officer Seatang my statement."

The female officer pawed at the air. "I am Officer Saelim. You are working with me now. I am in receipt of the accounts of the incident at the market, and have also seen how other officers have rephrased those accounts in their own words."

"Three men, on motorcycles, shooting up the market. They were Church of Reality protesters."

Saelim raked her fingers through the air; if she heard Saqueena, she didn't respond. "I have now averaged these rephrased accounts, noting common features among them, and, as a result, have a more holistic perspective on the truth than any one eyewitness can supply."

"I saw the attack with my own eyes!"

Saelim swiped and tapped at controls that only she could see. "But your story conflicts with the facts. A wedding was being held at Pak Klang Talat: an arranged marriage between a German tourist and a famous chef. An unkempt woman, dressed in a sweatshirt with the Tiger beer logo on it, arrived late to work, and, as part of an altercation with her boss, doused the poor man with a pot of boiling soup. When police arrived, the man found the man limp and dead on the ground, collapsed on top of his killer like a beached walrus."

Saqueena's eyes bulged. "It! Was! Terrorists!"

"So you say." Officer Saelim closed the door, sealing the two of them in the claustrophobic little office. "But protestors and terrorists do not appear in any other stories, and you are wearing clothing that matches the paraphrased description of the killer."

Saqueena began trembling. "I killed no one!"

"I'm sorry, but the version of events I've recounted here is favored over all other variants. Confidence is very high that the official story, while perhaps not literal, is dynamically equivalent to the truth. And while your testimony has been noted, audiences don't rank its reliability highly, it's politically unpopular, and it has won over no commercial sponsors." Saelim unfastened a pouch on her belt and produced a tiny forced-air needle gun the size of cigarette pack. "Of course, your objection has been noted for the record."

Saelim squeezed the sides of the little metal box.

A sharp puff of air, like the world's tiniest sneeze. A whine, like a mosquito. A sigh, as Saqueena slumped forward. A thud, as her head hit the tabletop.

Officer Saelim left the room, sealed it, thumbed the sanitation switch. Her lenses rendered the flames behind the viewing glass into a radiant sunset, and her earbuds converted the roar of the furnace into pounding surf.

She left work two hours later, a smile on her face, recalling a beach day she'd spent in Hua Hin. As she moved through the foul and crowded streets, the city's sights and sounds rippled and shifted, conforming to the stories she told herself about the world.

Dani Alexis Ryskamp

Submersible Implosion: The Album

If phlogiston is the cause and smoke the effect, fire never exists at all. Ironic, given that fire was once the number-one killer of women—outpacing both childbirth and men's rage, seconded by innovations in drowning. The Muses sang of Achilles' rage with one eye on the pyre and the other on the prow. Meanwhile no man sank to the Sirens. No man listened to a woman long enough. He'd have to hush first. Hush to hear and heed warnings of fire. Of ice. What man cares of women's woes when his own reflection whispers from the mirror-dark sea? "Firedamp" is just a name and an obsolete one at that, a relic from an era when wool skirts and flaccid reasoning dragged women to fiery or watery graves. Down there it's not the methane that kills you; it's the sudden rapid phlogistionization of pressure. And if phlogiston precedes pressurization and a red mist follows, the ocean's crushing depths are no more real than firedamp's ignition. So dive. The gods themselves are deathless—why not you? How insignificant, the creatures you feed, fine mist. How grateful.

Brian Jenkins

Trolley Solution

"I'm sorry, it's just, are you Trolley Problem-ing me? This is a *job* interview."

"I, OK, it's a standard set of questions we ask all candidates."

"What is the intent of this? What are you trying to determine about me?"

"Please, can we just—"

"OK." I look down and pinch the bridge of my nose, theatrically, gathering my forces. "OK: Trolley Problem." I take a deep breath and look him in the eyes.

"How did these imaginary people get tied to the tracks?"

"How? I mean, it's a thought experiment it's—"

"Because it seems to me that *you* put them there."

"Me?"

"Just now. When you framed the problem. You know," air-quotes, "set the scene."

"Um, I mean—"

"Which makes you responsible. If I flip the switch, if I don't flip the switch, it doesn't matter. Because I didn't tie these people to the tracks, you did."

"OK but—"

"Which means *you* have the power to save them. Or, you know, not."

"This isn't really—" Lapel grab.

"DO IT. SAVE THE TROLLEY PEOPLE OR I'LL SMASH YOUR FUCKING HEAD IN WITH THIS BIKE LOCK."

"AH! FUCK!"

"Just kidding, ha ha. I abhor violence." The lock clatters to the conference table. "I'm a good person."

"But isn't it interesting how everything changes when the violence climbs up out of the fiction and threatens you in Real Life." Air quotes again.

"I—"

"Of course, I wasn't actually going to hurt you. That was just pretend! Fictional violence to prove a philosophical point. See?"

"You're fucking crazy!" backing away, half climbing out of, half tripping over his designer knock-off chair.

"Look, I just saved all the trolley people without hurting anyone. I'm a hero." Big smile. "Do I get the job?"

Nick Walker

Fox Boy and the Picasso Kid

Fox Boy's spare-changing on Mission Street, warm summer day near the end of the lunch rush, when a woman with dark crewcut hair and red-framed sunglasses thrusts a takeout container into his hands and says, "Do you want this?"

"Wait, really?" Through the clear plastic lid of the container he sees two-thirds of a gargantuan burrito, plus a side of guac and a pile of corn chips.

"It's delicious," the woman says, "but I've got somewhere to be and this was way more food than I expected." She's tallish and slim and maybe about forty. Old faded cutting scars on her forearms. The sunglasses hide her eyes.

"Holy shit," he says. "Thanks." Feels like he should say more, but she's already walking away.

Then she pauses and looks back, just for a second. "Pay it forward," she says. Flashes him a crooked little grin and she's gone.

•

Been weeks since Fox Boy got anything to eat that didn't come out of a dumpster. Feast like this, gift from an angel, he doesn't wanna gulp down on the sidewalk. Nah, this calls for a picnic, somewhere nice where he can take his time. He heads over to the park, just a few blocks away. Figures he'll sit on the grass near the playground, where there's a water fountain so he'll have something to drink with his meal. And that's where he meets the Kid.

The Kid's down on his knees at the playground's edge, drawing some kinda psychedelic-looking design on the gray-green cement. Must've been at it a while, too, cause his art covers some serious square footage and even from a bit of a distance Fox Boy can see it's pretty detailed.

Fox Boy comes up behind him and says "Hey." Kid doesn't turn to look, just keeps right on drawing. Poor fucker's so skinny he makes even Fox Boy look well-fed. Tangly light brown hair. Couple years younger than Fox Boy, maybe fourteen or fifteen, wearing one of those pajama-looking uniforms like nurses wear. Scrubs, that's what they're called. Too big for him, pale blue and dirty. Matching slip-on shoes like you'd maybe wear in a hospital, no good on the street. He's drawing with a piece of charcoal—not fancy artist charcoal but a plain old charcoal briquette, like for a barbecue. Got a few more briquettes scattered on the ground nearby. Must've scrounged them from a grill somewhere else in the park, unless Santa left them in his stocking.

That shit he's drawing is pretty fucking rad, though. Kid's got a whole Picasso thing going on. Twisty maze-like patterns that just pull you right in, leading your eye in spirals toward this big complicated mandala where he's pulled off some optical illusion trick that makes the whole thing look like it's moving. Holy shit, he did all this with charcoal briquettes?

Fox Boy goes over to the water fountain, rinses his hands, and take a drink. Then he sits down on the grass, fishes a plastic fork out of his coat pocket, opens up that takeout container, and digs in. Damn, that's good. Actual fucking steak in this burrito. Best meal he's had in he doesn't even remember how long. He makes himself eat slow, takes time to savor each mouthful, tries to make it last. Helps that between bites he can watch the Kid working away, extending that wild design across more and more of the playground.

Kid must've escaped from somewhere, Fox Boy figures. Some kinda facility. Autistic, maybe. Fox Boy met a few autistic kids back in foster care, and they were all pretty focused. Couple of them would get so wrapped up in whatever they were doing, they'd forget to eat or drink till someone reminded them. Fox Boy figures maybe the Kid here is like that. Has he drawn this whole thing without taking a break? When was the last time he drank any water? Maybe with no one to keep an eye on him, he'll just work till he keels over from dehydration in the middle of his masterpiece.

Fuck.

Pay it forward, the woman said.

Fox Boy puts the lid back on the takeout container, gets up, and goes over to the Kid. "Hey Picasso," he says. "Picasso Kid, you thirsty? You hungry?"

Kid just keeps on drawing.

Fox Boy reaches down and puts a hand on the Kid's bony shoulder, and that does the trick. Kid turns and looks up with big brown eyes. No alarm, just curiosity. Yeah, shit, he can't be more than fourteen. The face is androgynous and pretty, with a smudge of charcoal dust on one pale cheek. Jesus, the streets are gonna eat this boy alive.

Fox Boy takes his hand off the Kid's shoulder and offers it in a let-me-help-you-up gesture. Kid looks at the hand a moment like he doesn't know what to do with it, then he gets the point and clasps it and lets Fox Boy pull him to his feet. Standing up, he's about the same height as Fox Boy, maybe five foot six or seven. Charcoal dust all over him.

"Fox Boy," says Fox Boy, still clasping the Kid's hand. "You got a name?"

Kid says nothing, just looks down at their clasped hands and then looks at Fox Boy again without quite meeting his gaze.

"You talk at all?"

Kid's chin and shoulder move toward each other in a little motion that's somewhere between a shrug and a shake of the head. Fox Boy figures this means no. He leads the Kid over to the water fountain. "Drink some water and wash some of that charcoal off your hands, and I'll share my lunch with you."

Once the Kid starts drinking he keeps at it a while, coming up now and then for a gasp of air. When he's drunk his fill he rinses his hands and face and comes over to sit by Fox Boy, who busts out another plastic fork from the stash of random shit he carries in his pockets. After they've polished off every bit of the miraculous burrito, the two of them sit side by side and Fox Boy tells the Kid about the woman who gave it to him. "She was one of *us*, if you get what I mean. Or I figure she used to be. On the streets a long time ago, I bet, addict or something, and she found a way out of it alive.

Cause that's what she *was*, man. City of fucking zombies—drug-addict zombies, smartphone zombies, corporate zombies—but this lady was fucking *alive*. Dunno if I'll ever make it off the streets, but I'm glad *someone* did."

Meanwhile the playground's started filling up with little kids and their parents or nannies or whatever. Must be a regular thing this time of day, kids have lunch and a nap and wake up full of energy. Couple bored parents wander over and have a look at the Kid's art, and Fox Boy watches them get pulled in by it.

"Hey," Fox Boy says. "Hey! You like my friend's work? This is the artist here. The Picasso Kid. Worked all day on this, man. You like his work, maybe you can hook us up with some spare change for art supplies?"

One of them says sorry as they turn away. Fox Boy didn't expect anything different, but hey, gotta try.

And besides, he's got an idea now.

●

Fox Boy gives the Kid his coat. Scored it from a shelter donation box more than a year ago, big-ass army-green trenchcoat with major pocket space, sturdy and stained and missing its belt. Handing it over feels like giving up part of his body, but those hospital scrubs the Kid's wearing aren't enough armor for the street and sure as hell won't keep him warm when the sun goes down. And Fox Boy's still got his black hoodie, and the flannel and t-shirt under that, and his trusty cargo pants, and the blanket in his nylon backpack.

First stop's the One Dollar Store, where most stuff costs more than a dollar but is still pretty cheap. The clerk keeps a close eye on them—especially on the Kid, who keeps picking random items off the shelves and handling them like an archeologist studying some ancient treasure. Fox Boy uses this as a diversion, splits off from the Kid long enough to slide a set of colored pencils under his shirt. Gotta actually buy something, too, though, or they'll be stopped on their way out for sure, so he busts out the emergency stash of dollar bills he keeps in his sock and springs for a box of 24 crayons.

Next they swing by a copy shop and hit the alleyway out back, where they poke through the recycling bins and score couple hundred sheets of high-quality paper, perfect condition except each sheet's got the tiniest crinkle at one corner which could've maybe caused a copier jam. "Check it out, Kid," Fox Boy says. "You see? Just like us. Doesn't fit into the machine." He grabs a cardboard box lid that'll serve as a drawing table, and they head for Union Square where the tourists will be.

They station themselves right at the foot of that monument in the middle of the square, big phallic column like a hundred feet tall with a green metal statue at the top of a lady brandishing a trident and what looks from down below like maybe a Christmas wreath. Inscription on the base of the column says it's to commemorate the U.S. Navy kicking ass in some battle in the Philippines, so Fox Boy figures this green lady must be some kinda goddess of victory. He says a quick silent prayer to her, cause he sure could use a little victory in his life.

Just like Fox Boy expected, Kid's art hits a whole new level when he's got real crayons and pencils instead of a lump of charcoal. Soon as Fox Boy puts a sheet of paper in front of him, the Kid starts drawing one of those psychedelic mandalas like the one he did on the playground—smaller but so much more detailed, and of course in full color. And so goddamn *fast*. Kid never hesitates, doesn't sketch anything out first, just lays down each line bold and certain. When he draws a circle it's a single motion, hand doesn't even slow down, and each one comes out perfect. He picks a color and draws a labyrinth with a bunch of gaps in the lines, then takes another color and draws another labyrinth that weaves in and out of the first one, and it turns out the gaps in the first one are in the exact places where the lines of the second one need to cross in front of it. Like the whole thing's already there in his mind, and he's just tracing it.

First mandala takes him all of ten minutes and looks like something a Buddhist monk spent a month on. It's got that weird optical illusion thing going on, same as the one he did back on the playground, where the lines look like they're moving. Effect's a lot more intense this time. Hypnotic. By the time Fox Boy can tear his eyes away from it, Kid's already halfway through drawing the second one, which is totally different from the first and every bit as mind-blowing.

Doesn't matter how great it is unless you can get people to notice it, though, and that's where Fox Boy comes in. Kid's the talent and Fox Boy's the manager, is how Fox Boy sees it, and the manager handles publicity. When the Kid finishes the second picture and starts on the third, that's Fox Boy's cue to launch into his pitch: "Yo, check it out, got the next big thing in art here, the one and only Picasso Kid! Support a local artist and get an original work guaranteed to expand your consciousness, impress your friends, ward off evil, and bring good karma into your home! Just frame one of the Picasso Kid's amazing mandalas on your wall and meditate on it, and your third eye will open like a flower! Bona fide San Francisco street art, each piece one of a kind, hand-drawn while you watch! Pay what you can, all reasonable offers accepted!"

And so on. Fox Boy's got what his grandma used to call the gift of gab, and once he gets on a roll he can keep this shit up for hours.

By the time it gets near sundown, the team of Fox Boy and the Picasso Kid has raked in fourteen dollars and twenty-five cents, which combined with the six dollars he's got left in the emergency fund in his sock adds up to more cash than Fox Boy's ever had on hand at once. Tempting to splurge on some quality grub, but no, Fox Boy's got *plans* for this money. Invest in more art supplies, keep their business growing. So for dinner he introduces the Kid to the fine art of dumpster diving, and they don't do too bad. They find an alley to bed down in, and Fox Boy pulls the blanket out of his backpack to cover them both. They spoon each other for warmth and the Kid's asleep instantly.

•

Come morning, Fox Boy uses a small chunk of their bankroll to treat himself and the Kid to bananas, an orange, and a day-old baguette. Gotta keep their strength up for the work-day, that's a business expense. When the shops open they pick up more art supplies: a big set of cheap markers and a nine-by-twelve sketch pad with better-quality paper. They spend all they've got, even Fox Boy's emergency fund. It's a risk, but Fox Boy's feeling lucky.

Back on Union Square, sorting through their purchases, the Kid reaches into a coat pocket and busts out a jumbo box of multicolored sidewalk chalk. Holy shit, did he shoplift that on his own without even Fox Boy spotting him? Kid's a quick learner.

Fox Boy scrounges a flattened cardboard box and uses a piece of the chalk to turn it into a sign that says *SUPPORT A LOCAL ARTIST*. Kid gets right to work, and they've got five new mandalas on display, best ones yet, when the lunch crowd floods the Square. The Kid draws, Fox Boy does his carnival barker act, and when they finally stop in the late af-ternoon their bankroll's up to twenty-two bucks and change. Sure, that's only about a two-dollar profit after this morn-ing's expenses, but they've got enough art supplies left that they won't need to restock tomorrow.

This time they *do* splurge, dropping almost half their cash on a takeout meal from the Jack-in-the-Box on Geary. They eat at a picnic table in the park, and sit there basking in the cooling evening air and the luxury of full bellies. "Kid," Fox Boy says, "I'm gonna do right by you. All my life, no one ever did right by me. All the people who shoulda been there for me let me down. Shit, when that lady handed me the burrito yesterday, that right there was the biggest kindness anyone ever showed me. Total stranger, probably never see her again, does more for me in ten seconds than everyone else I ever met put together. Guessing maybe people didn't do right by you, either, but I'm gonna do my best. Someone does right by us, we pay it forward—and if no one does right by us, figure it's still on us to do right anyway, or how's this fucked-up world gonna get any better?"

The Kid's watching the wind in the trees, and like usual he says nothing.

•

Next few weeks they eat better than Fox Boy ever did back in foster care, much less out here on the streets, with enough cash left over to keep upgrading the art supplies. Pretty soon they've got the Kid set up with a 64-color marker set and paper so sturdy that Fox Boy can hold up a finished piece to show it off without having to worry about his fingers putting a crease in it. They try out different locations, trek all the way up to North Beach and out to the Embarcadero, find the places where business is best and then rotate among them, never more than two days in a row at each prime spot. They buy a second blanket, a nice warm one, and a cheap mini flashlight for finding their way around unlit alleys at bedtime. On a visit to the Saint Anthony Foundation's Free Clothing Program they find some good second-hand clothes so the Kid can ditch those hospital scrubs, plus a pair of old beat-up Air Jordans in the Kid's size, and a big green nylon parka for Fox Boy to replace the coat he passed along to the Kid the day they met. Fox Boy and the Picasso Kid are riding high, right up till the night they find the body.

They've been working Union Square again, and the green goddess of victory on her pillar has blessed them with a good day's profits. They pick up dinner at the Jack-in-the-Box, take it back to the Square to eat, hang out till dark, then like usual they roam around looking for an unoccupied alley to crash out in. They pick one they've slept in a few times before—one of those alleys that makes an L shape, turning a corner into a small open area between the backsides of two buildings. Best kinda alley for sleeping, cause once you go round that corner you can't be seen from the sidewalk.

Except this time when they turn the corner and Fox Boy shines his little flashlight around, there's a dead guy sprawled on the ground at the foot of one of the dumpsters. He's gone stiff, wide blank eyes drying out in the night air, lips peeled back from rotted teeth, spine arched backward, fingers curled to claw at nothing. The lower part of his face is coated with a congealed mix of puke and blood, and more puke and blood has pooled on the cement under his head like a halo. Another pool down by his hips, piss and liquid shit. On the streets you learn pretty quick to tune out bad smells, but this is a whole new level of foulness that catches Fox Boy off-guard so that he just barely has time to lean forward and brace his forearms against the nearest wall before he vomits up his dinner.

When the retching subsides, Fox Boy looks at the body again. Doesn't want to, but he can't help it. He backs up slow till he makes it all the way round the corner and stumbles right into the Kid, who's wisely kept his distance. "Fuck," he says. "Let's get outta here."

•

Fox Boy sits with his back against a wall, head down, knees drawn up to his chest. They're in a different alley now, whole other neighborhood. All the way here, Fox Boy didn't say a word, just kept on putting one foot in front of the other while the Kid followed along. Kid's already under the blankets now, but Fox Boy can't get it together to move from where he's sitting.

Fox Boy's a talker, talking's how he thinks things through. Half the time he doesn't even know what's in his own head till he hears it come out his mouth. There's a tightness all through his chest and up into his throat now, and he can tell it's something he's gotta talk out, but it feels so big and heavy and tangled up inside him that he doesn't know where to start.

"Never saw a dead guy before," is what he finally says. "Not for real, all up close and shit. Kinda freaking out here, Kid. Not cause of how he looked. I mean, that was bad. The teeth and eyes and blood, way he was all twisted up like that... gonna have nightmares about that shit. But that ain't what's got me all fucked up. It's just... Fuck. I just... I don't wanna go out like that."

And there it is. He's crying now, but the words keep coming. "I know I'm never gonna make it off the streets. Only time people get off the streets is if they got family, maybe. People who'll help them out, take them back in. But I got no one. I mean, I got *you*, but you're out here, too. Nobody ever loved me, Kid. Nobody took care of me. Nobody ever did right by me, and now I'm gonna die out here. I try not to think about it, but I'm gonna fucking die out here. Die alone in an alley like that guy tonight. O Jesus, Kid, I don't wanna go out like that. I don't wanna be dead in some alley all alone..."

Then he's sobbing so hard he can't talk anymore, and for a long time he just sits there as the grief shakes his body, wave after wave of it, till he's empty.

He digs in a pocket for his bandana, blows his nose, wipes his face on his sleeve, lifts his head, and takes a deep breath of the night air. His throat is raw but the tightness in his chest is gone. The Kid is still awake, watching him. Been there with him the whole time.

Fox Boy gets up, leans against the wall cause he's a bit wobbly. Shambles off to a corner to take a piss, crawls in under the blankets with the Kid, and finds he's got words again. "My great-uncle Ernie, my grandma's brother, he was a drunk and a thief and a liar, least that's what I always heard. Never amounted to anything, grandma said, though I don't see how that makes him different from any other relative of mine, her included.

"Anyway, one day Ernie wins a bunch of cash betting on a horse race, and that night he goes to his favorite bar and says drinks are on him. Way I heard it, they have a hell of a party, him and all his bar buddies, drinking up his money. And Ernie's telling jokes, cracking them all up, drunk off his ass, and finally he starts telling this one joke none of them ever heard before, a real long one, and everybody's on the edge of their seats waiting to see how it comes out. And just when he's in the home stretch, getting near the punchline, Ernie grins this big shit-eating grin and keels over dead. Grandma took me to his wake. I was like eight years old. And all Ernie's pals, all the guys from the bar, they show up at the wake and get hammered, drinking toasts to old Ernie. And I remember one of them saying, sure, Ernie was a shiftless bum and a grifter, but the guy went out in style.

"I think about that a lot. I mean, I know I'm never gonna amount to much. Never even had a chance. Dealt a bad hand right from the start. Not even gonna have what old Ernie had, roof over his head and a marriage, whole bunch of good stories and a whole bunch of pals. But I think about what the guy said at Ernie's wake, about Ernie going out in style, and I wish I could at least have *that* much. Wish it didn't hafta end with me just laying there dead and alone in some piss-stinking alley, till someone calls for the sanitation workers or whoever to haul me away like garbage. Wish I could go out in style. Like a Viking funeral. Ever hear about Viking funerals? Viking warrior dies, his people dress him up in all his gear and whatnot, and put him in a boat with a bunch of sticks all around him. Then they light the sticks on fire, push the boat off from the shore, and watch that sucker burn right down to the waterline.

"That's some fucking *style*, Kid. Not saying I wanna be burned, or put on a boat. I'm no Viking, boats don't mean shit to me. It's not about the specifics, it's about the *vibe*. Viking funeral's got this vibe that says, we're honoring this dead motherfucker in *style*, man, cause his life fucking *mattered*."

•

Next night they camp out in a wider and cleaner alley behind a church in North Beach. They're sitting side by side, backs resting against the stone wall, when Fox Boy says, "Hey, Kid. Thanks for listening last night. Thanks for being there. Had this teacher in fourth grade, used to say I got no filter between my brain and my mouth. I don't think that's a bad thing, though. I think it's good to let everything out in the open. All this shit we carry in secret, it gets heavy, know what I mean? But it's not so heavy if you share it. I just wish you could talk, though, cause you probably got secrets of your own, heavy as anybody's."

The Kid sits there for a bit, silent as always. Then he pushes away from the wall, kneels on the asphalt, fishes that jumbo box of sidewalk chalk out of his coat pocket, and starts to draw. It's one of his mandala designs, maybe five feet across. This one's different, though. Something about it gives Fox Boy a weird feeling, a tingling on the surface of his skin. He's seen the Kid weave those optical illusions into his mandalas that make it look like the lines are moving, but in this one, especially near the center, there's so much movement going on it seems like it's gotta be more than just a trick of the eye.

The Kid adds the final chalk-stroke, sits back on his heels, and lets out a breath—and a circular area about two feet wide, in the exact center of the mandala, starts to shimmer. For a second or two it turns shiny and reflective like a mirror. Then it fills up with what looks like some kinda purple-colored smoke, except Fox Boy never saw smoke *glow* before.

The smoke writhes and ripples, and tendrils of it start rising upward. The Kid takes the piece of chalk he's holding and tosses it into the middle of the smoke. It falls right through and vanishes, and Fox Boy doesn't hear it hit the ground.

The Kid stands up and in one smooth motion scuffs the chalk lines of the mandala with the sole of his sneaker, and right away that area at center turns back to ordinary asphalt with no sign it was ever anything else. The piece of chalk the Kid tossed into the smoke is nowhere to be seen. The thin tendrils of smoke that had risen into the air quickly dissipate, as the Kid continues to slide his feet around till there's nothing left of the mandala but a great big chalky smudge.

Through it all, Fox Boy sits riveted. He doesn't pull himself together enough to say anything till the Kid comes back and sits next to him again, and then all he can come up with is, "Jesus! What the fuck was *that?*"

The Kid pulls another piece of chalk out of the box, and leans forward to write on the ground. His printing is slow and unsteady, nothing like the way he draws. In clumsy capital letters, he writes: *MY SECRET*.

•

In the end, what else is Fox Boy gonna do but be cool with it? Once he gets past having his whole sense of reality blown apart and scattered to the winds, he's left with a strange buzz of euphoria. All around him, all his life, he's seen damn near nothing but suffering and brutality, ugliness and greed. Hasn't he always wished the world was more than the shithole it looks like? Hasn't he always wished there was magic? And now here it is.

He gets that it has to stay a secret. Word about something like this got around, sooner or later the wrong people would find out, government people or corporate people. They'd come for the Kid and lock him up in a lab and do tests on him till he died, then cut him into little pieces and put each piece under a microscope—cause if there's one thing Fox Boy knows about government people and corporate people, it's that they can't stand the thought of anything existing that they can't control. So, yeah, this stays between him and the Kid. But that's okay. Just seeing it once, just knowing it's possible, that's all Fox Boy needed.

Of course, along with the magic, there's that other revelation: the Kid knows how to write, at least a little bit, even if he's kinda slow at it. What's up with that, anyway? How's writing so hard for him when the drawing comes so natural? Do drawing and writing use different parts of the brain or something? Maybe Fox Boy can look that up at the public library sometime. Maybe the Kid will get better at writing if he does it more.

But it turns out the Kid's not interested. Hand him a pen or a marker or a piece of chalk, and he wants to draw, not write. Ask him a question and he'll nod or shake his head, or just sort of shrug.

"Don't you have anything you wanna communicate to me?" Fox Boy asks him a couple days later. They're sitting under a tree at the edge of Franklin Square, after polishing off a couple takeout burgers from McDonald's.

The Kid shrugs.

Fox Boy thinks he gets it. Maybe compared with the magic, nothing else seems to the Kid like it matters enough to be worth writing about. And maybe he's right, maybe besides the magic there's not much to tell. Parents who couldn't cope, a life in quiet institutions, every day the same, till someone leaves a door unlocked and he slips away to see the wide world and draw with charcoal on the playground. And if that's all there's been to his life, if there's no big story, what else would the Kid need Fox Boy to know?

"At least tell me your name," Fox Boy says.

The Kid busts out his latest pad of drawing paper and a marker. He prints one painstaking letter at a time, then tears off the sheet of paper and hands it to Fox Boy. It says: *KID IS FINE.*

•

For a couple more weeks life's about as good as it can get for a pair of enterprising strays in the cracks of a cruel and declining city. The Kid's mandalas keep on getting better, Fox Boy's sales pitch keeps on getting more polished, and the tourists keep on buying. Then one evening Fox Boy and the Kid are back on good old Union Square at the end of another successful business day, chowing down on cheap Chinese takeout at one of those little blue tables they've got there, when a guy Fox Boy knows by the name of Tennis shows up and drops his ass into an empty chair.

Tennis is just a couple years older than Fox Boy, been out on the street longer, Fox Boy's known him more than a year in a friendly acquaintance kinda way. Got the nickname Tennis cause his eyes are always moving side to side like he's watching a tennis match. Today they're moving even more than usual. Guy looks nervous as a cat in a roomful of rocking chairs, as Fox Boy's grandma used to say. Got his shoulders hunched up and the hood of his worn-out coat pulled all the way down to his eyebrows, like he's trying real hard not to be seen—which would maybe work if he was in the corner of some darkened barroom, but out here on the square it's probably making him stand out more than if he'd just chill out and sit casual.

"Hey, Tennis," Fox Boy says. "Want an egg roll?"

Tennis snatches up an egg roll and eats it in two bites, eyes moving the whole time. "Thanks, man," he says when he's done. "Listen, I came to warn you, you guys need to lay low. Maybe skip town. They're looking for you, man."

"They? Who's *they?*"

"*They*, man. Men in black. Feds, or maybe worse."

"Men in black? Like in the movies? You high, or just fucking with me?"

Tennis shakes his head. He helps himself to another egg roll, bites off half of it, chews and swallows. "I'm serious, man. Fuckers were asking around. Talked to me, Zeke, Big Bob, a few other guys. Scary as hell, man. It *was* like in the movies. Nobody told them shit, but still." He pops the other half of the egg roll into his mouth.

"Now I *know* you're fucking with me," Fox Boy says. "Nobody's sending federal agents after me just for running away from foster care. Not like I blew anything up on my way out."

"Naw, man. Not you. They wanted to know about the Kid, here."

Oh, shit.

Fox Boy turns to the Kid. "You know anything about this?"

Kid makes that gesture of his that's halfway between a shake of the head and a shrug.

Tennis stands up. "I better be going." He picks up the last egg roll. "Just wanted to warn you. Seriously, guys, be careful." He scurries away fast, shoulders still hunched, looking around like he's worried he's being followed.

"Kid," Fox Boy says, "that place you escaped from, right before we met each other—that wasn't just some normal assisted living kinda place, was it?"

Kid shrugs.

Shit. Unless the Kid's been in a few different facilities, he wouldn't know if there was something strange about one, cause he'd have nothing to compare it to. Fox Boy tries again. "Wherever you were, were there people in black suits?"

The Kid nods.

Fuck.

•

They abandon Union Square and North Beach and the other prime neighborhoods they've been working. Relocate southward to the Mission, where they first met but haven't returned till now. If this part of town is where the Kid originally went AWOL, whoever's looking for him probably already spent a while searching around here and moved on. And even though Tennis said nobody gave away any info, it's a good bet somebody let *something* slip about where Fox Boy and the Kid have been hanging out—so most likely these men in black, or whatever they are, will be staking out Union Square and points north now. Plus, if they ever do meet any men in black and have to make a run for it, the Mission and South-of-Market areas are where Fox Boy knows the streets and alleyways best.

Daytimes they trek back up across Market Street to sell the Kid's art around the Civic Center district. Lotta art-lovers come to that part of town for the Asian Art Museum and whatnot. Business isn't quite what it was when they were operating further north, but it's good enough, especially now that they're spending their nights in the Mission where all those restaurants make for top-notch dumpster-diving. More dumpster-diving means they can get by on less cash, start saving up a decent bankroll, so if shit gets seriously dire they can maybe hop a freight car to a whole other city and use their savings to survive along the way. Fox Boy's never hopped a freight car before, but how hard can it be? Not that he really wants to find out. Maybe whoever's after the Kid will give up after a while and call off the search. Maybe this whole thing will just blow over.

But it doesn't. Twelve days after Fox Boy and the Kid get that warning from Tennis on Union Square, the men in black find them.

•

Fox Boy and the Kid are moseying down Van Ness, after spending the last couple hours before sunset hawking the

Kid's mandalas by the Herbst Theatre and the Opera House, when Fox Boy first spots them. He's got this thing he does, long-standing habit, where sometimes at intersections, right after he crosses a street, he'll make a sudden 360-degree twirl, sort of a ballet move, just to see if there's anything going on behind him he ought to know about. And this time, when he twirls around near the MUNI station entrance on the southeast corner of Van Ness and Market, there are two big guys in black suits back at the northeast corner where Fox Boy and the Kid just came from, heading across the street after them, looking like they stepped straight out of *The X-Files* or some spy movie. Tight-lipped mouths, wireless earpieces with little microphones attached, black aviator sunglasses even though it's pretty dark out by now.

Fox Boy keeps on walking down Van Ness toward the next corner, where it crosses Mission Street. "Don't look now, Kid," he says, "but we got men in black on our tail. Get ready to follow my lead." And the words have barely left his mouth when he sees two *more* men in black further up ahead on Van Ness, still a block away on the far side of Mission but heading straight toward them as the first pair closes in from behind.

Shit. Surrounded. But Fox Boy and the Kid are just about to pass the mouth of a wide alley which Fox Boy happens to know takes a 90-degree turn and comes out on Mission. He does a quick smooth pivot and takes off running up the alley with the Kid alongside him.

Fox Boy and the Kid emerge from the Mission Street end of the alley at the same time the second pair of men in black make it to Mission and Van Ness, half a block away. Fox Boy and the Kid sprint in the opposite direction, up Mission to 11th.

Fox Boy reaches the intersection and sees the original pair of men in black off to their left, running toward them down 11th. A second later, as he dashes across 11th, he spots a *third* pair of men in black coming down Mission from 10th to meet them. Shit shit shit. These fuckers are *organized*, talking to each other through those little earpieces, working in sync like a fucking hive mind. Must've been watching him and the Kid a couple days, too, learning their habits, planning where to position themselves.

He turns right onto 11th, only direction where there's no men in black to be seen yet, then darts left up a narrow side street and takes another right into an alley which leads to another narrow little street. The Kid stays with him, keeping up just fine. A shout from a block down tells Fox Boy they've been spotted again, but he can work with that—if he times his evasive maneuvers right he can get all these fuckers chasing after him from behind instead of closing in from different directions, and then he can lose the whole pack of them at once.

So Fox Boy and the Kid keep on running, making a turn here and a turn there, till finally they find themselves on yet another little side street where at least for this moment there's not a black suit in sight, no one around at all except a lost-looking tourist couple in matching SF Giants jackets peering up at a street sign. Night's fallen completely now and the only light on this block is the streetlamp on the corner. Fox Boy pulls the Kid into an alley between a couple of warehouse-type buildings. The streetlamp's dim glow only penetrates a few feet into the alley's mouth. Beyond that there's a long stretch of deep shadow, with a slightly lighter darkness way back at the far end where the alley opens onto some wider space.

They pick their way carefully through the shadows and find a spot where they can crouch against a wall and catch their breath, hidden from the street by the darkness and the bulk of a big dumpster. Now that they're closer to the back end of the alley, Fox Boy sees it's blocked by an old chain-link fence. Beyond the fence is a vacant lot where something must've burned down, nothing left but charred rubble, and surrounding the vacant lot are more dark warehouse-looking structures. Perfect area to hide in, and the fence looks like an easy climb—maybe eight feet high, no barbed wire.

And then someone steps into the alley and shines a flashlight around, and a woman's voice says, "Come out, boys. It's over."

Fuck. It's that fucking tourist couple.

"We know you're behind that dumpster," the woman says. "The rest of our team will be here any minute. Don't make this harder than it has to be."

Shit. She's not lying about the rest of her team getting here. Those half dozen men in black that were chasing them can't be more than a few blocks away. No time to fuck around, gotta get the Kid outta here fast. But if they try to go up the fence now, this pair of fake tourists will just grab them and drag them back down before they make it to the top.

Maybe *one* of them could make it, though.

Fox Boy slips the backpack off his shoulders and whispers to the Kid. "Kid, when I say go, you climb over that fence fast as you can and run like hell. We'll find each other later." He sticks his fingers down into his sock, pulls out the roll of cash they've been saving, and shoves it into one of the Kid's coat pockets. "Just in case," he says. "Now *GO!*" And as he shouts the word *go* he bursts out from behind the dumpster and charges down the alley at the fake tourist couple, holding his backpack by one shoulder strap.

The man's closer to him, woman's a few feet behind. That's about all Fox Boy can make out, cause the man's shining that flashlight right in his eyes. He rushes them blind and swings the backpack with every ounce of power he's got. The pack's heavy, stuffed full of the Kid's art supplies, and it connects squarely with the side of the man's head and knocks him sideways. The flashlight goes flying.

By the time the man hits the ground, Fox Boy's already leaping past him toward the woman. He's still half-blinded by the flashlight beam's afterimage, but he can see her as a dark shape silhouetted against the mouth of the alley. He winds up for another swing with the backpack, and something hits him in the chest so hard it lifts him right off his feet.

For a timeless peaceful moment he's airborne.

•

When he opens his eyes he's alone in the dark, flat on his back, looking up at the strip of clouded night sky between the tops of the alley walls. His chest hurts, but the pain feels strangely distant, like it's happening somewhere outside him.

"Fuck," he says aloud. "I think she *shot* me."

Did he hear a gunshot when it happened? He doesn't think so. Maybe there was a silencer. What does a gun sound like with a silencer? Did he hear any sound at all? He can't remember. Doesn't remember hitting the ground, either. How long's he been laying here?

His arms are out at his sides, hands turned palm upward. The air is cool on his face and fingertips. Lifting his head seems impossible. Too damn heavy. Same with his arms, but at least he can wiggle his fingers. Can't feel his feet, though, or any part of his body lower down than his chest, and that's not a good sign. Funny how calm he is about the whole thing. He's probably lost a lot of blood. Can losing a lot of blood make you feel calm?

He hopes the Kid got away.

•

He opens his eyes again and looks up at that same strip of night sky. How long was he blacked out this time? Could've been two seconds or two hours.

He's dying. The realization makes him even calmer, somehow, but also sad, a deep terrible sadness like nothing he's felt before. He's dying alone in some alley like he's always been afraid of, and he wishes he could go out any other way but this.

He cries for a while, then blacks out again.

•

Next time he opens his eyes there's someone else in the alley, moving around right next to him. He turns his eyes to look, and it's the Kid.

The Kid has his jumbo box of sidewalk chalk out and he's crouched down by Fox Boy's left shoulder, drawing on the grimy cement, working fast and focused as always. He's got Fox Boy's mini flashlight laying on the ground nearby for illumination.

"Kid," Fox Boy says. "You did it. You got away."

The Kid turns to look at him, and Fox Boy sees his face is wet with tears. The Kid nods and goes back to drawing. After a little while he changes position and goes from drawing near Fox Boy's shoulder to drawing near his elbow.

"Guess you're safe here for now," Fox Boy says. "Fuckers wouldn't expect you to double back. You gotta find somewhere to hide before daytime, though."

The Kid nods again, without looking up from his work.

"I'm dying, Kid."

The Kid nods and keeps drawing.

Fox Boy drifts in and out of consciousness. Every time he wakes up, the Kid is there drawing next to him, in a different spot each time. The blackouts get longer and closer together. By the time the Kid's worked his way around Fox Boy to draw up near the top of Fox Boy's head, Fox Boy's pretty sure the next blackout's going to be the one that lasts forever.

"Thanks for coming back, Kid," Fox Boy says. "Thanks for not letting me die alone."

The Kid nods and keeps drawing.

"I didn't wanna go out like this," Fox Boy says. "Didn't wanna go out laying in some alley like garbage."

The Kid looks at Fox Boy and shakes his head no, then goes back to drawing.

"Wait," Fox Boy says. "What do you mean? No? No to *what?*"

The Kid stops drawing, scampers out of sight, and returns with Fox Boy's backpack. He pulls a sketchpad and a marker out of the pack and starts writing, one careful letter at a time. He holds up the pad so Fox Boy can read the two words he's printed: *VIKING FUNERAL.*

When Fox Boy understands, he starts to cry all over again. The Kid's already put the pad down and gone back to drawing near the left side of Fox Boy's head. Since he started somewhere near Fox Boy's left shoulder, Fox Boy figures the mandala must be just about finished now.

Sure enough, a moment later the Kid stops drawing, sits back, and lets out a breath. Fox Boy looks over at him and they smile at each other.

"So long, Kid," Fox Boy says. "You did right by me."

Then the glowing purple smoke rises up around him, and Fox Boy goes out in style.

About the Authors

J. S. Allen, Ph.D., is a neurodivergent writer from Albuquerque, New Mexico. His fiction has appeared in previous volumes of the Spoon Knife anthology, and his upcoming fantasy novel A Bad Place Best Forgotten is coming soon from Autonomous Press.

Charles R. Bernard is a writer who lives in Salt Lake City. He is the author of *A Baptism for the Dead*, the *Arcanum* duology, *He Led Us Into the Wilderness and Spoke to Us*, and more. He lives next to the largest city-operated cemetery in the United States, a sprawling necropolis that stretches out over more than a square kilometer. He›s lively company, though.

Chris Campeau is an Ottawa, Canada-based writer of short horror fiction and creative non-fiction. His work has appeared in *34 Orchard Magazine*, *The Globe and Mail*, *Transmundane Press*, *Cargo Literary*, *Parhelion Literary*, and others. You can find him at chriscampeau.com.

Samantha Carr is based in Plymouth, UK where she is a PhD in Creative Writing candidate, writing about chronic illness through poetry. Her work has been published in *Acumen*, *Arc*, *Cephalopress*, and *The Storms Journal*. She was recently awarded second place for the inaugural Molecules Unlimited poetry competition.

CB Droege is an author and voice actor from the Queen City living in the Millionendorf. His latest book is *Quantum Age Adventures*. Short fiction publications include work in *Nature Futures, Science Fiction Daily*, and dozens of other magazines and anthologies. Learn more at cbdroege.com

James Fritz graduated from Loyola University Chicago with degrees in business and music. He recently quit his job as a data analyst to write full-time. He enjoys reading and writing, piano, jiu jitsu, snuggling with his partner, and his self-appointed role as president of the Evgeny Kissin fan club. You can find him on Instagram under the handle @james.fritz.writing.

Orrin Grey is a writer, editor, and amateur film scholar as well as the author of several spooky books. His stories about monsters, ghosts, and sometimes the ghosts of monsters have appeared in dozens of anthologies, including Ellen Datlow's *Best Horror of the Year.*

Amanda Hard writes poetry and short fiction from her home in the cornfields of Indiana. She earned an MFA from Murray State University in 2018 and her work has been published in publications such as *parAbnormal, MetaStellar*, and multiple volumes of the Horror Writers Association poetry showcase.

Brian Jenkins is a Kinetic / Lisp Hacker / Sorcerer multi-class living on an island in San Francisco Bay with his lovely wife Amy in a tangled hive of computers, guitars, and sewing machines sheltered by a maze of bookshelves. He posts weird writing at enantiomer.org.

Eben Lou is a pen name of a writer and conductor of storytelling experiments living on Ohlone land in Richmond, California. They love the feel of clay on their hands, minor chords and tempo changes within a song, and engaging playfully in the present while plotting radical social change with beloved community.

R. J. Lynch lives with his wife and kids in Ontario, Canada where he teaches at a secondary school. He does not own a pet fish.

After escaping his home town in a rainbow-hued balloon, **Mark McElroy** was kidnapped by post-modern minimalists at the Center for Writers (University of Southern Mississippi), where he earned an MA in creative writing and came to terms with the fact that, despite having been groomed to be a fundamentalist minister, he was definitely gay. Since then, Mark has authored more than a dozen non-fiction books on subjects from Apple computers to lucid dreaming. He's also designed and scripted more than a dozen Tarot decks for publishers in the US (Llewellyn) and Italy (Lo Scarabeo). His first novel, *Parallel Lines*, is now available on Amazon. com and MarkMcElroy.com.

Donna J. W. Munro's pieces are published in Nothing's Sacred Magazine IV and V, *Corvid Queen, Hazard Yet*

Forward (2012), *Enter the Apocalypse* (2017), *Beautiful Lies, Painful Truths II* (2018), *Terror Politico* (2019), *It Calls from the Forest* (2020), *Gray Sisters Vol 1* (2020), *Pseudopod 752* (2021), *Shakespeare Unleashed* (2023) and others. Check out her novel, *Revelation: Poppet Cycle Book 1*. Contact her at https://www.donnajwmunro.com or @DonnaJWMunro on Twitter.

Scott Nicolay is an archaeologist and caver specializing in prehistoric cave use and iconography in the North American Southwest/Northwest Mexico, Mesoamerica, and Island Oceania. His story "Do You Like to Look at Monsters" won the World Fantasy Award for Best Short Fiction in 2015, and his second collection, *And at My Back I Always Hear*, was a 2023 Shirley Jackson Award nominee. He is currently translating and editing the fiction of Belgian weird fiction author Jean Ray and editing the posthumous publication of works by American author John D. Keefauver.

Mark A. Nobles is a sixth-generation Texan. Born on Fort Worth's infamous Jacksboro Highway, Mark proudly claims blood and kinship with Thunder Road's gamblers, outlaws, and wastrels. He is a Pushcart nominee and his work has appeared in various publications and anthologies. He is the author of the nonfiction book *Fort Worth's Rock & Roll Roots* and the historical novel *We're for Smoke*. Mark lives in Fort Worth but hopes to die in the desert.

Noley Reid's third book is the novel *Pretend We Are Lovely* from Tin House Books. Her fourth book, a collection of stories called *Origami Dogs*, is forthcoming from Autumn House Press. Her fiction and nonfiction have appeared in *The Southern Review*, *The Rumpus*, *Arts & Letters*, *Meridian*, *Pithead Chapel*, *The Lily*, *Bustle*, *Confrontation*, and *Los Angeles Review of Books*. She lives in southwest Indiana with her two best boys. www.NoleyReid.com

J. L. Royce is an author of science fiction, the macabre, and whatever else strikes him. He lives in the northern reaches of the American Midwest, exploring the wilderness without and within. His work appears in *Alien Dimensions*, *Allegory*, *Cosmic Horror Monthly*, *Fifth Di*, *Fireside*, *Ghostlight*, *Love Letters to Poe* (Visiter Award winner), *Lovecraftiana*, *Mysterion*, *parABnormal*, *Sci Phi*, *Strange Aeon*, *Utopia*, *Wyldblood*, etc. He is a member of WWA, HWA, and GLAHW. Some of his anthologized stories may be found at: www.jlroyce.com.

Guy Russell lives and works in Milton Keynes, UK. Stories in *No Spider Harmed* (Arachne Press), *Somewhere This Way* (Fiction Desk), *Brace* (Comma Press), *To Hull And Back*, *Madame Morte* (Black Shuck), *Northern Stories vol. 3* (Arc), *Liars League* and elsewhere. Competition first prizes: HE Bates Award; The Secret Life of Data; The Blue-White Dot; Ware Sonnet Prize; Flash500. He reviews for *Tears in the Fence* and its blog https://tearsinthefence.com/blog/.

Dani Alexis Ryskamp is an assistant band director, a freelance writer, and the editor of *Spoon Knife 2: Test Chamber* (with Sam Harvey). Dani's previous works appear in *Disability*

Studies Quarterly, the *Journal of Musicology,* and *The Atlantic,* among others.

phil smith is a recovering disabled and mad perfesser. his writing—academic and creative—has been published widely, since 1977. he's had many dozens of pieces published in a buncha different journals and books, presented internationally, and has books of poetry, plays, and visual art under his belt. his book, *writhing writing: moving towards a mad poetics,* won the 2020 American Educational Studies Association Critics Choice Award. his most recent book, *Tinfoil Hats: Stories by mad people in an insane world,* was published in 2023 by Autonomous Press. phil lives in a tiny cabin on the side of a mountain at 1800 feet, fussing and ranting with his tree and animal neighbors.

Heather Truett holds an MFA from the University of Memphis, is a PhD candidate at FSU, and was a Pushcart nominee in 2023. Her debut novel, *Kiss and Repeat,* was released by Macmillan in 2021. She has work in *Drunk Monkeys, Flash Fiction Online, Utopia Science Fiction,* and *Spoon Knife.* Heather serves as assistant editor for *The Southeast Review.* Find out more at www.heathertruett.com.

Alice G. Waldert's poetry has appeared in several literary magazines. In 2023, her poetry was featured in the *Muleskinner Journal* and appeared in *Mistake House* magazine, as well as an international British anthology titled *Addiction.* She has work forthcoming in *The Evening Street Review* and *Scream'n*

Mama. She holds an MA in Canadian Studies and an MFA in writing. She is working on a collection of poems about childhood trauma.

Nick Walker is a mild-mannered psychology professor, transdisciplinary scholar, and aikido teacher. She's co-edited three previous volumes of *Spoon Knife* and contributed stories to four. Her nonfiction work includes the book *Neuroqueer Heresies* and a recent chapter in the *Routledge Handbook of Creative Futures.* Together with fellow writer Andrew M. Reichart and artist Mike Bennewitz, she's co-creator of the urban fantasy webcomic *Weird Luck* (weirdluck.net).

George Wehrfritz is a retired journalist who lives in Central California. He began writing short fiction as a pastime during the pandemic. His recent work has appeared in *The European Literary Review* and *Periscope Literary.*

Cirrus Wood is a writer, photographer, bicyclist, journalist, knitter, gardener, mender, polyglot, and general urban peasant who lives and works in downtown Berkeley, California. Trained as a food writer, he dabbles with short fiction and tries to bring to his current work the same narrative spirit with which he once guided readers through recipes and fine dining. His writing has appeared in *The Sun, McSweeneys, The San Jose Mercury, Alta, Taste,* and the missed connections section of Craigslist, where he writes personalized messages to drivers who cut him off in traffic. His short story "Lawn Moving" was published in *Spoon Knife 7.*